A DARK AND SINFUL DEATH

Also by Alison Joseph

Sacred Hearts
The Hour of Our Death
The Quick and The Dead

A DARK AND SINFUL DEATH

Alison Joseph

HEADLINE

First published in 1997
by HEADLINE BOOK PUBLISHING

10 9 8 7 6 5 4 3 2 1

British Library Cataloguing in Publication Data

Joseph, Alison
A dark and sinful death
1. Agnes, Sister (Fictitious character) –
Fiction 2. Nuns – Great Britain –
3. Detective and mystery stories
I. Title
823.9'14 [F]

ISBN 0-7472-1873-0

Typeset by
CBS, Felixstowe, Suffolk

Printed and bound in Great Britain by
Mackays of Chatham PLC, Chatham, Kent

HEADLINE BOOK PUBLISHING
A division of Hodder Headline PLC
338 Euston Road
London NW1 3BH

For my mother
From whom I learned to be a mother

ACKNOWLEDGEMENTS

I would like to thank Craven Yarn Services of Keighley, and the sisters, staff and pupils of New Hall School in Chelmsford, and St Mary's School in Shaftesbury. I would also like to thank Cllr. Irene Ellison-Wood and Cath Rowen of Keighley. Lastly, I wish to thank Mike Fielden of the Leeds Probation Service, and PC Cliff Ashton of West Yorkshire Police.

I have no way, and therefore want no eyes; I stumbled when I saw.

King Lear, William Shakespeare

Chapter One

She was sitting in the middle of the room. The walls had been splashed with black paint, and there were fragments of paper where the girls' work had been torn away. The windows were daubed with black too, thickening the darkness of the night outside. Paint dripped from the workbench. She watched it, staring vacantly as the splashes counted time in the silence of the room.

Agnes still had her hand on the doorhandle. 'Joanna?' she whispered.

Joanna continued to watch the black droplets scatter as they hit the floor.

'Miss Baines?' Sister Teresa said, at Agnes's side.

'Did you do this?' Agnes asked.

Joanna slowly lifted her head and gazed at Agnes and Teresa. Her hands and face were smeared with black. In front of her was an arrangements of objects: a vase of flowers, sickly winter carnations and dried roses drooping haphazardly; a bowl of apples, overripe and wrinkled. In front of the vase there was an animal skull. At the side a candle was burning, so low that its falling wax had engulfed the candlestick. The flickering light was reflected in the darkness of the windows, in the shadows of Joanna's face as she stared at Agnes and Teresa.

'I'll get someone,' Teresa said to Agnes. 'You stay here.' The door closed behind her.

'Joanna . . . ?' Agnes wondered what to say. She realised she hardly knew her. Joanna Baines. Miss Baines, who taught art part-time at the school; who was considered to be a very private person; who was adored by the girls. She worked in the gardens of the school in her spare time, and never set foot in the staffroom. She had a young, open face; probably not yet thirty, Agnes thought.

Joanna stirred and seemed to focus on Agnes, then looked at

the desecrated art work in front of her. 'Those poor girls,' she murmured.

'Why . . . ?' Agnes began, hearing footsteps hurrying up the stairs.

Joanna turned anguished eyes to Agnes as if seeing her for the first time. 'There is nothing . . . First him – and now me . . . there is nothing . . .'

'I found the Head,' Sister Teresa said, breathlessly, coming back into the room. Sister Philomena appeared behind her. She was short and slightly hunched, and now she peered at the scene before her through tiny glasses balanced on her nose.

She turned to Agnes and spoke in her customary bark. 'Mops?'

'S-sorry?'

'Buckets?'

'Well,' Agnes faltered, 'I'm sure in the kitchens . . .'

Sister Philomena made a sudden dismissive flapping gesture with both hands. 'Staff,' she barked. 'In the morning. Leave it now. You, Baines —' her voice softened, and she held out one hand to Joanna. 'Come now, come with me.'

Joanna stood up and allowed herself to be led from the room. Their footsteps faded away.

Agnes looked at Teresa and screwed up her nose. 'Mops,' she barked. 'Buckets . . .'

Teresa flapped her hands. '"Staff,"' she echoed. They left the room, shutting the door behind them.

'"You turn us back to the dust and say, Go back O child of Earth . . . For a thousand years in Your sight are like yesterday when it is past . . . You sweep us away like a dream, we fade away suddenly like the grass . . ."'

The psalm murmured through the chapel, merging with the soft patter of the rain on the windows. Agnes had woken that morning with a sense of dull depression, echoed by the chill of the school's stone corridors, the grey of the skies, the wintry presence of the moors whenever she'd glanced out of the window.

'"Our iniquities You have set before You, and our secret sins in the light of Your countenance . . ."' Agnes glanced up at Father Elias, the school chaplain. His dark brows met in a deep frown, and his eyes were closed. His voice rose and fell with his recitation, his head bowed, his thick black hair falling across his face.

2

'"As from Dust did you come, to dust ye shall return . . ."'
The words seemed wrapped in melancholy.

Afterwards in the corridor, Sister Teresa took her arm. 'Sister Philomena wants to see us at twelve.'

'But it's Ash Wednesday. We're supposed to be reflecting on our sins.'

'Nonsense, Agnes, it'll take you more than a day for that.'

'How well you know me after such a short time.'

'State of operations,' Philomena announced as they walked into her room. She gestured to two chairs opposite her desk. Her office was generously proportioned, carpeted in warm green. Outside Agnes could see the wind shaking the bare branches of the chestnut trees along the drive.

'Miss Baines – queer old show, eh?' The Head peered at a button on her suit. She adjusted it, then looked at Teresa.

'I happened to be passing, that's all,' Teresa said. 'I heard an odd noise, and then I called Agnes because she was nearest and because – well, I wasn't sure what I should find . . .'

'Paint all over the shop. Still, all right as rain now.'

'But – all those paintings . . .' Agnes began.

'Plenty more. Heaps of them in the cupboards. Dogs and cats and whatnot, fluffy things, you know.'

'How's Joanna?' Agnes asked.

'And a rabbit. Think it's a rabbit. Although –' She turned to Teresa. 'Anteater perhaps? Short ears for a rabbit. You lived in the tropics, what d'you think?'

'Um, well . . .' Teresa hesitated. Agnes didn't dare look at her.

'Capybara.' Philomena picked up a mug from her desk and squinted into it. 'Beyond me why any of the girls should want to paint a capybara.'

'Perhaps it was a rabbit,' Agnes said.

Philomena peered at her. 'D'you think so? I do hope you're right.' She stood up. 'Ears rather short, that's all.'

Agnes and Teresa stood up too. 'And Joanna?' Agnes tried again.

'Baines? Bolted. Set up a room for her here last night. No sign of her this morning. Her third years sitting there like lemons. Had to teach them myself. We all drew a vase.' The door shut behind them, and they were alone in the corridor as the bell rang for lunch.

* * *

They took their trays of soup and bread and cheese to a table tucked away in the far corner of the dining room.

'So what did Philomena mean?' Teresa said as they sat down.

'Joanna's vanished.'

'Ah yes, the mystery of the disappearing art teacher,' a voice said.

'Colin Furse,' Teresa said looking up. 'I might have known you'd have the gossip.'

'History, you see,' Colin replied, joining them. 'And I have very little gossip. Only that she was upset about something and then went. Don't suppose you know why?'

'We saw her in the art room, last night. Yes, she was quite upset.'

'Can't think what it can be. She's such a quiet old thing, isn't she. The girls have started speculating. Elopement seems to be getting the keenest odds.'

'How do they get to hear of everything?' Agnes asked.

Teresa buttered her bread roll. 'It's astonishing. Some kind of Jungian collective radar. And it always involves men. I'm amazed you survive in this atmosphere, Colin.'

'I positively thrive in it, Sister. I see Charlotte Linnell's back with us, at least.'

Agnes glanced across at a noisy group of sixth formers. Karen Phelps was nursing an injured elbow from hockey. Zoe Webster was trying to grab her sling, and Claire Doylan was fighting her off and giggling. Charlotte Linnell was staring at her plate.

'Depends what you mean by "with us", I think,' Agnes said.

'What's the story there?' Colin asked.

'She's been absconding in the evenings, won't tell anyone where she's going. She was sent home last week for a few days. Now she's back, but she won't talk to anyone, and she's clearly unhappy.'

'Is she in your house?' Colin asked.

Teresa nodded. 'We've tried to get her to talk to us. It's hopeless. She's carrying some secret burden.'

Colin surveyed the room. 'Like Joanna,' he said. He turned to the two women. 'Do you think this place is more neurotic than most, or does it just reflect the national average for nutcases?'

'We were probably average until Agnes joined us,' Teresa said. 'Now we're off the scale.'

'On the contrary,' Agnes said, 'I've brought a measure of sanity

4

and reason which was sadly lacking before. I'm surprised you haven't noticed.'

It was Wednesday afternoon. The rain had eased, and a light mist had settled on the higher slopes, clinging to the bare gorse. Agnes followed her familiar path across the moor, leaving behind her the fading shouts of the school playing fields. She wondered what had become of Joanna. On a couple of occasions in the past she'd met her during her walks, and they'd exchanged a few words, during which she'd learned that Joanna lived across the moor from the school and sometimes walked all the way home rather than taking the bus.

Agnes strode on, climbing higher, away from the town. The wind gusted suddenly, icily. She paused to catch her breath, and was aware of a figure emerging from the mist towards her.

'Good afternoon, Father,' she said, as Elias came into view.

He looked up, startled. 'Oh, Agnes.' He halted next to her.

'Admiring the nothingness again?'

'I never said it was nothingness,' he said.

'Last time I met you up here, you said you liked the moors because they had a total disregard for anything human.'

'I said I liked the fact they existed before us and they'll exist after us.'

'So does that make you a nihilist or just a misanthropist?'

He smiled. 'And what are you?'

'Me? Just generally melancholic, I think.'

'Still missing London?'

She nodded.

'The girls like you.'

'I think they're just mystified by me, actually.'

'Perhaps. I think they find me pretty odd too.'

'It was a good service this morning.'

'No it wasn't. The start of Lent – what sense does it make to them? I can't convey any of it in a way that might inspire them.'

'I've always liked Lent.'

'Even when you were a kid?'

'Yes.' Agnes smiled. 'Not the giving things up, although we didn't have much of that anyway, being a household of excess. But I liked considering my failings.'

'And do you still?'

'Do I still what?'

'Consider your failings?'

'Oh, yes, I've got loads now.'

He laughed. Above them the clouds drew closer as the daylight began to fade. He glanced at her. 'Do you think it makes any difference? Lent. Reflecting on one's failings . . .'

'Yes, of course. It's about being reconciled to God –'

'But what does that mean?'

'Well, I suppose –'

'That's what I can't convey.' A squirrel rippled across their path, and Elias gazed after it. 'I feel like you,' he said. 'Out of place.'

'What is your God, then?'

Elias looked at her. 'God is –' he began. 'God is just Beingness. The charge between atomic particles, the distance between one galaxy and the next.'

'And what about love?' Agnes said.

He considered her for a moment. The wind caught his hair, blowing it across his face.

'If you really believe as you do –' Agnes hesitated. 'It must make your job very difficult.'

'Maybe. But it's a safe place, at least.'

They stood in silence.

'Well,' Agnes began, after a few moments, 'it'll be getting dark soon, and I'd better –'

'Yes, of course.' He glanced at her, then set off away from her towards the school. The sweep of the moors was shaded indigo in the twilight. Agnes could see below her the lights of the town, the silhouette of Father Elias as he descended the hill; in front of him the school, its dainty turrets echoing the rougher outlines of the mill chimneys across the valley. Agnes turned away and continued her walk, unwilling to return, in spite of the darkening sky. She looked at the shadows of the trees on the slope beyond, and quickened her pace.

She thought about Father Elias. She thought about his bleak vision. He was only in his thirties or so, she thought. She wondered how he'd come to be a school chaplain. She wondered what he meant by 'a safe place'. She wondered what had happened to upset Joanna. She wondered what topic to choose for this week's French conversation classes. She wondered, again, how to approach Charlotte to find out what it was outside the school

6

that was exerting such a powerful attraction.

It was dark when she at last returned to the school. She'd missed supper. The hallway was unlit. The girls were all tucked away in their houses. Agnes could hear a phone ringing in the office. She opened the door and in darkness picked up the receiver.

'Um – hello . . .' It was an uncertain male voice.

'St Catherine's School,' Agnes said.

'I wondered if you could get a message to someone. One of the girls.'

'Yes, of course.'

'Charlotte Linnell.'

'Oh – yes. Certainly.'

'Just say that Mark phoned. Mark Snaith. Um – the message is – it's difficult really. Could you tell her that I can't do – oh, I dunno. Just ask her to ring me, could you? That's all.' The line went dead.

Agnes walked through the main building and out into a courtyard to Milton House, of which she was the Assistant Housemistress, an idea which still made her want to laugh. She unlocked the door to her tiny room, switched on lights, put the kettle on to boil, then changed her mind and opened a miniature fridge, in which there was a half bottle of Petit-Chablis. She pulled the cork, and poured a glass, which misted with condensation. She poured water into a saucepan and set it on one of two tiny electric rings, then opened a cupboard and searched for pasta and sauce.

When she'd first been shown her room at the school, she'd been horrified to find it had no fridge or cooker. In two days she'd installed both, and a toaster. She'd wanted to install a telephone line too, but she'd sensed a certain frostiness from Sister Philomena at the idea that she might wish at times to escape from the communal life of the school. No one else, it was made plain to her, needed a private telephone line. But then, as Agnes had explained to Teresa at the time, she hadn't asked to be sent away from London, away from the work she enjoyed at the hostel for homeless kids, away from her friends, exiled to a chilly Yorkshire convent school to do a job for which she was singularly ill suited.

She waited for the water to come to the boil, gazing absently at her brand new mobile phone, which was sitting on her desk and which now rang suddenly.

'Agnes?'

'Julius – I was just thinking of you.'

'You always say that.'

'Maybe it's always true.'

'How alarming.'

'No, I was just thinking about London and wondering how I came to be here.'

'Through your exemplary obedience to the wishes of your order, wasn't it?'

'There's no need to laugh.'

'Agnes, would I laugh at you?'

'What do you think?'

Julius laughed. 'And this is your mobile number, eh? So I could be talking to you anywhere?'

'Anywhere. I might be in the bath for all you know.'

'Isn't science wonderful?'

'Expensive, too. I'm always recharging the batteries, it costs a fortune.'

'Lucky you have one, then.'

'Hardly a fortune. And now Sister Philomena knows it's there, it won't last long.'

'I thought your French lawyers made sure it was watertight.'

'They hadn't met Sister Philomena.'

'What's that beeping?'

'The batteries, again. It's such a bore.'

'Why don't you get a proper phone?'

'Because it didn't seem worth it. It's not as if I'm here for long.'

'Agnes –'

'They can't make me stay, Julius.'

'Is it still that bad?'

'Julius, I can't bear it, I'm supposed to eat communally, I can't wear jeans, there are offices for the nuns at least three times a day, chapel for the girls every day—'

'What's wrong with daily offices?'

'Nothing in themselves, of course, but – I'd got used to having privacy.'

'Perhaps that's why they moved you.'

'It's as if I'm not trusted to conduct my spiritual life without them supervising it the whole time. I feel like a child again.'

'Is that such a bad thing?'

'You didn't know me as a child. And the girls, Julius, they all stand up when I come into a room. They're so polite, and restrained, and – and so bloody English and repressed and—'

'And you'd rather have our crazy hostel residents?'

'At least I'm useful there, I'm really needed. This lot are so privileged—'

'And immune from suffering? Surely not.'

'It's all so well mannered here.'

'I imagine you were the same at their age.'

'Perhaps that's just the problem. Hang on a minute . . .' She turned the heat down and added some fusilli to the water. 'You were saying?'

'Nothing really.'

'Do you miss me?'

'It's part of my spiritual training not to.'

'Perhaps one day you'll tell me how it's done.'

'There was one thing, actually. Someone's been trying to get hold of you. James Lombard.'

'James – good grief.'

'Is he the one who was the friend of your father?'

'Yes.'

'Who was like an ally when you were a child, you said.'

'Fancy you remembering that.'

'And you were really fond of him, but he moved to the States.'

'Julius, you know everything.'

'He wanted your address. He's going to write.'

'To me? How odd.'

'Did I do the wrong thing?'

'No. No, I'd love to see him again. But – I can't think why he'd want to see me.'

'He said he had memories of your family.'

'Yes – but they're not the sort of memories one would want to re-live.'

Later she heard the sixth formers returning to their rooms, and went to look for Charlotte.

Charlotte was sitting at her desk in her pyjamas. She looked up as Agnes came into the room. Agnes noticed the teddy bears arranged under huge posters of Keanu Reeves and Brad Pitt. She looked tired, Agnes thought. 'I – er – took a phone call for you. During supper.' Charlotte gave nothing away. 'From Mark,' Agnes went on, 'Mark Snaith.' Charlotte's eyes widened. 'He said, can you phone him. Something about not being able to do – to do something. He didn't say what. I said I'd tell you.' Agnes turned, calmly, to go.

'Was that all?' The girl's voice was barely a whisper.

Agnes turned back to her. 'I imagine,' she said, 'that he didn't want to give anything away to a stranger. If you had a secret arrangement for this week that he's now having to cancel, he'd hardly have told me, would he?' She smiled. Charlotte looked bewildered. Agnes said gently, 'If you need to talk about anything, you know where I am.'

'But you –' Charlotte began.

'No,' Agnes said. 'Not me. I'm not going to judge you. If you want to talk, I'll listen. Goodnight.' She closed the door softly behind her.

'Gaping bloody hole in the timetable,' Agnes heard Philomena saying as she walked into the staff room next morning. 'Counting on you. You'll cover, won't you?' Iona Gish, the head of art, nodded. 'And go easy on the tropical animals,' Philomena added. Iona looked at her blankly. 'Ah, Sister Agnes,' Philomena said. 'Nash?'

'You mean Pamela Nash?'

'Funny turn last week.'

'Yes, I know, she had a fit or something.'

'Talked to the quack, he says, tell the parents. Write them a letter, you know the form. Nothing to worry about, fell into a dead faint, won't happen again, keep an eye out, that sort of thing, all right?' Philomena nodded benignly at Agnes and then left the room.

'It's a bit much for you,' someone was saying to Iona, 'that you have to cover for Joanna.'

'I suppose no one knows whether she's coming back.'

'Was she ill?'

'She seemed fine to me. Quiet, as usual, but nothing odd.'

'And Miss Baines was terribly poor,' Clemmie Macintosh was whispering to a group of fellow fourth years who had gathered around her in the classroom. 'And she had no garden and that's why she was so fond of our gardens, and why she looked after the roses every day, because roses are for romance and she had no one to love her –'

'Clemmie, that's enough thank you,' Agnes said. 'Perhaps, *mesdesmoiselles*, we can begin our French conversation now.'

'Maybe she was thwarted in love,' Agnes heard someone whisper.

'*Bon, aujourd'hui, nous allons faire une dictée . . .*'

'Perhaps he jilted her. And now she's gone and –'

'Killed herself?' The whispering shrank to an awed hush.

Agnes spoke. 'Frankly, girls, I'm amazed that you could find the disappearance of one of your teachers to be more fascinating than French dictation.'

'They can't stop talking about it,' Agnes said, back in the staff room.

'The Maths Fives reckoned it was unrequited love.'

'Oh, the French Threes were for elopement.'

'And suicide.'

'Yes, we had suicide. I blame the English department.'

'Why us?' asked Jean Pagnell, a tall woman in a tweed suit.

'Too many nineteenth-century novels. It gives them melodramatic ideas.'

'Nonsense,' Jean said. 'Although, come to think of it, my group of fourth years couldn't decide between nervous exhaustion and what they called a decline. Oh dear, I'd better stick to T S Eliot and Maya Angelou from now on.'

The bell rang for afternoon classes. There was a chaos of books and bags and departing staff, and then quiet descended. Agnes got another cup of coffee, and flicked through the local paper.

'Allbright's Mill facing redundancies,' she read. 'William Baines to retire.' She read on. 'William Baines, owner of Allbright's Mill, has announced that he is to hand over control of the business to his daughter, Patricia, and her husband, Anthony Turnbull. "We aim to keep Allbright's as a main player in the twenty-first century yarn industry," said Turnbull.'

'Baines,' Agnes said.

'Sorry, Sister?' The school secretary, Mary Watson, was making a cup of coffee.

'Baines. William Baines.'

'Oh, Allbright's. My sister-in-law used to work there.'

'But it's the same as Joanna Baines.'

'Joanna . . . ?' Mary thought for a moment, then shook her head. 'I can't see there'd be a connection. Joanna's never mentioned it. And it's a very common name round here. You see, the Allbright Baineses are a different lot altogether. You know it if you've met an Allbright Baines.'

That evening Teresa knocked urgently at Agnes's door.

'Leonora,' she gasped as Agnes let her in. 'There, look!'

Agnes looked out of her window and saw a small figure with a suitcase striding purposefully down the drive in the yellow lamplight.

Agnes sighed. 'This must be her fourth attempt this year. Thanks, Teresa.' Agnes pulled on her coat and ran down the stairs, out of the hallway, up the drive.

At the gates, the girl turned her head and smiled. 'Hello, Sister.'

'Leonora –'

'How nice of you to come and say goodbye.'

'Leonora, you can't keep running away.'

'Oh, but I can.'

Agnes paused to catch her breath, leaning against the heavy wrought iron of the gates. 'Is it so bad?'

The girl's exquisite manners never faltered. 'Oh, Sister, you mustn't take it personally. You've all been very kind, but you see, I belong at home. They need me.'

'And how were you going to get there at this time of night?'

'I appreciate your concern, Sister, but really I can manage.'

Agnes stepped in front of her, and took her arm, glad that she was still taller than the child. She began to propel her back towards the school.

Leonora was chewing her lip. Her eyes were quite dry. She swallowed, then said, 'It's really a terrible waste of your time, Sister, I'll only do it again.'

'I'm sure you will, Leonora. But I have my job to do, you must understand that.'

Leonora nodded, but her face was white with anger. She said nothing more all the way back into the school, all the way to her tiny room. Agnes waited while she changed into her pyjamas and

12

brushed out her long blonde hair. A wisp of hair floated against her cheek, and Agnes saw there were tears in her eyes. She bent and kissed the top of her head. Leonora turned her face away and got into bed.

We need an armed guard on this door, Agnes thought, closing it behind her. So much unhappiness, she thought, remembering what Julius had said, wondering why Julius was always right. She walked back along the darkened corridors to the main building, thinking she should tell Sister Philomena. She could hear voices at the main doorway, and the porch windows seemed to be lit with an odd blue light. As she approached, she realised she could see a police car through the open doorway. Philomena was talking to a policeman. Colin Furse was standing in the doorway.

'What's happened?' Agnes asked Colin.

'They've found a body,' he said.

'What?'

'No one we know. In the little stream that runs across the top of the moor up there, by the crag. They had to let us know because we're the nearest dwelling. And because he was murdered. Stabbed. They'll be up there all night, apparently. Sister offered my services to the police, being a man and all that.'

'And did they jump at the chance?'

'Strangely, they declined.' His smile seemed to take some effort. 'Perhaps they can afford enough torches of their own.'

On Friday morning, Agnes glanced out of her window while brewing coffee and making toast, and saw Leonora wandering aimlessly across the lawn. She left her half-made breakfast and hurried downstairs to the garden. Leonora looked up from the bare rose bushes and smiled.

'It's all right, Sister, I'm still here.'

'I'm glad you are, Leonora.' Agnes breathed in the wintry February morning, wondering if the girls had picked up the events of last night on their super-sensitive communications network. 'I was thinking we should have a chat,' she said to Leonora. 'I know you don't think it'll do any good. But I'm afraid I insist anyway.'

Leonora shrugged. 'If you must.'

'How about next week? Wednesday tea-time. In my room.'

Leonora brightened slightly. Agnes's room had acquired a mythology amongst the girls, as if they sensed that each new consumer durable installed there represented a triumph, that somehow the toaster and kettle and phone were on their side in the endless quiet rebellion which made up their school days.

'OK, then.'

'Four o'clock?'

'OK. Thank you, Sister,' she remembered to add, as the bell rang for the first lesson.

Agnes lingered in the gardens. 'These were all hers,' a voice said. She looked up to see Elias approaching.

'All whose?' she asked.

'Joanna's.' He gestured to the neat circles of rose bushes that now shivered in the breeze. 'She would, you see,' he said. His voice was low. Agnes could hardly hear what he was saying. 'All this, all neat and pruned. It's like her, to have everything ready.' Elias looked up with sudden intensity, and she noticed the lines of pain around his eyes. She realised that he must have sought her out.

'You were in the art room' he said at last. 'The other night . . . When she –'

'Joanna, you mean? Yes. Teresa heard a noise and called me.'

'Would you mind – might I . . .' He shifted on his feet, staring at the dull black leather of his shoes on the bare winter grass. He raised his eyes to her again. 'Do you have a moment – now? There'll be no one up there.'

Agnes followed him back into the school and up the narrow staircase to the art room. He pushed open the door. All was neat and clean, washed with thin sunlight. 'You wouldn't know anything had happened,' she said.

'What did she do?'

How do you know, Agnes wanted to ask him. She went over to the window. 'This was all covered in paint, black paint. You can see traces by the frame. She'd torn the paintings off the wall and covered them in black paint. See the table leg, all black? That's where it was.' Elias ran his fingertips across the workbench. 'Oh, and she'd arranged some objects, like a still life.'

Elias looked up. 'A still life?' His voice was unsteady.

'Y-yes.'

'What objects?'

'There was fruit, and flowers –'

'These?' Elias moved swiftly about the art room, gathering the vase from a corner shelf, the bowl, now empty of apples. 'These flowers?' He arranged the dry roses carefully in the vase.

'And a skull.'

'A skull?' He smiled then, as at some private joke. He looked suddenly younger.

'A sheep's skull, I mean, not a human one. Why is it funny?'

He shook his head. 'It's not. Not really . . . A skull,' he said, and his lips twitched with amusement as he looked for it.

'There it is.' Agnes brought it down from the paint shelf and handed it to him.

He held it in his hands. 'She would,' he murmured.

'She said something, when we found her.'

'What did she say?'

'Something about there being nothing. Nothing for her. "First him, now me," she said.' Elias's gaze met her own. Agnes went on, 'I – I know no more than that. I'm just telling you what I heard her say.'

'Yes.'

'Is – is she in trouble?'

Elias turned the skull over in his hands.

'I mean, I know it's not my business,' Agnes went on.

'No, It's not.' Elias began to dismantle his arrangement, putting the objects back in their places. He took a last look at the skull, then replaced it carefully on the shelf. He opened the door for her, and they walked back down the staircase in silence. They came out into the gardens, and wandered towards Joanna's roses.

'Will she come back soon?' Agnes asked him.

He shook his head. 'I doubt it. Although –'

'What?'

'This man they found on the moors last night . . .'

'The – the dead one?'

'Yes. Snaith.'

'Sorry?

'Mark Snaith.'

Agnes felt herself losing her balance. 'Mark – Snaith?' She put out her hand, grasping at thin air.

'The murdered man. He was Baines's gardener. He was only twenty-two,' Elias was saying.

'How do you – ?'

15

'And the worst thing, somehow . . .' Elias stopped and ran his fingers along the bare thorns of a rose bush. 'The worst thing was, that his eyes had been put out.'

Chapter Two

'Hello, yes, I'm enquiring about the Snaith murder – on Morton's Crag, last night . . . All right, then the incident room . . . in Bradford? Can I have the number then?' Agnes tucked the phone under her chin and waved one hand madly over the toaster which was puffing blue smoke into her room. She reached across to grab a pen and paper, and wrote down a phone number. 'Thank you. Goodbye.'

She opened the window, pulled two charred pieces of bread from the toaster and dialled the number.

'Hello, yes, I'm enquiring about the Snaith murder – Mark, yes, that's right. I'm Sister Agnes, I work at St Catherine's School, yes, that's right. The thing is – one of our girls was seeing this man . . . Yes, I think so . . . Charlotte Linnell, sixth former . . . And she doesn't know what's happened, and I'm not supposed to know about her relationship, and . . . yes, I thought you'd say that. Yes, OK. Thank you, officer.'

It was four o'clock. Agnes went across to the main school and knocked on Sister Philomena's door.

'Sister—' she began.

'Agnes?' Sister Philomena gestured to a seat.

'It's all rather tricky.'

'Well?' Sister Philomena's smile was friendly.

'The police phoned just now,' Agnes lied. She saw Philomena frown, and carried on, 'um, in the office. I happened to answer it . . .' Philomena picked up a Biro and turned it over in her stubby fingers. Agnes took a deep breath and said, 'The murdered man, on the moors – you see, they found someone's name and phone number on him.'

'And?'

'Charlotte Linnell.'

'Oh.'

'She has no idea he's dead. And they'd like to see her,' Agnes said. 'The police, I mean. I said I'd check with you, but that after supper would be OK. I've arranged, with your permission, to take Charlotte to the police station. I thought it would be fairer on her to have the discussion away from the school. With your permission of course.'

Philomena studied the Biro in her hands.

She knows I'm lying, Agnes thought.

Philomena looked up and Agnes was aware of being appraised by the small, beady eyes with their heavy brows. 'Permission granted,' Philomena said, her gaze still fixed on Agnes. The words were like a move in a game. Her chair scraped back as she stood up. 'Nash?' she barked.

The two women's eyes met. Agnes thought she saw the glimmer of a smile.

'Um, just about to do it, Sister.'

Agnes went to Mary Watson's office, which was empty. She opened a filing cabinet and picked out a folder, flicking through the names until she found 'Nash, Pamela. Date of birth, 22 July, 1982'. She turned to the section marked medical history. Under 'Fits, Fainting, Epilepsy', the parents had written 'None'. There was an address in Cyprus, and Agnes noted it down. She put the folder away, composing in her head the letter she would write, both informative and reassuring at the same time. 'Dear Flt Lt and Mrs Nash . . . I am writing to let you know . . . there is no cause for concern . . .'

'Baines,' she saw on the edge of a file, under the drawer divider marked in neat Biro, 'STAFF admin'. She pulled it out, amazed that it was so easy, then remembering that these were the non-confidential files. Baines, Joanna, it said. Date of Birth, 15 September, 1967. There was an address on the other side of town. Under next of kin, it said, 'None', in big handwritten letters. Then Joanna had added, 'In case of emergency, contact Mrs Patricia Turnbull'.

Agnes blinked. She stared at the page for a while. Then she wrote down Joanna's address from the file, and Patricia Turnbull's too. She looked up Father Elias, found he wasn't there, closed the drawer and left the office.

At six-thirty that evening, Agnes licked the gum on an envelope and sealed the letter to Pamela Nash's parents. She put it down on her desk and took a sip of cold coffee from the mug beside her. She got out her notebook and looked at the names she'd written there. Joanna Baines, Patricia Turnbull. She picked up the local paper that she'd removed from the staffroom and carefully cut out the piece about Allbright's Mill, and William Baines handing control of the mill to his daughter Patricia and her husband, his son-in-law, Anthony Turnbull. She stuck the cutting into her notebook.

And Elias, too, she thought, still bewildered by the conversation she'd had with him earlier that day. How did he know what Joanna had done? And how did he know about Mark Snaith on the moors? And in everything he'd said, his words had betrayed a familiarity with Joanna, with Snaith, with Baines – 'Baines's gardener,' he'd said, as if she'd know who he meant. And the urgency of his tone, as if he had to know, absolutely had to know, what Joanna had done, even to the extent of recreating it.

Agnes turned from the desk to the window. It was drizzling. The thin rain made tiny beads of light against the glass. It was time to find Charlotte.

She was in her room, and looked up reluctantly as Agnes opened the door. 'Charlotte? May I have a word?' Agnes sat on her bed. 'It's about Mark.'

Charlotte coloured. 'What about him? Has he phoned again? I've tried but he wasn't there. He's never there . . .'

'Charlotte – was he a gardener for William Baines?'

'Y-yes. How do you –'

'How old was he?'

'Twenty-two. On January the 14th. Why?'

'Charlotte, I think there might be bad news. The police wanted to see you.'

'The police? Why?'

'I've arranged for us to meet them at the police station, I don't want everyone here gossiping.'

Charlotte had paled. 'Wh-what do you mean?'

'They found a man on the moors. Dead. He was called Mark Snaith. It may not be the same one . . .'

Charlotte was sitting bolt upright on her bed, staring blankly at Agnes. 'It's not the same one,' she said, her voice flat.

Agnes stood up. 'It may not be,' she said, taking Charlotte's arm. 'Let's go and find out.'

'Oh God,' Charlotte murmured, as they went out to the car. 'I knew this would happen.'

Agnes scanned the blank walls of the interview room. A plastic cup of coffee sat untouched in front of Charlotte, as she listened to what the policewoman had to say. Her face was expressionless. She looked up as she was asked a question.

'I said, how long had you known him?'

Charlotte looked at Agnes.

'I'll go outside if you like,' Agnes said.

'No. No, it's OK. I'd known him since last summer term, when a group of us from school went to help with the community centre on the estate. You know, the Millhouse estate. And then he asked me to a club . . .' She glanced at Agnes again.

'Were you going out together?'

Charlotte picked up a paperclip from the desk. 'Sort of. After that it was the end of term, but last term he got in touch, and we went out together. One Sunday. And it was really lovely . . .'

'And you continued to see each other?'

She twisted the paperclip between her fingers. 'Yes. It was a bit difficult to organise . . . Yes, we did see each other.'

'Did he indicate that he might be in danger?' the policewoman asked.

Charlotte shook her head.

'Was he happy in his work?'

'He used to grumble about Mr Baines, but that's normal, isn't it, when you have to work for someone.'

'Is there anything else you can think of? Any fights he got into, anyone he fell out with? He lived on Millhouse, it's quite a rough estate.'

'No. Although –'

'What?'

'I didn't know him very well. Although we – although we were close – there was something a bit – he was a bit secretive. Sometimes.' She put the mangled paperclip back on the desk.

The policewoman scribbled in her notebook, then looked up. 'Do you think it was drugs? That can make people secretive.'

Charlotte shook her head. 'No. Definitely not. He was really anti all that, he knew someone who'd really messed up their lives with heroin, he was dead against it.' She glanced at Agnes, then added, 'Apart from the odd joint, you know . . .'

'Do you know a lad called Billy Keenan?'

Charlotte chewed her lip, then nodded. 'He was involved with the sports centre.'

'Do you know if there was any trouble between him and Mark? Might Mark have been afraid of him?'

Charlotte hesitated, then said, 'No. Nothing like that. Mark was a gentle person. Like those birds he was watching up on the moors, he really cared about them –' Her eyes welled with tears.

'Birds?'

'There was a pair of peregrine falcons, he was devoted to them, knew everything about them, he was like that, a gentle person –'

'On the moors? Is that why he was there, watching the birds?'

'Yes. No, maybe, I don't know, I hadn't seen him for days.' She wiped her eyes. 'I can't believe he's . . . will there be a funeral? Can I see him?'

The policewoman exchanged a glance with Agnes. 'There'll be a funeral eventually.'

'Can I see him before that?'

'In the circumstances . . . sometimes it's better to remember someone how they were in life,' the policewoman said.

'Why? What's happened? What did they do to him?'

The policewoman hesitated, then said, 'They – whoever killed him – they damaged his face rather badly.'

'I don't care, I still want to see him—'

'Charlotte,' Agnes interrupted. 'There'll be time.' She stood up.

'We can arrange for you to see someone, a counsellor,' the officer said.

Charlotte shrugged.

'My name's Janet Cole.' She scribbled a phone number on a piece of paper. 'You're very welcome to phone us any time.'

Agnes led Charlotte to the car. As they set off back to the school, Charlotte said, 'It was the moors.'

'What about them?'

'He was always going up there on his own, watching for those birds. I knew something like this would happen, I had a feeling . . .'

Agnes braked as a fox froze on the road in front of them. Its eyes flashed startled green, then it darted away. Agnes accelerated again as the gates of the school came into view.

It was Saturday morning. The bus dropped Agnes on the edge of the industrial estate. She pulled her cashmere scarf around her face, and buttoned up the neck of her coat against the frosty air. A single tall chimney rose up against the hillside, and next to it the blackened yellow stone of the old mill. Agnes saw, in the neglected façade, a huge archway, carved with the letters ALLBRIGHT'S MILL. She stared at the letters, wondering what had brought her here. She went through into a courtyard. On three sides the mill buildings towered over the old cobblestones. The fourth side looked out across the town, across the old terraces which made a grid across the valley, the newer estates sprawled in the distance. The chimney towered above the mill, above the town, like a huge flag planted in virgin territory, as if to say, this is ours.

Agnes thought about the millions of tons of fleece that had passed through the archway, to be made into yarn and sold on; about the thousands of workers who had passed through this courtyard, and upon whose labour the town was built. And now Baines was handing over to his daughter; and his gardener, Mark, had been found murdered on the moors.

All last night Agnes had tried to comfort Charlotte in her terrible grief. Something had been worrying her, some thought at the edges of her mind. She'd settled Charlotte into sleep, at last, and gone to bed herself. Sheep's skulls, she'd thought, as she'd drifted into sleep. Sheep's skulls and withered roses. On the day that Mark was found dead, Joanna had disappeared from the school. Joanna Baines, who seemed to have disowned all family; but who had named Patricia Turnbull on her personnel file.

Agnes opened a door into the old mill building. Inside it was dark. The broken windows shed a thin light, picking out the puddles of rainwater on the expanse of empty floor, the brooding structures of rusting machinery, the wisps of fleece, the discarded bobbins that were scattered here and there. Above her she could see the mainshaft that ran the length of the ceiling, that would have driven the spinning machines in their hundreds. The silence seemed to be filled with the echoes of the past. For a moment, Agnes thought she heard footsteps on the floor above.

Agnes went back out into the courtyard. The door creaked shut behind her. She walked through the yard towards the new industrial site, leaving the old buildings behind her, and came upon a wide, sleek, single-storey building. She could hear a low hum. Above the glass door, the name ALLBRIGHT'S was engraved on a silver metal sign. The machine noise was louder here. Agnes tried a door marked 'Reception'. It was locked. Behind it she knew there must be people, manning the machines that never stopped. She tried the door again, pointlessly, then wandered back to the old building. It was only then that she noticed a lone light coming from one of the old windows on the first floor. She quickened her pace, went back through the creaking door and up the staircase, which was broad and solid, built to contain the comings and goings of a workforce of hundreds. Now it echoed with her solitary footsteps. A carved mahogany sign on a door said 'Wm. Baines'. She knocked at the door. There was no answer. She knocked again, then opened the door.

A man was standing in the room by the fireplace, his back to the door. He was tall and thick-set, and had a shock of untidy grey hair. A coal fire burned in the huge blackened chimney. The office had bare floorboards, stacked up with piles of paper. A large oak desk stood by the window. Beyond, Agnes could see the same view across the town she'd seen from the courtyard. She knocked loudly on the open door and the man turned. He had a broad, square face and dark eyes half hidden under thick grey brows, which frowned now on seeing her.

'Yes?' he barked.

'Hello. My name's Sister Agnes.'

'And?'

Agnes took a step towards him and held out her hand. He ignored the gesture. 'What do you want?' he said.

Agnes hesitated. 'I'm from St Catherine's Convent,' she said. At the name she saw his expression flicker with recognition. She took a deep breath and went on, 'One of our staff, a young woman called Joanna Baines, seems to have vanished, and I thought you might know where she's gone.'

She was unprepared for his reaction. In two strides he crossed the room, grabbed hold of her arm and propelled her towards the door. 'Joanna Baines?' he cried. 'I know no such person.' He led her back down the staircase, dragging her down each step. 'The impertinence of it,' he said, pushing her out into the courtyard, then shouted again from the doorway, 'I know no such person.' She heard the door slam, heard his footsteps recede up the stairs behind it. Her hand went to her arm where he'd gripped it with such force. You know it when you've met an Allbright Baines, she thought, rubbing her arm, turning across the courtyard, going back through the archway to the bus stop.

'Father –' Agnes called to Elias across the crowd of girls. He didn't hear above the noise. 'Elias,' she called again, pushing through the bustle until she caught up with him.

He turned. 'Yes?'

'I'm – I'm sorry about my third years.'

He frowned. 'Sorry?'

'In Chapel this morning. They were restless. I thought you might have heard them giggling. Monday morning, I'm afraid.' She smiled.

He looked at her, distracted. 'Oh, it's OK. Can hardly blame them.' He turned again, and began to walk along the corridor and Agnes walked with him.

'Are you joining us for coffee?' she said.

'No.'

'Oh.'

They reached the main doorway. Agnes watched him put on a pair of woollen gloves.

'Elias –' He looked at her, waiting. 'How's Joanna?'

'I've no idea.' He turned to go.

'Also –'

'What?'

'Mark Snaith,' Agnes said.

'What about him?'

'He was seeing one of my sixth formers. Charlotte Linnell. They had a relationship of some kind.'

Elias stared at Agnes. 'Baines's gardener and one of your –' He shook his head. 'How did that happen?' He looked away. A frown shadowed his face. He turned back to her again, made as if to speak, then shook his head and went out of the heavy front door.

Agnes gazed after him. Her hand went to her pocket and she pulled out a letter she'd received that morning. It was addressed in a clear, even hand, and stamped 'James Lombard' on the back.

It had a local postmark. She put it back in her pocket and went into the staffroom.

'You think what?' Colin Furse put down his mug of coffee and looked at Agnes.

'I think it would be a good idea to do some local history with the girls.'

'This is all I need on a Monday morning. The curriculum is already over-stretched –'

'You could make room for it somewhere, couldn't you?'

'I thought you sisters knew to leave the teaching to us.'

'The mills, for example.'

'Which mills?'

'I mean, when you think that this area owes everything to the wool industry –'

'I see, not only local history but a Marxist analysis too. And I thought I knew all about nuns.'

'Allbright's, for example. They do visits for school parties.'

'I bet they do. And do you think the girls want to be dragged around some dusty noisy old mill?'

'I think they'd learn a lot.'

Colin laughed. 'I suppose I *am* doing the Industrial Revolution with the fourth years.'

'There you are, then. Look, here's the address to write to, and the phone number's at the bottom there.'

Colin looked at Agnes. 'And what's in it for you?'

'Me?'

'Why are you so keen to visit Allbright's mill?'

'Oh, you know, us soft Londoners, we need to see a bit of real life from time to time.'

Colin took the piece of paper she held out to him and glanced at it. 'Well, it's not a bad idea, I suppose.' He looked up at her again. 'You really are a most unlikely person to be an assistant housemistress, you know.'

'That's what I tried telling them,' Agnes laughed, getting up. 'They never listen.'

At lunchtime Agnes went to her room and made herself a sandwich. She sat at her desk, took a paperknife and slit open the letter from James Lombard.

Dear Agnes,

It seems presumptuous to write to you after all this time, so I apologise in advance if this letter disturbs your peaceful life. You will remember I knew your parents well, particularly your father. Our friendship deepened after his move to the States, because by then I was living in Manhattan, and we saw a lot of each other.

After his death I learned he'd bequeathed me several of his possessions – some paintings, ornaments, the odd family photograph, that kind of thing. I was touched by this, and kept them, eventually transporting them over here when I moved back to England and settled in Yorkshire.

The reason for this letter is that I am now packing up my house to move abroad again, for various reasons, and I do not wish to burden myself with luggage. I have been looking at Aylmer's things and wondering what to do with them, and in the end I decided it was not my right to dispose of them, particularly as I fear your mother did not have a say in their bequest. You will understand what I mean by this. I then contacted your family lawyer who gave me your London address, and I spoke to a charming colleague of yours who let me know where you are now – practically on my doorstep, it turns out.

As I said, I hope this is not an unwelcome intrusion into your life. If it is, then please forgive me, and simply let me know you are not interested in renewing my acquaintance. I will understand. If, however, you could spare the time, I would be delighted to entertain you here for lunch, and if you want to look over your father's things and reclaim them as your rightful inheritance, no one would be more pleased than I.

I look forward very much to hearing from you.

Yours, James

Agnes read the letter through twice, then folded it away. She leant her head on her hands and stared out of the window.

Aylmer, she thought. Everyone else called her father Emile. Perhaps Aylmer was his real name, she thought. Another thing I didn't know about him.

There was never a time when she didn't know James Lombard.

A frequent visitor to their house, someone who'd make her father brighten by his very presence. Her mother resented him for this. When they went into business together, Emile and James, her mother would call him 'that Lombard man'. The business was very successful.

James Lombard. He's known me all my life.

Or rather, he's known me for the worst part of my life.

Perhaps it's best never to see him again.

She got out the letter again. It would be ungrateful, she thought, not to see him. Although as for him returning all this stuff of my father's, it's not as if I can own any of it anyway. I'd have to hand it all over to Sister Philomena. Let's hope there are no furry animals in the paintings.

Agnes laughed, out loud. She looked at the phone number, picked up her phone. Then she put the phone down, folded up the letter and put it back in its envelope. There was nothing to be done. Not yet, anyway.

She glanced outside. A group of girls was wandering towards the hockey pitch. Leonora Talbot was trailing at the back, dragging her hockey stick, staring at the ground, her long blonde hair tied back. Agnes remembered wearing her own hair that way at that age. Perhaps if she looked through James's photographs, she'd find that version of herself preserved for posterity.

She glanced at her watch. It was time to discuss French local government with the fifth years. She yawned.

At tea she went to the sixth-form common room. Charlotte Linnell looked up from her corner and smiled wanly as Agnes sat next to her.

'Well?' Agnes asked. Charlotte was pale, her eyes ringed with sleeplessness.

'Well what?'

'It must be awful.'

'It is.'

'Does praying help?'

Charlotte shrugged. 'No. He's dead, isn't he.'

'Do you want some time at home? I can arrange it. I've talked to Sister Teresa, we've got to tell your parents in any case, they're bound to blame us –'

The girl shook her head. 'I'd rather be around the places we knew together.' Tears filled her eyes.

'Charlotte, you can't take exams in this state –'

'I'll be OK. Really.'

'Have you got friends you can talk to about it?'

'A bit. But no one really understands.' She swallowed. 'I just hope they catch whoever did it.'

'We'll talk to the police again if you like.'

'Sister Philomena said she didn't want word of this getting out.'

'She has no right to interfere in your grieving. If it helps you, we'll talk to the police. Tomorrow.'

Charlotte nodded.

'And if there's anything else I can do –'

'Really, there's nothing. I've just got to get on . . . Father Elias has been really great . . .'

'Elias?'

'He came to see me today. He listened. And we talked about death. It kind of helped. He said if I wanted we could go to the place on the moors where – where it happened. When I'm ready . . .'

'How does he know where it happened?'

'Everyone knows Morton's Crag. It's up above the track across to the estate. That's where the nest was, the peregrine falcons, he called them his birds . . . Elias said he'd take me up there.' Her eyes filled with tears again.

It was twilight when Agnes returned to her room with a stack of marking. She put it on her desk, and took off her coat. She glanced out of the window, at the outlines of the moor, hollowed by the fading light. She put her coat back on, picked up a torch and left, locking her door behind her.

She climbed the path away from the school, thinking that Joanna must have done this every day. The track was still visible. A halfmoon appeared from time to time behind scudding clouds, and the wind caught at her scarf.

For some reason she remembered Elias's words. God is the space between atoms, between universes. She thought of God in the gusts of wind, in the blades of grass. She thought of her childhood image of God, bearded and paternal and human. She thought of Leonora's hair, and James Lombard.

James Lombard. A memory, of being about seven, of being in

28

Provence and taking her pony out to the paddock, and her parents and James coming to watch. The feeling of delight as her pony sailed perfectly over a series of jumps – then turning to see her audience share her triumph. Her father had gone. Her mother had wandered over to the greenhouses. Only James was there, clapping, smiling, praising her as he helped her from her pony, both of them pretending to ignore the tears that rolled down her cheeks.

Agnes joined the track that led down to the estate, dashing at her eyes with the back of her hand. She felt suddenly angry. How dare Philomena put the publicity needs of the school before those of Charlotte? It was quite clear that Charlotte cared deeply about Mark, and was more involved in his life than she was letting on. They'd go to see that nice policewoman tomorrow, whatever Philomena thought. And Joanna – had she resigned? Was Philomena appointing another art teacher?

And Mark. Agnes stopped and glanced around her. The moon had vanished. She felt suddenly alone in the gathering darkness. What was Mark doing up here that night? Just walking, like I am now? Like Elias?

Below her the lights of the estate spread a yellow haze across the valley. She quickened her pace towards it, descending the hill until she reached the road. She took a scrap of paper from her pocket and read it in the lamplight. Number 18, Merton Way. Joanna's address, copied from the file. She turned into the main avenue of the estate, aware of shouts, a car engine, loud music. A dog appeared from nowhere and sniffed at her heels. She heard growling, then there were shouts.

'Fison – leave it.' She heard laughter, and turned to see three boys of about eleven.

'He won't hurt yer, Miss.'

'Unless he feels like it,' one of them said. They laughed.

The dog left Agnes and jumped up at the boys.

'Do you know where Merton Way is?' Agnes asked.

'Aye, just down there.' They pointed, vaguely. 'Why d'yer want to know?'

'I'm just looking for someone.'

'It int' Dodds, is it? Only t'coppers came, not five minutes since. Took him away, they did.'

'Smackhead, him.'

29

'You've missed him now.'

Agnes smiled. 'No, it's not him.'

'D'you smell burnin'?' one asked.

They twitched their noses. 'It'll be the Warren. Again.'

'There might be a fire engine.' They ran, the dog at their heels.

Agnes followed the road in the direction they'd pointed. The houses were all semi-detached, laid out in neat rows. Some were boarded up, some had windows smashed. The name 'Chub' was painted several times along the street. On number 18 someone had sprayed 'Kris'. The house was in darkness, the curtains drawn.

Agnes turned to go. Under a streetlight at the end of the street, a man was standing, quite still, his face partly hidden in the shadows. He was thin and slightly stooped, wrapped in a thick coat. Against the light she could see the angle of his nose, the little squares of red and yellow on his tartan scarf. Agnes walked quickly away from the estate, towards the town. When she glanced back the man was still there, standing, motionless, staring at Joanna's house. Agnes hoped she'd be able to find a bus to take her back to the school.

Chapter Three

The girls clustered at one end of a huge bank of spinning machines, shouting to each other across the noise. Clemmie MacIntosh put her hands over her ears and giggled. Two women in earplugs and overalls watched her, then exchanged a weary glance and turned back to their work.

'We produce on average between ten and twenty tonnes of yarn here a week, depending on what our customers want.' Their guide was a smart young man whose badge said Malcolm Hollins, Sales Assistant. He spoke in tones of pride, as if he was somehow personally responsible for the inexorable process that transformed the huge mass of raw fleece into boxes of neatly wound thread.

'Look,' he said, moving closer to the girls. He tucked his finger behind one of the tubes that circled in rows and Agnes saw the thread across his fingertip become visible. He took his finger away and the thread vanished again, twisting at top speed on to the tube, like the hundreds along the same line, like the thousands on the neighbouring banks of machines.

Agnes felt slightly sick. 'Where does it all go to, all the yarn?' she said.

'It depends. Abroad, a lot of it. Cheap suiting. The stuff that's knitted up ends up as jumpers, leggings, you know, market stalls, that kind of thing. Eastern Europe, that's a big market now.'

He led the group away from the noise of the machines. Agnes saw a woman in overalls and earplugs move down the banks of spinning tubes where they'd been standing, checking for broken threads.

'My great uncle was killed here,' Cathy Phelps said cheerfully.

'Your what?' The smart young man blinked at her.

'My great uncle. He was only a boy, it was his job to crawl under the machines taking out the fluff. He got caught in one. Horrible death.' She smiled, charmingly, at their guide.

'Are you sure?' Colin Furse asked her.

'My mum told me. He was my grandfather's older brother.'

'But hang on,' Colin said, 'that's only a couple of generations ago. He wouldn't have been old enough –'

'1938, it happened,' Cathy looked at Malcolm Hollins. 'He was only fourteen.'

'Ah, well,' Malcolm said, smiling slightly nervously, 'that would have been in the old mill. We'll have a look at that on our way out.'

'It made my mother's father leave the mills altogether. After the war he was determined not to go back. The family got no compensation or anything. Grandpa became an engineer in the motor industry.'

'What was his name, the boy who died?' Agnes asked.

'Charlie. Charles Rudge.'

'Rudge?' Malcolm Hollins asked. 'Now that's a local name. Maureen,' he called across to one of the women working by the machine. She came over, pulling her ear protectors from around her head, glancing uncertainly at the group. 'The name Rudge – from round here, isn't it?'

She looked from face to face, then said, 'Aye, the Rudges. Aye, I know of them.'

'Did you ever hear of a Charles Rudge?' Malcolm went on. 'Worked here. He died in the thirties –'

The woman peered at the badge on Cathy's blazer, then looked up. 'Aye. Before my time, but weren't there a girl, called Matilda?'

'Yes,' Cathy said, 'my mother's aunt. Grandfather's little sister.'

'My mother talked of her,' Maureen said. 'Didn't she marry late – one of the Wilsons?'

'Yes, she married a George Wilson. I have cousins who are Wilsons.' Cathy was pink-faced with delight.

'My mum's sister married a Wilson,' Maureen said, again addressing the badge on Cathy's blazer. 'They go back a long way, here.'

'So –' Cathy hopped from one foot to another. 'So – that means you and I must be related – by marriage, anyway.'

Maureen slowly raised her eyes from Cathy's blazer to her face. The hum of the machines seemed to grow louder. 'Aye, well, yes, s'pose we are,' she said at last. She put her ear protectors back on and went back to her machines.

'Well, who'd have thought,' Malcolm said, smiling fixedly around the group. 'Some real history, there, eh?'

Colin Furse nodded. 'Um, yes, um – history, yes.'

'Let's go and look at the dye process,' Malcolm said.

The group set off. Cathy glanced back at Maureen, who was moving slowly along the lines of bobbins, then ran to catch up with the group.

Agnes hesitated by Maureen's machine. Maureen looked up at the clock, exchanged a few words with someone who came to replace her, then walked across the floor towards the staff rest room. She noticed Agnes. 'Clever girls,' she said, nodding towards the departing group.

'Yes. St Catherine's Convent.'

'Ah. You a nun then?'

'Yes. I am.'

Maureen nodded. 'Idea I had once, when I were a girl. Read a book about one once. But we're chapel, though, we are. Round here, you'll find everyone's chapel. The Baineses were always chapel, always took on chapel.'

'And the Turnbulls?' Agnes said quickly.

Maureen looked at the spotless lino floor. She glanced up again at Agnes. 'That remains to be seen. If there's anybody left to see it.'

'They're laying people off, I hear.'

Maureen shrugged. 'We've been lucky under old Mr Baines, he's kept this place going as best he can. And in profit. In my view, Mr Baines could stay on for a good few years yet, barely sixty, him, and at least he knows the trade . . .' She stopped, and fiddled with the ear protectors around her neck.

'You mean, the Turnbulls don't?'

'It's not for me to say,' she said. 'Only, wi' Mr Turnbull there, I don't see how you can make your money in the building trade and then come in and run a mill in times like these.' She shook her head. 'Our Robert says I should be lookin' out for another job – though, as I said to 'im, where's anyone going to find another job these days.' She looked at her watch.

'I'm sorry, I'm keeping you,' Agnes said. 'I must go and find my group. They'll be in the old mill by now.'

Maureen smiled at her. 'If you're going in there, watch out for the ghosts.'

★ ★ ★

'You missed the dyeworks,' Colin Furse whispered to her.

'Was it good?'

'All state-of-the-art Italian computers. Apparently we've all got to wear navy blue and beige next year.'

'. . . and this was all powered by water in the eighteenth century, and then later, steam,' Malcolm was saying.

Agnes looked around her at the empty expanse, at the puddles of oil and rainwater, the broken window panes set in rotting frames of classical proportion. From the floor above them came the sound of footsteps, a hollow echo on the bare wooden boards.

'Ghosts,' giggled Clemmie MacIntosh. 'Maybe it's your great-uncle, Cathy.'

Agnes thought of William Baines in his office above, pacing the floor, pausing from time to time to stare out of the window at the view, the same view surveyed by his ancestors. She imagined Baines's grandfather looking out at his estate stretching out before him, seeing landscaped gardens symbolising wealth and progress, terraces of workmen's cottages built by him in the philanthropic spirit of the age. And what did William see? Council offices, housing estates, a patch of derelict land; a hotel and leisure centre, part of the ring road; all on land that had once been his birthright. It wasn't so much ghosts of the departed that suffused this dank air, Agnes thought, but ghosts of the still living.

The girls piled back into the coach, laughing, unwrapping biscuits, scuffling over who was to sit with whom. Clemmie started up an animated discussion about whether Malcolm Hollins had a nice bum. As the coach pulled out of the driveway and on to the road, Agnes, sitting right at the back, noticed two police cars drive up to the mill and into the courtyard.

Back at the school the girls dispersed to their afternoon activities. Agnes went to her room. She took James's letter from her desk and read it again, then picked up her phone and dialled his number. It was answered by a pleasant, elderly voice.

'Hello, is that James Lombard?'

'Who is speaking?'

'It's Agnes.'

'Agnes. How good of you to call.' His voice was as she remembered it, but perhaps slightly more East Coast.

'I got your letter.'

'Thank you so much for telephoning me.'

'You suggested that we –'

'I suggested lunch, didn't I?'

'Yes.'

'Saturday?'

'That would be lovely.'

'You're not to expect anything fancy. I live rather simply now. Nothing like your banquets in Provence.'

Agnes laughed. 'They were hardly banquets, James.'

'About twelve thirty for one? You have my address. Turn off the Addingham Road, go down into the village and mine's the second house on the right. There's a phone box opposite, you can't miss it.'

Agnes scribbled down his directions.

'I'll be lovely to see you,' she heard him say.

'I look forward to it.'

Agnes rang off. She stared at her phone. Lunch with James Lombard. In Yorkshire. How odd. Just from picking up the phone and saying yes.

There was a knock at her door. Charlotte stood there. She came into the room wordlessly and sat down. At last she said, 'I can't work.' She stood up and went over to the window. 'I can't think. I can't sleep.'

'Janet Cole said –' Agnes began, but Charlotte went on.

'I just keep seeing his last hours, his last minutes, his last breath . . .' She broke into sobs, standing by the window, her hands across her mouth.

'When we went to the police – ' Agnes tried again.

'What do they know? What are they doing?' Charlotte turned round sharply. 'Nothing. That Janet Cole – she said nothing.'

'They were up at the mill this lunchtime, two cars, I saw them.'

'So? Does that bring the murderer any closer to being caught? Does that bring Mark back?' She collapsed on Agnes's bed in a fit of sobbing. Agnes went to her and rested her hand on her shoulder.

'No,' Agnes said softly. 'Nothing will bring him back.'

'What did they do to him?' Charlotte sat up, raising her eyes to Agnes, waiting for the truth.

Agnes sat down next to her. 'For some reason – his eyes – they felt he shouldn't – they had to –'

Charlotte sat quite still. The colour had drained from her face. Her voice was barely audible. 'How can they – how could they – how can God forgive . . .' She turned to Agnes. 'I'll never sleep again, how can I, knowing that someone's out there who –' She stood up and walked unsteadily to the door.

'Charlotte . . .' Agnes went to her. 'You must get away, surely, go home, give yourself time –'

'Why? Where is there to go? I'd rather be here. You see, don't you –' Charlotte opened the door – 'they've just got to catch whoever did it. Then maybe I'll sleep.' She went out into the corridor and back to her own room.

Agnes went and sat at her desk. Outside the sun was setting, searing the sky with red. And what if they don't, Agnes thought. What if they never catch the murderer?

And even if they do, that young boy is still dead.

She got out some French essays and stared at them for a while. At ten past four there was a knock at the door. Leonora came in and stood, waiting. Agnes gestured to a chair. Leonora sat down with exquisite poise, her hands clasped neatly in her lap. She looked up at Agnes with her clear blue-grey eyes.

'Tea, I think,' Agnes said.

'As you please, Sister.'

'Or something stronger? A glass of wine, it's a little early I know but even so . . .'

Leonora's poise faltered slightly, then she shook her head. 'Tea would be lovely.'

Agnes put her kettle on to boil, then sat down opposite her. 'Well, let's begin.'

'There's no point,' Leonora said.

'So you say.'

'I don't wish to be rude, but I have to get home. I'll do it one day, you can't stop me.'

'There's just one thing I find a little odd,' Agnes said. 'You see, speaking from my own experience of running away, it's not that difficult, is it?' She glanced at the girl, then continued, 'What I mean is, if you really wanted to get home, you'd be there by now.' The beautiful eyes narrowed slightly. Agnes went on, 'What I wanted to ask you, Leonora, is not, why do you keep running away, but why are you so determined not to succeed?'

'What do you know about running away?' Leonora asked in a small voice.

'Rather a lot, I'm afraid. Violent husbands, well, only one – then my first order which was disastrous. And various smaller attempts since. Not a good record. I fear it's in my blood. Started, of course, by having parents who didn't give a damn. You see,' Agnes went on, 'if I'd run away from home, it would have been some weeks before my parents had even noticed.'

'Poor you,' Leonora said, politely.

'And I wondered, whether, perhaps, in your case –' Agnes looked at the girl sitting there, at her calm composure. 'You see, what I wondered was, whether perhaps you're happier with the fantasy of running back home than with the reality of what it would be like when you got there.'

Leonora smoothed her skirt on her knees.

'Which made me think that perhaps you feel, as I did at your age, that if only you could do the right thing, everything at home would be lovely and happy, instead of –'

'Did you call me here to reminisce about your unhappy childhood?' Leonora's expression was one of perfect calm.

'No,' Agnes said. 'I called you here because you're so clearly miserable and I want to help.'

'It's very touching that you choose to identify with me,' Leonora said, 'and it's been lovely talking to you.' She stood up. 'But really, I've got an awful lot of prep to do before tomorrow. I'm so sorry not to be able to stay longer.'

Agnes sighed.

Leonora hesitated by the door. 'You see,' she said, 'you can't stop me running away.'

'In that case,' Agnes said, getting up and opening the door for her, 'here are some tips. Speaking as one who knows. One, don't pack a huge suitcase. Two, go in the hours of daylight when the trains are running and you can get a cab. Three, avoid public routes of escape. There's a gap in the hedge behind the kitchens, leads straight on to the back drive. I noticed it a couple of weeks ago when I was planning my own getaway.'

A smile spread across the girl's face, and for a moment her eyes sparkled with life. Then the polite composure returned. 'Thank you, Sister,' she said. She walked away along the corridor without looking back.

Agnes went to her fridge and pulled out a bottle of chilled white wine. She rummaged in a drawer for a corkscrew, just as the phone rang.

'Sweetie, it's Athena.'

'Extraordinary,' Agnes said, 'I was just opening a bottle of Chardonnay.'

'Telepathy, darling.'

'You mean you can sniff out a decent white wine all the way from London?'

'Heavens, darling, you have no idea of the extent of my talents. And how's life up North?'

'Dreadful. These girls – I've never seen such hard cases.'

'But surely, compared to all those poor delinquent baby junkies you rescued in London –'

'They were a doddle compared to this lot.'

'At least they must be polite and well-behaved.'

'You should see their politeness in action. It's deadly. I'm beginning to realise the British kept their whole empire in subservience just by being polite.'

'That and a few guns too, perhaps. Anyway, the point is, how do you fancy dinner on Sunday?'

'But I can't escape from here.'

'No, I mean up North. There. If they have any decent restaurants, that is.'

'Well, they do, but –'

'Simon's discovered a little gallery in Leeds by the canal, he's very excited about it, wants to talk business, don't ask me, sweetie, but he's insisting we both go.'

'What does Nic think?'

'Oh, Nic's coming too.'

'Doesn't he trust you with Simon?'

'More to the point, do I trust Simon with Nic? Anyway, apparently there's a decent hotel somewhere around there.'

'There's a Harvey Nichols too.'

'Harvey – ? No, sweetie, no. You must have made a mistake. What do those Northerners want with a shop like that?'

'Athena, you're terrible!'

'Do you know, I'm beginning to look forward to this expedition after all. Anyway, Sunday evening, just you and me, dinner – what do you think?'

'I can't wait.'

Old friends, Agnes thought, switching off her phone. She thought about her friend Athena, living her London life, shopping, working in an art gallery, going to restaurants, more shopping. It made her feel lonely.

That evening Agnes slipped into the chapel. She sat alone, in the front pew, and contemplated a painting that hung there, of St Catherine praying before her death. She thought about Charlotte in her anguish, locked in the horror of Mark's last moments. And now I've told her the truth, she thought, about his eyes. I've only made it worse.

Nothing will bring him back, she thought, raising her eyes to the stained-glass altar window. And You, she said, addressing the image of Heaven that was depicted there, once again You deal humanity a blow, a random act of violence that shatters several lives by destroying one. Once again You allow our imperfections to take hold, You allow the consequences of our frailty to unfold before You. And You do nothing. You do nothing in the face of Mark's murder, of Charlotte's grief. Of Joanna Baines's flight. Of the thousand incidents of human tragedy that happen every second in this world. You wait, and You ask us to believe in You, the God of Love; You ask that we should have faith and You promise us redemption. And is it likely, Agnes asked the window, that Charlotte will reward You with her continued trust? What is Your promise to her, now?'

In the chapel there was silence.

Am I wrong to be angry with You? Agnes asked. Elias would say I am. He'd say my anger is like the tantrum of a child, standing on a beach and stamping its foot at the sea because the tide has come in and washed away its sandcastle. The futile wringing of hands, he'd say, in the face of the implacable Oneness of the divine.

And should I not pray, then? Should I not pray for Charlotte, for Joanna, for William Baines? For Mark and his family? And should I not pray for whoever it was who killed Mark? And pray that they be found?

That they be found. Someone must have seen Mark set out that evening, someone must have known what he was intending to do, whom he was intending to meet. Somewhere there must be a reason; somewhere in the chaos there must be order.

Agnes imagined Elias pitying her for trying to see a pattern in the void. She looked up at the window. In daylight, with the sun streaming through it, the altar windows showed God as Light, with His Son and Mary and the apostles. Now in the darkness it showed nothing at all, just the lines around the panes of glass, a random leaden web against the night.

On Saturday morning Agnes chose her clothes carefully, eventually settling for a cream silk shirt and black trousers and jacket. She borrowed the community's ancient Metro and set off in good time, heading away from Leeds and then taking the Addingham Road as James had instructed. The morning's drizzle was clearing, and she felt a sense of escape. She wished the car had a radio, so that she could tune to a music station and sing along. Not that she ever knew the words.

She parked in James's drive. It was a two-storey cottage, with thick stone walls and wide, elegant windows. She rang the bell. Then the door opened and James was there, and they found themselves smiling at each other; he hugged her, and kissed her on both cheeks.

'You haven't changed,' he laughed, ushering her into his hallway. The house was warm, with polished wood panelling and thick pale carpets.

'Since I was seven? Surely I have,' she replied.

'Well, maybe since then. Can I get you a drink?' She followed him into his living room. He seemed less tall than she remembered, and very thin, but graceful and upright. He was wearing blue jeans and an expensive Guernsey sweater, which made him seem somehow frail.

He poured them both a sherry and they sat down opposite each other. Sunlight fell on the polished floorboards, on the plain cream sofas and the Chinese silk rugs.

James raised his glass to her. 'On the other hand,' he said, 'I've changed beyond recognition.'

'Nonsense . . .'

'Go on, say it,' he laughed. 'My hair's white –'

'You were always blond –'

'– and these wrinkles –'

'They're nice. Everyone has wrinkles.' She remembered now his blue-grey eyes, the lightness of his expression. She tried to

40

remember whether he'd always looked so fragile, his skin so papery.

'I've aged,' he said, and his face grew serious.

'We all age.'

'Yes, but – anyway,' he said, brightening again, 'what news? How's your mother?'

Agnes sighed. 'Just the same. As far as I know. Her nursing home sends me the occasional bulletin.'

'Antibes, isn't it?'

'I think so.'

'You think so?'

She raised her eyes to his and saw only sympathy. Suddenly she wanted to cry. 'You know how it was,' she said, trying to keep her voice level.

'Yes,' he said. 'I know how it was.' He stood up. 'Lunch? It's only cold ham and salad. I'm more decrepit than you realise.'

He led her through to the dining room. She sat at the large mahogany table, while he brought warm bread rolls from the kitchen.

'My greatest fear,' he said, 'was that when your father left, you'd feel responsible for your mother.'

'Why did that frighten you?'

'Because I knew she'd never let you go. You'd have given up the rest of your life.'

'I have anyway.'

'Yes, but not to her.'

'It's funny, I never talk about it to anyone. The fact that she's still alive, that we don't communicate apart from birthday and Christmas cards –' She stopped, blinking back tears. 'I'm sorry,' she murmured. 'I can't think why I'm so overcome.'

'Don't apologise,' he said gently. 'After all, who else is going to understand? Who else is going to remember how awful it was for you?'

'Yes, but was it? Sometimes I think perhaps it wasn't too bad, that someone less selfish than me would have made it work.'

'Agnes – all the time I spent with you – the worst thing was seeing you take it all upon your shoulders. I used to talk to Aylmer about it, later, but by then he was – he didn't really – he was mentally somewhere else.' He poured white wine into her glass. 'She sends me Christmas cards too,' he added.

'Does she?'

'Yes. After Aylmer died, I kept in touch with her. I had to, there were various business things I was taking care of – I think she grew to resent me less. This Christmas just gone, she was quite effusive – for her, anyway. Inviting me to visit, even. I might just do that.'

'So why are you going abroad?' Agnes buttered a bread roll.

'Oh, things to sort out. I'll end up back in the States, but I'm planning a long trip. A kind of holiday in fact, unusual for me. Would you like salad dressing?'

'But why clear out this house?'

'I'm planning to rent it out. I've got two old friends who live nearby, the Campbells, they're going to keep an eye on it for me. Your father's things are valuable, I didn't want them lying around while I was gone.'

'You know I can't own anything. I've taken a vow of poverty.'

He smiled. 'How appealing. Shall we just put everything in the trashcan now, or do you want to take a look at it first?'

Agnes laughed.

After lunch Agnes sat with her coffee in the sunny living room while James brought her father's things to show her.

'Your inheritance,' he said, taking something from a box and unwrapping it. It was a Chinese vase.

'Ming, of course,' laughed Agnes.

'Imitation, I'm afraid. But very pretty. And these . . .' he unwrapped two framed photographs. 'You've got to have these,' he said, 'they're no good to anyone else.'

She saw two black-and-white images of herself. In one she was a toddler, with ringlets and a lacy dress, standing with her parents, one on each side. In the other she was about fifteen, her hair tied back, wearing a tight-waisted dress with a full skirt which fell in perfect folds.

'Who took these?' she asked.

'I've no idea. But your father wanted me to have them.'

'Why you?'

'I'm not sure exactly, but – ' James wrapped them up again and handed them to her – 'I think he couldn't face what he'd done. In leaving, I mean. He didn't want your mother to have them, and – he couldn't bear to give them to you. It would mean facing up to his own failings. Perhaps. Anyway, they're yours.'

She sat with them on her knee.

'There are some other things. Look – this clock.'

Agnes stared at it. It was a brass carriage clock, so familiar it hurt. 'I remember that. We had it in the Paris apartment, in the window. It has those four spheres that go round and round, I used to watch it . . . I used to think it would wind down eventually, I'd sit there and wait for them to slow down, I couldn't see why they didn't.' She looked up and laughed.

'It belongs to your mother. And look, some silver teaspoons. These are valuable. There's some Meissen as well, it's upstairs.'

Agnes was shaking her head. 'I can't.'

'You really can't own anything?'

'Well – strictly, no. I have a trust fund set up by some lawyers long ago, after my divorce settlement, but that's different. This stuff here, if I take it, it all goes to the order.'

'But what if –' James hesitated, then said, 'I'm sorry, it's presumptuous.'

'You were going to say, what if things don't work out and I need to leave the order.'

'That's precisely what I was going to say. But I'm sure you'll never need to.'

'Do you really think that?'

James looked at her for a long moment, then shook his head. 'No. I don't. Unless you've really changed, and I don't think you have.'

She smiled. 'It's such a relief.'

'What is?'

'To be with someone who knows me. Only Julius –'

'Who's Julius?'

'The priest you spoke to on the phone. He's known me since – since I was married.'

James fell silent, wrapping up the vase and putting it in its box. Then he said, 'I tried to stop that, you know.'

'My marriage?'

'I tried to tell your father it was a disaster.'

'But you'd gone by then, you were in the States.'

'I heard about it. I was horrified. I knew your husband's family. Terrible people.' He shook his head. 'I'm sorry.'

'It wasn't your fault. It was my decision.'

'They pushed you into it.'

'I wanted to go. It seemed preferable to staying where I was.'

'I feared for you.'

'With reason, it turned out.'

'Does your mother –?'

'She knew he was violent. She's never admitted it.' Agnes glanced down at the photos in her lap, at her younger selves. 'It makes me feel like a monster,' she said.

'What does?'

'That I can't – that she doesn't . . .'

'My mother sent me away to school when I was seven.' James smoothed the creases in his trousers. 'We were living in England then. And it's not that I didn't forgive her, because I did. I hope I did. But – I always felt after that, that I could never love her as much as I should. It left me with this feeling, that I was somehow unnatural. Kind of monstrous, as you said.'

Agnes nodded. 'Yes. That's what it is.'

They sat and smiled at each other. Then James stood up. 'Shall we have a ritual burning of this stuff now?'

Agnes laughed. 'I've got to get back for chapel. But I'll take the vase and the photos.'

'Do you always break your vows so readily?'

'And I'll give you my solicitor's address – you can send the spoons and the porcelain to him, in trust, should I ever feel the need to follow my instincts to bolt over the wall.'

At James's door he took her hand. It was growing dark, and the birds were twittering in preparation for the night. 'I hope I'll see you again soon,' he said.

'I'd love to,' Agnes said.

'Don't leave it too late,' he said. Agnes glanced at him. The twilight seemed to age him.

She kissed his cheek, then got into the car and drove away.

On the way home she stopped at a flower stall and bought some scentless hot-housed pale yellow roses. She unpacked the vase and arranged the roses within it on her mantelpiece, then placed the two photos one on each side of it. She glanced out of her window, expecting to see Leonora making her way once again up the drive, to see her standing by the railings dreaming of escape. For some reason she imagined her in a tight-waisted dress with a full skirt that fell in perfect folds.

Chapter Four

In chapel that Sunday Elias seemed more preoccupied than usual. His sermon was half-hearted, and he never raised his eyes once from his text. Agnes found herself scanning the pews in boredom. Charlotte was standing with the sixth-form, her head bowed, her face sallow. Afterwards Agnes caught up with her in the corridor.

'Charlotte, you can't go on like this.'

'What else can I do?'

Agnes took her arm and led her to their house, ushered her into her room and put on the kettle.

'Charlotte – whatever you want to do, you must do. If you want to carry on with your exams, then we'll support you in that. If you want to go home and come back next year to take them, no one will blame you.'

Charlotte was shaking her head, muttering. Agnes made out the words, 'I just want to see him.'

Agnes went to her and took her hands. 'It won't bring him back.'

Charlotte raised her tearful eyes to her. 'Whatever state he's in, it can't be any worse than the way I see him, I keep seeing him, whenever I close my eyes, it can't be worse than that. Whatever he suffered, I have to know . . .' She buried her head on Agnes's shoulder.

'I'll phone Janet Cole,' Agnes said. 'I'll arrange it.'

'And Elias said it would help.'

What does Elias know, Agnes thought, standing up, going to the kettle and making tea.

'Also –' Charlotte was dabbing at her eyes with a handkerchief – 'also, I prayed last night, because – because I didn't know what to do – he told me not to tell, but last night it seemed I better – I don't know . . .'

Agnes took milk from her fridge. Charlotte was silent again.

'What is it?' Agnes said.

'Just that he was – he said he was meeting someone –'

'Billy Keenan?'

Charlotte nodded. 'How did you know?'

'When Janet mentioned his name – there was something about your reaction, that's all.'

'He said he was going to meet him.' Charlotte took the mug of tea Agnes handed her.

'Mark was going to meet Billy?'

'On the night he died. I phoned him the day before, he couldn't see me that night, he said he was meeting Billy, they were going up to the moors.'

'Were they friends?'

'Not really. That's why I remembered. David said –'

'Who's David?'

'Mark's brother. He's an artist. He said there were bad feelings between the families that went back years.'

'Why should Mark meet him?'

'I don't know. They were doing this sports club thing at the community centre, they were both trying to get that off the ground, so maybe they were getting on better.'

'Charlotte, shouldn't you tell the police?'

'They know. David told me. I spoke to him yesterday. He said they were questioning Billy because Mark was seen getting into his car that night.'

'Oh. Right.' Agnes sipped her tea.

'And you see, Mark needed a lift up to the moors because someone said they'd seen someone behaving suspiciously around the ledge, up on Morton's Crag.'

'Suspiciously?'

'The peregrines. People try and take the eggs, apparently. They lay rope over the ledge before spring, so then they can move in quickly when the eggs are laid. Mark told me. He'd been tipped off and he was in a hurry to get up there before dark, and according to David it was Billy who offered him a lift.'

'Charlotte, you shouldn't feel burdened by all this. If the police already know –'

Charlotte put down her mug and turned to Agnes. 'I want to see him.'

★　★　★

46

At eight o'clock that evening, Agnes walked into a high-ceilinged, white-walled, marble-floored space and scanned the tables for Athena. Her eye was caught by a scarlet-sleeved arm, waving madly.

'Sweetie! Over here.'

Agnes bent to kiss her friend. 'You smell different. What happened to the Miss Dior?' she said, as the waiter took her coat.

'Oh, no no no, far too old fashioned. I'm wearing Calvin Klein now, it's what all the young people are wearing, poppet. I decided that after all these years, it was time to get younger again. And Nic gave it to me, so who am I to argue?'

'Where is he?'

'Oh, darling, it's such a shame, he had to stay in London after all, his son, you know, Ben, needed to stay over at the flat, and we thought it was best if they caught up, you know, bonded over beer and Chelsea – or is it that other one, Dagenham or something, it's all lost on me, I'm afraid.'

'So, let loose in Leeds, Athena, what are you going to do?'

Athena sighed theatrically and looked at the menu. 'I mean, Leeds, sweetie, of all places. Hardly the place for a romantic adventure. Gosh, look at this menu, proper food. Mmm, I fancy the red mullet terrine myself. What was I saying?'

'You were musing on the possibility of a romantic adventure.'

'The funny thing is, darling, it's just not what I want. Not any more. Nic's so sweet and lovely and – and real, somehow. So surprising.'

'So your morals have got older and your perfume's got younger.'

Athena giggled. 'Something like that. Heavens, guinea fowl too – I had no idea civilisation extended this far north.'

'How long are you staying?'

'Oh, just till tomorrow, we're meeting Gavin, he owns the gallery. But we'll be back.'

The waitress appeared, and they gave her their order.

'This really isn't too bad,' Athena surveyed the restaurant. 'Maybe you shouldn't feel too exiled after all.'

'Exile isn't just about restaurants,' Agnes sighed.

'No. You're right.' Athena sipped her wine, then frowned. 'What is it about, then?'

'I'm not sure. We're both exiles, you and me.'

'Yes, but it's OK.'

'It's OK in London. But here – you see, there's a difference between being an exile and being someone who doesn't belong. Yesterday I saw someone I hadn't seen for years, and it made me realise –'

'Who?'

'He's called James. He was a friend of my father, a business associate. He lives near Ilkley. And it was terribly strange to be with someone who's known me since I was little. I kept wanting to cry. It was such a relief. And then I went back to the school and it seemed like a pretence again.'

'Are you seeing him again?'

'He phoned this morning. He's invited me to supper on Wednesday.'

'The father you never had.'

'Athena, really.'

'Funny I've never noticed this before in you, this need to be looked after.'

'In London there's you. And Julius. And the community's different there, they leave me alone.'

Athena poured herself more wine. 'So it's a need to escape, then? They'll let you out soon, won't they? Don't you get time off for good behaviour?'

'But it's not as if I could go, not now. You see, one of my girls was seeing this young man, secretly, and he was found dead on the moors, and as you can imagine, she's in a terrible state. And at the same time, there's an art teacher, and I think it's her father who employed this young man, and she's vanished. And if she is an Allbright Baines then I seem to be the only one who's saying so, apart from our chaplain, Father Elias, who definitely knows more than he's letting on – what's so funny, Athena?'

'Same old Agnes, then.'

'No really, it's serious – you must see, Athena, that I have to find out what's going on.'

'Oh, absolutely, sweetie. Yes, the terrine for me, and – snails? You never said you were having snails.'

The waitress placed an exquisite arrangement of shells and butter in front of Agnes.

'I so rarely see civilisation, you see, Athena. I expect they had them flown in from Bourgogne, especially. Which is odd as they're two a penny up on the moors. You can crunch them underfoot up there.'

Agnes dropped Athena at her hotel, then joined the Leeds ring road towards Bradford. She watched her windscreen wipers splash against the rain, and thought about Athena returning to London the next day, back to real life. She envied her.

At St Catherine's she found Leonora, sitting on the wall by the school gates. Agnes got out of her car and sighed. 'Leonora, what did I say about suitcases?'

Leonora shrugged. 'It's only a few things.'

'It's hardly the weather for it.'

'I like the rain.'

They looked at the night sky, at the muted edges of the clouds. 'If you leave it a few days,' Agnes said, 'I might just come with you.'

Leonora looked down at Agnes and smiled. She jumped down from the wall, and Agnes took her suitcase, and they walked back along the drive towards the school.

'But the girl is tormented by not knowing,' Agnes protested on the phone next morning. 'No, of course they weren't married, but for Heaven's sake, she loved him, he was her boyfriend, and now he's been killed and she can't begin to grieve until she's seen him . . . what do you mean, only next of kin? No, I can see it's not – no, of course I don't think it's a circus . . . right. Goodbye.'

Agnes hung up. She stared out of her window. She sighed, got up and went out of the school, across the courtyard, to Elias's flat, and knocked on the door.

'You've got to help,' she said as he opened the door. 'Charlotte wants to see the body, she's in a terrible state, I've been on the phone all morning, they all say no. Anyone would think I was suggesting bringing a coach party. It can't be any worse than what she's imagining, can it?'

Elias stood in the doorway. 'No, it can't. Have you got the number?'

Agnes handed him a piece of paper.

'Leave it with me,' he said.

They sat in the back of the car, Charlotte and Elias, as Agnes

49

drove them to the mortuary. No one spoke.

They trooped silently into the building, and were greeted by a young woman who led them along gleaming corridors. She took them through a swing door and asked them to wait.

Charlotte turned her fingers round and round in her hair. Elias ambled to the window as if he knew the room. Then the young woman came back and held the door for them to go through. Elias glanced at Agnes, then accompanied Charlotte through the door. Agnes was left, waiting.

She sat on a beige plastic chair and looked around her. It seemed to be a workroom. There were tables in one corner, and shelves above them, cluttered with glass jars, plastic bags, cardboard boxes. Agnes wandered over to them, wondering whether it was unusual for people to see the bodies of their loved ones, surprised that no special place was provided for grieving relatives.

She saw a label on one of the boxes. 'Mark Snaith', it said. She took it down and opened it. It contained a pair of muddy binoculars, a rather filthy handkerchief, a Biro, a bus ticket. A dry-cleaning ticket for a garment that Mark would never see again. A dentist's card with an appointment time written on it. A life cut short, Agnes thought. A young man fully expecting to collect his dry cleaning, go to his dentist – and now there is no Mark Snaith. Agnes stared at the objects, these Things Left Behind. It was difficult to grasp, this sudden non-existence. There was a piece of white card at the bottom, and she picked it out.

'Mr and Mrs A. Turnbull', she saw printed on it in curly script, 'Request the pleasure of your company on Tuesday, 5th March, at 7.30 p.m., for a private viewing of artworks by David Snaith.' There was an address.

Tuesday, Agnes thought. She scribbled down the address and phone number, replaced the card in the box and put it back on the shelf. She went and stared out of the window, as the door opened and Elias was there, supporting Charlotte who was near to collapse. Agnes ran to help him. Charlotte struggled against them both, making a low moaning noise in her throat, grabbing the door handle as if trying to go back, trying to return to Mark, fighting Elias and Agnes as they propelled her back to the corridor.

'No, no,' Charlotte was crying, as they left the building. Elias was murmuring to her.

Agnes unlocked the car. 'He's dead,' she heard him say.

* * *

They led her to Agnes's room. In the car she'd quietened, and now sat, passively, on Agnes's bed.

'She shouldn't be alone,' Elias said.

'She can sleep here,' Agnes tidied some books from her floor. 'I can get a spare mattress, if you'll help me carry it.'

They went out into the corridor. 'Do you think we did the right thing?' Agnes asked him.

'I'm sure we did.'

'How did he look?'

'Dead.'

Agnes glanced at him. 'Did he look awful?'

'No, just dead.'

'His eyes—'

'They'd closed the lids. It was OK.'

'She seems horror-stricken.'

'It's the finality of it, that's all. She's had to say goodbye. It's tough.'

I hope you're right, Agnes thought, you with your certainties, your knowledge of death. They carried the mattress back. Charlotte was sitting exactly where they'd left her.

That night Charlotte stirred and murmured in her sleep. Once she cried out Mark's name. Agnes watched her settle back into sleep, wondering what demons were haunting her dreams. She thought about Elias, and wondered what it was that drew him to Charlotte's anguish, that made him speak with such authority about death; that gave him such a bleak view of life.

She found she was wide awake. She got up and put on a jumper. Charlotte stirred and muttered again. Agnes padded silently to the window and sat in her chair, watching the shifting darkness of the sky. She wondered what was Elias's connection with Joanna, with Allbright's. Her eye fell on her two photographs, lit by a streak of light from the courtyard, and she thought about James, his kindness to her, his concern for her all those years ago. In her sleep Charlotte turned over, and Agnes thought about the letter she ought to write to Charlotte's parents. She imagined Charlotte's mother awake too, sitting quietly by a window in another country, seeing the same dawn, missing her daughter. She imagined her own mother, insomniac as ever, watching the sky turn grey. She wondered what her mother thought about during her sleepless nights.

She felt weary, stood up, yawning, covered Charlotte up gently with an extra blanket and went back to bed.

Chapter Five

Setting off from the school on Tuesday evening, Agnes wished Athena was with her.

'What a hoot, poppet,' Athena had said on the phone. 'Yes of course you can pretend to be from our gallery. You can even borrow my name, if you like. What a shame I'm not there, I could come too and pretend to be you. I'd be utterly convincing as a nun, what do you think, sweetie?'

Athena was always so much better at these things, Agnes thought, turning on to the Otley Road. She drove past tall hedges, beautiful old houses tucked away behind stone walls. She checked the directions that she'd been given on the phone, turned up a drive and saw a bright white building, the front of which was mostly glass. Several cars stood in the drive. She pulled up behind a BMW 318, and parked behind it with a wave of envy which she knew was sinful.

She got out of her car, pulling her black pencil skirt down, hoping there wouldn't be hours of standing up as she'd chosen her highest-heeled shoes, still only a modest couple of inches but unfamiliar. As she passed the BMW, she noticed a baby seat strapped into the back of it.

She rang the bell, and the door was opened by a man dressed as a waiter. A hubbub surged behind him. She smiled warmly and said, 'Agnes Bourdillon.' It seemed to be enough, and he stepped aside to let her pass, indicating someone collecting coats at the foot of the stairs.

The hall was broad and light, hung with framed pictures. Agnes glanced at them as she handed her coat to the petite, dark-haired waitress, who slung it clumsily over one arm and then smiled. 'The reception's through there, the ladies if you want it is that door there.'

'Thanks.'

'Unless you want the one with the Jacuzzi,' the girl went on. 'Which is upstairs. Though I don't s'pose they'd thank me for telling you.'

'I think I'll save that for later,' Agnes smiled.

The bathroom was cool, blue and marbled. Agnes checked her face in the mirror above the basin, then carefully applied an expensive red lipstick. Agnes Bourdillon, she thought. It's ages since I've called myself that. It was odd how her husband's surname tended to follow her around. Agnes Bourdillon, she thought, looking at the image of herself that the mirror held up to her. Tailored skirt, red lips, smart white shirt. It's a disguise, she thought. An illusion. I'm allowed that.

She went back out into the hall, noticing that the pictures on the wall were cheap prints; a Victorian street scene, warm lamplight, crinolined ladies, hurrying carriages. A past that never was, thought Agnes. She went towards the noise.

Almost immediately she found herself face to face with the first work in the exhibition. It showed a standing group of men facing out of the picture. The outlines were scratchy and muted, in shades of charcoal. Behind them a few desolate lines suggested a mill. The next picture was similar. The third showed a group of women; the same dark colours, the same faces ingrained with dirt and pain.

At a distance from the pictures, glasses clinked, people chatted. The room was huge and light, and gave on to a conservatory. The doors were open to the chilly darkness of the garden beyond, but the room was warm.

'Wine, Madam?'

Agnes turned. It was the girl who'd taken her coat, now holding a tray. Agnes took a glass of white wine.

'They're good, aren't they?'

Agnes noticed the straightened black hair and wide-set eyes heavily coated in eye-liner. 'Yes,' she said. 'Yes, they're very good.'

'Not that this lot give a toss,' the girl went on. 'Look at them all. What are they like, eh?' Agnes glanced at the crowd. 'I've known Dave for a while now,' the young woman said. 'We were at college together.'

'Dave?'

'David Snaith. The artist. He's around somewhere.'

'Nina, it's time for the buffet, don't you think?' A tall woman in

54

elegant black appeared. 'And can we have some wine at the far end of the room, thanks so much.'

Nina turned to Agnes and winked, then sauntered down the room, her tray swaying on her hand.

Agnes drifted towards a crowd grouped at the far end of the exhibition, wondering whether the artist was amongst them.

'. . . patronage, you see, the only way forward.' A booming male voice was holding forth next to one of the works. '. . . tradition among us mill owners, fostering the arts, looking after the new young voices upon which, after all, the future of British culture depends. Isn't that so, darling?' A man in an expensively cut suit was holding out one arm towards the woman who'd just given her orders to Nina. He had thinning grey hair and a broad, amiable face.

'Isn't what so, Anthony?' the woman said.

'I was saying that your father's family had always supported the arts, and we intend to maintain that tradition.'

'Yes, dear, of course. What can have happened to the food, do excuse me, those girls are just hopeless . . .'

Anthony Turnbull beamed expansively at the few people gathered around the painting. 'Ah, David, dear boy,' he said as a thin-faced young man appeared. 'We're all dying to hear what you have to say about this.'

Turnbull was indicating a three-dimensional piece, set in a heavy frame. Various objects were half-submerged in a background of thick muddy oil paint. Agnes saw an antique beer bottle; some kind of spinning bobbin; a sheep's skull.

'Well?' he said.

David flinched, stared at the floor, then at the piece. He wore a loose white shirt in fine cotton, and his hair was short and well cut. At last he looked up at the crowd. 'What did you want to know?'

There was a silence which Agnes broke. 'I wondered,' Agnes said, 'how such an abstract work could be said to relate to the more representational themes in the other pieces?'

David looked at her with eyes which were a dark stony grey. 'It doesn't,' he said.

Turnbull laughed. 'That's the problem with modern art – one has to work so much harder. Ah, the food, I see. My wife has worked her magic with the staff at last . . .' He shepherded his following away from the paintings. Agnes was left standing with David.

'I keep seeing sheep's skulls,' she said, conversationally.

'Oh yeah?' He stared at the floor.

'Someone I know called Joanna Baines –'

He flashed a glance at her. 'How do you know Joanna?'

'I work with her at St Catherine's.'

'She's left.'

'She was working with sheep's skulls.'

'So? It's the nineties.'

Agnes glanced at him, but he wasn't smiling. 'How do you know Joanna?' she asked him.

'Who are you?'

'Sister Agnes. I'm a nun.' Athena would have managed to keep her cover for longer than five minutes, Agnes thought with regret.

David was surveying her. Then he shook his head. 'Nice try,' he said, moving away.

'Me and Elias – Elias Parnell – we're very concerned . . .' Agnes followed him.

'Elias can get stuffed,' David said, beginning to merge with the crowd who were gathered around the buffet table. 'And while he's at it, he can give me back the key to her house.' He disappeared into the throng at Turnbull's side, and a moment later Agnes heard snatches of conversation: '. . . the post-industrial legacy . . . the worker as participant in the gaze . . .'

'He's not that forthcoming, is he?' Nina was at her side, struggling with two trays of empty glasses. 'Help me with these will you?' Agnes took a tray and followed her into the kitchen. 'I'm off duty now, gotta go back to my little girl.' Nina went into the hall and took her coat from a row of hangers. 'You couldn't do my apron, could you?'

Agnes untied her apron strings.

Nina gestured to the prints on the wall. 'He's a nice bloke, Anthony, but he doesn't know much about art. I mean, look at these – not worth the frames they're in.' She laughed. 'Victorian ladies and happy millworkers and cobbled streets – give me Dave's work any day. And this one, look –'

Agnes saw a smiling housewife standing by a kitchen range.

'She looks like my mum, she does. Only my mum looks more interesting.'

'Your mother – but you're –'

'Black?' Nina's eyes danced.

'I just meant –'

Nina laughed. 'My mum's white. And I'm black.' She pulled on her coat.

'I was asking David about the sheep's skull.'

'Oh, that. I prefer his portraits and stuff. He got into that abstract stuff when he met Jo, his girlfriend.'

'Jo?'

'Joanna Baines, Patricia's sister.'

'And she's his –'

'Crazy about each other. Surprised she's not here, but then, she hates her family.'

'But I had no idea – you see, I work with Joanna.'

'You know Jo? How come?'

'I'm from the convent. I'm one of the sisters.'

Nina stared at her, then grinned, then started laughing. 'You're nothing of the kind. Not you. Not like . . .' She gestured at Agnes's skirt, and shoes, then laughed some more.

'David didn't believe me either.'

'I'm not surprised. Ooh, I must go, I'm going to be late.'

Agnes followed her outside. She pointed her car key at the BMW which unlocked itself with a display of flashing lights.

'Is that – is that yours?'

'Shouldn't it be? If you're allowed to be a nun then anything's possible.'

'Wouldn't mind one of those. Or maybe the 528.'

'Now that would be nice. Although I've been thinking about a Saab Convertible.'

'With a baby seat?'

Nina laughed. 'Maybe not. What car do you have?'

Agnes pointed at the Metro. Nina giggled, then clapped her hand to her mouth. 'Rude of me to laugh,' she said.

'Oh, feel free. It belongs to the school. Not my choice at all.'

'Trade it in for something decent when the nuns aren't looking,' Nina said.

'I might just do that. Listen –' Agnes hesitated. 'Um, I don't know how to say this. Mark's death . . .'

Nina's smile faded. She opened the passenger door and put her bag on to the seat. 'What about it?'

'David must be very upset.'

'What do you think?'

'You know Joanna's vanished from the school?'

'No, I didn't know that. I don't know her very well.'

'Does David know where she is?'

'Really, love, I've got to go. Ring me, if you like. Are you nuns allowed to use the phone? I'm at the mill.'

'At Allbright's?'

'Yeah, I used to be a sales secretary there, but now I'm in the main office. Now that Patricia's there. And I usually help out at a "do" like this, a bit of extra dosh.' She got into her car.

'One more thing – this art of David's?'

'Yeah?'

'Why did Turnbull choose to promote him?'

'Family,' Nina said. 'You know what they say about blood being thicker than water.' She slammed the car door, revved the engine, turned the car with a squeal of tyres and roared off down the drive.

Agnes watched the two red dots of light recede. She went back into the house, shivering with cold.

'She's gone, has she?' Patricia was in the hall, a bottle of champagne in one hand, a tray of glasses in the other. 'Good, I hate to keep her out late – you couldn't help me with this, could you?' Agnes took the bottle she held out to her. 'I'm so hopeless with those corks, they frighten me for some reason, I'm sorry, I don't think we've been introduced, I'm Patricia Turnbull, and you are –?'

'Agnes. Agnes Bourdillon. Is there a cloth anywhere, it makes it easier to hold the bottle?'

'Ah, my lovely wife,' Turnbull boomed, as they came back into the room. 'And some even lovelier champagne –' The cork popped, loudly. 'Expertly done.' He smiled, appraisingly, at Agnes.

'Agnes Bourdillon,' Patricia said.

'From?' Turnbull's eyes searched Agnes's face.

'She's a nun.' David stood at her elbow, smiling.

'A nun?' Turnbull laughed.

'Yeah,' David went on. 'She works with Jo at that school.'

Turnbull was studying her closely. 'Is that so?'

Agnes met his gaze. 'Yes,' she said. 'It is.'

'Well well.' His gaze held hers, then he smiled back. 'And isn't she supposed to be here?' He turned to his wife. 'Your sister – I thought she'd be here?'

Patricia shrugged. 'I expect something kept her away.'

'Something obviously did.' Turnbull turned to David.

'Don't look at me, mate,' David said. 'You know she hates this kind of thing.' He walked over to the drinks table and loudly snapped open a can of beer.

'Artists, eh?' Turnbull's attention returned to Agnes. Patricia took the champagne and headed to the conservatory where the crowd still mingled. Agnes wondered what to say.

'And how did you get to hear about David's work, then?'

Agnes took a deep breath. 'It's a long story,' she said. 'Through the school.'

'Joanna?'

'Not exactly. One of my sixth formers knew David's brother.'

Turnbull faltered. 'Terrible business,' he said. He picked up his glass of champagne and drained it. 'Terrible,' he said again. Agnes followed his gaze to where David stood, leaning heavily on the drinks table. 'I asked him if I should call this off, but he wanted to carry on. Brave man.'

'Did you know Mark well?'

'He worked for us. And for my father-in-law. He was our gardener for a while. And before that he worked in the mill. Before it became ours.'

'I saw in the press that your father-in-law has retired.'

'Yes. Can't get away from reporters. Wanting to know my plans for the mill. Luckily they haven't made too much of – of Mark. It's important to keep the good name.'

'Of Allbright's?'

'Yes. Difficult time for the yarn business. Very difficult. Need local support more than ever.'

'Of course, the family must go back years.'

'Yes, but I'm a bit of an incomer. No background in textiles, you see, made all my money in property. I'm sorry, I must be boring you, can I get you a drink?' He took her arm and steered her towards Patricia who still carried the tray of champagne, took two glasses and handed one to Agnes. He raised his glass. 'Cheers,' he said, his eyes meeting hers. She noticed they were a soft grey, like James's.

'Are there many sisters at the school?' Turnbull was asking her.

'No. Not these days. Six of us.'

'Falling vocations, I suppose.'

'Yes.'

'I was raised a Catholic, you know.' He was smiling into her eyes. 'Another reason to tread carefully in Baines's country. They're all chapel here.'

'Do you still believe?'

He sipped his champagne. 'Yes. Yes, I do. I'm not very devout or anything. Not like you people.'

Agnes laughed. 'It's not that simple,' she said.

'I'm sure it isn't. One of these days I'll – oh, my wife beckons. Do excuse me.' Turnbull left her side, and Agnes found herself alone. She went to look for David, who she found sitting on the stairs in the hall, drunk.

'I was sorry to hear about your brother,' she said.

'Why're you sorry?' he slurred. 'Did you do it then?'

'And it's true, I do know Joanna. I work with her at the school.'

'So you say.'

'You know Charlotte, apparently. One of our sixth-formers.'

'Charlotte – she were going out with Mark. Sort of.'

'Yes.'

'Poor kid.'

'She told me the police were talking to Billy Keenan.'

'They've got nothing on him. They've let him go. And if anyone knows owt else about him, they'll not say. He's safe enough, that bastard Keenan.'

'David – why did Joanna leave us?'

He looked at Agnes, trying to focus.

'Is it about Mark? She hasn't been back to the school since Mark was found—'

'Dead. Found dead. On the moors. Say it.'

Agnes met his gaze. 'Found dead,' she said. 'On the moors.'

'With his eyes put out.'

'Yes.'

'Go on, say it.'

Agnes kept her voice level. 'With his eyes put out.'

David made a kind of sob in his throat. He put his hand over his face. 'And they'll never find a bloody thing. Everybody on that estate, they're just doin' their own thing. Only themselves to please. They'll not say who did it, even if they know.'

'Do you think people know more than they're letting on?'

David shook his head and laughed, mirthlessly. 'Who knows. They have their own rules there.'

'Tell me one more thing, David. Is Joanna frightened of something?'

'Listen, lady, I don't know who you are. I'm just the performing monkey here, I'm just Art in the service of Commerce, just playing my part in this farce – and you turn up here and ask me about sheep's skulls. Is there any reason I should tell you anything?'

Agnes scribbled her phone number on a piece of paper. 'No reason at all. But if you change your mind, I'm on this number.'

David squinted at the note. 'Are you for real, then? This really is the convent?'

'It's my mobile. But, yes, I am from the convent. And if I don't get back there soon, there'll be words from Reverend Mother.' Agnes turned on her heel and headed for the door, aware as she walked away from him of David staring after her.

Her car engine spluttered into life. She thought about Nina's BMW. Surely it wasn't so bad coveting someone's car if you liked the car's owner?

Her head was spinning. Everyone seemed to know everyone else. David and Joanna, Turnbull and Mark. And Charlotte. And Joanna was indeed an Allbright Baines.

And if Joanna is Patricia's sister, why does she live on such a rough estate? And why isn't she an inheritor of the mill? I know no such person, Baines had said.

And David knew Elias – and Elias had a key to Joanna's house.

She pulled up at the school, and drove round to the car park, passing the chaplain's flat. There was a light still on at the window. Agnes walked towards it. She hesitated, then turned and went into her house.

'Elias?' Agnes's voice echoed in the early morning stillness of the chapel. He was standing behind the altar, arranging candles for the first service of the day. He looked up and saw her.

'How's Charlotte?' he said.

'Better. She seems calmer. She's determined to do her exams this year.'

'Sometimes it's the best way.'

'Elias – I, um, was at the Turnbulls' last night.'

'The Turnbulls'? How odd.' He stared at her.

'Yes. Anthony was doing a private view of some of David Snaith's work.'

'You surprise me.'

Agnes scanned his face, but his tone was neutral. He busied himself with the holy water, the chalice. 'Was Jo there?' he asked, suddenly.

'No.'

'Oh.'

'David sent you a message.'

Elias smiled. 'I expect it was rude.'

'He said you can return the key to Jo's house.'

'Did he?'

Agnes studied him. 'Elias – why has Baines disowned Joanna?'

He looked up. 'What makes you think that?'

'Because Patricia and Turnbull have inherited the mill, and Joanna hasn't. And also –'

'Also what?'

'I went to the mill. Last week. I met William Baines. He threw me out. I was asking about Jo.'

'You did what?' Elias's face betrayed anger.

'I was concerned, that's all,' Agnes said.

'Why? What business is it of yours?'

'Well – it seems only normal . . . I mean – I found her in the art room, she was upset, I was worried about her –'

'Enough to go snooping around her father's mill?'

'Yes, actually.'

Elias unfolded a linen cloth and placed it on the altar. 'Is that why they moved you from London, then?'

'What do you mean?'

'Because you were always looking for distractions?'

'I don't know what you—'

'Meddling with other people's lives . . .'

'Elias, this is undeserved. I thought you'd understand, as you knew her too. As you obviously care about her. I was going to ask you to let me have the key to her house, in case there was something there . . .'

'Why should I do that?'

'I just thought—'

'She won't be there.'

'Oh. Right.'

'If you want to know about Jo, you can always talk to David. Now you know him.'

'Well, hardly—'

'Now you're so in with the Turnbulls.'

Is that what this is about, Agnes thought. This sudden attack. Because I've got too close.

He had his back to her. Agnes walked round the altar until she was facing him. 'Who do you think killed Mark Snaith?' she said. He continued to arrange the cloth. 'Or perhaps you don't care. Perhaps you think it's just another tale from the urban war zone.'

He went to place the chalice and the host on one side.

'Perhaps murder is nothing to you,' Agnes snapped. 'Perhaps it's just part of the random universe of your post-modern God.'

There was a crash as Elias dropped the decanter of wine. He stared at his feet, at the spreading red stain on the polished floor, his hand cupped as if to hold the bottle still. Then he turned to her.

'Do you think that's how I am?' His voice was a whisper.

Agnes bent to pick up shards of glass. 'I'm sorry –' she began, 'I didn't mean –'

He knelt down next to her and gathered up some larger pieces. 'She won't be there,' he said.

'I just thought there might be – I wanted to find out—'

'If you want to, then we'll do it. David Snaith can wait for his bloody key.'

Chapter Six

'Limits after all,' Sister Philomena said, thumping her tray down next to Agnes at lunch. Agnes waited for the reprimand. 'Starving away to bloody nothing,' Philomena went on, retrieving her bread roll from the other side of the table. Agnes realised she was not the subject of this particular discussion.

'Who do you mean?' she asked.

'The Swann girl. Look.'

Agnes glanced across the dining hall to where Rachel Swann, a fifth-year member of her house, was sitting in front of a very small salad.

'Hasn't touched it,' Philomena said.

'We had this last year,' Teresa said.

'Been watching her,' Philomena said. 'Yesterday she ate one small helping of cornflakes, dry, two digestive biscuits and several cups of black tea. Wasting away to bloody nothing. And one of our brightest girls. Time to call a halt, what?'

'Well,' Teresa began, 'she's had counselling, and I spoke to her last week, and we agreed that she'd think about what I'd said.'

'Think about it? Be dead before she'll think about it. Parents?'

'They're foreign office.'

'Your bag then, Sister. Up to you, old chap.'

There was a thin rain falling when Agnes and Elias set out across the moor that afternoon. Grey clouds blotted out the sun. Agnes was hot and breathless, hurrying to keep pace with Elias. 'Perhaps you're right,' she said.

'Right in what way?' It was the first time he'd spoken.

'That she won't be there,' Agnes said.

'We'll see,' he said, raising his voice against the wind as they reached the path that led down towards the Millhouse estate.

Agnes loosened her scarf around her neck, in spite of the rain which flattened her hair and dripped into her eyes.

Elias turned the key in one lock, then another. The door opened a crack.

'Something's blocking the other side.' He leaned hard against it and pushed his way inside. Agnes heard him say, 'Oh Christ.'

The place had been ransacked. An upturned table had been placed behind the door. In the living room the sofa had been slashed, the curtains hung in shreds from their rail. The television had gone. Agnes and Elias went from room to room, dazed by the chaos, the outpouring of hatred that had alighted, randomly, on this one place before moving on. In the bedroom there was a stink of perfume. Empty cosmetics bottles littered the floor. A pile of clothes lay across the bed, soaking wet.

'Do you think she's seen it?' Agnes whispered at last.

Elias was opening the door of the tiny second bedroom. 'I've no idea. Oh God,' Agnes heard him cry. 'Bastards. What good did it bloody do them? Not this as well . . .'

Agnes saw curtains pulled from the walls, drawers pulled out. Then she noticed paintings ripped from their frames, an easel overturned, tubes of paint squeezed out across the room, smeared over the walls.

'Subhuman, worse-than-mindless bloody yobbos . . .' Elias was muttering, picking his way across the mess. He bent and picked up a canvas that had been slashed in half. Elias began to search feverishly for the other half, his hands working through the wreckage, the unnamed stickiness, the stench of urine.

'Elias – be careful . . .'

'Here it is.'

He held up the other half and Agnes saw a bowl of golden apples in oils, a vase of yellow roses.

'Still life,' Elias said. There were tears in his eyes.

'Shall we tell the police?' Agnes said. They stood in the kitchen, washing their hands under running cold water.

'What good will that do?'

'You mean this happens all the time?'

'Look.' Elias pointed outside. Agnes could see, through the shabby net curtains, the row of houses opposite. On the roof sat

two boys, levering tiles away from the beams, throwing them down
to a boy below who was stacking them into piles.

'What difference is one trashed house going to make?' Elias
dried his hands.

Agnes took the towel he passed to her. 'All this hatred and
violence and destruction –' she began. 'If someone was actually
to get killed . . .'

Elias picked up the two halves of Joanna's painting. 'Like Mark,
you mean?' He glanced across at the kids on the roof. 'As far as
they're concerned, it's just another day.'

They came out into the street. The boys started jeering at them
and throwing bits of broken tile.

Elias stood by the door, the key in his hand. He glanced at
Agnes, then at the smashed front window. He shrugged, locked
the door, pocketed the key.

On the moors the rain had eased, and the twilight was pricked
with stars. Elias's pace had lost its urgency, and he walked slowly,
staring at the ground ahead.

'I didn't realise –' Agnes began.

'What?'

'That she was working as an artist.' Elias was silent. 'Had they
trashed much of her work?'

'Sorry? Not really, no, that room was just a storeroom.'

'So – does she have a studio somewhere else?'

'What – oh, um, yes. No.'

'Hadn't we better search for her there, then?'

Elias glanced at her. 'She won't be there.'

Agnes looked at him, at his profile shadowed by the fading
light. 'Well, where else might she be?'

Elias's fingers touched the side of his coat, where the torn
painting was folded away. He shook his head.

The path across the top of the moor narrowed, and Agnes fell
into step behind him, as the sky grew dark and the lights of the
town spread out beneath them. Elias stumbled, stopped. They
stood there, as the wind whispered through the bare grass. Elias
blinked, looked at the ground. Agnes reached her hand out
uncertainly to him.

'We'll find her,' she said.

Again, he shook his head.

'You know this skull business?' Agnes asked him, putting her hands into her pockets.

'What about it?'

'David Snaith put one in his work.'

'That doesn't surprise me.'

Agnes fished out some gloves and put them on. 'Perhaps we should pray for her.'

'Perhaps.'

'Do you?'

'Do I what?'

'Pray for people.'

'I used to.' He started off down the hill again.

'But not now?' Agnes walked next to him.

'False hopes,' he said. 'I try to avoid them.'

'So – do you believe anything at all?'

'Hardly anything.'

Agnes dropped behind him as the path narrowed. When she caught up with him again, she said, 'Nothing at all?'

He stopped and looked at her. 'The best we can hope for is to find stillness in the face of suffering.'

Agnes looked at him. The wind blew his hair over his eyes. 'And does that kind of faith sustain you?'

'It's not for long, is it?'

'But what about joy? What about celebration, what about thanksgiving? Isn't that what God wants of us too?'

Elias looked at the lights spread out beneath them. 'Once I thought that.' He turned and set off away from her, towards the school. 'Not any more,' she heard him say. She thought perhaps he said something else, but the wind caught at his words and carried them away.

She went to her room, changed and set off again in the community car. James let her in and kissed her on both cheeks. 'The Campbells are here, the friends I mentioned. I wanted you to meet them, I hope you don't mind. And Evelyn's done most of the cooking.'

'Nonsense, Jim, I just helped a bit.' An elegant, middle-aged woman emerged from the kitchen and shook Agnes's hand warmly. 'I gather he's known you since you were a baby.'

Agnes laughed. 'It sounds ridiculous,' she said.

'No it doesn't, not at all. Joss, this is Agnes – or is it Sister Agnes?'

'Just Agnes is fine.' Agnes shook hands with Joss, who was grey-haired with an angular, weathered face and a kind smile.

'And how do the photos look?' James said, handing her a glass of wine.

'Lovely. I'm so glad to have them,' she said.

They sat down to a lamb ragoût with baked potatoes and salad.

'St Catherine's, is it?' Joss asked her. 'Good reputation, I believe. Nice place to teach?'

'Um, yes.' Agnes glanced at James.

James smiled. 'Agnes is an exile, you see. She's a Londoner by instinct.'

Evelyn laughed. 'No wonder, then.'

'It's fine,' Agnes said. 'Never a dull moment, between the crises and the dramas. I'm amazed anyone passes their exams at the end of it all.'

'So what are the current dramas?' James asked.

'Well – we have an art teacher who's mysteriously disappeared. Joanna Baines –'

Evelyn put down her fork. 'Joanna Baines – not William's daughter?'

'From the mill, yes.'

'I had no idea she was an art teacher,' Joss said.

'Yes, we knew that, dear, don't you remember, at the funeral she said she was teaching –'

'I didn't associate it with that school, I suppose. And she's vanished, you say?'

'Does everyone know everyone else around here?' Agnes asked.

James laughed. 'It's a very small community. And the Campbells have been here for years.'

'That's not strictly true,' Joss said, 'we had all that time in the States, we only settled back here last year.'

'Yes, but you count. You get to play bridge with the Radleighs, for example.'

'It's hardly an honour,' Evelyn laughed.

'It's a tiresome bore,' Joss said, pouring Agnes some more wine. 'So when you say vanished . . .' he said.

'She seemed upset, and then one day she didn't turn up for

work. And we've had no word from her.'

'Of course,' Evelyn said quietly, 'it's the anniversary.' She glanced at her husband who was twirling the wine around in his glass. 'Their mother died almost a year ago,' she went on. 'Cancer. It was very sudden, a terrible shock. Barely in her sixties. The family took it very badly, William in particular.'

Joss stood up. 'I'll clear the plates, shall I?'

'He's handed the mill to his daughter,' Agnes said, as Joss carried a stack of crockery into the kitchen.

'Yes, I'd heard,' Evelyn said. 'And her husband. It's very odd.'

'Grief,' James said. 'Does terrible things.' A loud crash came from the kitchen. 'I'd better go and help,' Evelyn said. Agnes, left alone with James, had the impression he was about to speak to her. He glanced at her a couple of times, but remained silent.

'There's a call for you,' Mary Watson called to Agnes in the staff room next morning. 'Nina Warburton.'

'Nina – but – oh. Right.' Agnes went to the phone.

'Hello, is that Agnes? We met at the Turnbulls—'

'Yes, of course, I was going to ring you.'

'Well, I wondered if you wanted to come out for a drink tonight. I can get babysitting for Rosie, and the thing is, I can't talk now but what with you knowing Jo, and Mark and everything, and I thought you'd be someone I could trust—'

'Of course.'

'I've found these files. Here. About Mark. Are you free tonight?'

'Yes. Where?'

'There's a pub near where I live. The Queen's Arms. It's on the corner, you go down the hill from the mill, I'll give you the address.' Agnes wrote down the details. 'Eight o'clock?'

'Fine. See you then.'

Agnes hung up and returned to the staff room. Philomena was there, consulting her watch. It was a huge man's watch with a broken strap. She put it back in her pocket and turned to Agnes.

'Talbot girl, Leonora – one of yours?'

'Yes,' Agnes said. 'What's happened?'

'Missing. Supposed to be in English this morning, no sign. Bolter?'

'Well, yes and no.'

'Your bag, old chap.' She swept away.

'Your bag indeed,' Colin said, watching the diminutive form speed away along the corridor. 'How does she do it?'

'Do what?'

'Philomena. The way she moves. Look. It's as if she's on wheels.'

'That's my morning, then. Searching the grounds for a fourteen-year-old escapee. It's my own fault. I was the one who told her that the best time to run away is when you can catch a train.'

'So she'll be on her way to Manchester by now, and it's your own fault.'

'Great, isn't it?'

'And it's raining. Happy hunting.'

'She's got a letter, Sister,' Clemmie Macintosh shifted from one foot to the other. 'That's all I know. She took it and went off somewhere.'

'Where?' Agnes squeezed the rain out of her hair. 'I've spent the last hour looking for her.'

'I don't know, Sister, I'm sorry.'

'Did she pack a bag?'

'No. She's always packing bags, so I noticed it was a bit unusual.'

'Even worse. Thank you, Clemmie, you may go.'

What will the child's parents say, Agnes thought, striding through the school to the entrance hall, if she tells them that the only thing she learned at school was how to run away? She glanced out of the front door at the rain. The drive stretched away from the school like a sheet of steel. A lone figure was standing at the gates. Then she slowly turned and began to walk back towards the school.

Agnes sat on the low wall by the entrance steps. Leonora approached, glanced at Agnes, then sat down next to her. Rain dripped from a broken guttering above them, splashing on to the gravel a few inches from their feet. They both watched it for a while.

Then Leonora said, 'I hate them.' She glanced sideways at Agnes, then produced from her pocket two damp, crumpled pages. 'Look,' she said.

Agnes took it. 'Darling Leonora,' she read out loud.

'As if they give a shit.'

Agnes handed the letter back to the girl. 'Tell me what it says.'

Leonora put the letter in her pocket. '"Darling Leonora, I'm so happy, Daddy's met a lovely new girlfriend so now it doesn't matter if I've been screwing someone else for bloody yonks, lots of love, Mummy" . . . I hate her. And him, why couldn't he have stood up to her, why didn't he fight to keep it all together instead of just going off and finding someone else . . . I hate him.' Her eyes were quite dry. 'I expect Mummy's already planning some bloody double wedding for them both, "Oh, do let's have a marquee, so suitable for a summer wedding, and so much easier for the caterers . . ."'

'They've got to get divorced first.'

'Do you think they will?' Leonora turned her blue eyes to Agnes. 'Did yours?'

'It wasn't the done thing in our circles. My father drifted away. Well, when I say drift, several thousand miles away.'

'At least you could blame him.'

'Him? Not him. I thought it was my fault. For years.'

They sat in silence again. The guttering continued to drip. After a while Agnes found a clean handkerchief and handed it to Leonora, who dried her face, which was wet with rain and tears.

Nina arrived at the pub late, wearing a huge black fun-fur coat. 'Sorry,' she said, flinging her coat on to the leather bench. 'Had to take Rosie over to Mum's and it got late. What'll you have?'

'I'll get these,' Agnes said, getting up.

'Half a lager then, please.' Nina settled down at the table.

'I don't suppose you're used to pubs,' she said when Agnes returned.

'I had a mis-spent youth,' Agnes laughed.

'It's a bit of a dump, this one.'

'I like it. It's a change after St Catherine's.'

'What's it like there?'

'Total chaos, in the middle of which they're all supposed to do fabulously well in their exams to justify the huge fees. Eating disorders, divorcing parents, promiscuity . . .'

Nina laughed. 'To think what I missed out on. Local comprehensive for me. Nine GCSE's, three A levels, French, English and Art, went on to college, had a baby. Retrained as a secretary through that job creation thingie. Joined Allbright's about a year ago. That's me so far. What about you?'

'How long have you got?'

Nina laughed again. 'Well, how long have you been a nun?'

'Hmm, let's think. Nearly half my life.'

'At that school?'

'Thank goodness, no. I've been in London for years.'

'And before that?'

'Oh, you know, just a privileged French upbringing and a violent husband.'

'Right.' Nina was surveying her closely. 'I suppose your friends get to know when you're joking.'

'My friends, what few there are, know that I'm a very serious person.'

'Hmmm. Perhaps.'

'Shall we get to work?'

'Yeah, sure. Look –' Nina pulled a file out from her bag. 'I found this at Allbright's yesterday. According to this stuff, Mark was threatened.'

'When? By whom?'

'There was a race relations tribunal a couple of years ago. An Asian bloke claimed unfair dismissal on race grounds, and Mark and another bloke helped him bring a case. And then after that there were threats against Mark and his mate. It's here in Mark's file.'

Agnes took the file and flicked through it.

'You can borrow it if you want,' Nina said. 'There's another one, here, miscellaneous press cuttings, there's a bit in it about the tribunal hearing.'

'What were the other two guys called?'

'The bloke who was sacked was called Mehfuz. Mark's mate who helped was called Ed. Ed Longley. The guy who was threatening him is called Billy Keenan. I know him, he still works at the mill, his mum does too, Maureen. She's a nice lady, but I don't rate him much. He's NF, he is. And said to be handy with the matches.'

'Have the police seen these files?'

'Yes, they went through loads of stuff about Mark. They've had Billy in for questioning too, but they let him go. David was really angry.'

'Do you know him well, David?'

'Used to. But I don't go around so much with that crowd.'

'You know his girlfriend?'

'A bit. Patricia's sister.'

'She seems to have disappeared.'

'Baines threw her out, I heard. Maureen told me, she said her friend Kitty was there when it happened, saw everything.'

'Does anyone know why?'

'All anyone knows is that after Mrs Baines died, old Mr Baines just wasn't the same and got it into his head to hand the mill over. And that's what he's done, and no one's really happy about it. I mean, I like Anthony, and Patricia, they're good to me, but there's rumours that they're going to lay people off. Don't go away, I need the ladies.'

Agnes watched Nina fight her way through the smoky crowd, then opened the press cuttings file. There were a few shabby photos marking various anniversaries and celebrations. There were two yellowing newspaper clips, one reporting that a settlement had been made in a race relations case. There was a photograph of some kind of sports team, a group of young men, posed in rows. Agnes read the caption at the bottom: 'West Yorkshire Amateur Athletics Association . . . Allbright's Mill Cross Country Team.' A boy was holding a trophy. She read the names. 'Mark Snaith, Edward Longley, Richard Worth, David Snaith . . .' She closed the file again.

'What are you doing Saturday?' Nina asked, coming back to the table.

'Nothing much.'

'I'm meeting Patricia in town, for tea, about four. Why don't you join us?'

'Sure, I'd like to.'

'She's a nice woman. Another drink?'

'Yes please, I'll have a –'

'You're driving, aren't you? I'll get us both a mineral water.' Nina stood up.

'Thanks. Must it be mineral water?'

Nina turned. 'Are you always like this?'

'Only when they let me out.'

'Seems to me, you need someone to keep an eye on you. Ice and lemon?'

Agnes watched her by the bar, envying her grace and youth, wishing that she'd been so at ease with herself when she was that age.

'There. Ice and lemon.'

'But no gin?'

'You're driving.'

Agnes sighed. 'Yes, Mum.'

Nina watched her sip her drink. 'Maybe it was having a baby,' she said suddenly.

'Maybe what was?'

'That changed me. I used to be like you. I used to get tanked up and then race my boyfriend home along the ring road. I had an MG in those days, and he had an Alfa Sud.'

'But how did you—?'

'You're going to say, how can I afford it? How can I pay for my BMW?'

'Yes.'

Nina took a deep breath, then said, 'When my Dad died, he left me some money. He said I should spend it – a gift to the living.' She smiled at Agnes. 'He said it was for living with. So I did.'

'Including racing around the ring road?'

Nina laughed. 'I was young then.'

Agnes sipped her mineral water. 'How old is she, your daughter?'

'Three and a bit. Rosie. She's lovely. Best thing that ever happened to me.'

Agnes sighed. 'Well, I don't think that particular path is open to me. I'll have to find another way to grow up.'

'Listen, when I said – I didn't mean – it was just about being kind of – dangerous –'

'I'm not supposed to be dangerous. I'm supposed to have given myself up to the service of the Lord, just like you've chosen to put your child's needs first. Well, not just like it, obviously, I just meant, it's sort of equivalent, not the same, obviously . . .'

Nina started to laugh. 'What are we like, eh? Nothing in common at all. Look at us – I'm young, I'm a mum, you're—'

'White, old and celibate?'

Nina laughed. 'That's about it.'

'And past reforming. Out of the question to be redeemed by motherhood – and, it seems, too immature and hopeless to settle down and become a good nun.'

'I never said that.'

'No, but I did.'

Nina fished her piece of lemon out of her glass and nibbled at it. 'I bet you're quite a good nun. I bet your God doesn't mind the odd drink or two.'

'If it was only that—'

'I bet He wants us to have a good time. I mean, why put us here if He didn't mean us to enjoy it?'

'Do you go to church?'

'No. Not me. Not now.' She sighed. 'I used to go with my Dad.'

They sipped their drinks. Nina looked at her watch. 'I'd better go soon.'

'Do you think Joanna knew Mark Snaith well?'

'I've no idea. She knows David pretty well.'

'They've trashed her house, you know, up on the estate.'

'It doesn't surprise me. Those Millhouse lads have their own rules.'

'And do those rules include murder?'

Nina frowned. 'Sometimes I wonder. Sometimes I think, if Mark had got caught up in something he shouldn't have . . .'

'What, though?'

'I've no idea.'

'He worked for Baines.'

'And for the Turnbulls too. Patricia was quite friendly with him.' Nina reached for her coat.

'You see, I keep thinking – Joanna disappeared from the school on the day that Mark was found. And she hasn't contacted the school since, and – and she seemed so upset.'

'But it's not as if she's vanished without trace. If she had, the family would be more worried, wouldn't they?'

'True. Oh dear, none of it makes sense. Perhaps it's best just to leave it to the police.'

'Hmmm.' Nina flipped a beer mat between her fingers.

'So what do you think?'

Nina drained her glass, then looked at Agnes. 'I'll tell you what I think. I think the Millhouse estate is full of some well dodgy characters. I think if someone had it in for Mark, it might go back to this tribunal thing. I think something has frightened Jo, but the family don't want to think about it. And I think David's dead scared for Jo, and dead upset for his brother, and he can't think straight.' She put on her coat. 'And I think, if David could think straight, he'd see that Turnbull is playing some kind of game with him, and, being Turnbull, he's playing to win.'

'And the prize?'

Nina gathered up her bag. 'Who d'you think? Jo, of course.'

Chapter Seven

'So I suppose you'd have to say, we've been a total failure as a family. Shall we have Darjeeling or Ceylon?' Patricia Turnbull squinted at the menu.

'Darjeeling would be lovely,' Agnes said. 'And maybe some cinnamon toast?'

'Loads of it,' Nina said. 'And I'll have a Diet Coke please. And you're having orange juice, OK?'

'But you're having Coke,' Rosie said, kneeling up on her chair.

'It's bad for you,' Nina said.

'Why?' Rosie had tight curls of hair fastened into bunches, and she was wearing a pink sweatshirt and leggings.

'Because you're little.'

'I'm not, I'm big. I'm big now.'

'You're having orange juice. And take your gloves off.'

'But they're my froggies. I want to wear my froggies.'

Nina removed Rosie's green woolly mittens and put them in her pocket.

'I want one of them.' Rosie pointed at a display of fancy biscuits. 'One of them dinonsors. Please, Mummy.'

Nina sighed. 'OK, you can have one of those.'

Rosie smiled, charmingly, at Agnes. Agnes smiled back.

'A total failure,' Patricia resumed. 'A great disappointment to Father, and to Mother too, probably, if she could see us. Perhaps she can. Are you really a nun?'

Agnes longed suddenly for the days of compulsory habit-wearing. She glanced down at her cream Aran sweater and jeans. 'Yes. I really am a nun.'

Nina laughed. 'Agnes says they go around in disguise these days.'

The drinks arrived and Nina helped Rosie with her juice. 'See, you've got a special cup and a straw, lucky you.'

'And you work with Jo?' Patricia said.

'I did, before she disappeared.'

'We're so worried. I've spoken to your convent. The Head there, Sister Phyllida or something – odd woman, isn't she? And there's no answer at her house, and we've asked Daddy, but he hasn't seen her for weeks. We're sure David knows where she is, because he seems so unconcerned. We thought we should report her missing, but David was dead against it. Practically threatened Anthony when he suggested phoning the police.'

Agnes poured two cups of tea. 'Maybe she just had to get away.'

Patricia sighed. 'I mean, yes, I know we were all rather hard on her, Father especially, all this business with the mill, I had no intention of taking it on single-handed, thank goodness for Anthony is all I can say, if I'd known that I'd be the lone inheritor of the mill I think I'd have emigrated or something.' She laughed, a polite, empty laugh. 'And poor Daddy, there he is with three children, you'd think he'd feel he could rely on us all, but after the business with Marcus, and now Jo—'

'Marcus?'

'My brother.'

'Your – your brother?'

'I've ate his head.' Rosie proudly displayed her gnawed biscuit.

Patricia smiled. 'Oh, here I am chatting away as if I've known you all my life, it's Nina, you see, she's been so good for me. I've had no one to talk to about it all, dear Anthony just wants to get on with it now, make the best of it, bless him, but really, it's all been so terrible, poor Daddy, I thought it might kill him, the strain of it. Still, at least he can rely on me now. Since Mother . . .' Her eyes welled with tears.

Nina glanced at Agnes. 'Patricia – listen, don't get upset –' she touched her hand. 'Here, have some toast.'

Patricia took a cotton handkerchief from her bag and dabbed at her eyes. 'Something about Mother dying . . . that's what seems to have done us all in. She must have held us all together without us even noticing.'

'Mummy, why's that lady crying, Mummy, that lady?' Rosie asked loudly.

'And then,' Agnes said, taking two slices of toast, 'there was Mark Snaith.'

'Yes. There was. Poor poor Daddy. The police were up at the

mill again the other day wanting to question him. I sent them away as soon as I could, he's not a well man, still so upset about Mummy, it's not long after all, not yet a year since she died, and then all the business with Marcus – it's been a terrible time for us, really.'

'Is Marcus younger or older?'

'Marcus is the middle. I'm the eldest, then Marcus, then Jo. Jo's an artist, I suppose it shouldn't surprise me if she didn't want to take on the responsibility of the mill, although God knows she needs the money, more than we do, ironic isn't it? Anthony's other businesses bring in more than enough. Still, he seems happy. He's always liked a challenge, my husband. And a bit of a gamble, too.'

'He bought a lottery ticket the other day,' Nina laughed. 'He got me to show him how it worked.'

Patricia smiled. 'Nothing surprises me about him.'

'I think we need more cinnamon toast, don't you?' Agnes said, catching the waitress's eye.

'I've told Agnes my theory about the tribunal and Billy Keenan,' Nina said.

'Oh yes. It's a whole industry now, this race relations business,' Patricia began, then looked at Nina. 'At least,' she said, brightly, 'that's what Anthony's always saying.' She helped herself to some more tea.

'Perhaps we should speak to your father about it,' Agnes said.

'He's so frail, poor dear.'

Agnes remembered his grip around her arm as he'd shown her the door. 'Still,' she said, 'if it helps this Snaith business . . .'

'Perhaps you should just take the file to the police,' Patricia said.

'They've seen it,' Nina said. 'I showed them when they came in last week. And Agnes is going to mention it again, aren't you?'

'Well, then, we've done what we can, haven't we?' Patricia took another slice of toast, her composure regained.

'May I ask what happened to Marcus?' Agnes said.

'Poor dear Marcus. It was something about Mother's illness, it seemed to send him off the rails. I suppose he was closer to her than anyone else. And then – he upset Daddy, really badly, around the time that Mummy was dying. He said something hurtful. He accused Daddy of being to blame – for Mummy's illness – and Daddy ordered him out of the house. And the stupid thing is, he

81

took Father at his word. So proud, you see. And he's never come back. Jo took his side, which made things worse, after what he'd done. He was always difficult, it didn't surprise me that when it came to a real crisis he bottled out. I think it's up to Marcus to approach Daddy, and until he does, well, I think it's important that someone supports Daddy. So when Daddy handed over the mill, he didn't include Marcus. It's my brother's own silly fault, I'm afraid. It wouldn't take much for Daddy to welcome him back. And actually, when Jo refused her share of the mill, I wasn't surprised. It's typical of them both to make a stand like that.'

'Where is he now?'

'He lives over towards Manchester, the other side of Halifax. He married last year. He doesn't see us.'

'Is Jo in touch with him?'

'Probably.'

'Has anyone asked him where she is?'

Patricia shook her head. 'It was so awful, last year – you can't know – it's left terrible scars. Daddy won't hear his name. That's why when Jo went off too, he took it so badly. Now there's only me . . .' Patricia looked tearful again.

Agnes thought for a moment. 'Our chaplain, Elias, said—'

Patricia blinked. 'Elias?'

'Elias Parnell.'

'Did you say –? Surely not. Did you say chaplain? You mean at your school? Now that really is extraordinary.'

'Yes, I did.'

'Elias a priest? Perhaps it's not the same Elias Parnell. Good looking, thick black hair, nice eyes, early thirties?'

'Yes—'

'Same age as Marcus in fact, they were at school together.'

'Elias and—?'

Rosie suddenly started bawling. 'I want my dinonsor.' She waved a soggy piece of biscuit in fury. 'I've ate his legs now and now it just looks like biscuit, and I want my dinonsor . . .'

'You were saying,' Agnes turned to Patricia again. 'Elias and Marcus—'

'And I want another one instead, can I, Mummy, can I have another, I want my dinonsor . . .'

'Hush, Rosie, shush, there's no need for this—'

'There was a terrible tragedy,' Patricia said, wincing at Rosie's noise. 'It drove them apart. They were best of friends, and then it all stopped, and we didn't see Elias again –'

'I want my dinonsor—'

'Listen, Rosie, it was just a biscuit, and now you've eaten it, and that's it, OK? That's what happens to biscuits.'

'But I want my dinonsor . . .'

'What tragedy?' Agnes leaned as near to Patricia as she could.

'It was a riding accident. We used to keep horses, and they'd ride out regularly, Marcus and Jo, and Marcus's girlfriend Katherine, and Elias – oh, and Daddy's dog, Greer; he was devoted to Elias, they adored each other . . .'

'Rosie, for Heaven's sake, look, there's two straws now for your juice, do you want some more?' Rosie quietened, and Patricia lowered her voice.

'And anyway, one day – Katherine – there was a terrible accident. She tried to take a jump, apparently, and the horse stumbled, and they both fell, and – and the horse crushed her.'

'How terrible. When was this?'

'It was a few years ago now, let's think, Daddy got rid of all the horses after that, it must have been five or six years ago, I think. They were all excellent riders, they'd take off over the moors. Marcus wouldn't talk about it afterwards. They couldn't cope with it, him and Elias, it was the end of their friendship. And the odd thing is, I'm sure old Greer still misses him.' She finished her tea. 'A priest? I wouldn't have predicted it, although his family were strongly Catholic, I remember that. Do remember me to him, won't you, I always had rather a soft spot for him.'

'Mummy, is that lady going to cry again?'

'She's not That Lady, she's Patricia—'

'Why?'

Nina looked at Patricia and Agnes. 'Shall we go?'

'I'll get the bill,' Patricia said.

As Patricia went over to the cash desk, Nina sighed. I'm sorry.'

'I don't know how you cope,' Agnes said.

'Look, take this, it's the phone number for Ed Longley. He left the mill in 1988 so it might not be current. We should catch up soon – how about Monday lunchtime? At the mill?'

'Fine.'

They left the tea room, buttoning their coats against the chill of the evening. The shops were still brightly lit.

'Well,' Patricia smiled, 'you must know everything about us now.' She offered Agnes her gloved hand. 'If anything comes to light about Jo, I'll let you know. Can I give you a lift?'

'I brought my car, thanks.'

'And we're walking, aren't we, Rosie?'

'No.' Rosie flapped her frog mittens at Agnes. They watched as Patricia disappeared into the crowded street, an elegant figure in tailored coat and high heels.

'See you Monday,' Nina said. 'Come on, Madam.'

'Supper,' Philomena said, meeting Agnes in the main corridor as she arrived back at the school and taking her arm.

'I thought I might go to my room – I rather need privacy this evening, time to think.'

'Think? Nonsense.'

They took their places in the queue in the dining hall.

'And the car.' Philomena placed a roll and butter on her tray. 'Never there these days.'

'Yes, I'm sorry, I've rather needed to be out and about –'

'You and your needs. Privacy? No such thing.'

'Surely solitude is a necessary part of –'

'The Lord is everywhere. Cream of chicken,' she added, taking a bowl of soup.

'I didn't mean privacy from the Lord,' Agnes said.

'Just as well. Anyway, the Old Bill. Cheese?'

Agnes stared at Sister Philomena. 'Did you say Old Bill?'

'Huge feet,' Philomena went on. 'Loads of them.'

Agnes took a deep breath. 'The police were here? Today?'

'Carpet filthy. There she is.' Philomena pointed across to the Sixth Form table, where Charlotte sat, pale and silent.

'Thank you so much, Sister.' Agnes left her tray of soup and cheese and crossed the room. Charlotte looked up with relief when she saw it was Agnes. 'They were here,' she began, tearfully.

'I know. Come with me.'

Agnes took her arm and led her from the dining hall. As she left she could see Sister Philomena standing in the queue, trying to carry Agnes's tray as well as her own.

'So what did they want?'

'There's another woman,' Charlotte said, then burst into tears.

Agnes put the kettle on to boil. 'Mark had another woman?'

'They said had I heard of someone called Lianna Vickers.'

'And had you?'

Charlotte nodded, then burst into renewed weeping. 'She's someone from the estate. Yesterday she went to the police station and told them she was going out with him.'

'Why did she wait until now?'

'I've no idea. Probably involved in something illegal. Knowing her.'

'Anything else?'

'No.'

Agnes cut some bread into slices and put them into the toaster. 'I suppose it's all round the school now.'

'Sister Philomena did her best, but –' Charlotte took a tissue from the box that Agnes passed her. 'I had to tell them, they all wanted to know.'

Agnes sighed. 'Perhaps I'd better visit this Lianna Vickers. Do you know where she lives?'

'I've been to her house once. It's a tip.'

'Can you give me the address?'

'David'll have it.' She began to cry again. 'Her, of all people – the idea that Mark might have – she's a – she's a slag, she's the kind of girl who'd – not Mark. Not him.'

A thin sun touched the chapel windows and flecked the altar with blue and green.

'How great is your goodness, O Lord . . .' Elias recited the psalm, his head bowed as he read from the text. 'Blessed be the Lord, for He has shown me the wonders of His love in a besieged city.' Elias threw the words away as if they had no meaning. 'Love the Lord, all you who worship Him –' for a second he raised his eyes, and met Agnes's gaze, then looked back to the book. 'Be strong and let your heart take courage, all you who wait for the Lord.' She wondered if the tone of irony was deliberate, or just the inflection of his voice.

It was after three when Agnes finally was able to return to her room. She took the number that Nina had given her and dialled it. A young woman answered the phone.

'Hello, is Ed Longley there?'

85

'I'll just get him.'

There was a pause, then a male voice said, 'Hello?'

'I'm phoning about Mark Snaith,' Agnes said. 'My name's Agnes, I'm a friend of his brother's.'

'Oh.'

'You worked at the mill?'

'Yes.'

'And you were involved in the tribunal with Mehfuz?'

'Yes, but that was – Oh. Right. D'you know, I hadn't thought . . . it were all so long ago, that, and we never took the threats serious, like – who did you say you were?'

'Sister Agnes. I'm a nun, I've – I've become involved with the Mark Snaith case.'

There was a silence. Then Ed said, 'D'you know, it never occurred to me, I saw it in the papers and that.'

'I wondered if we might meet.'

'Yeah, sound. Do you know the Old Gatehouse on the Silsden Road?'

'No, but –'

'I play darts there, I'll be there tomorrow night.'

'Fine. See you then.'

'You're meeting Ed Longley tonight? Fast worker, you are.' Nina's office was bright and spacious. Two wide windows with aluminium frames let in the midday sun.

'Seems so,' Agnes replied. 'He hadn't made the connection between the tribunal and Mark's death. Are you free this evening?'

'Bit short notice for Rosie, I'm afraid, but you can fill me in afterwards, can't you?' Nina put a file down in front of Agnes.

'What's this?'

'Billy Keenan's personnel file.' Nina was almost whispering.

'Anything in it?'

'He's had loads of warnings. He's National Front for sure.'

'Does it say so here?'

'No, but he's picked on loads of people, all of them Asian.'

'What's he like with you?'

'I don't have much to do with him. He's been civil enough, I s'pose, but that's not the point. Those NF boys choose their targets. You can borrow that if you want.'

'Won't it be missed?'

'I'm reorganising the office. Old Mr Baines has kept his office over in the old building, you see, and there's various files there that Mr Turnbull wants me to move over here, seeing as he and Patricia are going to be based here, and Mr Baines is bound to retire officially soon once Turnbull's properly in charge. So all the files are in boxes around the place, one more isn't going to matter.'

'Is it just you doing all that?'

'Yes, I'll be working late most nights, there's loads to do. Turnbull seems to be in a real hurry to get the files over here, he keeps bringing me more boxes and telling me to list the contents, and it's all really dull, invoices, VAT stuff, that kind of thing.'

They heard footsteps on the staircase, and then a voice called, 'Nina, any chance of a sandwich?' as Anthony Turnbull appeared in the office. 'Good heavens, it's you.' He smiled at Agnes and shook her hand. 'I had no idea you were such good friends, you two.'

'Oh, we go back years.' Nina turned away from him to get her coat, and winked at Agnes.

Turnbull relinquished Agnes's hand. 'And I believe my wife entertained you to tea on Saturday.'

'It was very kind of her.'

'And you know someone she used to know, some chap, friend of her brother's.'

'Elias, yes.'

'She was sure I'd remember, but all that was before my time.'

Nina was standing by the door. 'What kind of sandwich, Mr Turnbull?'

'Oh, anything. Not beef. Anything else. Oh, not prawn either.' He was still studying Agnes. 'Perhaps you could get something for our visitor too.'

'I thought I might go with you –' Agnes said.

'I'm sure Nina is quite capable of carrying three sandwiches.' Agnes and Nina looked at one another. Nina shrugged, went out of the room.

Turnbull took a packet of expensive cigarettes from his pocket, waved the packet in Agnes's direction as if anticipating her refusal, then lit one.

'Thank you, I will,' Agnes said.

Turnbull smiled as he offered her the packet. She took a cigarette and he leaned over and lit it for her.

'You surprise me,' he said.

'It used to be only Gauloises,' she said, 'but my good taste has been diminished by exile.'

'I thought perhaps nuns didn't –'

'Didn't smoke? Or didn't drink? Didn't lie, cheat or steal? We're only human.'

'Evidently.' His gaze didn't falter.

'So,' Agnes said, 'how's your new life as a textile baron?'

'Challenging. Or terrifying. Depending how honest I'm being. Like you, I'm only human.'

Agnes laughed. 'It must be very difficult.'

'It could be worse. At least I know some of the staff now, like Nina, and the sales team, and I've had meetings with all our customers, and the Baines name helps enormously, with Patricia on board. And even some of the shopfloor are familiar to me, from my work with the sports centre on the estate.'

'So you're part of that too?'

'We applied for lottery funding last year, we already had the matching funds, I helped them put the application together. And we got it. So it should be full steam ahead. And sports, you see, it's the ideal thing for an area like this, lots of bored teenage boys hanging about. We've got a community centre up the hill, it's been there for years, but it's barely used because it's so often vandalised. If we extend it into a sports centre, the kids'll think it's their own, they'll feel part of it. I'm sure of it.'

'Wasn't Mark involved?'

'Yes. And quite a few of the lads from the workforce here. It'll help, I think, with staff relations. Mark will be missed, though.'

'Bacon and avocado OK?' Nina came into the room. 'Or else there's mozzarella and tomato, and something else, what was it, ham and mustard? I'll put the kettle on.'

'Ladies first.' Turnbull held out the three plastic packets to Agnes for her to choose from. She took the nearest, not reading the label, aware of him watching her still.

'Cigarette?' Ed Longley produced a packet of Silk Cut.

'No thanks, I don't smoke.' Agnes smiled at him.

'Course not, stupid of me. Though it threw me when you walked in, in a nice skirt and that, not wearing that – you know, what they wear.'

'Habit.'

'Aye. Would've taken you for just an ordinary bird. No offence. Thing is, you see,' Ed took a long pull on his pint, 'lost touch wi'him when I left the mill. Mark, I mean.'

'When did you last see him?'

'Must have been . . .' he sipped on his beer. 'Must have been a good couple of years now. We were never great mates at best of times. I mean, nowt bad between us, don't get me wrong, just not in t'same crowd.'

'But the tribunal?'

'Y'see – a lot was made of it at the time, but truth to tell, it weren't a big deal. Our mate Mehfuz was told they didn't need him no more, it was when Baines was shutting down a lot of the wool spinning in favour of acrylic. Didn't think owt of it at the time. Several of the lads went then. Then a few months later, Baines takes on a couple of lasses. And I think Mehf must have spoken to someone about it then, but y'see, no one could prove it were unfair. We knew the girls were cheaper, but that's how it is round here. Old story. Their jobs were a bit different to the old jobs because the machinery was new.' He downed a large amount of beer, then wiped his upper lip on the back of his hand.

'So how did it come to be a case?'

'I think we'd have done nowt if it hadn't been for Billy Keenan. Nasty bit of work, him. Started spreading it around that him and his mates had, like, had a bit of a word wi' old Baines. And Billy starts goin' on like it's a victory for the NF lot. And then Mehf thought about this, and we thought, it's worth a go, just to wipe the smile off Keenan's face. So we took it to the tribunal and we won. Sort of, anyway, Baines settled.'

'And Mark?'

'He were a good sort, Mark. Sense of fairness, him. Also, he liked the idea of getting even with Billy, there was some old feud went back years with them two.'

Agnes took the photo of the athletics team from her bag. 'You're in this, too,' she said.

Ed took it and stared at it. He smiled. 'Sure am. There I am. Just a nipper when you come to think of it.'

'And Mark.'

'Yeah. And Dave, his brother.' He smiled. 'And Reg.'

'Reg?'

'Reg Naismith, our trainer. He were one in a million, he were. There.' He pointed at an older man standing at the back of the team. 'I wonder what happened to him, he must be a good age by now, he were knocking seventy even then. But he kept us on our toes, he did. Bit of a terror, too, like. After I injured my foot, I had to leave, I were too scared of him. He were just ordinary, though, Reg, just lived on the estate like everyone else, worked in the mill till he retired, rare thing these days. But he had summat, don't know what it were – we'd have done anything for him. Yeah, all right, lads –' he made a thumbs-up sign at the waiting darts team – 'be right with you.'

'So – do you think Mark's death might be connected with this tribunal?'

'To be honest, I doubt it. It were a long time ago, now. And a lot were made of it at the time, but really, it were nothing much.' He drained his glass. 'There were some lads from the other estate, Cartmel, saw it as an excuse for some trouble. Me and Mark were called some names. A couple of the pubs wouldn't have us for a while in case of trouble. But it blew over. No, whatever's happened to Mark is summat else. Maybe he's been mixing it lately with some dodgy types. Y'see, I lost touch with him, like I said. Yeah, y'all right, Barney, I'll be right wi' you –' He stood up and offered Agnes his hand. 'I don't really know what he were up to. But if there's owt else I can do, you know where I am.'

As Agnes crossed the pub she heard a chorus of whistles coming from the darts team. She didn't turn round.

In her room that night, Agnes lit her candle and knelt in prayer. She settled her thoughts, aware of images floating in her mind, of James's smile, his clear grey eyes. Of Anthony Turnbull. She jumped as the phone rang.

'Hello?'

'It's Patricia. I'm sorry to disturb you.'

'Patricia? What's happened?'

'I thought you should know. We've only just heard ourselves. Someone was found dead, on the estate. Earlier today.'

'Dead?'

'The thing is, he was just an old man, nothing to do with us or anyone. Anthony said to tell you –'

'Anthony?'

90

'You see, it's obviously some kind of random serial killer, you know, some nutter. He was killed the same way as Mark.'

'His eyes?'

'Yes, but you see, nothing to do with your Charlotte or our Joanna or anything. Just an old man, Reg someone, Reg Naismith I think. It's really very reassuring.'

'Reg –'

'And when I finally got through to the police they confirmed my view that it's one of those psychopath kind of things.'

'But Reg Naismith used to work at Allbright's.'

'Oh, well, everyone used to work at Allbright's. The point is, it's nothing to do with us. Anthony's terribly relieved, and so am I. Because it's quite clear that whatever's happened to Jo is separate from Mark. Do you see?'

'Yes. Yes, I see.'

'I'll speak to you later, maybe? I'll be at the mill if you're passing.'

'Right, thanks. Bye.'

Agnes sat at her desk. She took out the photo of the athletics team and stared at it. Mark Snaith. Reg Naismith. Did someone out there have some terrible methodical plan? she thought. Was there order in the chaos after all? Or is Patricia right, just some kind of random killing. Perhaps it's just coincidence. If I'd never seen this photo I'd probably be agreeing with her. Probably.

She got up suddenly and went out into the freezing corridor, finding she was hurrying down the stairs, towards the chapel. She reached the door. Slowly she walked towards the altar, shivering in her pale nightdress as the moon cast thin shadows on the stone around her. Two deaths. Two similar, savage deaths. And You expect me to make sense of it? She approached the East window and stared up at the darkened image of God. But what kind of God are You? You leave us here, Your so-called Creation, Your People, You abandon us here and leave us to get on with it, and when it all goes wrong, as it's bound to do because we're only human, what do You do? Nothing. You let a young man and an old man die a horrible death, and You do nothing. And what about the others, the countless others across this world of Yours, the man who sees his brother shot down next to him in battle, the woman who holds her hungry baby in her arms, helpless as its life fades away, the child who sees its parents killed before its eyes? And what about the killers, war-crazed village boys driven mad by fear, or the mercenaries brutalised beyond humanity – or some lone person even now wandering the moors out there, capable, perhaps, of killing again? And still You demand that we believe, that we hope? What the hell do You want us to do?

Agnes wasn't sure if she was speaking out loud or not. She sat on the altar step, suddenly exhausted. Her eyes welled with tears. 'What do You want me to do?' she whispered, and her words broke the chapel's silence.

Chapter Eight

Agnes crept late into assembly. She wished it was one of Elias's days for leading prayers, so that he'd be hiding away behind his hair, oblivious of any interruption. Philomena was mid-sentence as Agnes tried to take her place at the end of a pew. She broke off, looked up at Agnes, took out her watch with its dangling strap, squinted at it, put it back in her pocket and then continued:

'. . . they have dug a pit before me,
but have fallen into it themselves.'

Agnes caught Teresa's eye and, despite her fatigue, almost laughed.

She went to the staff room, made some coffee, and pretended to read a newspaper.

'Sister.' Philomena sailed across the room towards her.

Agnes looked up. 'I'm sorry about my lateness this morning.'

'Bad example to the girls.'

'Yes, I know.'

'And your House on duty this week.'

'Yes. I've put up the prefect rota.'

'So, back in the mess, eh?'

'I'm sorry?'

'No skulking in your quarters this week. Sharing the trough with the rest of us.'

'Yes, of course, Sister.'

'How's the Swann girl?'

'I've arranged to meet her in about three minutes.' Agnes stood up, relieved to have an excuse to leave.

'You wanted to see me.' Rachel Swann stood by Agnes's door. Agnes ushered her inside. She stood, tall and awkward, in the middle of the room, her long fringe of chestnut hair falling across her face.

'Won't you sit down?'

Rachel sat down on the nearest chair.

'Would you like some tea or coffee?'

Rachel shook her head. Agnes drew up a chair and sat down opposite her. 'How are you?' Agnes began.

'Fine, thanks.'

Agnes sighed. 'Sister Philomena is concerned about your eating.' Rachel said nothing. 'Or, rather, your lack of it,' Agnes went on. 'Apparently this happened last year too.'

'They've told you all about me, then?'

'I share their concern, that's all.'

'I'm fine. I ate breakfast this morning, didn't your spies tell you that?'

Agnes got up. 'I'll tell you how things stand, Rachel. You can eat or you can not eat. That's your choice. Personally, I feel it would be a terrible waste if you starved to death.'

'That's what they all say. A waste of a brilliant pupil. Think of those A grades I'm going to win for the school, my scholarship place at Cambridge to study medicine, not to mention my brilliance at music too.'

'How's the music going?'

'Which one, piano or violin?'

'Both.'

'I just passed my Grade Eight with distinction in both. Didn't you hear? It was announced in assembly.'

'I try to avoid assembly.'

Rachel glanced at her, then fell silent.

'I didn't mean a waste of a brilliant pupil,' Agnes said, sitting down opposite her again. 'I mean a waste of a human life. It seems to me that everyone's so dazzled by your brilliance they've lost sight of the person behind it.' Rachel brushed her hair from her eyes. Agnes went on, 'If you choose not to eat, the school plans to admit you to hospital again.'

'They can't.'

'It seems, they can.'

'I won't go.'

'You'd better eat then.'

Her lip trembled. 'They can't send me back there, it was horrible last time, food the whole time, people watching you eat, it's gross, it's just disgusting, I won't go.'

'It's not my approach,' Agnes said. 'And if it came to it, I'd fight them too. But we're responsible for you, Rachel. Sister Philomena's watching you fade away to nothing. She doesn't know what else to do.'

'I won't go. I'll take them to the European Court of Human Rights.'

'You'd probably win as well.' Agnes stood up and opened the door for her. 'You see, we can offer you all the counselling you want, all the care and concern in the world. But it's still up to you.'

Rachel stood up to leave, pulling her cardigan around her.

'Even if you want it all to stop,' Agnes said, as the girl hesitated in the doorway, 'it doesn't have to be you that stops. It can be everything else. The music, the exams. Just stop. As it is, it's you that's trying to call a halt, when everything else is just carrying on, dragging you with it.'

Rachel looked up at her. She shook her head. 'What would they say? I can't just stop.'

'They'd have to accept it, wouldn't they? They can either have a gifted daughter who's at death's door, or a healthy daughter who they've yet to get to know. It'll be an adventure for them, to meet you for the first time. "Hello," you can say to them, "I'm Rachel. You don't know me, I'm not the Rachel who's going to be a brilliant brain surgeon and give concerts with the Berlin Philharmonic in between operations. I'm Rachel, this one. I'm going to be—"The possibilities are endless, aren't they? "I'm going to be an international body-piercing artist. I'll head up a UN peace-keeping force in Bosnia. I'll be a mother of five, all by different fathers – I'm going to be a lazy slob who does nothing at all—"'

Rachel was laughing.

'"—I'll be all or none of the above,"' Agnes went on, '"but what I am, is your daughter. And it's time you got to know me."'

Rachel's eyes filled with tears. She looked at Agnes, tried to say something, then shook her head and went out of the door. Agnes heard the door of her room slam behind her.

'Her parents insist she's gifted,' Teresa said at lunch. Across the dining hall, Rachel sat, sipping on some soup. 'She was advanced a year, she's very young to be taking A levels.'

'I think hospital is the worst thing we could do.'

'Agnes, it was hell last time. She got down to under five stone. We had to. We tried everything else, nothing worked.'

Rachel gave up with her soup and sat staring at her bread roll.

'She is very bright,' Teresa said.

'Yes, but at what cost?'

Rachel glanced around, stood up and left the dining hall.

Agnes finished her last piece of cheese. 'Perhaps there's something to be said for my parents after all. They wanted me to be pretty and marriageable and not too bright. At least I ate.'

'Sister —' It was Charlotte, standing at her elbow.

'What is it?'

'Can I have a word?'

They left the table and went out into the corridor. 'You see, I got a phone call today.' Charlotte kept her voice low. 'From Anthony Turnbull.'

'You know Turnbull?'

'Through Mark. Through the Sports Centre. He was asking me about some papers.'

'What papers?'

'Mark was treasurer of the committee, he kept various files.'

'But why is Turnbull asking you—'

'Mark had some papers which he needs, and with Mark not being there any more . . . he's looking for them. That's all.'

'Do you know where they are?'

'Haven't a clue. He knew I was helping with typing stuff, which I was, but only the odd thing, on the computer here. But when I told him that, he was really angry. As if he thought I was lying. It upset me.'

'Well, he knows now.' Agnes looked at Charlotte. She was pale, chewing her lip, scuffing the floor with one toe. 'How are things these days?'

'OK.'

'I'm here if you need me.' Agnes watched her go, her retreating form clothed in grief. She turned and went into the staff room.

'Phone message for you, Sister,' Mary Watson said. 'Some woman with a Greek name, said she was risking returning to the frozen north against all her instincts, and could I let you know.'

Mary handed Agnes a scrap of paper, pursing her lips.

'Sweetie, they told you! I had my doubts. Saturday, how about lunch?'

'Lunch would be lovely, Athena.'

'That woman on the phone was rather prickly.'

'Athena, it may have escaped your notice, but some of the people who live here actually quite like it. The odd one or two, anyway.'

'Takes all sorts, sweetie. See you Saturday.'

Agnes put down her phone, then picked it up again and dialled a number.

'Hello, David?'

'Who is it?'

'Sister Agnes.'

'Ah, the so-called Sister Agnes. And what can I do for you?'

'I'm sorry to intrude—'

'So you should be.'

'I don't know how to say this, but—'

'Go on.'

'Reg Naismith.'

The line went quiet. Then David said, 'Yes. I know.'

'The same as—'

'The same as Mark. I know. And where do you come in?'

Agnes took a deep breath. 'I have this photograph.'

'What photograph?'

'It's of your athletics team, from the mill.'

'What, with Mark? Am I there?'

'Yes.'

'And – hang on a minute. You mean, Reg's there too.'

'Yes.'

Agnes heard him breathing. Then he said, 'Have you told the police?'

'Not yet. I'm going to pop in there tomorrow morning.'

'It won't change anything. They think it's just coincidence.'

'Do they?'

'Doesn't mean they shouldn't catch the bastard.'

'No. David?'

'What?'

'If it's not coincidence . . .'

'Now there's a thought. Someone working their way through the team. After all these years. Two down, eleven or so to go. Including me.' He gave a sharp bark of laughter. 'What are the chances, Sister?'

'I don't deal in chances.'

Again, his silence. Then he said, 'Has Jo been in touch?'

'No. Should our Head appoint a new art teacher?'

'Don't ask me.'

'David –'

'What?'

'You are in contact with her, aren't you? You do know where she is?'

'You've been spending too much time with Sugar Daddy Turnbull, haven't you?'

'I'm concerned for Jo, that's all.'

'He's very unsuitable company for a nun. Under all that jollity lurks a rotten heart. To listen to him, you'd think I'd bricked poor old Jo into a wall with only a grille for communication.'

'Whereas in reality—'

'What's reality? It's all illusion, you people should know that better than the rest of us.'

Agnes smiled. 'He's been asking Charlotte about some papers.'

'Oh, that again. He's been on about those ever since Mark died. There was a box of stuff from the sports centre at Mark's place, he reckons. But after Mark died, his place was done over. Usual ritual on Millhouse. The papers have vanished, along with other stuff. Turnbull thinks it's a conspiracy against him. He should know it's just boredom. Cosmic boredom.'

'One more thing.'

'What is it?'

'Do you know Lianna Vickers?'

'A bit, yes.'

'Do you know where she lives?'

'Why?'

'Can I be blunt?'

'It's the only language I understand.'

'Mark was seeing her.'

'What, "seeing" seeing her?'

'So she says. She told the police.'

'At the same time as Charlotte? The old devil.'

'Charlotte's upset, she wants me to visit Lianna, and she said you'd know where she lived.'

'Yes, sure. Hang on a minute.'

He came back on the line and Agnes took down the details.

'So you really do work with Jo?' he said. 'At the school?'

'Yes, I do.'

'Honest to God?'

Agnes laughed. 'Isn't God an illusion too, as far as you're concerned?'

She heard the catch in his voice. 'You tell me how your God can do that to my brother.'

'I believe –' She stopped. 'David, I have no answers.'

'It's lucky I had no faith,' he said. 'I'd have lost it by now. Keep in touch.' He hung up.

She went to the office, and made copies of the tribunal papers that Nina had given her. She copied the press photo of the athletics team three times. She closed the lid of the copier and turned to go.

'Oh, Elias . . .'

'You look busy.'

'Yes. I was just doing this, I'm going to see the police in the morning.'

'You're a great one for Doing, aren't you.' He smiled, faintly.

'At times, yes.'

'Admirable.'

Agnes felt she was being laughed at. And how long have you really known the Baines family, she wanted to say. 'There must be times when action is the best way, don't you think? For example, when people are in danger, maybe – then, surely, the right response is to take action?'

'But it's illusory, Agnes – the feeble strivings of humanity in the face of inevitable tragedy –'

'Don't you have hope, Elias? Don't you believe in anything?'

Elias met her gaze. 'I believe I'm here. Now. I believe that eventually I won't be.'

'And God?'

'That is God.'

'And love, and compassion?'

'Ah, yes. Love, compassion.' He took a few steps towards the door.

'We're born with compassion,' Agnes said, keeping her voice level against a rising wave of anger. 'It's the natural state of the human heart. And I know terrible things happen to knock it out of us, but isn't faith on our side? Doesn't our faith allow us to hold on to our compassion? Isn't that what we should strive for, not stillness in the face of suffering, but compassion instead?'

'I wouldn't know.' Elias's expression seemed to have shut down. Their eyes met, briefly, then he turned and left the room.

Janet Cole pored over the photograph of the athletics team. She ran her finger along the list of names. Then she placed it on the desk with the tribunal papers that Agnes had brought.

'It may be helpful,' she said. 'It's difficult to tell at this stage. We've already spoken to a lot of the names there. It's such a tight-knit community, you see, everyone's connected to each other.'

'And the tribunal? And Billy Keenan?'

Janet sighed. 'That name comes up time and time again. He was the last person to see Mark alive, which doesn't help.'

'So I heard.'

'He gave him a lift that night. Claims he dropped him off near the crag, he was driving across the moor to some club or other. We have a record of his arriving at the club.'

'And Mark was bird-watching?'

'He was keeping tabs on a couple of peregrine falcons, yes. There were sightings of a man up there, behaving suspiciously towards the nest. Apparently if someone wants to rob the eggs later in the year, they start preparing now.'

'And Billy dropped him off there?'

'That's what he said. No one else saw him, that's the problem. We've had Billy in a couple of times. But then, those Keenans know this place like it were their second home. We've had him in before, suspected arson, never proved.'

'Where was Reg found?'

'In the hallway of his house. He'd let in his attacker, there was no forced entry.'

'Not on the moors then?'

'No.' Janet chewed the end of her pencil. 'He'd been stabbed, like Mark. And the eyes were the same.'

'How did –'

'A knotted rope, tightened. Not very nice.' Janet dropped the pencil. 'How's Charlotte?'

'She seems to have settled down. Our chaplain's helping her, he seems to know a lot about grief and loss. She wants me to find out about Lianna Vickers.'

'Oh. Yes. We had to ask her about that, I'm sorry. This girl, Lianna, she might be making it up, sometimes people get fixations, usually with murderers, but sometimes with the victims. It becomes a sort of fantasy. And I'm afraid Lianna's grasp of reality is pretty thin at the best of times.'

The estate still looked desolate, despite the chilly sunlight which flashed across its windows. Agnes was glad she'd worn a thick shetland jumper under her coat.

She knocked again on the door. The remnants of a creeping rose clung to the outside of the house, as if trying to drain the life from it. She heard movement inside, and a voice said, 'Wha'you want?'

'Lianna?'

'I said, Whaddya want?'

'My name's Sister Agnes. I wanted to ask you about Mark. Mark Snaith.'

The letterbox lifted a crack. 'Who sent ya?'

'No one. I'm a nun.'

'A what?'

'Can't I come in?'

'I'm not supposed to – oh, all right then.' The door opened a fraction, and Agnes saw a mop of bleached hair and eyes thick with mascara. The door opened slightly wider, and Agnes found herself in the dimly lit hall, with Lianna turning the key in the lock again behind her. The cheap turquoise of the carpet was littered with unopened mail. Lianna went into the front room. The curtains were still drawn, and the sun filtered through the floral pattern, casting a flat orange light. The room smelt of soap and smoke. Lianna flung herself into an armchair and looked at Agnes.

'Nun, did you say?' She laughed, flapped her hand towards Agnes's clothes, reached for a packet of cigarettes, lit one with a slight tremor in her fingers, and then laughed again. 'And,' she said, drawing deeply on her cigarette, 'you wanna talk about Mark.'

'Yes,' Agnes said. She noticed how thin the girl was, stick-like in hipster jeans and a white T-shirt.

Lianna suddenly looked up at her with huge dark eyes, the lines around them accentuated by the smears of make up, despite her youth. 'I don't know owt about it.' Again her fingers trembled as she smoked.

'Lianna – I didn't come here to worry you or frighten you. I'm not from the police. The only reason I came here is –' Agnes breathed in the stale air. 'You see, I know someone called Charlotte Linnell. She says she knew you.'

Lianna nodded. 'Yeah, I remember. She were soft on him, weren't she? Poor cow. She were from that school, with the –' She stopped, and her face lit up. 'Oh, you. A nun. Now I see. That school.' She giggled, and for a moment she looked very young.

'She's very upset.'

'Daft bint. What did she think?'

'That he loved her.'

Lianna seemed to age again. She finished her cigarette and stubbed it out hard in an overflowing tin ashtray. Ash spilt across the arm of the chair. 'Yeah, well, who knows? He certainly in't goin' ter say now, is he?'

'Did you know him well?'

'Well enough.' She dabbed at the spilt ash.

'Do you know why anyone should want him dead?'

Lianna looked at Agnes, puzzled. She shook her head slowly.

Agnes took the photograph out and held it out to her. Lianna took it and stared at it. 'Where d'you get this?'

'From Allbright's.'

'I wanted a photo. After – when I heard, like. He lived across there, I went to have a look, see if I could find summat of him.' Lianna jerked her head towards the window. Agnes moved to draw the curtains back, but Lianna held her arm to stop her. Agnes sat back in her chair. Lianna lit another cigarette.

'You'll find nothin' there now,' Lianna said. 'They'll have had it all, pipes, wirin', flamin' roof an' all.' She looked at the photo again. 'Wasn't he the one – that Reg something, didn't they do 'im the other night?'

'Reg Naismith, yes.'

'He lived here too, down Knaresborough Place, over t'other side.'

102

'Was Mark still in touch with him?'

'Dunno. Never saw 'em together. He never mentioned him.'

'Lianna, you must have some idea – people must be talking about it. They were killed the same way.'

'The eyes, you mean?' Lianna chewed on a fingernail.

'You went to the police.'

'Yeah.'

'Why?'

'Thought I'd better. I knew him, Mark.'

'You said you were involved with him.'

'I was.'

'Charlotte was upset.'

'Poor cow.'

'Why did you go to the police?'

Lianna took a long drag on the end of her cigarette and stubbed it out in the filthy ashtray. At last she looked up at Agnes. 'Listen, when you live as I do, you get so's you don't care about owt. But I'll tell you this, and I've not told a soul, 'cos no one'd give a toss one way or t'other what happens to me. But when Mark came to me, it were like nothin' I'd ever known. It were soft and warm and gentle and – and it were like he loved me. It were fuckin' brilliant. And now there's some bastard out there who knows what it's like to hear that man, my Mark, pleading for his fuckin' life.' She lit another cigarette, the lighter flame juddering in her trembling hand. Her eyes flickered with defiance. 'And I'm not living with that. While I'm alive, that bastard's days are numbered.'

Agnes watched her for a moment. 'What did you tell the police?'

'What I knew. Which weren't much. About me and Mark. They asked me if anyone had anything against him. I said –' the light in her eyes deadened again. 'I said no. 'Cos it were secret, right, him and me, so even if –' she shook her head. 'I told them nowt.'

'You mean there's someone who might be jealous of him?'

Lianna laughed. 'Jealous? Nah. If I play around, right, it's me who gets me head kicked in.'

'So you don't know anyone who might be a threat to Mark?'

She drew hard on her cigarette, then looked at Agnes. 'I were goin' to tell them about the sports centre. Wish I had now.'

'What about it?'

''Cos I've had it now. In for a penny.' She smiled emptily. 'What's to come can't be worse than what I've already been through.' She took another drag, then said, 'That sports centre, right, that Mark were doin' with Anthony Turnbull, the one who owns Allbright's mill now. Well, they were on that committee thing, right, and Mark were in charge of t'money, and he said it weren't right. The money. He said it were goin' astray. But he couldn't prove owt, 'cos all them statement things all seemed OK, but he said there were things what didn't quite make sense. And then he's found dead, right. And what I reckon is, only I'm diggin' me own grave by tellin' you, is that it's all to do with Billy Keenan. Them Keenans always hated the Snaiths, goes back years, it do. Even his mum, Maureen, right, and she's a nice bird, she's sound she is, she wouldn't pass the time of day wi' Mark and Davey's mum. And Billy Keenan was the last one to see him alive, right.'

'The police already know that bit.'

'Aye, well, someone had to tell 'em in the end.' She put out her cigarette, twisting the stub down into the ash. 'Perhaps someone else told 'em about the money too. But if it gets back it were me, then I'm history, me.' She giggled. 'Perhaps there's a heaven and I'll meet Mark there, and we'll live happily ever after.' Her face lightened, and she raised wide eyes to Agnes. 'You know about these things, don't you, do you think that might happen?' Agnes looked at her open, childlike face, and for a moment it seemed possible. Then Lianna giggled again. 'Mind you, eh, there in't no shaggin' in heaven, so that's no good to me.'

They laughed, then fell silent. Agnes said, 'This money – would you have any proof?'

Lianna shook her head. 'They've had it all, you see, Mark's place has been done over. You'd have to search through the wreckage. They've probably done Reg's place by now, I saw them police guarding it last night, but them kids get in anyhow. Do you know . . .' her voice faltered. 'When they found Reg he were sprawled across his hallway. His neighbour found him. He'd tried to get help. They reckon he survived for a while, after – afterwards. Strong for his age, they said.' She glanced up. 'Din't help him, did it.' She reached for her packet of cigarettes. 'When I go to sleep at the end of a night, I think, well, there you are then. Survived another day. Another day older, another day nearer . . .' She shook her head. 'I gave up long ago. If it hadn't been for Mark . . .' She blinked back tears.

'Do you want me to go?' It was all she could think of to say.

'Charlotte,' Lianna said suddenly, 'she were just the same as you. She visited here a couple of times, with Mark. Before he – before he came to me. I used to imagine her, sneakin' back to her posh bloody school.' Lianna stood up and went over to the window. She twitched the curtain back an inch and peered out. 'It's when you have nowhere to go. Nothin' to do. No way out. That's what gets you in the end. Yeah, you'd better go, don't want you to be here when he . . .'

'When who?'

Lianna shrugged. She let the curtain fall across the window again.

Out in the hall, Agnes held out her hand for her photo. Lianna passed it to her. The tremor in her fingers was worse.

'Go on, out now,' she said.

'Who are you waiting for?'

Lianna whirled around in a dance of startling grace. 'I'm waiting for my man,' she said.

Agnes walked away across the estate. Once she glanced back. The windows of the little house seemed to echo Lianna's same empty grin, the same mask of despair. Agnes pulled her coat around her against a sudden gust of wind.

Chapter Nine

'Have you seen the papers?' Nina rummaged in her bag, then flung a heap of newsprint on to the mahogany, narrowly missing a beery puddle.

Agnes picked up her glass in one hand and one of the papers in the other. 'They're going for the serial killer bit, then,' she said, reading the headlines.

'We're all in danger, apparently. Random nutcase, could strike again anytime, we must all be on our guard. Isn't it wonderful?' Nina took a large swig of wine.

'Wonderful? Why?'

'Because usually it's women, so then you get all this stuff about not going out after dark and not on our own and keeping to well-lit areas – but now it's men, in't it. And they can't say that, can they? So they don't know what to say.' She gulped more wine. 'You're a bad influence, you are. This is my second trip to the pub in less than a week.'

'It's not just me. You must have friends –'

'Most of my mates live over towards Leeds. Apart from Jay, Rosie's Dad.'

'Are you – is he –?'

Nina laughed. 'We always confuse people, me and Jay. He's a great Dad, Rosie adores him. We see each other loads. But we don't live together. That's just how we are.'

Agnes sipped her drink and scanned the papers again. 'They don't seem to think Mark and Reg are connected. Other than by chance.'

'Perhaps they're not. Did you tell the police about the photo?'

'I gave it to them. I've kept a few copies.'

'And the tribunal?'

'I mentioned it to Janet Cole. She was interested in Billy Keenan, they know him. Although, his involvement in the tribunal is just hearsay, isn't it?'

'People know who's NF and who isn't.'

'And I spoke to Lianna Vickers, she lives on the estate. Mark was her lover. Sort of. And involved in the sports centre. She said that Mark thought there was money going astray from the funds for the centre. She had no proof though, and she was frightened of people coming for her if word got out that she'd told me.'

'They're all like that up there on Millhouse. Do you think there was any truth in it?'

'I don't know. I would have thought it's quite difficult to steal that kind of money without anyone noticing.'

'Perhaps that's why Turnbull keeps going on about Mark's papers.'

'Hmm. Another drink?'

'You know, for a nun, you're bad, you are. Just the one, then.'

Agnes stood by the bar. She glanced back at Nina, who was sitting quite still, her face set in an expression of anxiety.

'What's up?' Agnes said, returning with their drinks.

'What do you mean?'

'You seem fed up.'

'I had a hard day, that's all.' She drained her old glass and took the new one.

'At Allbright's?'

'It's tough there these days. To be honest, it's not been making huge profits for years, no one is these days, but Baines knew his job, kept one step ahead. But Turnbull knows if he's going to keep it going, he's got to make it more efficient. In a way, I don't blame him, but it means re-equipping, laying people off. And I'm the only one who knows about the redundancies, but the others know I know, and I can't tell them. It's really hard. And today –' She stopped.

'What?'

Nina sighed. 'I was all alone in the office at lunchtime, and Mr Baines came in. There wasn't a soul around in admin, and you can't get across to the mill floor very easily from my office, and . . . I suppose I was stupid to be frightened.'

'Nina, what happened?'

'He's – he seemed to be off his rocker, that's what. I mean, you've met him, he was OK, wasn't he, he's always been in his office in the old mill, he'd bob in and say hello to the older staff, and – he was respected, you see. Even the younger lads, people he had tough words with – you knew where you were with him. He were honest, that's what it was. Dealt with you straight. And now –' she laughed, uneasily. 'Stupid of me to be scared.'

'What happened?'

'He wasn't making sense, he came in to the new admin block, he's never come in since Pat and Anthony took over, and he marched in, and saw me, and it was like he was trying to tell me something really important. And I said, what is it, Mr Baines, and he said – you see, half of it didn't make sense, he sat down opposite me and said, "It's too late now." But he was kind of smiling. Then he asked me the time, and I told him. And he nodded, like it made him happy. And he was filthy, really looked like he needed a wash.'

'But he was calm?'

'Yes. But I'm not sure he knew who I was. After a while he got up and started looking through a box of files, there's a heap of stuff that Anthony had brought over from his office. Old bits of paper, share certificates, that kind of thing, goes back into the last century. Anthony thought he might frame some of it, you know, like people do, hang it in reception.'

'And Baines was looking through it?'

'Sort of. But he was smiling, and laughing. He picked some things out, looked at them, put them back, like he knew them all. He probably does, it's his father's stuff, and grandfather's.'

'What did you do?'

'I wanted to call for help, he was so weird, in fact, it made me think there should be an alarm or something in that office, and I was just wondering whether to yell out of the window when he got up, and kind of smiled, and said, thank you, Nina. And then he walked back down the stairs, calm as can be.'

'Did he go to his office?'

'No, he went straight out. There's a path that leads up to the moors from here, he went that way.'

'On foot?'

'Yes, he's known for his walking, it's a couple of miles across the moor to his place from here.'

Agnes frowned and sipped her drink. 'Did you tell Turnbull?'

'Yes, and Patricia, they both came back from lunch. Anthony said he should put in an alarm in the office. Patricia was really worried, and later I heard her discussing it with him, and they were arguing. But Turnbull's terrible too at the moment, he's been flying into rages with the staff, like he's really stressed.'

'Where does Baines live?'

'In the old family pile, up by West Moorside. They've always lived there. Patricia said her mother wanted to move nearer town, but her father wouldn't have it. He said the Bainses had always lived there and always would.'

'He's a great one for tradition, isn't he?'

Nina finished her drink. 'If you've lived through what he's lived through – trying to keep his mill going on the old lines, with the old staff, employing the old families, and it gets more and more difficult until you're barely breaking even – what else is there? It's all right for Turnbull, he's a newcomer, he can tear it all to pieces and start again. But for Baines – you see, he'd have felt ashamed to do what Turnbull's doing. Even though it's the only way Allbright's is going to survive.'

'Do you think that's what's driving him mad? Seeing his son-in-law change everything so fast?'

Nina took some lip salve out of her bag and applied it to her mouth. 'I'm not sure. He always said the mill needed new ideas.' She pressed her lips together. 'Maybe. I've got to go.'

It was cold out in the street.

Agnes reached her car. 'Do you want a lift?'

'No ta, I live just over there. And anyway, this week's serial killer is targeting men. Next week you can give me a lift.'

'Nina, it's not funny.'

'No, probably not.'

'Nina – could I look at the stuff that Baines was looking through?'

'Sure, pop in next week sometime. Monday? You can help me go through it. See ya.'

Agnes watched Nina stride away. The streetlamps streaked her fake fur coat with gold.

At the school she found a message in her pigeon hole, sealed in an envelope. She unfolded it as she walked up the stairs to her room. It was from James.

Dear Agnes,
   I didn't mean to write this to you, but it's proved impossible

to say it any other way. Even writing it is tough. The fact is, I'm ill. Very ill. My doctors have given me two years at the most, maybe less.

Agnes let herself into her room, went straight to her desk and switched on the light.

I won't go into detail. I first had the primary cancer diagnosed some years ago and was successfully treated. That was then. These days I take what they give me for the pain, which, thankfully, is bearable. I've had all that modern medicine can provide, but that stage is over. Inoperable, is the word they use now. It's a question of waiting.

I'm sorry you have to read this. I seem to find this business of dying a lot more straightforward than the people I have to tell. Perhaps with your faith, you might find it easier too, but I regret to say, the religious people of my acquaintance have often been the worst, railing on my behalf against a God I don't believe in. One or two have even blamed me for not believing enough, as if somehow true faith guarantees immortality. On good days I find it amusing. As you know, I have no faith to speak of, which, oddly, can be quite comforting.

I'll close now. Again, I'm sorry. Come and see me soon.

Love, James.

Agnes sat at her desk. She read the letter again. Two years. Or less. She read it again. She picked up her phone and was about to dial his number, when there was a very faint knock at her door, and she looked up. She hadn't closed her door and Elias now stood in the doorway, hesitant and uncertain.

'I'm sorry – I wasn't sure –' He took a few steps into the room. 'The thing is, you're right,' he said.

Agnes put her hand to her forehead.

'About compassion,' he went on. 'I've been – I was up on the moors all day. You're right. Joanna –' He turned and looked at Agnes. 'Are you all right?'

'Not really, no.'

'What is it?'

Agnes shook her head, then got up, went to her cupboards

111

and poured two glasses of whisky.

He took the glass she handed him. 'I was walking on the moors and I thought, you're right, about taking action. So, I think we should visit William Baines.'

'You think what?' Agnes sat down with her glass. She wondered whether Elias was already drunk.

'Or rather, I think we should visit his house. When he's not there.'

'You are drunk.'

'No, I thought about it. Joanna has a studio there, and she might still be working. David's saying nothing, the Turnbulls are obviously in the dark. And then, I thought, her father. Who else?'

'But he won't hear her name. And why his house, in his absence? Why can't we just ask him?'

'Because it won't work.'

Agnes remembered what Nina had told her about the current state of William Baines, but said nothing.

'Also,' Elias went on, 'I gather he's quite upset about the mill. Handing it over. I mean, Patricia's OK, but she's not the brightest of women.'

'By the way,' Agnes said deliberately, 'she asked to be remembered to you.'

Elias blinked. He glanced around the room, as if newly aware of where he was. 'Did she?' He spoke carefully, waiting for the next question.

'More whisky?' Agnes said.

He handed her his glass, still searching her face.

'So,' Agnes said, lightly, pouring him another drink, 'this plan to visit the Baines family house – what do you hope to gain?'

'You see –' Elias put his hand to his brow. 'That's where most of her work is. I thought there might be – oh, I don't know. It all made sense up on the moor.'

'Clues?'

He took his hand from his face and looked at her. He nodded. 'Yes. Clues.'

'OK,' Agnes said. 'When?'

'Sunday night. Day after tomorrow. He always plays bridge with some old friends. We can go in my car.'

'But what if – I mean, he might not go that day, particularly if he's not quite himself – and what if we're caught, and –' Agnes picked up her glass, put it down again. 'What I mean is, it's all so ridiculous, isn't it? Doing it by stealth?'

'Agnes, it won't help if William sees me face to face.'

She stood up and went to pour herself another drink. Then she turned to him and said, 'Patricia told me. About the accident . . .'

'She knows nothing about it.' Elias's face was pale.

'And Marcus –' Agnes went on.

'I said she knows nothing. Whatever she told you, it's not – it doesn't – I don't want to talk about it.' His eyes were dark and pleading, shadowed with suffering.

'Sunday night, then,' she heard herself say.

He put down his glass and stood up. At the door he turned to her. 'Thanks,' he said. She heard his footsteps recede along the corridor.

Alone in the silence of her room, Agnes poured another drink. She read James's letter again, then picked up her phone and dialled his number.

'Did I wake you?'

'It doesn't matter, I don't sleep that well. You – um –'

'I got your letter.'

'I'm sorry.'

'Sorry for dying? James, we're all dying.' Suddenly she wanted to laugh, and she heard him laughing too.

'I don't know why that should be funny,' he said at last.

'No. Neither do I. James – two years is quite a long time.'

'Long enough. I'm going to travel.'

'Yes.'

'While I'm still quite fit.'

'Yes.'

'Will you come and see me soon?'

'Tomorrow?'

'Agnes – could you make it Sunday?'

'Sure. After chapel, one-ish.'

'See you then.'

She drained her whisky glass, then picked up Elias's empty glass as well. She turned the glass in her fingers, wondering whether it had been a dream, that Elias had appeared in her room and suggested they break into Baines's house. It was a crazy plan.

She stood up and ran soapy water to wash the two glasses. She thought about his anger when she'd mentioned the accident. This trip to Baines's house isn't about Joanna at all, she thought. It's about Elias. Whatever whispered to him on the moors today, it wasn't Joanna's demon. It was his own.

She knelt in prayer, and in her mind she saw James, his courage and humour. He'd always been like that; even when she was young, he'd been calm and funny, and outspoken when necessary but not often. She found there were tears in her eyes, and realised she was crying not for him but for herself, that something should have been given to her only to be taken away again. It's not fair, she wanted to cry, like a child grasping at a toy out of reach.

'Go with him, sweetie,' Athena said. It was Saturday lunchtime.

'What?'

'It's obvious. He wants to travel, you're upset about losing him, go with him. Shall we have the halibut?'

'Athena – I can't –'

'Why not? I would. Mind you, it's a bit too platonic for me, no romantic adventure . . .'

'He's like a father, or an older brother at least – or a best friend.'

'Much better for travelling. No lovers' tiffs, plain sailing, a world cruise, I assume he's got pots of money?'

'Yes, but . . .'

'There we are then. Maybe salmon, mind you, I only eat wild salmon these days, I saw this documentary about pink colouring –'

'Athena – I'm a nun.'

'Sweetie, I know that.'

'So it's obvious –'

'It's obvious to me that you're very unhappy.'

Agnes was about to speak, then grabbed the menu and scanned it. 'Skate wings, that's what I'm having. And Chablis.'

'And I'm paying.' Athena waved at the waitress. 'Business is looking up. Simon has an eye for these things. We've got an artist in the gallery who makes art out of fruit. Eastern European, Romanian or Armenian or something. She kind of sprays fruit with plastic-y stuff and paints it funny colours, silver and turquoise and things. They are selling really well. Surprising really. And what happened to your art teacher, the one who vanished?'

'Well, she's still missing. But someone else has been found killed, so it's all rather grim.'

'And that priest . . .'

'Oh, him.'

'Well?'

'If you must know, he's suggesting we break into the family home of the woman who's vanished, Joanna, because her paintings are there. And her boyfriend, David, who's also an artist, won't say where she is, but we think he knows and he's protecting her. In fact – Simon might like his stuff.'

'Simon is in love with the North, sweetie. As long as your friend can splash a bit of paint or something, Simon'll show him, I swear.'

'And he's good. It's not just paintings, it's three-dimensional stuff too, *objets trouvés* kind of things. Still life.'

'I don't believe it – did you say still life? Simon's desperate for some work for our second room, to accompany the fruit things in the big space. Quick, give me his number.' Agnes scribbled David's phone number down and passed it across to her. 'It's absolutely the thing at the moment,' Athena said, scrutinising the piece of paper. 'Like the plastic fruit. Ludmilla's idea was that the fruit dies inside the structure, so it turns from being life to being death, but it looks just the same. I'm afraid it's all beyond me, it just reminded me of hats.' Athena refilled their wine glasses. 'And is he gorgeous?'

'Is who gorgeous?'

'This priest of yours.'

'Oh, Athena, honestly!'

'Celibate, of course. There's always something, isn't there?' Athena sighed and gave their order to the waitress.

'Elias, he's called. And it's quite clear he's in some terrible conflict of his own.'

'Just your type then, sweetie.'

'Athena, shut up.'

'Obviously, this Jo is some kind of childhood sweetheart who he still yearns for, and he's worried about her, and wants to find her, but at the same time he's worried about what will happen when he does. And we forgot to order mineral water.' Athena waved wildly at the waitress. 'In fact, it was probably something all going wrong with this girl that turned him into a priest.'

'There was a riding accident –'

'There you are then.'

115

'I'm not sure he and Jo were – he's not romantic, you see. He's more existentialist.'

'Oh well, that's the end of that, then. You can't fancy an existentialist, poppet, even a gorgeous one. Even if I did know what it means.'

The mineral water arrived and Athena took a long drink from her glass. 'No, it's quite clear to me, poppet. When James asks you, you must say yes.'

'I'll say no such thing. I owe it to my order to be committed, I made my vows –'

'And do you owe it to your order to be miserable, to be unable to throw yourself into your work because it doesn't feel right? Do they really want someone who's resentful because she feels she's living half a life?'

'They want me to grow spiritually through my commitment, through transcending my own desires for the greater good.'

'Seems to me, sweetie, if we can be happy, and live life well, then that is for the greater good.'

'Anyway, Athena, James won't ask me. So it doesn't matter what I want.'

'Absolutely, sweetie, you know best.'

Out in the street, Agnes gave Athena a hug. 'I must run, Athena, I'm due back at the school in twenty minutes. My house is on duty.' She glared at her smirking friend. 'It's not funny.'

'Your house is on duty. And you prefer that to a world cruise. Of course it's funny. Oh, you poor, poor sweetie, I shouldn't tease you, you're right of course, the world does need people who stay put regardless. I'm just glad it's not me.' She kissed her extravagantly on both cheeks, and then teetered away into the Saturday shopping crowd.

At tea-time Agnes went to the staff room. There was a message saying that David had called.

'You phoned.'

'Agnes, hi. Yeah, a friend of yours phoned me earlier, Simon, runs a gallery. Nice of you to think of me.'

'I like your work.'

'Thanks. Listen, if you ever fancy it – I don't know if you God-botherers drink . . .'

'What do you think?'

'I'm in the Woolpack most nights, do you know it, in town?'

'I'm sure I can find it.'

'Tonight if you like.'

'I'm afraid my house is on duty. But next week, maybe?'

'I'm always there.'

She was crossing the courtyard back to her room when Charlotte came up to her.

'What happened, what did she say?'

'Who?'

'Lianna, you know, what did she say?'

'Charlotte, come and sit down somewhere.' They went to the deserted common room and sat on beige armchairs.

'She wasn't his girlfriend, was she?' Charlotte sat on the edge of her seat, pulling at her skirt.

'No,' Agnes said.

'They didn't – they hadn't . . .'

'Charlotte –'

Charlotte's fingers worked at her skirt. 'It didn't mean anything, it can't have done, he said I really mattered to him. He said I was beautiful. Once he did. And she's so – she's so – I've been to her place, it's a real dive, and she smokes all the time. And other things.'

'Mark was a nice person, wasn't he?' Agnes said. Charlotte nodded. 'Gentle, and kind . . .' Charlotte was biting her lips. 'I think Lianna doesn't know many people like that.'

Charlotte flashed Agnes a glance. 'So I'm supposed to be charitable, am I? She can borrow him because she has a horrible life.' Her eyes filled with tears.

'Charlotte, that's not what I meant.'

'And – and I bet she knows more about how to – how to – and she's really sexy, isn't she, and really thin, and it's just because I wasn't very experienced, I knew he'd go and find someone else, someone who could – who knew –' Her sobbing drowned out her words. Agnes went to her and put her arms around her. In five years' time, she wanted to say, you will have survived this. But Lianna . . . Agnes thought about Lianna in five years' time. She held Charlotte close.

It was a fine afternoon when she pulled up opposite the phone box and parked in James's drive. He came to the door, hearing the car, and ushered her inside. She glanced up at him, and wondered whether the fact she knew he was ill made him seem more frail.

'I've made some lunch,' he said.

'You needn't have.'

'I'm not an invalid.'

She followed him into the dining room.

'Have you been in chapel all morning, then?' he asked, setting bread and butter on the table.

'I've been very glad of it today,' she said.

'Do you mean there are some days when you aren't?' He went to the kitchen and brought out two plates of soup. They sat opposite each other.

'I just meant, especially today.'

'Because of seeing me?'

'Yes.' She glanced up and caught his frank, clear gaze.

'What has He got to say about me, then?'

Agnes laughed. 'Do you want an apology?'

'No, not exactly. Though I would like to know how long.'

'I'll ask Him next time.'

'And He'll say nothing.'

'I thought you didn't believe in Him.'

'I don't.'

'James—'

'What?'

'If you don't believe, then—'

'What?'

'In your darkest moments, I mean—'

'You mean who do I speak to in the wee small hours when it's cold and dark and I'm scared?'

'You see, I can't imagine being without that dialogue, not being able to lay everything at His feet.'

'Even if it makes no difference?'

'But it does. It's the act of handing everything over that changes everything. It's the path to – to redemption, to acceptance.'

'If you don't mind my saying so, you don't seem very accepting.'

'Oh, you don't want to take me as an example.'

James smiled. He met her eyes, and seemed to be about to say something, then noticing their plates were empty, he got up to refill them.

After lunch he brought the coffee through into the living room. Agnes sat on the sofa and curled her legs under her. He poured the coffee in silence, then sat in the armchair next to the empty grate.

'I'll be setting out quite soon,' he said at last.

'Where will you go?'

'France, to start with. And Barcelona, maybe northern Italy too, I've an old friend in Verona I'd love to see before . . .' He sipped his coffee. 'And then the States, I've things to clear up there, and if by then I'm – I'm too – I can't—' He passed his hand over his eyes. 'It's not the dying, you see, the dying seems OK, it's the bit in between, I don't know how that's going to be, and in the darkest moments, that's when I find I'm cold and shivering, when I think about the pain and the illness and . . .' He shook his head. 'Still, that's yet to come.'

'James – are they sure?'

'Sure about what?'

'That you're dying. That it's two years.'

'They reckon I've got one good year left, after that it could be a slow decline, or it could be very sudden. The treatment has put a lot of strain on my system, it may turn out that I'm weaker than they thought . . .'

Agnes got up and poured another cup of coffee. 'James – might you not come back here, then?'

'No. I might not come back.'

'But . . .'

'I know.'

The afternoon sun through the trees cast flickering shadows. 'Agnes,' James said at last.

'Yes?'

'I think you should visit your mother.'

'You think *what*?'

'I know it sounds odd . . .'

'Here we are, saying the first of many goodbyes and you tell me I should visit my mother.'

'Please hear me out. Your mother isn't going to last for ever. And if she dies before you've seen her again, you're going to feel terrible. I know you are. Whereas if you come with me to the South of France, you can begin the process which will allow you to move on from it all, with some kind of resolution.' He stood up

119

and fetched the brass clock from the mantelpiece and put it down in front of her. 'You can give this back to her.'

Agnes blinked back tears, staring at the clock. 'You're the only one who has any idea how it was,' she said at last. 'There'd be these sudden bursts of kindness, of endless treats and new expensive dolls, and then nothing for weeks, months, maybe, and I'd be treated as a nuisance and she'd be ill again, and then some governess would arrive to look after me and keep me away from her, and then she'd fall out with the governess and say no one was good enough for her daughter and then there'd be another doll . . . There was one in particular, I loved that doll, more than the others, I don't know why, it was porcelain, and very beautiful, in a long white dress . . . I don't know where she got it. I used to imagine her choosing it specially for me, it was a kind of story I told myself, the day my mother went to the shops and chose me a doll. When I got married, I took the doll on my honeymoon. Isn't that an odd thing to do, I wonder why I did that?'

Agnes's voice faltered and she burst into tears. James came and sat down next to her. She took the handkerchief he passed her, and dabbed at her face.

'Did you . . .' she began, 'did you say if I come with you to the South of France?'

He nodded.

'You mean you'd be there too?'

'I didn't expect you to do it on your own.'

'James – why?'

'Why am I asking you to come with me?'

'Yes, why?'

He stood up and went over to the window. 'Everything I do, from now on, is the last. The last time I see a Chabrol movie, the last time I hear a live performance of Bartok's third piano concerto, the last – possibly the last – the last thing I do for your father.'

'For my father?'

'I'm the only living person who can make amends.'

'On his behalf?'

'On behalf of both of them.' He came and sat down next to her. 'I just think you should visit her. And if I'm there, it'll be OK, she's quite nice to me now.'

'In Christmas cards.'

'It's a start.'

They both laughed.

'And then, after Antibes,' James said, 'you could come to Italy, and then the States, I was thinking of going by ship.'

'And is this for my father too?'

'No. This is for me. And for you, actually. You can meet some of his friends, tie up some loose ends. And it's on condition that as soon as I get ill you deliver me into the appropriate medical hands and come straight home.'

'I might be quite a good nurse.'

'I won't have it, Agnes.'

Agnes took a sip of cold coffee. 'The problem is, that I can't. It's simply not possible. The order won't accept it.'

'Is it up to them?'

'Yes. I – I owe them my obedience.'

'At any cost?'

'But it's illusory, James, this self, this person with individual wants and needs. That's what I was trying to tell Athena. The self is endlessly greedy, always wanting more, essentially restless, whereas if you hand everything over, and stop listening to the self, and start listening to the stillness instead, then – then . . . You see, that's what I was trying to tell Athena when she said I should go with you, that the greater good is all about accepting what is, rather than ceaselessly striving for what might be.'

'Who's Athena?'

'She's a friend.'

'How did she know before I'd even asked you?'

'She said I was unhappy, that's all.'

'She's bolder than I am.'

Agnes smiled. 'She's bolder than most people.'

'So she says what other people only think?'

Agnes looked at him, then said, 'Maybe happiness isn't what we're here for.'

'But if one gets the chance, surely one should seize it. If your God has put us here, surely we should celebrate what He gives us?'

'He gives us the Now, that's all. The moment.'

'And if the Now includes the possibility of a cruise to the States, isn't it right to say yes? I'm sorry, Agnes, but your Athena has made me bold too, and if I thought you were happy in your order I wouldn't dream of saying all this, but to see you – as you are . . .'

'You mean, if I was to say no it would be a denial of God's plan for me, not an acceptance of it?'

'Yes. And I don't even believe in Him.'

They smiled at each other. James reached across to the clock and wound it, and set it down again. They watched the four spheres spinning, the mechanism springing smoothly into action.

'I wonder what Elias would say,' Agnes said after a while.

'I don't expect you to decide now, I'm not going for a month or two, you must take advice. You can ask Elias what he thinks.'

'I'm seeing him tonight, but we're breaking into someone's house, so there won't be much time for theology.'

James laughed. 'You see, you need me to keep you from your criminal tendencies.'

Agnes stood up to leave. In the hall, James helped her on with her coat.

'Agnes – I won't have this conversation again. You must take advice and decide when you're ready. Whatever you decide, I'll accept, please believe that. Don't feel you have to avoid me just because of today, I won't mention it again. Just let me know when you're ready.'

'Of course I won't avoid you.'

'Tea on Sunday, then?'

Agnes smiled. 'Tea on Sunday.' She tucked her scarf into her collar. 'Anyway, the only person I can talk to about this is Julius.'

'Will he be on my side?'

'Come to think of it, you're very alike. Perhaps I shouldn't tell him, he might want to go with you instead.'

'He can meet your mother, then.'

'He'd be great with my mother.'

James kissed her cheek. 'Until Sunday. We'll discuss golf next time, or bridge.'

'How very dull.' On the steps, she turned. 'James – Julius will tell me not to leave my order.'

'And will he be right?'

'He's always right.' Agnes kissed him, then got into her car and pulled out into the road. The clouds were edged with pink as the last of the sun sank lower in the sky and then was gone.

Chapter Ten

It was raining. Elias parked his car at the edge of the deserted moorland road and switched off the engine.

'Here?' Agnes could see nothing out of her window.

'I can't risk getting any closer.'

You just want us to get wet, Agnes thought, as they got out of the car and began to walk towards the house. An owl hooted. All we need is thunder and lightning now, Agnes thought.

'There might be thunder,' Elias said.

They approached the house. Agnes could hear dogs barking. Elias turned to her. 'You don't mind dogs, do you?'

Why am I here? Agnes thought. There was a wall which encircled the house. Elias turned away from the front drive, and followed the wall round to the side, until they reached a tiny wooden door draped with ivy. He lifted the latch, and it opened. Immediately there was a rush of barking and snarling and wet fur. Agnes flung herself back against the door, her arms across her face. When she next looked Elias was crouching on the ground with two black labradors jumping around him in glee, tails wagging.

'And where's Greer?' he was asking, fussing them. 'Where's your old Daddy, then?' She took a step towards him. He stood up. 'I said they were OK, didn't I?' His eyes were shining with tears. He set off towards the side of the house, the dogs jumping at his legs. They reached a back porch door, which opened easily. The dogs quietened as they went into the house.

It was pitch dark. Elias switched on his torch. Agnes saw Wellington boots on the tiled floor, fishing rods stacked against a wall. There was another door, also unlocked, then they were inside the house. A thin light shone through the bannisters from an upper landing. There was a damp smell; a low growling. Agnes heard Elias whisper, 'Greer?' He flashed his torch. 'Greer?' In the pale light Agnes saw a dog basket lying by one wall. A huge old dog seemed to be sleeping there, but its head was turned towards them, and it growled again.

'Greer, it's me,' Elias said, flinging himself down next to the dog. The growling stopped, and the dog opened one eye. Elias buried his head in its neck. 'I knew you'd wait, oh Greer, you waited . . . And now I'm back, and Kate, remember Kate . . .? Oh, I've dreamed of you so many times . . .' he murmured, through tears. With great effort the dog raised his head and licked his cheek.

The other two dogs sat to attention. The hall seemed vast, extending into shadow. There was a huge central staircase. Agnes could see the carved mahogany, the worn red carpet. In the heavy silence she could hear the rain against the windows. A clock chimed the quarter hour. Elias sat up. He patted the dog, then stood up, dashing tears from his eyes with the back of his hand. 'I knew he'd live for ever, that dog,' he murmured. 'Come on.' He set off up the staircase. Agnes followed him. The young dogs stayed in the hall, their tails thumping the floor.

They went along the first landing, then up another flight of narrow, uncarpeted stairs. 'How does Baines live in all this, all alone?' Agnes whispered.

'He's been rattling around here for years. He won't change.'

The upper landing was cluttered with furniture, a beautifully carved low table, thick with dust. The floor around the window was covered in leaves. Elias tried the second door along. It was locked. There was a shelf above the door, and Elias ran his hand along it. He picked up a key from the shelf and put it in the lock.

'If she doesn't want her Dad snooping around her work, she should change her hiding place,' he said. The door opened, and Elias ushered her in and switched on the lights.

It was a huge room, looking out to the front of the house. It was cluttered but not untidy. Canvasses in various stages of work were stacked against the walls.

'She didn't wreck her own art room, then, just ours,' Agnes said.

'Yes.' Elias pulled a canvas towards him to see what was behind. 'Typical of her. It's like the roses, all pruned before she left. She allows her madness into places where it'll do least damage. I remember this one,' he said, finding an old work stacked behind a new. 'Horses. She did loads of stuff about horses when I first knew her.'

'What, like Stubbs?'

Elias laughed. 'No, not quite. Look.'

He pulled out a small canvas, criss-crossed with scratchy charcoal colours.

'That's horses?'

'She used to say so. She'd take particular lines, like the angle of the back of the hoof, and repeat them.'

'So, has she moved on since then?' Agnes went to an arrangement of objects on a small table. There was a vase in rough porcelain, some drooping roses. A pink digital watch.

'Perhaps. Look, no skull,' Elias said.

'There's a watch instead. Do you think it's a clue?'

He laughed. 'I've no idea.'

There was an easel, a canvas in the early stages of work; rough outlines of light, the curve of the vase, a suggestion, in the brusque red lines, of rose petals unfurling. The numbers from the watch-face were pencilled in across the flowers. Agnes walked round it. 'She can't have been here for a while, the roses are entirely shrivelled up.'

'No, on the contrary,' Elias said, joining her, 'this is deliberate. It's all about decay, you see. If you're painting a rose like this, it becomes a representation of death. And anyway, you try getting fresh garden roses in March.'

'So this is work in progress?'

Elias went to a paintbrush that was lying on the easel. He wiped it on a rag. 'See, the brush is still wet.'

'We could –' Agnes began.

'What?'

'Shall we tell Joanna we've been here? Leave her a note?'

'There's no point now,' Elias replied. 'We know she's OK, don't we. We know she still comes here.'

'But the school –'

'That's not our business. She'll have to decide if she still wants that job in her own time.'

'But something made her run away—'

'We don't have to meddle in her life—'

'—connected with Mark's death.'

Elias looked at Agnes. 'So you say. But look at the evidence.

David seems to think she's OK. These brushes are still wet. She's obviously fine. You see, she was always a fragile person. Sometimes things just got too much for her. Especially after . . .' He blinked, shrugged. 'Maybe she'd just had it with teaching. It's like her to walk out whenever she needs to.' He smiled. 'Being totally selfish is one of her great talents.'

'She was very distressed in the art room that night.'

'She's often distressed. It drives her work. She's on to something with this still life stuff, it must have taken her over for a while.'

He began to put everything back in its place. 'You see, these skulls and flowers, they're part of the Baines family tradition. Goes back years.' He laughed, at some private joke. He surveyed the studio, everything orderly once more. They went out on to the landing. He locked the door, replaced the key, then turned to Agnes. 'I'll show you what I mean,' he said. She followed him to the end of the corridor. Elias grabbed a chair, jumped on to it, reached up and opened a trap door in the ceiling. He pulled down a ladder which was folded into the roof.

'Elias –'

'It's OK.' Elias started up the ladder.

'What if he comes back?'

'Then we fold the ladder up behind us and wait until it's safe to come out.'

'You're mad.'

'Come on.'

Agnes sighed and climbed the ladder. He reached out his arm and helped her into the loft. It was dark, with a thick dusty smell. The rain hammered on the roof. Elias was clumping across the rafters, muttering.

'They must be here. He wouldn't have moved them.'

His torch beam picked out a huge trunk; a roll of carpet; a regimental flag, half unfurled. A canvas.

'Here we are.'

They approached. Agnes saw two paintings leaning up against a tea chest. One was a still life, a kitchen scene; a cabbage, a dish of lemons and grapes. The other showed a young man sitting at a table piled with opulence, with jewellery, books. There was an ornate clock at one side. Placed at the centre of an open book was a human skull.

'Baines is crazy,' Agnes said at last. 'The doors unlocked, anyone could break in, these must be worth thousands.'

'He relies on the dogs.'

'People shoot dogs.'

'No one knows these are here.'

'But they're – sixteenth – seventeenth century?'

'Seventeenth. Spanish.'

'Someone must know about them.'

'The Baines family has always been Chapel.'

Agnes looked at Elias. 'I don't understand.'

'Some time last century, a young Baines, instructed by his father to find him some Continental Art, brought these back from his grand tour or whatever they did, having paid a sizeable amount for them.'

'Who told you about this?'

'No one.' Elias stroked some dust from a picture frame. 'I just know.'

'So why did they end up in a loft? And what's that got to do with being Chapel?'

'Agnes, it's obvious. These are so Roman Catholic, aren't they? So utterly un-Puritan. Painted by Jesuits.'

Agnes looked at the painted velvet of the table cloth, the cascades of pearls. 'So they hid them away.'

'Yes, for generations. Hannah, Baines's wife, wanted them displayed, but he stuck with family tradition.'

'And Joanna?'

Elias considered the paintings for a moment. 'You see,' he said, pointing to the man seated at the opulent table, 'this is a vanitas. A memento mori. The skull, and the clock together. A warning against attachment to worldly things. The inevitable passage of time.'

'And so she paints dead roses.'

Elias nodded.

'Elias – when did you first see these, then?'

He turned to her. 'A long time ago.' He looked back to the paintings. 'I like the cabbage best, in the kitchen one, look. A celebration of cabbage-ness.' He smiled. 'We'd better go, these bridge parties finish early.'

They replaced the loft ladder, closed the trap door, and hurried back down to the darkened hall where the dogs were waiting.

'Did you come here to set your mind at rest?' Agnes asked.

'Something like that.'

'About Joanna? Or about something more?'

He seemed to smile. 'Perhaps I just wanted to see my dog again . . .' He knelt down beside Greer's basket, and murmured into his fur. The dog lifted his head, blinking through ancient clouded eyes, and nuzzled Elias.

'Maybe he summoned me,' Elias whispered, getting to his feet. 'Maybe he was waiting to say goodbye.' His eyes welled with tears.

They left the way they'd come, the dogs subdued beside them. At the garden door the dogs stood to attention while Elias patted their heads. Then Agnes and Elias were out on the drive, walking back to the car. The rain had eased, and the air was fresh and damp.

Elias was enclosed in silence. They drove back to the convent. He parked in the car park and turned off the engine. As Agnes opened the car door, she heard him say, 'Thank you.'

She turned to him. 'What for?'

'Every time I've gone back, it's always been a dream. But now there's you to ask, to tell me it was real.'

They got out of the car and walked slowly down the drive. He turned off towards his flat in silence, leaving her to walk alone into the school.

She woke early on Monday morning. It was a bright, clear dawn, heralding spring. In the chapel, she found Philomena and Teresa already there. She joined her voice to theirs, finding peace in the familiar words, aware, inexplicably, of an image of a cabbage, perfectly executed, something to do with the Divine, with Creation itself. And God created Cabbage-ness, she found herself thinking, as Philomena chanted the final blessing.

Which, of course, He did, she thought, going into breakfast, trying to hang on to the thought in the noise and clatter, trying to recall the painting she'd seen last night with Elias. Cabbage-ness and Lemon-ness and Terracotta Pot-ness . . .

'Coffee?' Teresa said.

And Coffee-ness, Agnes thought. 'Yes please, no milk.' And Tray-ness and Plate-ness, and Dining Room-ness . . .

'You seem distracted.'

Agnes looked across at Teresa as they sat down at a table. 'Those

Jesuits knew a thing or two, didn't they,' she said.

'Which Jesuits?'

'I was thinking about Spanish still life painters of the seventeenth century.' Agnes sipped her coffee.

'You would,' Teresa said through a mouthful of cornflakes.

'I was thinking about Thing-ness.'

'Right,' Teresa said, eyeing her strangely.

'The celebration of Creation.'

'Of course. We talk about it all the time in the staff room.'

'It all starts with cabbages, you see.'

'Cabbages. Right.' Teresa was frowning now.

'If you paint a cabbage, then you're celebrating the thing-ness of it, aren't you? To paint something becomes an act of worship. And if it's something that was alive, like a cabbage, or a rose, then you're celebrating not only its essential nature, but its impermanence too. So in the act of painting, you're meditating on – on everything. On creation, but also on death. It's full of paradoxes, isn't it, because the painting acquires a permanence that the cabbage itself never had. So it's a kind of mimicry of God, to paint, yet also an act of worship in the face of God's greatness.'

Teresa put down her spoon. 'You know, every morning here, I have tea. Every single morning for more than ten years, I've had tea.' She pointed at Agnes's cup. 'Tomorrow,' she said, 'I'm going to have coffee.'

At eleven, Agnes knocked on Sister Philomena's door.

'Agnes, come in, sit down, what is it?'

'Joanna Baines,' Agnes began, taking a seat.

'Funny you should say that. Just had a letter of resignation from her.' Philomena waved a piece of paper. 'Writing back to accept, can't have all this bally AWOL all over the shop.'

'No, of course not.'

'Just as well you popped in. Swann child, Plan B, I think.'

'Sister, I cannot stress enough that if we send her to hospital –'

'Can't do a thing with her. Yesterday it was two Brussels sprouts, total.'

'But she's having counselling.'

'She had counselling last time, still ended up in hospital.'

'But –'

'No, Sister, it seems to me that Plan A is not working.'

'Give me time, please, she and I are talking—'

'We can talk to her all we like, it's no use if she's starving to death. She's thinner every time I look at her.'

'But—'

'I'll give you another day or two.'

'Thank you, Sister.'

Agnes spent the rest of the morning discussing the problems of the Paris suburbs with the fourth years, then at lunchtime she drove to the mill.

'I thought I heard you coming up the stairs,' Nina said, looking up from a heap of files.

'I brought you a sandwich.'

'How was your weekend?'

'Completely over the top.' Agnes sank into a chair. 'Terminal illness and world cruises and still-life painting and breaking and entering, and I can't really take it all in.'

'Normal convent life, then.'

'Any chance of a cup of tea?' Agnes took off her coat.

'The kettle's in that little kitchen there. Teabags on the shelf.'

'Any sign of Baines again?' Agnes asked from the kitchen.

'None at all. Quiet morning.'

'Was he looking for something?'

'Don't think so. Not seriously.'

'Which box was it that he went through?'

'This one.' Nina indicated a shabby cardboard box.

Agnes knelt on the floor and began to rummage through it. There were some Victorian shares certificates, a framed Memorandum of Association from 1885, an order addressed to Baines's Wool and Worsted Company, dated 1867. An ancient handwritten deed in the name of Wilhelm Albrecht, dated 1702, and framed in glass.

'He didn't take anything out, then?'

'No.'

Agnes went back to the kettle. 'Don't you have a teapot?'

'Oh, you with your fancy London ways. Teabags are good enough for the likes of us.'

'Have you got access to Reg Naismith's personnel records?' Agnes put two mugs on the desk and got out the sandwiches.

'Sure.'

'Did the police have a look at it?'

'Yeah, they did. You can borrow it if you like. Here. And this one, there's more on the athletics team in this one.' Nina passed her two files. 'Don't tell anyone, though. Oh no, I don't like prawn.'

'You can have mine – chicken OK?'

'Ta.'

There was the sound of footsteps on the stairs.

'Act natural,' Nina said. When Anthony Turnbull walked in, they were intently eating their sandwiches.

'Nina – and Sister Agnes. Again.'

'I'm afraid I didn't get you a sandwich,' Agnes said.

'I'm not hungry.' He smiled, and hung his coat carefully over the back of a chair.

'Would you like some tea? Coffee?' Agnes stood up. She glanced at the desk. The files she had taken were tucked into her bag, out of sight. She put the bag on the floor and folded her coat over it, then went to the little kitchen.

'Coffee please. Is it part of your religious duties to go into the community and make coffee for working people?' Turnbull asked.

'That's the problem,' Agnes said, finding mugs and instant coffee. 'It used to be nursing and teaching, but now that's being done so competently by the secular world, we have to find new markets to corner.' She handed him a mug.

'Did you sugar this?' He held out his mug to her, his eyes meeting her gaze. Agnes took it. 'Two please,' he said. She went back to the kitchen, put two very large spoonfuls of sugar into the mug, was about to add a third, a fourth, even, thought better of it, found a teaspoon, and returned to the room. She placed the mug on the desk next to him. 'It'll need a good stir,' she said.

Turnbull turned the spoon in his coffee, still holding her gaze. Then he turned to Nina. 'Still sorting, then?'

She nodded. 'The new stuff's OK, I just don't know where to put the old stuff.'

'I've yet to go through some of that, just leave it out for me.' He tasted his coffee, glanced at Agnes, took another sip. 'And what were you doing here?'

'Just escaping the routines of convent life,' she said.

'Are you allowed to do that?'

'I'm not supposed to want to.'

He smiled. 'You mean you're supposed to find fulfilment in the simple life, the everyday tasks . . .'

'Yes. Exactly.'

'And do you?'

'I wish I did.'

'Perhaps it comes with time.'

'Perhaps.'

He sipped his coffee. She glanced at her watch, then picked up her coat and bag, and stood up to go.

'Already?' He got up and opened the door for her. In the doorway he said, 'If you ever want to escape again, you could let me buy you lunch.'

'I always want to escape.'

'Wednesday, then?'

'Are you serious?'

'I'm always serious. I'd really like to talk about the religious life.'

'I'm not the person to ask—'

'I'll call for you at your school, twelve thirty OK?'

'But—'

'Please?'

She glanced up at him, then nodded. 'OK. Twelve thirty.'

'I'll walk down to the car with you,' Nina said, getting up, 'I've got to pick up some orders from the buyers.'

In the courtyard, Nina burst into giggles.

'You – having lunch with him!'

'It's research, Nina.'

'Pervy bastard—'

'I don't see—'

'—wanting to talk about "the religious life". Like what you wear under your habit.'

'But—'

'Or in your case, under your jeans. I bet Turnbull's hoping you wear big blue knickers.'

'Perhaps I do.'

'Nah, not you. I bet you wear black. Silk. And lace. That's what I think.'

Agnes laughed. 'But Nina, even if I did, who would it be for?'

'That's just the point. That's why I wear nice stuff. For me. For the feel of it.'

132

'And for Rosie's dad?'

She laughed. 'Maybe.'

'And you think Turnbull prefers big blue knickers?'

'Yep.'

'Perhaps he wears them himself.' Agnes unlocked her car.

Nina burst into more giggles. 'Are you really going to go?'

'Of course I am. It might shed more light on things.'

'That's not the real reason.'

'And it's ages since I was taken out for lunch by a rich man.' She laughed. 'Actually, the ones I'm wearing now are white cotton.'

'You'll have to do better than that on the day.' Nina was still giggling as she crossed the courtyard. Agnes locked her car again. She walked back to the mill, pushed on the old door, which creaked open, and climbed the stairs to Baines's office.

It was dusty and neglected. The desk was bare. There was an empty storage crate on the floor. The grate was still full of ash, and the hearth was stacked with files, scattered with soot. The room seemed weary with loss, with the passage of time. Agnes was filled with pity for William Baines, grasping at old certainties only to find they'd turned to dust. She shut the door and went back to her car.

That evening she sat at her desk in front of the files she'd gathered so far from the mill; the papers from Mark's personnel file, Billy Keenan's file, and the two new files. She flicked through them, then closed them all and went out. She got into the car and drove to the Woolpack pub.

She blinked in the warmth and the smoke, scanning the faces. David was sitting in one corner, hunched over a pint, alone. He looked up as she approached.

'You meant it, then,' he said.

'I always mean what I say. Can I get you another?'

'You certainly can.'

She bought him a pint and sat opposite him with a glass of white wine.

'You heard from my friends, then,' she said.

'Yeah, I'm meeting them in Leeds next weekend. It'd be ace to get a gig in London.'

'I hope it works out.'

'You like my stuff, then?'

'Yes. Some of it I liked a lot.' She took a sip of her drink. 'It surprised me that Turnbull financed that show of yours, though.'

David laughed. 'He knows nothing about art. Nah, it was just to keep an eye on me.'

'Why?'

''Cos he knows I know where Jo is. And he has this thing about her. And also, since Mark . . .'

'What about Mark?'

'He doesn't want me around as a loose cannon, so he's trying to buy me. I can see through him, and he knows that, he doesn't trust me. He's not what he appears.'

'So what is he?'

'He gambles, for a start. He's been doing gaming tables. A mate of mine's a blackjack player, sees him regularly. I don't think even Patricia knows. He's worried I'm going to tell.'

'And Mark?'

'This sports centre, these papers going missing, all that – there's more to that than anyone's saying.'

'And Turnbull thinks you might start digging for information?'

'He's wrong.' He gulped the last of his drink. 'I couldn't give a monkeys, me.'

'But–'

'Why should I?' His voice was suddenly loud. 'It won't bring him back, will it? He was all I bloody had and now he's gone.'

Agnes turned her glass round in her fingers. 'Your mother and father . . .' she began.

'Dead. My mum died of cancer when I was nineteen. My dad died in a car accident a couple of years later. Mark was all I had.' He got up and went to the bar. Agnes watched him leaning heavily, waiting for their drinks.

'It's a kind of club,' he said, coming back, placing her glass of white wine in front of her, two pints for himself. He sat down and took a long draught of his first pint. 'A kind of awful club. You see us regularly on the front pages of the papers, you can tell us by the blank looks of grief, the pleas to help us find the killers of our wives, husbands, parents, brothers. Children.' He drank some more. 'And we're grateful for the attention and the police and the press, and we cry in public and they photograph us – and then they go away. And then there's nothing. Nothing at all.' He flicked a beer mat over and over. 'They're talking of releasing his body for burial soon.'

'But if they found the person who did it –'

'Sure it would help. But don't ask me to look for him. I've been on the edge of bloody madness with this as it is.'

'It must help to have Joanna.'

He shrugged. 'I'm not sure "have" is the word.'

'But you're close?'

'She's got her own troubles at the moment.'

'But you must see her?'

'What's with your interest in Jo?'

'I saw her in the art room the night before she vanished. She was very upset, she'd tipped paint everywhere, she'd arranged a few things into a kind of still life –'

'Skulls and roses –'

'Yes.'

He shook his head and sighed. 'She's such a free spirit, she's stark raving bloody bonkers. That family of hers, her mother dies, so for some reason her father thinks she can inherit the mill with Patricia – Jo, a mill owner, it's like asking Sinead O'Connor to manage Manchester United. She's pure artist, her, and it drives her mad. And she thinks I'm getting too commercial, but at least I'm not lurking up on the moors living on nettle soup.'

'Do you love her?' Agnes asked quietly.

He met her gaze, and his eyes darkened with feeling. 'I love her more than any woman I've ever known,' he said at last.

Agnes hesitated, then said, 'On the moors—'

'She's there sometimes. Although I think she's staying with Marcus some of the time.'

'Where on the moors?'

'We have a hut, a derelict barn. She's adopted it. God knows who it belongs to. Don't tell a soul, will you, I'm only telling you because I trust you.' He started on his second pint. 'We meet there. If I'm lucky. I wait at the barn, then she'll appear, rip off my clothes and we'll have crazy, kinky sex. And then she vanishes again. You don't believe me, do you?'

'Well –'

'It's up to you. I never know when I'm next seeing her. She calls me on my mobile, when she wants me. I'm happy enough with that. Perhaps she loves me too, what do you think, you seem to know about these things?'

'I don't really, I'm a . . .'

'A nun. I know.' He leaned towards her. 'What do you think? Does she love me?'

'Perhaps. I really can't say.' Agnes reached for her coat.

'Don't go.'

'I must. And they'll be chucking you out soon, it's late.'

'I like talking to you.'

'Thank you.' Agnes stood up.

'I'm always here, you can buy me a pint any time.'

'David, it doesn't help.'

'It does. It makes it go away for a while.'

'And then it comes back worse.'

'Well, that's for later to worry about.'

Driving back to the school, Agnes thought of David, alone, wandering back to wherever he lived. Alone. She felt like crying.

She let herself in and poured herself a whisky, then took out the files from the mill and arranged them on her desk with the others. She opened Billy Keenan's. Amongst the routine papers she found a memo relating to an incident in 1992 in which, it said, Keenan had incited a group of lads to provoke another, resulting in a brawl. There was another memo about an event last December, involving Billy and his mother Maureen, and someone called Kitty Hanson. Agnes read the note.

Miss Hanson was clearly upset, but Billy claims he'd only been trying to help. His mother was supportive of Miss Hanson too, and Miss Hanson now appears quite fond of Billy, so at this point we are taking no further action against Billy. As always, he is under supervision, and we will see how his behaviour improves in the new year.

Agnes closed the file. She wondered what the incident was about. A vivid picture of Billy Keenan was coming together in her mind.

She started on the file on the athletics team that Nina had given her that lunchtime. It contained routine correspondence going back some years, concerning the team, its fixtures, its triumphs, occasional lists of members which changed over the years. Throughout it all, the name Reg Naismith, a thin, uncertain signature at the foot of letters, or printed at the head of the roll call. Agnes closed the file. An unremarkable life, to end so violently.

Agnes sipped her whisky, then picked up Reg's personnel file. His address was there, and she made a note of it. There were some memos concerning his certificate of long service, which he was awarded on his retirement last year. He'd joined the company in March 1939, and in October 1942 was called up on war service. He resumed his job at Allbright's in February 1946. There was a medical note concerning a period of absence from April 1947, suffering from 'nervous exhaustion'. Agnes wondered what that meant.

She closed the file, got up from her desk, and lit a candle for her evening worship. As she settled in prayer, she thought about David, drowning his grief in ale. She thought about Reg, his blameless life, his brutal ending unmourned. The candle flickered, and she saw once again the human skull of the still-life painting. She thought of Joanna's roses, etched across the canvas in crimson gashes, seared with the flashing digits of time passing. 'Lord, you sweep us away like a dream, we fade away suddenly like the grass . . .'

Perhaps she and Elias had found a clue after all.

Chapter Eleven

Philomena stared beadily across the dining hall. 'Anyone would think that girl had sealed her lips with Sellotape.'

'Rachel Swann?' Agnes could see her through the breakfast bustle, sitting straightbacked, resolute.

'Those cornflakes are untouched.' Philomena spread marmalade on her last piece of toast. 'Plan B, I think, Sister.'

'But Sister Philomena—'

'She's not eating.'

'Sending her to hospital won't work.'

Philomena arranged her knife on her empty plate. 'And is Plan A working?'

Agnes sighed. 'It's the nature of it, Sister, it's all about willpower and concealment. It needs time.'

'We don't have time. The girl's starving to death.'

'If we send her to hospital we'll just make her hate us.'

'She can hate us and live,' Philomena said, getting up from the table. 'Better than being awfully fond of us but being dead. Don't you think?'

Agnes watched her cross the room, saw her stop by Rachel's chair and rest her hand lightly on her shoulder as she exchanged a few words with her. There was something of steel in that touch, as if to say, I shall not let you die. However much you want to.

As she left the dining room, Agnes was called to the phone.

'It's DC Cole here.'

'Janet, how are you?'

'Did you meet Lianna Vickers?'

'Yes. I went to see her. What's happened?'

'She's been badly beaten up. A neighbour told us, we had to break in. She's in hospital.'

'How bad is it?'

'Couple of broken ribs, massive bruising.'

'Any idea who it was?'

'We've tried to take a statement. All she'll say is that it's *your* fault.'

'Me? But—'

'Could you pop into the station at some point today?'

'Well, lunch time, I suppose.'

'See you then.'

Janet Cole showed Agnes to a seat and sat down opposite her.

'Am I under arrest, then?' Agnes said.

Janet smiled. 'Doesn't take much observation to work out that you couldn't possibly have inflicted those injuries.'

'So what did Lianna say?'

'I asked her who did it. She wouldn't say. She said to ask you.'

'Well, off the top of my head I'd say it's either her pimp or her dealer. And they're probably the same person anyway.'

'So would I.'

'So why's it my fault?'

Janet produced a hand-written statement. 'She said you talked about something with her, and it reminded her of how things might have been.'

Agnes took the paper and read it. 'Did she say what we discussed?'

'She wouldn't.'

Agnes sighed. 'I caused her trouble. She was waiting for someone, her "man", when I was there. She wasn't supposed to let anyone in. And we talked about Mark Snaith.'

'I thought it must be that.'

'He was different, you see, he was nice to her, which made him unlike every other man she's known.'

'It's a dead loss,' Janet said. 'She'll never disclose who beat her up. It's happened before, and it'll happen again.'

'What will you do?'

'Us? We'll visit the estate, ask around, get dead silence from the neighbours, even though they'll all know who he is. He's probably local, from one of the neighbouring estates. And in the end Lianna will get stroppy and ask us to leave her alone.' She closed the file.

'She did say – she thinks there's something odd about the sports centre.'

'Oh, the rumours flying about that. And Mr Turnbull at the heart of most of them.'

'Are you taking them seriously?'

'The council is part-funding the scheme. Their auditors would know if there was a problem.'

'Lianna said Billy Keenan was involved.'

'They all say that. If there's any trouble up Millhouse, it's not long before the Keenan name comes up. Mind you, I had a word with Ed Longley.'

'About the tribunal?'

'Yes. He seemed to think it was water under the bridge. He's had no trouble from anyone. Also, as he said, it doesn't explain Reg. Mind you, he had his own ideas about that.'

'About Reg?'

'Yes, he was in the athletics team with him.'

'He spoke very highly of him to me.'

'Yes, me too. But then I asked if he thought anyone might have anything against Reg. And he said, yes, he could think of several. He said Reg ruled that team with terror, he said, everyone did so well because they were bloody scared of him.'

'Was he violent?'

'Ed said, only rarely. But yes, he was. Sudden rages. Couldn't stick failure. Any boy not pulling his weight and Reg Naismith would see that he knew it all right. Ed said he did OK until he injured his ankle, but Reg couldn't take weakness. He left after that.'

'I suppose there's always a cost to winning.'

Janet flicked the file cover with her fingers. 'Yes. I suppose there is.'

At two o'clock Agnes arrived in Nina's office, panting from climbing the stairs. Nina looked up from her desk. 'Didn't expect to see you – have they allowed you out?'

'I had to see Janet Cole. I was suspected of Grievous Bodily Harm.'

'Doesn't surprise me. D'you want a sandwich? Only cheese and tomato.'

'I'm starving. Thanks.' Agnes pulled up a chair and took the sandwich.

'So, who've you done over?'

'No one directly. Just that by meddling in other people's lives I've made them worse.'

'I'll make you some coffee.'

'If Turnbull finds me here again –'

'He's out of the office today. Otherwise you'd get invited for more than just lunch.'

'Oh, nonsense.'

'Talking of Turnbull,' Nina said, 'I was going to phone you.'

'Why?'

'Hang on.' Nina brought two mugs to the desk, sat close to Agnes and lowered her voice. 'I overheard Turnbull talking on the phone yesterday. Late in the evening, I think he thought I'd gone. He's often doing that, it's because he's still running his other companies, property and stuff. And last night, he was talking to this feller called Mel. Mel is the sidekick in his main property company, a kind of deputy. And I was sure I heard Turnbull say something about selling the mill.'

'What, Allbright's?'

'Shhh. I think so, yes, I'm not quite sure. He was going on about realising assets, and the textile industry going down the tubes. And then he said something about not breathing a word to Patricia, something about having not quite talked her round. I couldn't think what else he could mean. It might be another property, he's always going on about land values and things, but then why mention the yarn industry?'

Agnes sipped her coffee. 'It can't be what Baines intended.'

'It's unthinkable.'

'Baines must have built safeguards into the deal, don't you think, when he handed it over?'

'You'd have thought so. But it is true that these days, a lot of these mills have such a low turnover that their land value is worth more than the company.'

'Perhaps Turnbull was talking about redeveloping the old building, the derelict bit.'

'But he was going on about a working mill.' Nina sipped her coffee. 'Maybe you're right, he's always thinking big. Eh, it would be great, wouldn't it, that mill. You know, I've long had plans for that building. Every time I go past it, I think, arts centre, you know, with a café, and a cinema, and crèche, and – and –'

'An ice rink?'

Nina laughed. 'OK. And classes, aerobics, martial arts, I did karate for years, I could go back to it.'

'And a swimming pool.'

'You're on.'

'Japanese garden.'

'If you insist.'

'Go-Kart track.'

'I thought Scuba-diving tank . . .'

'Absolutely. And a rock-climbing wall . . .' Agnes saw the door was opening. The swish of cashmere camel coat announced the arrival of Patricia.

'Nina, I'm back a bit late, any messages . . . Oh.'

'Hello.' Agnes smiled at her.

Patricia continued to address Nina. 'Did you get on to Warmans about the colour mix-up?'

'Um, yes, they said they'd delivered what we asked for.'

Patricia flung her coat over the back of a chair. 'Our order didn't say black.'

'They said it did.'

'Who filled it out?'

'Alan must have done.'

'He knew we didn't need black.' She looked at her watch. 'Well, you can sort it out now, can't you, Nina? I'm sure your lunch guest was just leaving.' For the first time she looked at Agnes.

Agnes stood up and put on her coat. 'Yes, I was.' She smiled at Patricia and held out her hand. 'How nice to see you again.' Patricia stood, unmoving. 'I believe I'm having lunch with your husband tomorrow,' Agnes went on.

'I believe you are.' Patricia's gaze faltered.

'I'm not sure why.'

Patricia tried her brightest smile. 'Oh, he's always asking women to lunch. Completely indiscriminately. Most of them have the sense to refuse.' She gathered up her coat and swept out of the room.

Silence settled on the room. Agnes could hear the hum from the factory floor. 'Why did you mention it?' Nina said at last.

'It was the only thing to do. I thought I'd brazen it out. And anyway, it's not as if – I mean, I'm hardly likely to –'

'He's her husband. And he's flirting with you. Don't you know anything?'

'Flirting?'

'Of course. The way he looks at you . . .'

'He looks at everyone like that.'

'So?'

Agnes sat down. 'I thought it would help. To talk to him. To find out about Baines, and the family, and Mark Snaith, and this concern he seems to have about Jo, and the sports centre, and this gambling that David mentioned, and whether he's worried about the serial killer, and –'

'And his plans for the mill.'

'Yes.' Agnes looked at Nina. 'Oh dear. Perhaps you're right. Should I cancel lunch, do you think?'

Nina's eyes widened. 'Me? I never said you should cancel. Of course you're going to have lunch with him.'

'I need to talk to you about Joanna,' Agnes said to Elias on Wednesday morning after chapel.

Elias looked grey and weary. He'd conducted the service in a monotone, staring fixedly at the texts, never once raising his eyes. Now he looked at her.

'What about Joanna?'

'David says she's mad.'

'She was never stable at the best of times.'

'He thinks she might be staying with Marcus.'

Elias ran his finger along the edge of the wood panelling. 'That's up to her,' he said.

'But –'

'But what? There's nothing we can do.'

'David said –'

'David fancies himself as a tortured artist, and it suits him to have a crazy lover as part of the pose.'

'That's not fair.'

Elias stared at the floor. 'Maybe not.'

'Philomena's accepted Jo's resignation.'

'That's Jo's choice, then, isn't it?' He was looking beyond her, to the bustle of the corridor as morning lessons started.

'Elias –'

'What?'

144

'Did you think it was a dream? The next day?'

He met her eyes. 'No. It was real. It still is.' He set off along the corridor, not looking back.'

Anthony Turnbull pushed at the swish swing doors and ushered Agnes into the restaurant. 'Very special place, this,' he said. 'Mind you, I reserve it only for people whom I can trust to share my appreciation of it.'

That's not what your wife said, Agnes wanted to say. Instead she allowed him to help her with her coat.

'An aperitif?'

'Thank you, yes.'

Turnbull led her to the bar, which was all cream and chrome and glass, nodding affably at the waiters on the way. 'A Scotch, please,' he said. 'And a –'

'A dry sherry with ice.'

They took their drinks and went to sit down while their table was prepared. Agnes swirled the ice around in her glass. 'Don't they drink it like this in Yorkshire?' she asked.

'Well, I can't say I've ever had to ask for one before. Still, with your exotic background . . .'

'Exotic?'

'You have a hint of an accent.'

'I grew up in France.'

'Ah, that will be it then. I love France.'

Agnes sipped her drink and wondered why people said that, why people felt able to express affection for a whole country. Did they mean its landmass, its total population? Its roads, rivers, building sites, industrial estates, sewage systems, waste disposal . . .?

'What are you thinking?' Turnbull asked her.

'I was thinking about French municipal refuse collection,' Agnes said.

'Ah. Right.' Turnbull scanned her face.

They were shown a table by the window, looking out to a garden filled with rhododendrons, their new leaves warmed by the sun. They ordered whitebait, followed by poussin, and a bottle of Meursault. Agnes noticed as he lifted his glass that his hands were shaking, but he smiled at her and said, 'To the religious life.'

'Why?'

'To our redemption.'

Agnes allowed their glasses to chink, then said, 'I don't think you'll find redemption in a glass of wine.'

'No. Probably not.' Again he seemed troubled.

'And how's the mill?'

'Oh, OK. Hard work.'

'It must be difficult to see any real profit these days.'

He sighed, as if reluctant to embark on this conversation. 'It's very competitive. Foreign competition, we're working in narrow margins.'

'What will you do?'

'Well, keep going, of course.'

Agnes squeezed some lemon juice on to her whitebait. 'I would have thought you could rationalise that operation –' She glanced at him.

'Well, up to a point, of course . . . yes, I mean, there are some measures I'm thinking of taking to make us more competitive.'

'I mean, surely in a community like this, people must be prepared for change. If everyone carried on as they were before, no business would survive at all.'

'No, of course, you're absolutely right. And I am thinking –'

'What?'

Turnbull topped up their glasses. 'The thing is, Agnes – I may call you that, may I?'

'Of course.'

'The thing is, I'm coming to this business as a newcomer. A fresh eye. And these old families, they have great strengths, wonderful sense of history and all that – but it weakens them, the way they hold on to tradition. Baines has let things slide at Allbright's, just for the sake of tradition. Don't get me wrong, I'm a Yorkshireman myself, but our family was small, unimportant – and adaptable. My father worked on the railways, to start with, then went into management. I started out in catering, ended up in property.'

'And now textiles.'

'Yes. You can never tell.'

'How did you and Patricia meet?'

'When I was doing outside catering events. Silver service stuff. She was working for a classic car company over in Harrogate, I catered a few of their receptions, we got to know each other. Some years ago now.'

'And are you happy?'

He looked up. 'Well – um – I'm not sure – it's not a question one generally asks of a marriage, is it? Yes, I suppose we are. I'm not the most – I'm a difficult bloke to live with, Agnes. Patricia is very understanding. My work is my life, property is a knife-edge business these days, but there's a buzz about it, I love it. One minute you're facing bankruptcy, you take a huge risk and it pays off and you're sitting on several million quid.'

'So you're a gambler?'

He laughed. 'I certainly am.'

'I imagine textiles is a bit different.'

'Well, let's say, I'm having to learn a new approach.'

'Which do you prefer?'

'Put it this way, Agnes, if it wasn't for my property companies, the sports project would never have happened. I unlocked that money, I put up the venture capital myself, and I have to say, I'm proud of that, a lot of good will come of it.'

'Whereas the mill?'

'The mill? It'll be OK.' Their plates were cleared away. 'It's just, sometimes, when I walk through the spinning sheds . . .' He turned the stem of his glass between his fingers. 'Sometimes, I feel weighed down by it all. If you build up a business yourself, you can grow with it – but Allbright's, it's huge. It's like a giant –' he smiled at the simile – 'like some ancient giant I've woken out of sleep. And now I have to carry it on my shoulders.' He refilled their glasses. Again, his hand was unsteady.

'And are you?' he asked suddenly.

'Am I what?'

'A gambler?'

'Not as much as I used to be.'

'And do you miss it, like you miss the Paris dustbin lorries?'

Agnes laughed. 'My gambling was too dangerous. I don't miss it, no.'

'All gambling's dangerous,' Turnbull said. For an instant his face lost its affability. Agnes saw the worry behind his eyes, the tension around his mouth.

Their poussin arrived. Turnbull was fiddling with the two knives by his place so that they made a ringing sound against each other.

He looked up and met Agnes's gaze.

'Why did you invite me to lunch?' she heard herself ask.

'Because I liked you – because I felt you were someone –Agnes,' he said, his voice oddly loud, 'what do you think about forgiveness?'

'What do you mean?'

'I mean – if someone's done something really wrong, and it's leading them into – oh God, it's so difficult, I was awake all night imagining this conversation, working it out, and now – I was taught by monks, you see, I – I've never lost my faith, even though I've been lazy, not gone to church for years, but deep down . . . and now I find that I'm living in ways that aren't – that I can't . . .' He passes his hand across his eyes, which Agnes saw were reddened with tears.

'Anthony . . .' she said, softly.

He raised his eyes to her, shook his head.

'We're never lost,' she said.

He shook his head again, reached for his glass with trembling hands.

'What is it?' she tried.

She saw his expression harden, locking away his feelings.

'Do you really think you're beyond redemption?' She felt she was reaching across a chasm.

'I should never have mentioned it, I'm sorry.' He drained his glass, then refilled it.

'The church won't turn you away,' she said.

He gestured to the waiter for more wine, then turned back to her. 'I won't set foot in a church again.'

'But –'

'Please, no more. I thought you'd be able to – last night it all made sense. But now – I'm sorry . . .'

There was a chirping of a mobile phone. He snatched it from his pocket.

'Turnbull,' he said. His hands were shaking. 'What? Right. Yes. No, I don't care any more. Just do it. Do it, for God's sake, what else can we – right. OK.' He rang off. He was ashen, and his breath came in short gasps.

'Anthony –' Agnes's hand went towards him.

'No,' he almost shouted, clumsily putting out his hand to stop her, knocking his glass which fell against his plate, smashing glass and wine everywhere. He stared at it, his hands against his face, motionless. The waiter appeared, and Agnes asked for the bill. Turnbull put his signature to the chit, then sat, staring unseeing at the mess. Agnes helped him up, got their coats, led him to his car.

At the car door he appeared to notice her. 'I must go,' he said. 'Forgive me. Forgive . . .' he smiled at the word, then got into his car and drove away.

As Agnes's taxi drove up to the school, she passed another car leaving, slowly enough for her to see Rachel Swann sitting in the back, her eyes staring straight ahead.

'You said you'd give me time,' Agnes cried, bursting into Sister Philomena's office.

'Where were you?' Philomena looked up from her desk. 'Teresa and I searched everywhere.'

'We've failed her,' Agnes said.

'She'll live,' Philomena said.

'We've failed her.' Agnes left, slamming Philomena's door behind her.

'Agnes –' Teresa met her in the staff-room doorway. 'Rachel said we must find you, she was so upset, she said you'd promised to fight for her, we couldn't find you, I'm sorry . . . they'd got a bed for her. The medical team are so worried about her, it's just like last year . . .'

'It's not your fault,' Agnes tried to say, but the words were a whisper. 'I should have been here.' She turned away and hurried to her room to hide the tears that welled in her eyes.

She locked her door, picked up her phone and dialled Julius's number.

'I'm sorry,' she began to sob as he answered the phone.

'Agnes – what is it?'

'Everything.' Agnes couldn't speak for tears.

'My dear –'

'I'm sorry . . .'

'Don't be sorry.' Julius waited for the sobbing to abate.

'There's this girl here,' Agnes said at last, 'and I've let her down really badly, I said I'd fight for her and then when it came to it I wasn't there, and it's just like James, only the opposite, he really was there, he really did fight for me and now he's not going to be there anymore, and all these years I've lived without him and now just when I think it would be nice to – to have family – to have someone who – cares – not that you don't, I don't mean that, Julius – oh God, you're not in a meeting or anything, are you?'

'Well, apart from a room full of visiting Vatican dignitaries – no, I'm not in a meeting, and even if I was I'd send them away. Go on.'

Agnes took a deep breath. 'Oh Julius, it's all a mess. I want to go away, and James has asked me to travel with him, and I'd see my mother which is a good thing, and he's dying of cancer, so I could look after him, which is another good thing, but then this business with Rachel has made me think I can't just run away, everyone has responsibilities and mine are to my order . . . Aren't they?'

'You phoned me so that I'd tell you that there's no escape?'

'I phoned you because none of it makes sense. And there's the man in charge of the mill and something really bad is happening . . .'

'I wish you weren't two hundred miles away.'

'I wish I was.'

Julius laughed. 'When do you have to decide?'

'Not yet. I know what you're going to say.'

'Listen to the stillness. There'll be an answer in time. And phone me again soon.'

'I will.'

Agnes went to her bookshelves and took down a copy of Pascal's *Pensées*. She spent the rest of the day reading it. At eight she made herself some toast. At ten she crept out to the chapel and sat there for some time, listening, taking comfort from hearing only silence.

She returned to her room, and went to bed. She'd just turned out the light when the phone rang.

'Hello?'

There was silence on the other end, then a rough, uneven breathing.

'Hello?' Agnes tried again.

The breathing sounded more like sobbing. Then Agnes heard a voice.

'Agnes?'

'Who is it?'

'Nina.'

'Nina? What –'

The voice was barely recognisable. 'Help me.'

'Oh my God, where are you, what's—?'

'Agnes – someone just tried to kill me.'

Chapter Twelve

The headlamps of the oncoming cars splashed against the windscreen wipers. Agnes reached the ring road and put her foot down hard, cursing the convent's Metro. The speedometer wavered around fifty. Just get home, she'd said to Nina. Get home, lock the doors, wait for me there. She glanced at the scrap of paper on the seat beside her on which she'd scrawled Nina's address: 21 Kensal Terrace.

She turned off the ring road, into town, past the pub where they'd often met, recognising the corner where Nina had indicated her street. Kensal Terrace. She screeched to a halt, jumped out of the car, ran to Number 21. It was in darkness. She knocked gently at the door. There was no answer. She opened the letter box, and spoke quietly. 'Nina?'

She heard footsteps, a voice whispered, 'Who is it?'

'It's Agnes.'

The door opened a crack to allow her in. Nina was standing in the darkness, dishevelled, her eyes dark-ringed. She ran to slam the door and locked it behind Agnes.

'Where's Rosie?'

'She's staying overnight at Mum's, I was working late.'

Agnes took Nina's arm and led her into the kitchen. She switched on all the lights, found the kettle, set it to boil. She searched the cupboards for whisky, found none.

'Arnica,' Nina whispered. She was sitting at the table, shivering.

'This?' Agnes found a little bottle of homeopathic tablets, took one out carefully and gave it to Nina. Then she took off her coat and wrapped it around Nina, and led her to the armchair by the gas fire.

'Are you sure you're not injured?' Agnes put a match to the gas.

'I'm OK.'

'What happened?'

Nina shuddered. 'I was working late. There's an urgent order, it had to be processed before tomorrow to be sent off in the morning. I was over in the spinning sheds, then I came back to the office. It was dark, I switched on the lights, then someone grabbed me. They had a hand over my mouth, so I bit it hard, it was in a glove, it tasted of . . . kind of . . . like old dishcloths, ugh . . .' She put both hands over her face. Agnes saw she was shaking.

'It's all right,' Agnes murmured. She put her arm round Nina's shoulders.

Nina leaned against her. 'He took his hand away, he shouted something.'

'Was there just one?'

'If there'd been two of them, I'd be dead by now.'

Agnes met her gaze. 'Go on.'

'Then – I tried to get away, but he'd got both hands behind my back. And this thing went over my eyes, and it had – oh God.'

'What?'

'Knots. Like, two knots, one for each eye. And it was pushing on my eyes . . .' She broke off and began to cry.

'I'm calling the police,' Agnes said.

'In a minute. He got away, it won't make any difference now.'

'Then what?'

'I don't know how I did it, Agnes. My karate, you know, I had no idea I was so good . . . I kind of roared, right, not screamed, a really weird noise, and all the time I was thinking no one could hear, but I kept going and I could smell old dishcloths and I kicked out behind me, at kind of groin level, and I must have hit him, and he fell back, and I pulled the thing off my eyes, and he was shouting some kind of abuse and I turned round—'

'Did you see him?'

'No. He ran.'

'He ran off?'

'He had some kind of mask, like a balaclava, and as soon as I turned round he put his hand over his face and ran out of the door. So I followed, really hollering, but like I said, that office is isolated, no one heard, and he was really fast. I saw him climb over the back fence, up towards the rest of the industrial estate. Then I . . .' To Agnes's surprise, Nina started giggling. 'Then I fell over.'

'You fell over?'

'My legs gave way. I sat there, kind of stunned. When I could get up I couldn't think straight. I phoned you. You told me to come here. I did. I just got in my car and came home.' Nina was still laughing.

'I had no idea you were in the mill. You could have stayed there, there are people there all the time, you could have got help, phoned the police . . .'

'I wasn't thinking straight. I just wanted to get out. I kept thinking of Rosie, I kept thinking she was in danger . . .' Just as suddenly, Nina started to cry. They sat for a while. Then she said, 'It's weird, you know. I just knew I couldn't go and look for help.'

'Why?'

'I know what it was. I couldn't go to the spinning sheds, because –'

'Because what?'

Nina smoothed her hair with her fingers. 'Whoever did it knew where I was. Knew where to find me. So, whoever it was knows something about Allbright's. That's why I wanted to get out. I had to get away.' She shuddered again.

Agnes went over to the kettle and made a pot of tea. Then she went to the phone. 'Can I call the police now?'

Nina nodded. 'Yes. I'm ready.'

Janet Cole was the first to arrive, and sat sipping sweet tea with Nina, taking notes. Then another car, screeching and flashing, spilling out two more police officers, and then Nina and Agnes were driven to Allbright's. As they processed up the stairs to Nina's office, she began to shake, and Agnes put her arm round her.

'So it was here?' Janet asked.

Nina nodded. In the background the younger of the two policemen picked up the phone.

'And he was waiting –'

'Over there.' Nina's voice shook.

'Mr Turnbull, please,' the young man was saying into the phone. 'West Yorkshire Police, that's right. I'm sorry to disturb you, Madam – yes, the mill, that's right . . .'

'And then the events happened as you described?'

'Yes . . .' Nina was looking tearful again.

'No, Madam, nothing like that . . . An assault on one of your employees, Nina Warburton. Earlier this evening –' He broke off, looked at his watch – 'Last night, now, it being nearly three – if you can, Madam, and your husband, that would be very helpful. Would you like us to send a car?'

'And he ran out of this door?'

'It's the only one.'

'And down the stairs . . .'

Nina followed Janet to the landing. Agnes could hear Nina describing the path her attacker had taken across the courtyard. They reappeared. Nina sat heavily into a chair, leaden with exhaustion.

'The Turnbulls are on their way,' the young policeman announced.

'Where's Jeff?' someone said.

'He went to talk to the factory people.'

'Does this place run twenty-four hours a day?'

Nina nodded.

'And did the people over there see anything?'

Nina glanced at Agnes. 'They wouldn't, you see,' she said. 'The windows are high up, the machines are noisy. Anything could happen in the offices, they wouldn't know.'

Outside Agnes could hear another police car arriving, hurried footsteps on the stairs, and soon the room filled with people. Two men in suits were asking Janet questions. Someone was taking photographs. Nina was introduced to a police surgeon, a pink-cheeked woman, who sat her down and examined her face, round her eyes, the sides of her head. Into all this walked Anthony and Patricia Turnbull.

Janet stood up. 'Mr Turnbull, I'm sorry – and Mrs Turnbull . . .'

Agnes noticed that Patricia was immaculately dressed, her make-up flawless.

'Poor Nina,' Patricia was saying, looking across at her. She was sitting motionless, her eyes glazed over. 'What happened?' Patricia approached her, leaned over her.

'She's had enough, I think,' Agnes said. 'She's already had to go through it several times.'

Turnbull flopped into the chair next to Nina. Agnes noticed the same pale face, the same shaking hands, that she'd seen at lunch. 'Such a terrible thing,' he murmured. 'And in our mill . . .' He turned to Patricia. 'Thank God,' he said. 'Thank God she

156

got away.' His eyes filled with tears.

Janet appeared and pulled up a chair. 'It was just after eleven, Mr Turnbull, last night . . .'

Agnes took Nina by the arm and led her from the room. They sat on the stairs in the chilly darkness. Nina still had Agnes's coat around her. The noise from the room ebbed and flowed, voices rising and falling in interrogation, explanation. After a while Nina turned to Agnes.

'I want my mum,' she said.

It was after four when Agnes pulled up outside Nina's mother's house.

'Terrible time to wake someone,' she said to Nina.

Nina got out and knocked softly on the door, then produced a key and opened the door. Agnes followed her inside.

'Mum?' Nina was calling softly.

They heard a door opening upstairs. 'Nina? Is that you? What sort of time – what's up, love?' A tousled woman appeared at the top of the stairs, patting at her soft white hair.

'Mum, it's me. Something happened at the mill last night, someone broke in –' Nina turned to Agnes, then started up the stairs. 'We've been at the mill, I didn't want to go home. How's Rosie?'

'Fast asleep, I should hope. Is there someone with you?'

'Yes, she brought me back, a friend. She's just going. I'll sleep on the settee, Mum.'

'I'll find some blankets.'

Nina came back downstairs. 'She can't see very well,' she whispered to Agnes. 'Her sight's going. I'll introduce you another time.'

'Will you be OK?'

Nina nodded.

'Will you sleep?'

She shrugged. 'There's not much night left, is there.'

'But when you close your eyes –'

'Don't want to think about it. I'll get up early and go back to the mill, pick up my car.'

'Don't go back until you're ready. Turnbull'll understand.'

Nina smiled. 'He seemed worse than me.'

Agnes touched Nina's arm. 'Call me. Tomorrow, I mean, later today. I need to know you're OK.'

157

Nina nodded. 'Sure.' She gave Agnes a quick hug, then laughed. 'Do you think I'll need a police guard now?'

Agnes drove through the deserted streets, out of the town, turning off the ring road to take the route over the moors. In the east the night sky was edged with grey. A drifting mist softened the spikes of gorse and dead bracken. She drove slowly, thoughts eddying in her mind. Mark; and then Reg; and now Nina. The eyes, the knots against the eyes, the smell of old dishcloths . . . But Mark and Reg were stabbed. Whereas Nina – there'd been no sign of a knife with Nina's attack. And who would want her dead? Perhaps her attacker meant her to survive, chose not to use the knife. But why? And if it was a random event . . . Agnes braked against the swift shadow of an animal on the road. Nina was in her office, at dead of night. It was nothing to do with chance. Someone must have sought her out, with the intention of – of killing her, mutilating her eyes, strangling her . . .

And they had failed. It was incompetence that had saved Nina's life, a fear of being recognised. The brutality of the other two murders, on the other hand . . . they must have been carried out with absolute conviction. It didn't make sense. And there was Turnbull, weak with shock, his wife cool and composed by his side. She thought about how he'd been at lunch, steering the conversation to talk about – about forgiveness. Redemption. And Patricia – perhaps she went to bed in full make-up just in case; perhaps she'd been delighted to be summoned by the police at dead of night, because for once all that trouble had been worth while. Agnes thought of Joanna, the scatty younger sister, choosing instability as a role, to mark her out from her utterly poised older sister. And Marcus, the middle child . . .

The mist thickened as the road climbed higher. Agnes's thoughts drifted, muddled, obscure. David Snaith, his open smile, his raging grief. Marcus . . . Elias . . . Nina . . . knots across her eyes . . . Greer, the old dog . . . Elias. She thought about telling Elias what had happened in the mill. She imagined him, in his present mood, sloughing it off. 'And what is it to me?' he'd say, reasoning that it was just one of those things, entirely unconnected with Joanna's disappearance. Just further proof that all life is suffering. Or, she realised, he could just as easily seize upon it with sudden passion, insist that they tell Baines, run back to Baines's house and his

158

beloved dogs just to announce to Baines that it was all his fault, that since he gave up the mill everything was going awry, like the skull and the clock in his hidden paintings, the ticking away of time towards inevitable death . . .

Agnes stopped the car. She turned off the engine and wound down her window. She listened to the quiet, the whisper of the breeze. The mist was clearing. Agnes watched the sky fading into dawn. She recalled Joanna in the art room. 'First him, now me,' she'd said.

Agnes breathed in the freshness of the new day. Out there, she thought, someone intends harm. She shivered. She wound up her window, and realised that she must find Joanna. Before it was too late.

'You look terrible,' Teresa said at breakfast.

'Thanks,' Agnes said.

'You're drinking tea.'

'Uh-huh,' Agnes said.

'What's up?'

Agnes shook her head and stirred some sugar into her cup.

'You look like you've been up all night.'

'Maybe I have,' Agnes said.

'Why? It's not even exam time yet.'

'Exams?' Agnes looked up from her cup. 'Exams? Listen, I need my sleep. Sleep is important to me. If I miss my sleep, it's going to be for a good reason. Spiritual crisis at least. Or declaration of war. Or finding I've conceived a child by an angel. Exams . . .' She shook her head and returned to stirring her tea.

Teresa looked at her with an expression of pity. 'You haven't done an exam term yet, have you?' She patted her hand, got up and left the dining hall.

'*Quand je suis plus agée, je veux être un médecin.*'

'No, Helen, remember the French takes the future tense with quand, and no article at all with *médecin* . . .' Agnes yawned, heard the girl repeat the corrected sentence, glared out of the window. The sun was breaking through the clouds, throwing a slash of light across the purple of the moors. Mark Snaith, Agnes thought, wondering why his name had suddenly crashed into her mind.

159

Because he died up there. That's what it was. Reg was sought out at home, and Nina was tracked down at her work, and Mark – Mark was out on the moors in the middle of nowhere.

'*Je voudrais être professeur.*'

'Very good, Amy.' Which meant that Mark was lured to his death. Someone must have set a trap.

'*Moi, je veux bien être kangourou.*'

'Excellent, Alice.'

But the police had found no trace of anyone else. Only the binoculars, the mark of a solitary bird-watcher. And the fact that someone had noticed a man behaving suspiciously around the nest. And that Billy Keenan dropped him off in the car, everyone said . . . Agnes was aware that the class were all giggling.

'What is it?'

'Sister . . .' Clemmie stifled more giggles. 'Sister, Alice just told you she wants to be a kangaroo.'

After lunch Agnes found Charlotte sitting in a corner of the sixth-form common room. 'I know we've been through all this before,' she said, sitting down next to her, 'but who else would have known that Mark was up on the moors that day?'

Charlotte looked up from her book. She shook her head. 'I think about it all the time. He always went alone to the nest. He didn't want anyone else to know about it.'

'He can't have arranged to meet someone—'

'Unless it was this serial killer person.'

'But Charlotte, I've been thinking about it. Reg answered his door to someone. It was deliberate. And Mark must have been the same.'

'I've thought and thought. I've tried to remember if he had a meeting or anything, if he was worried about someone, or owed someone money.'

'Someone told him his birds were in danger.'

'Yes. Probably one of his bird-watching friends, they were always talking to each other.'

'And this suspicious man on the moors—'

'The police are still looking.'

'Then there was the community centre project—'

'I've been thinking about that, too.'

'Lianna said there was a problem about the money.'

'That's just stupid rumours, if she'd got involved she'd have known it was all straight up.'

'She said no one trusted Turnbull.'

Charlotte fiddled with one of her rings. 'That's just crap, everyone likes Turnbull. And he got us the money.'

'Billy Keenan gave him a lift.'

'Yeah, Billy bloody Keenan. Unless they find he killed Mark, which no one can prove, they can shut up about him. They just want a scapegoat, those estate people, the whole place is full of people doing nothing to help themselves but ready to criticise anything that might wake them up out of the – the mess of their lives.'

'I thought we might talk to her.'

'Us? Lianna?'

'She's in hospital. She got beaten up.'

'Well well. We can take her some grapes.'

It was after four by the time Agnes escaped, yawning, to her own room. She made a pot of Earl Grey tea, and sat at her desk. She picked up the phone and dialled a number.

'DC Janet Cole, please, it's Sister Agnes.' She waited.

Janet came on the line. 'Hi, I was going to phone you.'

'Did you get any sleep?'

'Not much.'

'How's it going?'

Janet sighed. 'We've tried to get witnesses. No one saw anything. The fingerprints tell us nothing, he was wearing gloves. Hard gloves, like footballers wear. It doesn't really make sense.'

'Do you think it's like the others?'

'No. Apart from the eyes.'

'The thing is, Janet, if it was a killing like the others—'

'She wouldn't have been around to tell us, you mean?'

'It does seem to be different.'

'We've been asking her about her life, a bit, you know, whether anyone might have it in for her. Have you spoken to her?'

'Not today.'

'Please try,' Janet said. 'Some time soon it's going to occur to her that she's survived a murder attempt. The fallout from that can be quite serious.'

* * *

161

Agnes finished her tea, just as the phone rang again.

'Agnes, it's Nina.'

'I was about to phone you. How are you?'

'Fine now.' Her voice sounded flat. 'I went into work but they sent me home to rest. Rest? Hang on. No, Rosie, I said no biscuit. Where was I?'

'You went into work.'

'Oh yes, anyway – hang on, OK, in a minute, no, leave the chair alone, Rosie, wait, oh for Heaven's sake, hang on a minute . . .'

The phone was put down, then Nina returned. 'Where was I?'

'The mill.'

'It's mad there. Turnbull's putting in alarms and security cameras and things. D'you know, I think it's not for my benefit at all. I think he thinks he's next.'

'But Nina – why would he think that?'

'It's just the way he's behaving, kind of obsessed.'

'Surely they came for you.'

'That's what the police think. I was cross-examined today about my private life. Rosie's dad, mainly. I almost laughed, the idea that Jay would come creeping around my work at dead of night. I suppose they'd go on about him just as much if he was a white guy, what d'you think?' Her voice smouldered with restraint.

'I suppose if someone's trying to kill you –' Agnes said.

'There you are then. Obviously nothing to do with colour.'

'And Turnbull thinks he's next?'

'He's panic stricken.'

'Perhaps whoever came for you was looking for him.'

'Listen, whoever went for me the other night couldn't have mistaken me for Turnbull unless they had all the gumption of a short-sighted ant.'

'And they knew you were there.'

Nina's voice suddenly changed. 'I just keep thinking, what if they'd succeeded? What would have happened to Rosie?'

'But they didn't succeed.'

'But when they come back –' Agnes heard a catch in her voice.

'They won't come back.'

'How do you know?'

'Where are you staying?'

'With my mum, I'm afraid to go home. For some reason.' Nina

sniffed. 'All I want, Agnes, is to feel normal again. Oh God, she's got the whole biscuit tin and she's taking a bite out of each. Rosie – listen, Agnes, I must go, I'll phone you soon, 'bye.'

Agnes lay down on her bed and closed her eyes. She realised she must have fallen asleep, because when she opened them again her clock said 20:32. She remembered she'd been dreaming of Joanna. She also realised she'd missed supper. Philomena would no doubt have noticed.

She had a shower, changed into fresh jeans and a jumper, and grabbed her coat. She crept down the back stairs of the school to the front door, got into the convent car, and drove to the Woolpack.

He was sitting hunched over a pint.

'Fancy a drink?' she said.

David Snaith looked up. 'Sister Agnes. As I live and breathe. An angel, bestowing good will to all men. Or in this case, just to me. Yes please.'

She returned to the table with his pint, and sat opposite him with a Scotch.

'So,' he said, 'how's things?'

'OK.'

'OK? That's not good enough. You're got belief, you've got a hotline to the Almighty, you're supposed to be able to hear cherubic singing and angelic harps.'

Agnes laughed. 'It's not that easy, I'm afraid.'

'You see? When it comes to it, you just cop out, don't you. All right, then, how are things at the coalface of existential doubt?'

'I think that's more a question for Elias.'

'I've tried asking him, God knows, but he just sighs and looks glum. Although, come to think of it,' he added, raising his glass, 'if you asked Elias whether he wanted one of these, you'd get the same response. Cheers.'

'Cheers,' Agnes said. She sipped her Scotch. 'How long have you known Elias?'

'Since I started seeing Jo, really. She said they worked together.'

'I think they go back longer than that.'

'You're telling me. Little glances, in-jokes. He has the key to her house for Chrissake. Luckily he's such a testy old bugger that she couldn't possibly fancy him. Otherwise I'd be jealous.'

'He's a priest, you know.'

David laughed. 'So that's all right then.'

'David – I wanted to ask you – the thing is, someone attacked Nina last night.'

'*Nina?*'

'At the mill. Late last night.'

'Is she OK? Was it – oh my God –'

'No, she's fine. And it wasn't stabbing. Although he did try – he had this knotted rope which he put across her eyes.'

The light faded from David's face. 'No . . .'

'She freed herself, he got away.'

'Bloody hell. Agnes, I can't bear it. It's bad enough, my brother, but knowing whoever did it . . . and now this . . .'

'David, I think Joanna knows.'

'Knows what?'

'I think she's more embroiled in all this than she's letting on.'

David slowly put down his glass. 'Great. On what evidence do you think this?'

'None at all. Just something she said in the art room that night.'

'Oh, right, you mean she just happens to know a crazy axe murderer who hacked to death her own lover's brother. Of course. Stupid of me not to work that out.'

'David, don't be angry, I don't mean that at all. Listen, Elias and I, we broke into Baines's house the other night.'

He looked up. A faint smile crossed his face. 'You – and him –' he laughed. 'And did the dogs eat you? I wish I'd been there. Or did Elias float above them and get in down the chimney?'

'Something like that. The point is . . . Joanna's still working there, isn't she?'

David bowed his head. He circled his glass on the beer mat. At last he looked up, his eyes dark. 'Is she?' he said.

'But – I thought – I mean – you said . . .'

'What did I say?'

'About – about when you see her . . .'

'The sex you mean?' He laughed, emptily. 'Ah, yes, the sex.'

'But aren't you, I mean, don't you—?'

'Of course we are. Of course we do. All the bloody time.'

Agnes felt suddenly exhausted. 'David – I need to know. Everything that's happened centres on that mill and that family. All this started when Joanna destroyed the art room and ran away. She knows, David, she must. She must know something at least . . . I just keep thinking, she and Turnbull seem to be connected

164

in some way.' She looked across at him, at the pain etched across his face. She picked up her coat and made to get up. 'I'm sorry, I'll go—'

'No –' He reached out and grabbed her hand. 'Don't go.' He let go of her hand as she sat back in her seat. 'Tell me, were the brushes wet?'

'Yes, they were.'

He nodded. 'And was it roses, dead ones?'

'Yes.'

He sighed. His hand went to the back of his neck. 'When I met her,' he said, 'we were like – it was like finding your other half. I know it sounds like one of those stupid things people say. But our work, our ideas . . . it was brilliant. I loved her. I *love* her. And she was so crazy, so full of life, drinking me under the table, so passionate . . . And she needed me too, she needed me to earth her. She still bloody needs me.' He blinked, took a gulp of his drink. 'And her work got better, mine got better, we were great. And now . . .' he rubbed the back of his neck. 'Now – she's shut me out, you see. Ever since this still-life stuff, which your saintly Elias seems to know so much about, I'm excluded from her work.'

'Do you see her much?'

'She comes to me.'

'The hut on the moor?'

'Yes. You thought I'd made that up?' He smiled faintly. 'But we don't talk.'

'David, she must be frightened of something. Or hiding something. Or someone.'

He drained his glass. At last he said, 'Yes.'

'I need to speak to her.'

'Don't we all.'

'David—'

'Why should I help you? I want to protect her.'

'Tell her – there's a rumour that Turnbull might sell the mill.'

David set his glass down. 'Turnbull? But – he can't. Surely. That's what she was most afraid of.'

'Joanna?'

'Yes. She told her father to make sure that the deal made it impossible to sell the mill.'

'It's only a rumour.'

'Still . . . Typical of that bastard.'

'David – if you know where she is . . .'

'But I don't, not any more. Apart from . . . And anyway, what I want more than anything is that she should be safe. Her family is bad for her. Her father's opted out ever since their mother died, her brother hides away with his new family, they've got a baby now. He doesn't see any of them any more apart from Jo. That mill is like some huge satanic force that drags them all down . . . I want her to be safe, Agnes.' Tears welled in his eyes.

'I need to talk to her. Nina's still in danger.'

'Don't ask me. I'm just the toy boy, the bit of stuff, I'm just used for my body.' He laughed, harshly. 'It's every man's dream, of course, and she's crazier than ever, needs it more than ever – does the most extraordinary things . . .'

'Does she love you?'

His eyes met hers. 'She says so. When she's crying out – when she's – when we're . . .' He closed his eyes, opened them again. 'Then she says she loves me.'

'Well then, she must mean it.'

David looked across at her. 'Are you sure you're a nun?'

'Being a nun doesn't stop you being human.'

He smiled. 'Another drink?'

'No thanks. I ought to go. I didn't sleep last night.'

'Listen, Agnes, I'll help you to meet her. It'll have to be the hut, I don't see her anywhere else now. Leave it with me, I'll phone you.'

'Thanks.'

As she stood up, he took her hand. 'Listen – don't tell Elias. About the hut.'

'Elias?' She smiled. 'Ever since we floated down the chimney *chez* Baines, he's been avoiding me.'

Chapter Thirteen

'Might have known you'd pop by. Still, makes a change from t'coppers.' Lianna was propped up on pillows, wearing fluffy pyjamas covered in pink ponies.

Agnes arranged some grapes in a bowl. 'You look very well.' She wore no make up and her skin looked clear, apart from a bluish mark over one eye.

Lianna laughed, and rolled up one sleeve. Her arm was swollen, purple and yellow with bruising, marked with weals, still scarlet and raw. 'And me ribs – it's all plaster under here,' she said, tapping her chest. 'He never gets the bits what show. Go on, then,' she said, turning to Charlotte, 'gawp away then. Summat to tell your friends when you get back.' Charlotte lowered her eyes and sat on a chair at the end of the bed. Lianna grinned and turned back to Agnes. 'S'pose they've sent you to get more out of me.'

Agnes laughed and sat on the edge of the bed. 'They know there'd be no point. It's not as if you'd tell me.'

'Not with her here.'

'I'm going to find a cup of tea,' Charlotte said, and disappeared along the ward.

'Don't be too hard on her,' Agnes said when she'd gone. 'She's very jealous of you.'

'You what?'

'Of course she is. You knew Mark. Charlotte saw you together. She's no fool. She knew that there was something special between you.'

Lianna shifted her position, wincing. 'Jealous?' She reached out her hand for a glass of water and Agnes passed it to her. 'Yeah, well. I s'pose we were special.'

'Charlotte loved him. She's only young. It's bound to hurt to know that he was never hers.'

Lianna handed the glass back to Agnes. 'Why's she come here then?'

Agnes took off her coat and arranged it over a chair. 'Mark was killed on Morton's Crag.'

'Yeah. So?'

'Who else would know he was there?'

Charlotte reappeared with three polystyrene cups and distributed them, then sat on her chair again. Lianna smiled at her, tried to take off the lid with her one good arm, failed. Agnes opened the cup for her.

'Yeah, well,' Lianna said at last, 'Billy Keenan drove him up there, didn't he.'

'Why?'

'Dunno. Said he was going that way, I suppose.'

'But they weren't close.'

'No.'

'Would Anthony Turnbull know?'

Agnes noticed Lianna wince.

'Turnbull? Why should he know?'

'Because the only thing that brought Billy and Mark together was his sports centre.'

Lianna shifted on her pillows. 'You'd better ask him then.' She sipped her tea.

Charlotte put down her cup. 'I'm sorry –' she began. She gestured vaguely towards Lianna's injuries.

Lianna shrugged.

'And –' Charlotte hesitated. 'Mark . . .' her eyes filled with tears. Lianna looked up at her, and for a moment the two young women were caught in each other's gaze.

'It's knowing there's someone out there . . .' Lianna said. Charlotte nodded. Lianna smiled at her. 'He were a man in a million,' she said.

'Rachel's been discharged,' Teresa whispered to Agnes at tea in the staff room that afternoon.

'Is she at home?'

'Home? No, she's here.'

'*Here*?'

'Don't shout. There's no one at her London house, they're all abroad.'

168

'But she's –'

'They said she wasn't ill enough.'

'What the hell does that mean?'

'I think it may mean that between you and Rachel, you've won this round.'

'Colonel?' Philomena's voice echoed across the staff room. 'Or Lieutenant?'

'Yes, Sister?' Agnes sighed.

'Swann chappie.'

'Neither, Sister. Rachel's father's in the Foreign Office.'

'Ah, thought so. Need to get on to them.'

'Yes, Sister.'

'Right away. I've been looking for you,' Philomena added, peering down at Agnes. 'Seems to have become my main occupation.' She swept away again.

'Colin's right,' Teresa whispered. 'Perhaps it's roller skates.'

That evening Agnes went to Rachel's room and knocked on the door.

'Who is it?'

'It's Agnes. Can I come in?'

There was no answer. Agnes pushed the door open.

Rachel was lying on her bed, staring vacantly at the ceiling. She looked pale, but the dark circles around her eyes had gone, and there was a spot of colour on both cheeks.

'How are you?' Agnes sat on the end of the bed.

Rachel shrugged.

'I brought you some fruit.' Rachel glanced at the bowl as Agnes placed it on her desk.

'How was the hospital?'

Rachel turned her face away.

'I'm glad they let you out.'

'You weren't there.'

'I'm sorry –' Agnes began.

'Sorry? You're *sorry*?' The girl turned to face her. 'When you promised? When you said you'd be on my side?'

'It would have made no difference. They were adamant –'

'It would've made a difference to me.' Rachel turned away again.

'I'm here now,' Agnes said.

'So?'

'What do you want to do now?'

Rachel didn't answer.

'You can go home. You can stay here.'

'It's not up to me, is it?'

'It's not up to anyone else, Rachel.'

'I never wanted to go to hospital, but that was decided for me. I never wanted to eat but they made me –' Rachel's voice choked.

'I'm sorry.' Agnes leaned towards her, but Rachel shrank away. 'Perhaps you should go home,' Agnes said.

'What's home?'

'I mean, go and stay with your parents for a while.'

'Why?'

'To get strong. To think about what you want to do with your life.' Rachel shrugged. Agnes reached for an apple and took a bite of it. 'Or maybe,' she said, 'you don't want a life. Maybe you want to die instead.'

'Maybe I do.'

'Well, let's talk about that, then. I mean, if you're going to choose to die, we've got to make plans, haven't we. We must work out where you're going to do it, somewhere where they'll let you starve yourself to death in peace.' Agnes took another bite of apple.

Rachel glanced at her.

'Obviously not here,' Agnes went on, 'too full of busybodies who want you to stay alive. Somewhere where no one gives a damn. Any ideas?'

Rachel was staring at her.

'And the funeral,' Agnes went on, 'let's get that all planned. If you're going to kill yourself deliberately, which you seem intent on doing, at least tidy up all the loose ends. Make a will, perhaps.'

'There's no need to laugh at me.' Rachel's voice was barely audible.

'Laugh? I'm not laughing. On the contrary, I'm serious. As serious as you are. If you're determined to kill yourself, who am I to stop you?'

'I wish everyone would stop going on about me killing myself.'

'So you don't want to die?'

'Course not.'

'Why aren't you eating, then?'

'I am eating. I ate in hospital.'

'And now? What have you eaten today?'

'Enough.'

'One digestive biscuit? Two?'

'You're as bad as they are.'

'Because I want you to live? To be well?'

'That's what they all say. They only care about food, not about me.'

Agnes stood up. 'Listen, Rachel. You're the only one who can do this. Firstly, if you want to go home, I'll arrange it.'

'I don't have a home.'

'Secondly, I'm leaving that fruit there. If you don't eat it, I don't care. If it all rots in the bowl, it's nothing to me. The only person you're hurting by not eating is you.'

'So why does everyone make so much fuss when I don't eat?'

'Because you want them to.'

'That's not true.'

Agnes sat down again. 'When I've been at my worst . . .' she began, then stopped. She remembered a lunch at the house in Provence, a bowl of tomato and basil soup placed in front of her, warm and fragrant, with a swirl of cream at its centre. Feeling hungry. Watching her parents, still absorbed in some endless silent conflict that had been going on for days. I have become invisible, she used to think.

'I must have been about your age,' she began again. 'I sat at this long table, with a white linen tablecloth, and I tipped a bowl of soup on to the table. All of it. Even though I was hungry.'

'Were your parents there?'

'Yes.'

'What did they do?'

'Nothing.'

'Nothing at all?'

'They didn't notice.'

'They must have been pretending not to notice.'

'I thought that at first. I waited. They had this way of talking to each other, because they were so used to having rows, and they knew each other so well, they used to argue in code. My father said, "Crystal." He was talking about the glassware, someone had put out the wrong ones. And my mother rang for Liliane, and said "My husband requests you to change the glasses." And I sat there in this growing puddle of soup and I realised they hadn't even noticed. And when Liliane changed the glasses, my father was inspecting the new ones, and my mother was busy disapproving of him, and Liliane cleared my place and laid a new cloth over the mess and poured some more soup for me and they didn't even see.'

'What did you do?'

'I ate the soup.'

Rachel put her hand over her mouth. 'Oh, I couldn't. I just couldn't have eaten it. Not after that.'

'What would you have done?'

'Me?' Rachel considered, animated now. 'I'd have punched my fist through a window. Something like that.'

'Yes, I thought of that. We had these glass doors between the two rooms. But I couldn't have risked it.'

'Risked what, the injuries?'

'Oh, no, I didn't care about hurting myself. But I couldn't have risked bleeding to death in front of them and them still not noticing. The last great gesture, totally wasted.'

Rachel started to laugh. 'Your maid would have just laid a new rug over the blood and carried out your corpse –'

'– and my parents would have been arguing about the cutlery by then.'

'So you sat and ate the soup.'

'And planned my own funeral.'

'I often do that.'

'The thing is,' Agnes said, 'it only dawned on me later in life, there's no satisfaction in your own funeral.'

'But at least then they'd realise – they'd have to notice . . .'

'Yes, but it's too late by then.' Agnes finished her apple and threw the core in the bin. 'They'd feel awful – but you wouldn't be around to see it.'

'You might be, watching from the ceiling, like a ghost.'

'Yes, but what's the point if it's too late to change your life?'

Rachel reached across to the fruit bowl and took a grape.

'Anyway,' Agnes said, 'we had a house guest. I couldn't have killed myself in front of him, they'd have reproached me for my lack of manners.'

Rachel giggled again. Then, carefully, she ate her grape.

'Your David Smurthwaite's a tasty geezer, isn't he, sweetie?' Athena poured tea into delicate cups.

'Snaith, not Smurthwaite. And I hadn't noticed.'

'Of course you had.' Athena leaned back in her pink armchair. In the background, Agnes could hear the muzak of the hotel foyer.

'He's very unhappy,' Agnes said.

'Sorrow is very becoming in a man.'

'And did you like his work?'

'Simon did. There were all these shipyard ones—'

'Can't have been shipyards.'

'Coalmines or something then, a bit colourless for me, but Simon's delighted. You greedy poppet, I wanted that éclair.'

'There are two, Athena.'

'And did he ask you?' Athena took an éclair and a strawberry tart from the cake stand.

'Did who ask what?'

'The world cruise, of course.'

'Yes, he did.'

'Wonderful, sweetie, so you're going, of course.' She looked up and caught Agnes's expression. 'Or rather, you're going to agonise about it for ages and then go.'

'It's not that simple, Athena, I can't just go, can I?'

Athena shrugged. 'I would.'

'You're not committed to a religious order.'

Athena giggled. 'Just as well.'

'It would ruin my life, Athena. To throw all this away, all this hard spiritual work of the last few years, all my attempts to try and live in God's service, to work towards understanding what God might want of me – if I just threw it all back at my order and took off with James, I'd be back to square one, wouldn't I? The order wouldn't have me back, and they'd be right. I'd have shown I was incapable of transcending my own desires, my own selfish wishes, that I'm just constantly clinging to what I want now, just Me, Now, instead of understanding that the self is temporary, illusory – and that you only find peace when you cease to listen to its constant demands.'

Athena was eating the second strawberry tart.

'I wanted that,' Agnes said.

Driving back to the school in the fading daylight, Agnes heard the chirrup of her phone.

'Hello?'

'Agnes, it's David. Can you meet me, now?'

'Where?'

'The Woolpack.'

'What's happened?'

'Something odd. I'm not sure . . .'

'I'll be there in fifteen minutes.'

'Look.' He pushed a photograph across the table to her. 'It was stuck through my letterbox, I found it when I got back from meeting your friends.'

She picked it up. It was the Allbright's athletics team. 'It's exactly the same as the one I've got,' she said. She turned it over in her fingers. It was printed on photographic paper, and looked new.

'Only this one's not a press cutting. And look –' David pointed.

There were no names listed underneath, but the faces were the same. Amongst them, Mark, David and Reg. And on each of the three, a line had been drawn in pencil circling their faces.

Chapter Fourteen

Agnes took a sip from her mug of cold tea. She wrote down the last name from the athletics team. She pulled her dressing gown around her. She yawned, closed the phone book, and then put the photograph back in the file. Longley, Snaith, Hanson, Pashley, McKinnon, Snaith, Styring, Weston, Graham, Adams, Bullock. And Naismith. There was no point finding a number for Reg Naismith.

In the phone book there were two Longleys, no Snaiths, two Hansons, one Pashley, several McKinnons, Styrings, loads of Westons, Adams, Grahams, and Bullocks.

And what would she say to them once she'd dialled their numbers? Do you know anyone in the athletics team who had a grudge against Reg and the Snaith boys?

And what if it was nothing to do with the athletics team? And how had someone got hold of the photo and sent it on to David?

She'd told David to go straight to the police with it. She hoped that's what he'd done, though it was more likely he'd stayed in the Woolpack for just another pint or two. Or three.

It was late. She stared at the files, thinking she really ought to go to bed. She pulled out Reg's file again and flicked through it. More names: his supervisor at the mill; the military officer responsible for his call-up; the other lads who joined up with him.

More names. She wrote them down. Jones, Coulter, Highworth, Chadwick. She stared at them. These names belonged to young soldiers, young men sent off to battle in 1942. They might be anywhere now. They might be living out their peaceful last years with children and grandchildren around them. They might be dead.

She opened the phone book, searched out Chadwick, Coulter, Highworth. There was no point trying Jones. There was an F. Chadwick, listed, with an address near the estate. And an M.

Coulter, also, judging from the *A–Z*, nearby. She wrote them down. She turned to Billy's file, wrote down his address and phone number, put all the files away, took off her dressing gown and went to bed.

'In the day of my distress I seek the Lord, I stretch out my hands to Him by night; my soul is poured out without ceasing, it refuses all comfort.'

In the chapel Agnes glanced around her, seeing Charlotte, Leonora and Rachel, their lips moving with the service. The words stayed with her, still ringing in her mind as she returned to her room and sat down at her desk.

She reached for the files, as the phone rang. She heard Julius's voice.

'I've been thinking about you,' he said.

'Thank you.'

'I don't want you to go away.'

'That's very kind of you.'

'Have you had any further thoughts?'

'All I know is that I should live in the service of the Lord.'

'So that hasn't changed?'

'You know me better than that. Of course it hasn't.'

'So the question is, does He want you to stay put or does He want to you visit your mother? And, more to the point, couldn't you do both? I could talk to your provincial about it, plead the case for a sabbatical—'

'And then what? I'd come back to the same difficulties, the same refusal to live in community—'

'Perhaps that's your path.'

They sat in silence. 'Julius . . .' Agnes said at last. 'It would be the same if it was you going away. If it was you asking me to come with you.'

'But I wouldn't go away. I'm someone who stays put.'

'I wish I was the same.'

'Perhaps—'

'What?'

'It might be helpful if you reflect on the good things about your religious life. You see – what I mean is, you going away – it may appear to be the right decision now, but if you stayed put, in the long term, you might be grateful that you didn't go. It might be that long-term, it's the right decision to stay.'

'But I'll be old, Julius.'

'Does it matter if it takes that long?'

'Yes, if I've spent all the time in between being resentful and full of rebellion – and it's not good for the order, either, if I'm like that.'

Julius was quiet. Then he said, 'I'm worried he doesn't care about you enough – to have put you in this dilemma . . .'

'But he does. He always has. He's only asked me because he can see I'm unhappy.'

'How noble of him.'

'Wouldn't you do the same?'

'Don't forget, I have to be your conscience too.'

'Only because I ask you to be.'

'Agnes –'

'Yes?'

'Just reflect on the good things. Please. For both of us.'

'What does Julius think?' James paused on the path that led away from the village. The moorland slopes dipped away from them, still bare and wintry.

'I don't know, to be honest.'

'He must want you to stay.'

'Yes. I think he does.'

'He's probably right,' James said, glancing at her. She walked at his side, her head bowed.

'Are the Campbells expecting me?' she said after a moment.

'Yes, I told them we were both coming.'

They walked in silence for a while. Agnes paused, taking in the beauty of the afternoon, the crisp air, the soft clouds nudging the shadows of the slopes ahead.

'You see,' she said, 'Julius imagines me being one of these old nuns you meet, full of wisdom and joy and peace, like Sister Katharina in the London community, you should meet her one day, she's extraordinary. She says things like, "Of course, the first fifty years were pretty tough . . ."' Agnes broke off, laughing. 'And you realise that she probably left all sort of opportunities behind, and she probably did her time in the laundry full of resentment, and she probably considered leaving countless times – and now she's very glad she didn't, and she's learnt so much from staying

177

put, and she's filled with the Holy Spirit, you should see her face when she's praying, just kind of radiant . . .' She sighed. 'And Julius has faith that I might be the same, when I'm about ninety. And I keep thinking – what if he's wrong? What if I continue to rebel, what if I don't come with you, and then I resent it, and start to shrivel up with bitterness – what kind of ninety-year-old will that make for? And what if I don't get to that stage, isn't it better to live now, to live with joy, with a sense of adventure?'

James paused at her side. 'I don't know –' he began. 'I can't say anything helpful.'

'Julius told me to think about the good things, and he's right, there are moments, even here, in chapel sometimes, or here on the moors, when it feels right, when I feel that I'm doing the right thing, and certainly in London, there've been moments in the community house, when I'm cooking for the sisters or something, when I've felt, just for a moment, a sense of being in the service of something greater than myself. It's a kind of freedom, being deprived of choice, it does allow one's spiritual side to grow and develop.'

'And yet we have choice.'

'Yes.'

'We continue to have to make choices.'

'Yes.'

'Until you get to the point I've reached.'

Agnes looked at him. The walk had tired him, and his face looked grey.

'You see,' he said, 'in the end, we die. And I'm not sure it makes any difference.'

Agnes smiled. 'Some help you are.'

'I did warn you.'

'Between you and Julius, I'm completely on my own in this.'

Evelyn kissed Agnes on the cheek and led her inside. It was a spacious house, with a wide hallway and an open-plan living room looking out on to an immaculate garden.

'Tea?' Evelyn said.

Agnes sat down, admiring the dashes of colour in the garden in spite of the wintry day.

'Joss has taken James off to show him his plans for a rose trellis,' Evelyn said, returning with tea things. 'It's so tedious,' she said, pouring two cups of tea and offering Agnes a slice of fruit cake. 'And poor old James isn't going to be here to see it, is he, those climbing roses take ages to get established. I think it's Joss's clumsy way of expressing hope, of trying to say that he's going to miss him. Which of course he is, poor dear.' Evelyn blinked back tears. 'And anyway, it's such a nuisance, it cuts down my space for the hives, I've got to move them further back, the bees won't like it. Oh, here they are.'

'Perhaps white roses would be more elegant,' James was saying. He took a cup of tea and sat down next to Agnes. 'And how were the Radleighs?'

Joss grunted.

'They were very welcoming, as usual,' Evelyn said.

'Full of gossip,' Joss said. 'Can't think why they think we want to hear what everyone in the village is up to. Who's extending their patio, who's traded in the Jeep for a Merc, who fell off their mount at the last hunt meeting – we don't know half these people, but they will keep on.'

'They told us about William Baines, dear, you were very concerned.'

Joss stared into his cup. 'Yes. William Baines. Though, frankly, it's none of their business.'

'They'd seen him at bridge the week before. He's not at all well, apparently. Not himself.'

'They should just leave the poor bugger alone,' Joss said, helping himself to a large piece of cake.

'Someone's got to look after him. With all his children having abandoned him.'

'They're grown up. What does he expect?'

'I thought –' Agnes hesitated. 'I thought Patricia was very loyal to him?'

'Well,' Evelyn said, offering more cake, 'apparently he was very unhappy about all of them. He was saying terrible things about Anthony Turnbull, her husband.'

'He said he thought he was capable of anything,' Joss said.

'What kind of anything?' Agnes took some cake.

'It's all hearsay,' Joss said.

'He's not himself,' Evelyn said. 'He wasn't really making sense. And he left early, they said. It's grief, about Hannah. I'm sure of it. He's kept it all buttoned up, and now it's driving him mad.'

'All the same,' Joss said. 'The poor man deserves better than to be fodder for the Radleighs' tittle-tattle. More tea, Agnes?'

Agnes noticed, once again, the tension in his face at the discussion. He handed her the cup clumsily, before she'd properly got hold of it, and it fell to the floor between them, splashing hot tea. Agnes jumped up in a rush of confusion, cloths were brought, apologies made, Evelyn insisted it was an old rug and really, not to worry, and had it scalded her?

'Don't worry about Agnes,' James said. 'I've know her spill a whole plate of tomato soup. Deliberately.'

Agnes glanced at him. He smiled back at her.

The moors were shaded with the last of the day when they set off back to James's cottage, refusing Joss's offer of a lift, promising to come back soon. They walked in silence, as the twilight deepened.

'I was only fourteen,' Agnes said at last.

James smiled. 'I was completely on your side. I almost joined in, just to give you support. But they wouldn't have noticed me either. And I felt sorry for your nice maid, having to clear it all up. I remember looking at Aylmer and Marie-Claude, locked in that terrible battle. And there you were, caught up in it all, an innocent bystander. I was very angry with them. I told Aylmer, afterwards, I tried to talk to him about it, but he wouldn't really listen. Guilt, I think. He knew I was right.'

Agnes knew that if she tried to speak she would burst into tears.

'I love this time of day,' James said, aware of her silence. 'Particularly now. This landscape is so – timeless. I like thinking how it will still be here when I'm not. It makes me feel insubstantial. It gives me hope that – that when it comes to it, it'll be easy to let go.'

'If Julius knew you –' Agnes was trying not to cry. 'If he knew how well you know me – he'd understand why I need – why I need . . .'

James touched her shoulder.

It was almost too dark to see the path, as they descended the hill towards the lights of the village.

'And Mary said, "Behold, I am the handmaid of the Lord. Let it be to me according to Your word."'

Agnes looked up, at Elias, at the window behind him, the white of the altar, the morning sun streaming in, glancing off the candlesticks with flashes of silver.

Let it be to me according to Your word, Agnes thought. Let me obey.

'It was all right for Mary, though, wasn't it?' she said to Teresa as they walked back to the staff room. 'I mean, it was obvious what she was supposed to do.'

'She could have said no,' Teresa said.

'No? How could Mary have said no? If an angel came to you and suggested that you might bear a divine child –'

'– I'd say no. Wouldn't you? I've gone to all this trouble to have an orderly life, and then that? Absolutely out of the question, I'd tell him. Go and pick on someone else.'

Agnes laughed.

'So,' Teresa said, 'what's *your* angel asking you to do?'

They were standing in the empty corridor.

'Either stay here. Or go away. In a good cause.' Agnes stared at her feet.

'And you can't tell which?'

Agnes nodded.

'I suppose compared to that, immaculate conception is a doddle.' Teresa squeezed her hand, and then left her at the staff-room door.

'This isn't a bleedin' lending library,' Nina said, at lunchtime. 'Marching in here, going straight to my files, helping yourself.'

'I was surprised to find you here,' Agnes said. 'I thought you'd stay well clear after your experiences.'

'I need the money. And the whole place is falling apart. The Turnbulls haven't been seen for days. No, you can't have Baxter, that's my mum's maiden name, she worked here for a few years. And you can't have Warburton either. And you didn't even bring me a sandwich.'

'I've spent the morning trying to coax a few words of halting French out of girls who in other circumstances can't stop talking. It ruins the appetite. I'm sorry, Nina.' Agnes sat on a chair with a heap of files on her lap.

'All those?'

'I'll bring them back.'

'Better had do.'

'Nina – are you really OK working here? I'm worried about you.'

'It's fine, honest. The coppers keep popping in, I couldn't be safer.'

'What does your mum think?'

'I've played it down for her.'

'But the newspapers?'

'She can't see to read them no more. I read bits to her.'

'But the radio – the local TV news –'

'I know, it's a matter of time. Maybe they'll have caught the bastard by then.'

'Maybe.'

Agnes left the mill and climbed the hill up to the Millhouse estate. She turned down Radcliffe Street and knocked on the third door on the right. It was opened by a woman whom Agnes recognised from the conversation in the mill with Cathy Phelps during the school visit.

'Maureen Keenan?' Agnes said.

'Aye.' The woman eyed her suspiciously. She wore a large pink jumper and woollen skirt, and her feet were squeezed into mauve slippers.

'I'm Sister Agnes. We met when our school visited the mill. St Catherine's.'

'Oh, aye, yes. I remember.'

'One of our girls, Cathy Phelps –'

'Aye, that one, said she was my cousin. D'you hear that, Kitty,' she called over her shoulder, 'never told you at the time, there's a girl at that school up t'hill, the convent one, says she's my cousin. Through the Rudges, them what married the Wilsons, t'other branch. Come through, love.'

Agnes followed Maureen into the front room. The television was on, with the sound turned down. A woman was sitting in front of it. She was thin and upright, with dark hair scraped back from her face.

'And what can I do for you, Sister?' Maureen said.

'I wanted to ask you about Billy, actually,' Agnes said.

Maureen's face fell. 'What's he done this time?'

'No, it's nothing he's done. I'm concerned that his name keeps coming up in this Mark Snaith business . . .'

Maureen sighed heavily and lowered herself into a chair. 'Weren't nowt to do wi' him, and everyone's pointing the finger. Take a seat, love. This is Kitty, my friend, we work together at Allbright's.'

'I'll put t'kettle on,' Kitty said, and went into the kitchen.

'So, where do you come in?' Maureen said.

'It's a long story, but one of my sixth formers was involved with Mark.'

'Poor kid.'

'And she said that Billy gave Mark –'

'I know I know, our Billy drove him up to t'moor, don't think I haven't heard it over and over again, them coppers have been coming here asking me, asking our Billy too, poor kid, all he'll say is, he dropped him off on the moor, that's all he knows. Last to see him alive, you see, in't that right, Kitty?'

'Poor lad,' Kitty said, coming back into the room, 'hasn't done nothing wrong. Sugar?'

'No, thanks.' Agnes watched Kitty return to the kitchen. 'I gather they knew each other through the sports centre.'

'That's right. It were good for our Billy, that, to get involved in summat like that. Not that it's come to much. Folks say they got all this money, but where is it, eh? Still all boarded up, that centre. They promised they'd have it reopened, all fitted out nicely.'

'Perhaps it takes time.'

'Time?' Kitty said from the kitchen. 'They'd had time enough.'

'They've not long had this new funding,' Agnes said.

'They could have made a start at least.' Kitty handed her a mug of instant coffee. 'They were talking about doing up that centre before Mother was even taken ill, and now she's gone and nowt's changed.' Her voice wavered. 'And that Mr Turnbull, I don't trust him, not one bit, Mother always said, if the mill got into his hands, it would be the worse for us all . . .'

'Now now, love.' Maureen got up and helped her friend into a chair. Kitty sat, biting her lip, her hands clasped round her mug of coffee.

'Do you think Billy would mind if I had a word with him?' Agnes asked.

Maureen sighed. 'He's had that many people wanting to have a word wi' him. I can tell when he's lying, he's my lad after all, and I know he's telling the truth.'

'I owe it to Charlotte —' Agnes tried.

'Well, you can try if you like. He's often down the pub, the Wetherby Stakes. Most nights.'

'What does he look like?'

'You can't miss him, our Billy. He's got his head shaved, like they do, you know, with kind of zig-zags in it, and he wears all designer clothes, don't he Kitty?' Kitty sat, staring at her fingers. 'And an earring. All I can say is, I'm just glad my old man in't around to see it, how these lads dress these days. And if our Billy isn't in t'pub, you can catch him at the mill, we'll be going down there later, won't we, Kitty?'

'Wha— oh, aye, yes.'

'She's in a world of her own,' Maureen whispered to Agnes at the door, as she showed her out. 'Poor Kitty. Lived with her mother all her life, just the two of them, and now her mother's died. Just a couple of months ago. Just before Christmas too, only sixty-eight. She's lost her bearings. I'm doing what I can for her, but she's taken it badly.'

Agnes tore a page from her notebook. 'Here's my number,' she said, writing it down. 'Just in case.'

Maureen took the piece of paper carefully and held it in her fingers. 'Sister, eh? We were your kind, once. My grand-daddy came from Ireland, fetched up here. He were taught by the brothers when he were little. Best education you could get, he used to say.'

Agnes continued up the hill, past a row of three shops, one of them boarded up. She turned off the main street, and came to a crossroads. On one corner stood a modern single-storey building in red brick with bright red railings. The windows had grilles bolted across them, the door was boarded up and padlocked. 'Millhouse Community Centre', the sign said. Agnes walked round it. Someone called 'Biker' had sprayed his name across the walls, along with 'Chub' and the 'Acid Girls'. The board across the door was fastened with a heavy padlock, and was scorched where it touched the floor. On the ground Agnes saw blackened silver foil, an empty packet of cigarettes. A filthy, discarded, football glove. Agnes bent and picked up the glove between her thumb and forefinger. She looked at it, then dropped it again, and set off back down the hill to the town.

On the way back to the school she bought some fresh bread and a bunch of early daffodils. She arranged the flowers in the vase that James had given her, so familiar that she'd passed her whole childhood without noticing it. Now she seemed to see it for the first time, illuminated by the bright splash of yellow, the promise of spring. The message of the Annunciation, Agnes thought, a promise of new life. Of salvation. No wonder Mary said yes. She ran her finger along the pattern of the vase, and her eye fell on the two photos that James had given her.

And what good is such a promise, she thought. What good is it to James, this promise of new life? What good is it to him, when this might be the last spring he sees, when these daffodils might be the last he ever sets eyes on? The clock, and the skull, and the roses, she thought, like Joanna's work, like the old paintings in Baines's attic, the Jesuit lemons, made all the more beautiful by their transience, and by our own impermanence. Perhaps for James, the daffodils this year are the most beautiful he's ever seen.

Oh Julius, she thought, surely it is better that, to celebrate each moment, than to wait patiently, steadfastly, for a spring that may never come.

She drew her curtains against the dusk, switched on her lamp, and unpacked all the files from the mill. She stacked them up on her desk. She'd taken all the names she could find, Styring and Coulter and Longley and Pashley and Snaith and Hanson and Chadwick and Highworth. A line of young faces from the athletics team; and now a stack of files on her desk. And somewhere, out in the world, real people, real, living people with their own lives, their own stories.

The phone rang.

'Agnes – David.'

'David. Did you go to the police?'

'She's phoned me. I'm going to the hut. She'll be there.'

'Joanna?'

'Who else. If you want to see her, you'd better get a move on.'

'What, *now*?'

'Yes, now. Before she disappears into the ether again.'

'How do I get there?'

'You know the Bingley road over the moors? You reach a crossroads, and there's a farm and a signpost to Baildon.'

'Hang on, I'll write this down.'

'There's a track just there, park your car and I'll meet you there.'

Chapter Fifteen

Agnes got out of her car and locked the door. The only sound was of the wind gusting across the moors. She stared into the darkness around her. She reached into her bag for her phone, for David's number, when she heard footsteps from the track, and a flash of a torch.

'Agnes?'

'David.'

'You were quick. Come on.'

She followed him up the track, stumbling over the uneven ground as his torchbeam swerved ahead of her.

'I told her what you said about the mill,' David said, breathlessly. 'About Turnbull selling it. That's why she'll see you.'

They turned off the track and descended a slope, coming upon a tiny cottage. There was a flickering light at its window. Agnes could smell woodsmoke.

David pushed the door. Joanna turned. She was standing in front of the fireplace in which there was a blazing fire. A blackened kettle hung from a hook. There were candles everywhere, balanced on the windowsills, the mantelpiece. There was rough rush-matting on the floor, and cushions, and a mattress draped with a multi-coloured quilt. Joanna was wearing a long velvet dress, whether cheap bazaar or Nicole Farhi it was difficult to tell. She smiled, then turned back to the fire.

'I was just making tea,' she said.

'Do you like our home?' David said, as they settled on cushions by the fire.

'Whose is it?'

'Typical bourgeois response of the so-called religious,' David said. 'It's ours. We've made it ours.'

'We did pay for it, David,' Joanna smiled, handing Agnes a mug of tea. 'He likes to think it's all revolutionary, all squatters' rights and anarchy, but actually we've got a deal with the farmer.'

Agnes looked at Joanna, remembering the last time she'd seen her. She was transformed now, her red hair piled on her head, her skin softened by the candlelight.

'I'm sorry about the art room,' Joanna said, suddenly serious.

'It was fine. Philomena had it cleared up in about ten minutes.' Joanna laughed.

'What happened?' Agnes asked.

Joanna handed David his tea, bending over him as he sat by the fire, allowing her hair to brush his face. He caught at her hand and kissed it, and she smiled into his eyes. She took her mug and sat down next to him.

'I just couldn't take it any more. I liked the school, I liked the kids, some of them, anyway. It wasn't about the school, it was about my father being so angry with me – but for some reason that's where I flipped. I suppose.'

'Where did you go?'

'Here to start with. Then to my brother's. He helped me calm down a bit, it's the same for him too.'

'Is that who you meant, in the art room? When you said there was nothing for you, first him, then you?'

'Is that what I said? Nothing?' She smiled. 'I suppose it must have been.' She turned to David, and he took one of her hands, as if somehow protecting her from Agnes. Agnes felt suddenly irritated.

'Did you take your photograph to the police?' she asked David. He flashed her a glance.

'What photograph?' Joanna asked.

'Oh – um . . .'

'Someone sent him a photo with him picked out, along with his brother and Reg,' Agnes said, watching her.

'But – what – why – you didn't tell me. What photo?'

'Really, it's nothing . . .'

'Nothing?' Agnes tried not to shout. 'You're probably in more danger than anyone, than Nina even, and you say . . .'

'Dave, what is this?'

'I thought we were here to talk about Turnbull and the mill.' David faced Agnes.

'It's all the same thing, isn't it?' Agnes felt her anger rising. 'Turnbull, and the mill, and the community centre, and the attack on Nina, and your brother's death, and Reg, and your photo, and Billy Keenan, and all these Chadwicks and Highworths and Styrings and everybody else whose families go back years and they're all tied up with the Baineses, with you, Joanna, and your father, and Marcus, and Elias . . . And you sit there trying to say that it's nothing . . .' She felt, surprisingly, as if she was going to burst into tears. She took a gulp of tea.

'How is Elias?' Joanna spoke quietly.

'About the same. Still burdened with misery.'

Joanna met her eyes. 'Poor man. Did he tell you about the accident?'

'Patricia did.'

David got up and stoked the fire.

'And is Anthony really trying to sell the mill?' Joanna asked.

'It's only a rumour,' Agnes said. 'But Nina's overheard him talking about it.'

'It's impossible. I know times are hard, God knows our whole family has seen the money drain away with each generation, but Daddy's made it work. He's determined it doesn't leave the family.'

'He's very upset, your father.'

'I know.'

'But can Turnbull sell the mill?'

'All I know is that Anthony is very angry with me. When all this came up, about our inheritance, I said that I didn't want to run the mill, I didn't want the money, what little there is, but what I did want – what I still want – is to have my name on all the documents. I've never trusted him, Anthony, and I thought it would safeguard things for Daddy. So that's all it is – my name. Technically, although I have no rights of ownership, I'm a signatory for any transference of ownership. And it's made him really angry with me. He's been phoning Marcus, asking where I am. Marcus won't tell him.'

'And what does your father think?'

Joanna sighed. 'He was very upset when I wouldn't accept my inheritance. He was furious. He wanted everything to be as he'd imagined it, a happy family taking over his life's work.' David sat down next to her again. 'He wanted it to be perfect. And I said no. I refused my birthright. I let him down. But I knew that if I didn't fail him, I'd fail myself. I learned from Marcus, you see, sometimes you have to save yourself. But at the time it was driving me mad. And now – now it seems, he's the one being driven mad by it. Poor love . . .' There were tears in her eyes.

'And your mother's death . . .' Agnes said.

She nodded, wiping her eyes. 'It's all mixed up in Dad's mind, and I think that's why he handed over all control to Anthony. But Pat, that's what I can't understand, I don't know why she'd agree, she's devoted to Dad, she wouldn't harm him, and she's named in the trust document. So unless she agrees too, they can't sell. And then I was speaking to Andrew, he's our family solicitor, and he said that Dad had to come to see him a day or two ago, and was in a real state, and kept saying that Anthony can't sell it, he can't, and Andrew said he had the impression that he wanted proof, somehow, he kept asking to see the trust document, but when he showed him he said, no, not that one, the old one. Andrew said he didn't know what he meant. And then Dad got really angry, apparently, and stormed out. I'm really worried about him.'

'Do you see him?'

'He won't see me. My work is at the house, most of it, and I used to go there a lot. But now he's – he's very angry with me.' She started to cry, and David took her in his arms.

Agnes finished her tea. After a while Joanna dried her tears. Agnes got up and went over to the hearth and placed her empty mug with the rest of the washing up in a bucket of water. She went and sat down again.

'Did you know that Charlotte was going out with Mark?' she asked Joanna.

Joanna nodded. 'It was a bit difficult, her being at the school.'

'We went to your house, Elias and I,' Agnes said.

'I know.'

'Who trashed it?'

'Just kids. They do that if anything's left empty for too long. I know who did it, there's a real nutcase eleven-year-old they call Beanie, and his gang. They were really sweet to me last time I saw them, that's how you can tell.'

'Is it still your house?'

'Nominally, yes. If it's still standing.'

'Elias has got that key,' David said.

'He's welcome to it.' Joanna smiled at him. 'He can keep an eye on it for me.'

'The accident – it seems to live with him still.'

'He severed all connection with our family. And when I joined the school, I was so pleased to see him again. I didn't know that's where he'd ended up. We had some lovely talks, he's so thoughtful, isn't he, I'd always enjoyed talking to him, in the old days, when he and Marcus . . . and then we all lost contact with him. And there he was, and at first it was awkward, but we got close again. Dave's jealous as hell, aren't you, love?' She pulled on his sleeve.

'Him? I've no reason to be jealous of him.' David forced a smile.

'He showed me the paintings in your father's attic,' Agnes said.

'When you broke into the house,' David said, acidly.

'You – when? What, in the attic?'

Agnes sighed. 'It's a long story. Something Elias wanted to do, I'm afraid.'

'He's always loved those. So have I. We'd go on at Dad to put them on show, but he wouldn't. Elias said they were too Roman Catholic for him, and I think he was right. Mum liked them . . .' Her voice trailed off. She took a cushion from the floor and pulled it around between her hands.

'Your brother,' Agnes began.

'Marcus – what about him?'

'Why did he move away?'

'He fell out with Daddy. When Mummy died. It all comes back to that, you see.'

'Won't he come back?'

'He's just like Daddy. Neither of them will budge. And anyway, he's happy now. He married last year. I was the only one invited. They've got a baby now, just a few weeks old, she's lovely.'

The log on the fire hissed and crackled, then quietened into flickering flame. Agnes gathered her coat around her. 'What will you do?'

'About Daddy? I don't know. I'm not sure there's much I can do. I can't talk to him any more. And my sister doesn't believe that Anthony wants to sell it. Marcus says we've just got to save ourselves, and I'm beginning to think he's right. I was in such a state a month ago, as you saw. I don't want to go back to that.'

They gazed at the fire for a while. Joanna took David's hand and stroked each finger in turn. Agnes put on her coat.

'Come and see us again. How is the school?'

'OK.'

'Did Philomena replace me?'

'I think she's advertised. You could still come back.'

Joanna shook her head. 'I liked teaching, but –'

'But she's relying on me to keep her, that's what.' David smiled. 'Come on, I'll walk you to your car.'

Agnes waited in the doorway while David gave Joanna a lingering kiss.

'Hurry back,' she heard Joanna whisper. Then she and David were out in the cold, picking their way back up to the track by the faltering light of his torch.

'Is she all right?' Agnes asked as they reached her car.

'Now she is, yes. Marcus helps, she's been staying with him since her father threw her out. When she's not up here.'

'Why isn't he –' Agnes began, then stopped.

'Sorry?'

'David,' Agnes said, 'please take that photo to the police.'

'It may be some silly hoax.'

'It may not.'

David brushed her sleeve. 'I know. I will, I promise. Tomorrow.'

'Promise?'

'Promise. I must get back.' He bent and kissed her cheek, then turned back to the track.

Agnes watched him go, the bobbing torch beam receding into the darkness. She got into her car. The engine seemed much too loud as she started it up and drove away.

Her alarm dragged her from deep sleep peopled with daffodils and skulls and blackened kettles on hissing logs. She lay in bed, trying to remember what day it was, recalling her conversation with Joanna, her fears for David's safety. And Marcus, something about Marcus.

She got up, showered, pulled on skirt and blouse, brushed her hair. Ahead of her, the rest of the day: chapel, then a meeting with Sister Teresa about a new girl who was joining their house for the summer term, a meeting with Sister Philomena and the head of music about the liturgy for Palm Sunday, more chapel, and two sessions of French conversation. She pulled back the curtains. It was a dull, damp day. This evening, she decided, she would go to the Wetherby Stakes.

★ ★ ★

192

Walking to the pub, in jeans and black cashmere sweater, she wondered whether she'd be confronted by several identically dressed lads with sculpted haircuts and earrings. A noisy cluster of boys was lurking by a games machine.

'Oi, Doddsy, mine's a pint,' one called out, his voice ringing across the pub. He had a zig-zag hair-cut and a pierced ear.

'Sit on it, Keenan,' another lad called back from the bar, to much jeering from the group by the games machine. Agnes approached the group. They eyed her as she drew near them, and their loud jostling subsided. Glances flicked between them.

'Billy Keenan?'

He studied her, his head on one side.

'I'm Sister Agnes,' she said to him, her gaze level with his.

He laughed, and his mates laughed with him. 'Sister, eh?'

'I called on your mother yesterday, she said I might find you here.'

'Yeah, well, that's mothers for yer, in't it.' The sneer was fixed on his face.

'I thought we might have a talk.'

'Oh yeah?'

'You're in luck, mate,' one of his friends said.

'Another older woman for you, eh, Billy?'

'I thought we might talk about Mark Snaith,' Agnes persisted.

'You did, did yer?'

'And about Anthony Turnbull.'

'What's he been saying?'

'He's a very worried man,' Agnes said.

'He's got reason to be an' all.'

'Billy – when it comes to it, who are the police going to believe? Anthony or you?'

'It in't going to come to that, is it?' Billy kept his posture of bravado, but his smile waned.

'I want to help, Billy,' Agnes said.

'Oh yeah?'

'Yes.'

Billy kept his eyes fixed on her. After a moment he said, 'You can buy me a pint if you want.'

They sat at a table away from his friends, who from time to time looked across and made loud comments.

'So Turnbull sent you, did he?' Billy took a long pull from his pint.

'No. The only reason I'm involved is that a girl at my school was involved with Mark.'

'I'd never have given him a fuckin' lift if I'd known it would lead to all this. Them coppers in't been off my back since the poor kid were found up Morton's.'

'Why was he there?'

'Bird watching, he said. A couple of falcons, he said. I didn't know him that well, our families weren't close, like. I'd got to know him a bit through this sports centre idea. That were sound, that were, folk'll tell you all sorts about me, but that were summat I believed in, me. Still do, if Turnbull hadn't . . . Anyway, that afternoon I said summat about driving up that way, I were visitin' a mate t'other side of Skipton, and he blagged a lift. Said someone had tipped him off about his nest. Fine by me, I said. I dropped him off by that road that crosses back towards Keighley. And the rest you know. Poor kid.' He knocked back more beer. 'I were shocked, I were. And them, over there, they can be laffin' and jeerin' now, but you should've seen them when we heard the news. We're no strangers to trouble, us Millhouse lads, but – but that were way out of our league, man.'

'Nina said–'

'And her, that's another one. Is she OK now?'

'She's fine.'

'Couldn't believe it when I heard. They said that were someone who knew the mill, but I don't know about that. Coppers swarming everywhere . . .'

'Have you seen Turnbull recently?'

Billy glanced over at his mates, who responded with thumbs-up signs and guffaws. He shook his head. 'Only around the mill.'

'Do you get on with him?'

'What's he said, then?'

'He seems very upset about something.'

'Did he drag my name into it?'

'No. I just thought—'

'Well you can think all you flamin' well like.'

'Billy, no one's accusing you of anything.'

'Aren't they?' His eyes narrowed.

'I'm just concerned that Turnbull might –'

'Might what?'

'Might do something stupid.'

Billy laughed, an empty, hollow laugh. 'Nah, not him. A coward, him.'

'I thought you might know what Turnbull is so afraid of.'

Billy smiled at her. 'That'd be telling, wouldn't it?'

'Billy, how can you expect the police to leave you alone if –'

'They won't leave me alone, them coppers, not ever. Not with my name. So I need all the advantages I can get, eh?' He stood up, drained his glass. 'Thanks for the pint.'

'Any time,' Agnes said. She watched him saunter across the pub to join his friends. She stood up, put on her coat, and left.

'What is it with Billy Keenan?' Agnes paced Nina's office the next day.

'He's a trouble maker,' Nina said, tidying her desk. The clock tower chimed five. 'And I'm off now. Do you want to come with me? I'm having tea with my mum.'

'I oughtn't to get back too late, I can't miss the evening office again.'

'It won't be late, I've got to get Rosie into bed.'

'But what is it with Turnbull and Keenan?' Agnes followed Nina as she locked the office and set off down the stairs.

'What do you mean?'

'I bought him a drink last night. He seems to think he has one up on Anthony, but he refused to tell me what it was.'

'It's all bravado with him. He's sweet as pie with me, but I know what he really thinks. Was it the Wetherby Stakes?'

'Yes.'

'NF pub, everyone knows that. Shall we go in your car? Mine's at home.'

Louisa Warburton cut the crust from a large white loaf, then tucked the loaf under her arm and proceeded to butter the first slice. She cut this off, then buttered the next.

'Nina tells me you work at the convent school across the moor?'

Agnes dragged her attention away from the loaf buttering. 'Yes, that's right.'

'And that Baines's daughter used to work there, but now she's resigned.' Louisa was looking towards her. She had the same broad forehead as Nina, the same neat chin and easy smile, but her gaze was vague and clouded.

'That's right.'

'I'd have done something special, only I have to stick to what I know these days.'

Agnes watched her move around the kitchen, her hands darting lightly, feeling her way.

Rosie was sitting by the fire, watching the flickering light behind the plastic logs. 'No, Mummy, little plaits, like Laura has,' she was saying to Nina, who sat behind her, combing her hair. 'And I want those bubbles, those pink bubbles, like Laura has on her plaits, OK, they're pink with all glitter on them, I want those, OK?'

Louisa placed the cups on the table, checking the position of each one with her fingertips, before carefully pouring the tea into each.

Agnes left as night was falling. Driving across the moor she saw a bird, circling, dark against the indigo sky. In her mind she saw Mark's binoculars, flung aside in his struggle for life, lying unseeing in the mud. The bird still circled, eyeing its prey, biding its time.

'Mine own eyes have seen the salvation, Which You have prepared in the sight of every people . . .'

Agnes repeated the familiar words, her voice joined to the voices of the other sisters. She looked up to the darkened window, and seemed to see again the circling falcon, poised in the twilight, watching, waiting.

'Lighten our darkness, Lord we pray . . .'

Agnes closed her eyes. She recalled Louisa Warburton, her guiding hands, her careful strategies for a life without seeing. And whoever had attacked Nina . . . Agnes touched her own eyelids as she thought about the knots pressing into Nina's face, as she saw again the binoculars, sweeping an arc through the air to land face down, sightless.

'Lord, may Your word be a lantern to our feet, a light to our paths and a strength to our lives . . .'

When the service was over, Agnes stumbled from the chapel and went straight to her room.

Why sight? Agnes argued with herself, arranging the files on her desk, lighting the little Anglepoise lamp, pouring herself a whisky. Why a knotted rope for Nina, why such horrific mutilation for Mark and Reg? Why eyes?

She opened the first file. Laurence Styring. Born 15 January 1954. Joined the mill March 1977. Left in 1991 to move to Northampton. Member of the athletic team. Married, two children. Allergic to penicillin.

Jim Highworth. Born October 1944. Had a son, also Jim, member of the athletics team . . .

Esther Hanson. Joined the mill in 1941. One daughter, Kitty.

Agnes checked the athletics team photo. There was a Hanson there, Alan, it said. He looked about 19. She must have picked up a different Hanson by mistake. She turned to the next file.

Ray Chadwick. Joined the mill in 1938, aged 16. Returned to the mill in 1946. He'd had a period of ill health soon after that, and died in 1956 of 'injuries incurred in armed service'. Agnes picked up Reg's file, and flicked through to the call-up papers. There it was, Ray Chadwick, signed up as a soldier when still a boy; never made it to his forties. She found the note she'd made of his address, from the phone book. F. Chadwick, it said. The address was the same as in the file, still Myddleton Terrace. There must be a relative still living, then. His widow? His brother? Agnes underlined the phone number.

She started on the next file. Stephen Pashley. Joined the mill in 1982, member of the athletics team . . .

And the next. Coulter, Ernest. Joined the mill in 1937, called up with Reg and Ray Chadwick . . .

This tells me nothing about Mark, she thought, closing the file. It tells me nothing about David, and why someone should have sent him the photo. It tells me nothing about Billy Keenan, and about Turnbull, and why he thinks he needs forgiveness. It tells me nothing about Nina.

She sat at her desk, sipping her whisky, her thoughts circling, all the time returning to the mill, to Allbright's. She stared at the heap of files before her. I could read every file in Nina's cabinets, she thought, and all I'd have is a litany of names, of lives, of histories unfolding towards an inevitable ending, after seventy years, or eighty, or forty, or thirty . . .

At the end of my life, she thought, I will be someone who stayed faithful to my order. At the end of my life, I will be someone who ran away from a convent in order to look after a dying friend . . .

At the end of my life there might be peace. There might be regret. At the ending of a life there might be sorrow, or pain, or violence. There might be a pair of binoculars lying in the mud while a bird of prey circles overhead.

Agnes got into bed and switched off the light.

Chapter Sixteen

Agnes stared at her bowl of cornflakes. The clatter of the dining hall seemed to be happening at a distance. Agnes was aware that Teresa had asked her something.

'Sorry?'

'I said, have you had any visitations recently?'

'You mean angels demanding that I do impossible things?'

'Something like that.'

'If only it was that straightforward. No, the Lord seems to have left me entirely on my own in this one.'

'Do you really think you might leave?'

'I don't know. I just don't know.'

Back in her room, Agnes made a pot of tea, then rummaged amongst her papers until she found the phone number for F. Chadwick. She dialled the number. After several rings it was answered, by a thin, elderly voice.

'Is that Mrs Chadwick?'

'Yes, Mrs Florence Chadwick . . .'

'I wonder if you can help me. I'm doing some research into the history of Allbright's mill, and I wondered if I might interview you. My name's Agnes . . .'

'Allbright's? Oh, dear, I'm not sure I'm the right person, I don't know, I haven't had much to do with the mill, my late husband, you see, after he died – and it was so long ago, and I never really worked there myself . . .'

'Really, any information is welcome.'

'But I know so little.'

'You must have heard your husband talk about it, perhaps, there must be things you'd remember from him?'

There was a little silence.

'When would you want to come?' Florence asked.

'Whenever's convenient to you.'

'Oh, anytime's convenient to me. I'm not going anywhere. Today, tomorrow . . .'

'Today? Early evening?'

'Well, if you're sure you won't be wasting your time. About seven, then?'

'That would be lovely. It's still Myddleton Terrace, is it?'

'That's right, number fifteen.'

'Thank you so much.'

'Goodbye.'

Agnes hung up. She glanced at the rota above her desk, which told her she was on house duty this evening. She got up and poured her tea, allowing herself to appreciate the mist of fragrant steam against the smooth curve of the cup in an attempt to quell the jagged anticipation of yet more conflict with the demands of school life.

At lunchtime she saw Charlotte on her own in a corner of the dining hall. Charlotte looked up as she joined her.

'Oh, Sister Agnes.'

'How's things?'

'OK.'

'Are you looking forward to the Easter holidays?'

'Not really.'

'Where will you go?'

'To Mum and Dad's. It'll be awful. They're so cross with me.'

'They're pretty cross with us.'

'It wasn't the school's fault I met Mark.'

'We could have prevented you seeing him.'

Charlotte looked at her. 'No you couldn't.'

'Well, you can understand their feelings. They want to protect you.'

Charlotte fell silent. After a moment she said, 'Like Mark.'

'What's like Mark?'

'The way he wanted to protect those birds. He really cared about them. And it led to him dying. It's not fair. What kind of God rewards people like that? His birds come back for the spring, and he goes up to see them, and . . .' She covered her face with her hands. 'It doesn't go away, Sister Agnes, it just gets worse . . .'

Her eyes filled with tears. 'It was only because he cared so much, it's just not fair . . .'

'Come on, let's sit quietly somewhere.' Agnes led her from the dining hall, aware of the stares and murmurs of the other girls.

Myddleton Terrace was part of the old town, facing away from the estate, a row of Victorian houses, of old yellow stone blackened by age and smog.

'They were building them estates after the war, but my Ray refused to have owt to do wi' em.' Florence Chadwick led Agnes into the small front room. She had tight white curls of hair and bright blue eyes. The room was neatly arranged, furnished in pink and cream. A fire burned in the grate. 'I couldn't see it myself, lovely new houses they were, and these weren't what they are now. Funny how things change. My nephew put that fire in for me last month. Wouldn't have been seen dead wi' one of them when I were first married, it were all the gas then. Cup of tea, love?'

Agnes followed her into the kitchen, which had bright white units and matching worktops. 'My nephew did this too,' Florence said. 'He looks after me, does our Danny.' She arranged two cups on a tray. 'I've looked out some bits and pieces for you,' she said, 'from the mill days. I don't know if they'll be any good. Is it for a book, then?' She led Agnes back into the front room.

'Sort of,' Agnes mumbled, sitting on the sofa.

'There's a lot of it about, these days. People tracing the past. Funny how things change. I'm not much use to you, really, love, my Ray worked there, but he were dead before he reached thirty-five.'

'I'm sorry to hear—'

'Aye, from the war. They should never have made him work, he should have been on the sick like Mrs Finch's boy down the road, never worked again. And my Ray were taken worse than him. Chest injury, y'see, shrapnel, wi' his lungs, and them fibres in the mill, in them days, terrible. Coughin' and wheezin'. Killed him in the end.' She stirred sugar into her tea, her fingers rattling the spoon.

'How terrible for you.'

Florence sipped her tea for a moment. She put the cup down then reached across for a photo album, which she offered to Agnes.

'I've put bits and pieces in there over the years.'

Agnes began to turn the pages. There were photographs, a group of soldiers, a smart man in uniform. 'That were him,' Florence said, following Agnes's gaze. Agnes saw a strong, angular face, short dark hair. Then there were several similar photographs, all depicting a long line of millworkers standing outside Allbright's. The mill seemed somehow alive behind them, the name still crisply engraved on the archway, the sunlight lending brightness to the stone.

'I never married again,' Florence said.

Agnes turned a page. She found herself looking at Reg's signature. 'Allbright's Amateur Athletics Team', the paper said. It was a roll call of names, most of which she didn't recognise. Ray Chadwick, it said. Ernest Coulter. Reg Naismith, July 1949. 'Reg was running the athletics team even then?' she said.

'It were the love of his life. Kept him going, I reckon. He didn't have much of a life aside from that. Great mates with our Ray, too.' On the next page was a yellowing press cutting. 'Allbright's Team: Victorious Return', it said. There were three men in uniform. 'There you are, see,' Florence was saying, 'Reg, Ray and Ernest. Brothers in arms, they were. Before the war, when they were just lads, they were the stars of the athletics team; and they all came back from the war together. Heroes, they were.' She smiled. 'Forgotten now, of course. Funny how things change.' She finished her cup of tea. 'And the war took its toll, that's what no one'll tell you now. The price them young men paid. Not only with their lives. Sometimes I thought the dead were the lucky ones. It were the walkin' wounded I felt sorry for. Like Ernest. He lost his sight in the end.' Agnes felt her cup fall from her grasp. 'Oopsy daisy,' Florence said. 'Lucky you'd finished.'

Agnes retrieved the empty cup from the carpet and placed it on the tray.

'And my Ray, of course,' Florence said. 'A slow death. And it weren't just the lungs, no. It were the mind, that's what no one saw. Them three boys, all of 'em, Ernest's wife Millie, she saw it too, there were summat different about them when they came back. Psychological, you'd call it now. People who knew Reg well, they saw it. He'd fly off the handle, for nowt. And my Ray were the same. Rages the like of which he'd never had before the war. Like a child, almost. Like he were lookin' to me to make it better, and I never knew what it were that were wrong, and I'd be pleadin' with 'im to tell me, what is it, love, and that just made him worse . . .' She broke off, blinking, breathless. 'It's a while since I've talked about these things, love, I'm sorry.'

'Go on.'

'And no one said nowt. And now I think, the wives, like – we suffered during the war, but in a way we suffered worse after the war, when our husbands were returned to us, and they'd changed. And we never knew what they'd been through, what they'd seen. Burma, it was, in the jungle. You heard things afterwards, you know, about the fighting there, terrible things. And them three lads, Ernie and Reg and Ray, they were closer to each other than they were to anyone else, I reckon, because they knew. Whatever they'd seen, whatever horror it was, they kept it to themselves. It were Millie I felt most for, Ernie lived to old age, she had that for the rest of her married life. A stranger, sitting at her table, sleepin' in her bed. Although at least they had their little girl. But you see, in those days, no one said owt. You couldn't talk about things in those days, like you can now, everything about people's married lives all over the newspapers these days, things you don't even want to know about.'

'Did Ernest stay at the mill, even when he was blind?'

'They retired him early. Poor Millie. She was stuck with him then, day in, day out. She grew to hate him, though she'd never say so. You didn't, you see.'

'Is she still alive?'

'Oh, aye.' Florence frowned. 'She's had a difficult time of it. Lives just here, on the corner, number fifty-four.'

'So Reg was all that was left of the athletics team.'

'He built it up again, though, Reg did. Got the younger lads involved, kept it goin' till he retired. He had staying power, did Reg. That's what they need now, those lads up on the estate there, someone like Reg to see things through. Teach 'em self reliance. And for that to happen to him. Poor man. Never deserved an ending like that. I were that shocked when I heard. Terrible. Bad goings on up there, I'll always be grateful to my Ray for staying put in this house. It were his mother's house, been in her family since it were built. We ripped out all the fireplaces, years ago, all the wood panelling and that, and now our Danny has paid a fortune to buy fireplaces that look just the same and put them back in. Funny how things change, int'it?'

Driving back to the convent, Agnes thought about the three friends, the scars of war. Shrapnel, mental problems. And Ernest had lost his sight, lost the use of his eyes. Something about this made her feel cold. She thought about Nina's mother. She wished she'd borrowed the Warburton file after all.

She got back to her room too late for supper. She found a note had been slipped under the door, sealed in a crisp white envelope. She switched on the light, sat at her desk, opened the note. It was from Philomena, as she knew it would be.

'Sister Agnes,' it began. 'Where are you? Here one minute and gone the next. Come to see me tomorrow at 11 a.m. Sister Philomena.'

Agnes sat with the note and read it. She got up and poured herself a whisky, then read the note again. She recalled former such meetings with other superiors, the catalogue of her failings, the insistence that she reflect upon her place in the order. Philomena might even suggest she leave. The thought brought her a huge sense of relief, that the decision might be made for her, that the order might eject her, might free her to go away with James after all.

She settled to her evening prayers. An image filled her mind of a pair of falcons returning for the spring.

She woke on Friday morning with a profound sense of peace. She lay in bed, watching the sunlight through the trees dappling the curtains, wondering why the prospect of meeting Sister Philomena should have the effect of calming her like this. At breakfast she joined her house.

'What's up?' Sister Teresa asked.

'What do you mean?'

'You've been wishing everyone a good morning. The girls'll be wondering what's going on. They rely on you not to speak until about ten.'

'I've got a meeting with Philomena this morning. About my bad behaviour.'

'Oh. Right.' Teresa looked at her. 'Terror, eh? It gets people funny ways.'

★ ★ ★

'What do you mean, you want my mother's file?' Nina's voice on the phone was indignant.

'I know it sounds crazy, but I keep thinking about Mark's binoculars lying in the mud.'

'And?'

'And one of Reg's friends lost his sight.'

'So? Did anything happen to him?'

'No, but –'

'Well then.'

'It's just, your mother . . .'

'What about my mother?'

'And her failing sight . . .'

'Agnes, it makes no sense at all.'

'No. Nina – it's just a hunch. Please.'

Nina sighed. 'OK. When can you come in?'

'Monday?'

'Listen, I'll drop it off Sunday, OK? But I must have them all back Monday morning, Turnbull's really itchy about missing files since I sorted them all, and he's doing a check then.'

Philomena appeared in her office with two polystyrene cups of instant coffee. She gestured to Agnes to sit, then sipped her coffee, pulled a face and tipped it into the rubber plant by the window. She tapped on the window, and a tabby cat appeared on the windowsill outside and pressed its nose to the glass. She bent down and made mewing noises at it, then turned to Agnes. 'Right. Bit of a chat, eh?'

Agnes waited.

'Of course, can't say I wasn't warned,' she said, sitting down.

'Warned?'

'About you.' She picked up the empty coffee cup, sipped from it, peered into it and put it down. 'Trouble, they said.'

Agnes waited.

'And they were right.' Agnes felt like getting up and walking out, but Philomena went on, 'Just like me, you see. Bloody struggle, whole bloody business. Isn't it?' She waited for an answer.

'Um – well, of course . . .'

'Terrible. Couldn't stick it myself. For years. Joined one order. Over the bloody wall after five years. Out in the world after that. Odd jobs. Haberdashery. Milliners. Dental nurse.' Philomena let out a sudden bark of laughter. 'Waste of bloody time.' She jerked her head towards the ceiling. 'Had other plans, didn't He. So here I am.'

Outside a fresh breeze stirred the branches of the trees. The horse chestnuts were showing new green buds. The tabby cat had clawed its way up a tree after a bird, and now sat there looking foolish.

'Life,' Philomena said. 'Like mud. Floundering about, all of us. Only He knows.' Philomena tilted her chin and fixed Agnes with her bright gaze.

Agnes felt a sudden overwhelming need to confide in her. 'But – but it's so difficult. I mean, how do we know?'

Philomena nodded. 'It's a complete bloody mystery.'

'And I can't change . . .'

'No no no. Not change. No point.'

'Then, I mean – how do I – what shall I . . .?'

Philomena stood up and went over to the window. 'Oliver Plunkett,' she said.

'What?'

'Silly moggie, he's always going after those birds. Stuck on a branch now. I'll have to get old Joseph out with his ladder again.' She turned back to Agnes. 'What were we saying?'

'About how one makes the right decisions . . .'

'Ah, yes. Thing is, you see, I realised, in the end – I saw that I didn't have to be happy. Blinding inspiration. Weight off my mind. I was free then. Free to be glum. Didn't matter a fig. And the funny thing was, once I'd seen that, stopped being glum. Queer old show.' She went over to the door and Agnes realised the interview was at an end.

'But it's not happiness I'm chasing.' Agnes stood up. 'I don't know how best to live, that's all.'

Philomena nodded. 'Mud,' she said. 'But at least He's got an aerial view.' She opened the door, and Agnes felt her gaze appraising her. 'Glum for years, I was,' Philomena said. 'Didn't matter a jot.' She smiled at Agnes.

Agnes realised that nothing had been resolved. 'But what shall we – what do you want me to do?'

Philomena shrugged, and smiled. 'Decisions. Damned illusions. Even my own.' She began to chuckle, and went back into her office and closed the door, still chuckling.

Chapter Seventeen

'Who dare argue against me?' Elias's face seemed set in defiance as he read the Palm Sunday lesson. 'Let us confront one another. Who will dispute my cause? Let him come forward. The Lord God will help me – who then can prove me guilty?'

The term was almost finished. Some of the younger girls had already gone home. The chapel echoed with Elias's words.

Afterwards Agnes walked on the moor. There was a freshness in the breeze, and the ground was soft underfoot. She watched the changing sky, the clouds fringed with light as the sun broke through. I could just stay here, she thought. I could just accept, stay in my tiny room, resign myself to the community routine . . . Our year would pass, and then the next, and soon it would all be over, and I would have been an obedient nun all my life. She thought of Elias, how he seemed to have relinquished his will to some higher force. Perhaps she should try to do the same, to accept whatever life, or God, put in her way. But Elias is so weighted down by it all. That isn't acceptance, she thought. That's just evasion. Evasion of life itself.

An image returned to her, of Jo's painting, of the withered roses and the clock face. She thought about the old still-life paintings in Baines's attic, the grapes, painted with such a sense of wonder that they seemed to glow with it; the lemons, shining with lemon-ness.

If I shut myself away, Agnes thought, it won't be an acceptance of God's will. It will be a refusal, a turning away.

And yet – she could almost hear Julius's voice – perhaps it's in the turning away that one comes to find joy, perhaps it's in the stillness of acceptance that one finds one's true nature, like the lemons and the grapes.

Agnes had reached the foot of a crag, and now stood in its shadow, listening to the wind buffeting the stone.

Life is too short to turn away from the chance to live with joy.

Or, life is too short to make a decision that turns out to be the wrong one.

Is there an answer? She wanted to shout out loud, so that the echo would carry her words across the valley; so that the wind might bring her an answer.

She turned back across the moors, descending towards the school. She was due at James's in less than an hour.

'Who'd have thought a mere American would know about afternoon tea?' Evelyn gestured to the table, which was carefully arranged with sandwiches and cakes.

'He's not entirely American,' Agnes said. 'Be charitable.'

'And anyway,' Joss said, 'wasn't Agnes's father American?'

'Not really. English, mostly. He just ended up living in the States.'

'It's a favourite occupation, I find,' James said, coming into the room with the tea tray, 'maligning my countrymen. A national English pastime. And after all we've done for you.'

'What have you done for us?' Joss laughed. 'Apart from smearing a sort of phoney junk culture on the surface of English life.'

'You don't care anyway, dear,' Evelyn said. 'You're far too much a Scot to care what befalls the English.'

Joss laughed and patted her hand. 'That's just the point. We know all about cultural imperialism.'

'I play golf, for Heaven's sake.'

'We all play golf, James. That's just globalisation. Even William Baines plays golf.'

'How is William?' James asked.

Evelyn glanced at Joss. 'We hardly see him,' she said.

'Do you have any news?' Joss asked James.

'Only from Isabel, my cleaner, she works for him too. She says he's pretty distraught. This mill business seems to have gone very wrong indeed.'

Evelyn sighed. 'Poor man. Such a noble spirit. But ever since his wife died . . .'

'It's the anniversary,' Joss said. 'Of her death.'

'Only a year? Surely not,' James said.

'Good Friday, she died.' Joss twisted his napkin around his finger. 'Last year.'

'It goes against all wisdom.' James began to pour the tea. 'Making huge life changes so soon after a bereavement. He should have waited. No wonder it's gone wrong, handing over the mill. He must be mad with grief.'

'I think that's just it.' Evelyn took the cup he handed her. 'Mad with grief.'

'And they were devoted, weren't they,' James went on.

'Oh, yes,' Joss murmured, staring at the floor, and Evelyn nudged him to indicate that James was holding his cup out to him. He looked up vaguely, then took the cup. 'Devoted. Hannah and William.'

'Which makes this anniversary all the more worrying, then,' James said. 'We must make sure we keep an eye on him.'

'Hannah and William,' Joss said again. He looked at his tea cup as if surprised it should be there at all. Agnes watched him. Then Evelyn took the cup from him and put it on the little table at his side. 'You were about to spill it, dear,' she said.

Joss looked up at her, took her hand and grasped it for a moment as their eyes met.

Later Agnes helped James wash up. The Campbells had gone, and the house was quiet with the evening.

'James?'

'Yes?'

'How long have Evelyn and Joss known William Baines?'

'Oh, years.'

'And have they always been close to him?'

'In the old days, yes. More recently, it seems that –'

'What?'

'I don't know. Evelyn said something about the friendship having changed. When they came back from the States, she said, it was different.'

'Perhaps time changes things.'

'Does it?' Agnes glanced at him, but he looked away.

'Hannah had died, of course,' she said.

'Yes. That kind of thing changes people. Perhaps that's all it is.'

'They're still fond of him.'

'They're good people. When I had to see my doctor last week—'

'James – you didn't tell me.'

'Oh, I see him so often these days, it's hardly news.'

'And?'

'They were very sweet, the Campbells. Made me cups of tea, allowed me to pace and rage and shake my fist at the sky, until the mood passed.'

'Tell me what he said.'

James was gazing out at his garden, at the darkness beyond. 'He said, if I'm going to do this trip, not to leave it till next year.' He turned to Agnes and smiled at her, and she saw his acceptance of the ending of his life. She wanted to seize hold of him, as if somehow she could make him immortal just by holding on to him. She touched his sleeve.

'I'll decide very soon,' she said.

He looked at her fingers on the cloth of his jacket. 'Perhaps I'll go alone,' he said.

'No!' the word burst out of her.

'What's the point of you tearing your life to shreds for the sake of a few months – maybe a few weeks . . .' He raised his eyes to hers and again he smiled. 'If you break your obedience vows and it turns out we get no further than two weeks in St Tropez, I'll never forgive myself.'

She laughed in spite of herself. 'At least you won't be around to care.'

He was serious then. 'Agnes, that's not what I want. I don't want to burden you with caring for a dying man. I want us to go before . . . before . . .'

She took his hands in hers. 'James, I'll let you know very soon. I promise.'

'Any more words of wisdom from Julius?'

'No. But then again, I haven't dared ask him.'

She got back to find that Nina had dropped off her mother's file, and a set of keys, with a note. 'I'm late in tomorrow, please return these yourself, I'm counting on you.'

The file was marked 'Warburton, Louisa'. 'Baxter' was crossed out. There were addresses, past and present, date of birth. Some notes related to tax and National Insurance. Details of her retirement, which gave a number and said, 'Refer to Pension Fund'. A certificate of maternity leave for 1973. A couple of sick notes. One mentioned glaucoma and someone had underlined this in red. Next to it, also in red, Agnes saw 'Refer to document A52N'. Agnes flicked through the file but couldn't find any such document.

She put on the kettle and settled down at her desk. She turned to Ernest Coulter's file. There were yellowing certificates of service which dated back to the war. Ernest had joined the mill in 1938 at the age of fifteen. In 1941 he'd been called up to join the Army. He'd returned to the mill in 1946. There was a certificate from the Army, describing in cold detail his medical condition on leaving. Facial injuries. She noticed a period of absence in the spring of 1947, and a doctor's note which mentioned nervous exhaustion. He returned to work in October 1947.

The similarity with Reg startled her. The same condition, the same length of absence. There were other periods of leave, one for a day to attend his daughter's wedding on 15 May, 1969. One for a funeral. Then she found a memo: 'Re. Coulter, Ernest. We have today agreed that due to his failing sight, he will be moved from machinework. We have agreed with Mr Coulter a programme of work which will be compatible with his disability.' It was dated July 1978.

After that there were papers to do with his early retirement and pension fund, and a doctor's certificate which gave details of his blindness. Again, in red handwriting it said, 'Refer to document A52N'. Again, no such document was in the file.

Agnes replaced the papers carefully. This daughter, she thought, staring at her heaps of files. The daughter's wedding, 1969, she thought, pulling out a file marked 'Press Cuttings, personnel'. There were a few jumbled, shabby cuttings. May 1969, she thought. Although there was no reason to believe that the Allbright's archives would extend to the marriage of daughters of workers, she thought. She saw 29 April, 1969. The story was about the mill's old drayhorses, and the photo showed two shire horses harnessed to an old-fashioned cart in the mill courtyard. She pulled out the next cutting. 'Athletics Team sees out Daphne in Style', the headline said. It was dated 20 May 1969.

'The boys from Allbright's Athletics put on a special show for a special girl last Saturday, when Daphne Coulter stepped out on her wedding day. And the lucky groom, Robert Snaith . . .'

Agnes stared at the yellowing newsprint. Daphne Snaith. Her father was blind. Her children . . . In her mind Agnes saw the binoculars, the curve of the arc as they flew up into the air, the mud splashing as they landed. Her children . . . If she had two boys . . . If . . .

Births, she thought, returning the cutting to its place. Births. From the press cuttings? Or perhaps it would be easier . . . If only she had the file . . . Her eyes scanned the heap of files. Snaith, D. She pulled it out. On the front it said, Snaith, Daphne. 'Coulter' was written on the front of the file, crossed out. Agnes rifled through the sheets of paper, her hands shaking. There were two certificates of maternity leave in her file, for a boy born 1971, named David. And in 1974, Mark.

She stared at the names, reading them over and over again, her mind struggling as an idea formed, a pattern took shape. Ernest Coulter lost his sight. Louisa Warburton lost her sight. Both were in the employ of the mill. And their descendants were Mark. David. And Nina.

Reg, she thought. It doesn't explain why Reg should also . . . And what was document A52N? And where was it?

Agnes put on her coat, gathered up all the files and went out. She drove fast.

The single-storey spinning sheds were floodlit across the courtyard, leaving the old mill in shadow. She went straight to the admin block, unlocking the door, then let herself into Nina's office and by the light of the torch carefully replaced all the files.

She remembered what Nina had said about Turnbull looking for a missing file, his insistence that it was something to do with Baines. Her torch beam scanned the boxes on the floor. Inland Revenue, she saw, VAT, Price Lists, Weavers Lists . . .

She stood up, switched off her torch and left the office, locking the door behind her. She slipped across the shadows of the courtyard and tried the door of the derelict mill, which opened. She ran up the stairs and tried Baines's door. It was locked. She tried key after key on Nina's bunch, until at last a brass Yale turned in the lock, and the door gave.

The room seemed huge and bare in the torch beam. The boxes of files distributed around the floor were gone. The desk was still there, its polished surface empty. There was a chair in one corner. There was nowhere to hide a file. She thought of Baines living out his last weeks in this room, torn apart by his loss, by the desertion of his favourite daughter. She remembered how he'd come to find Nina, saying it was too late, filthy, she'd said, really filthy. Agnes glanced at the empty hearth, the old bricks scattered with soot. Soot.

Agnes went to the fireplace and shone her torch up the flue. She reached up and ran her hands around the brickwork. She could feel nothing.

This is crazy, she thought. I'm looking for a document, and I've now convinced myself that Baines hid it up the chimney. I've allowed some kind of fantasy to get the better of me. She flashed her torch around the chimney again, and saw nothing at all. She was just about to leave when she heard a shout from the courtyard, then several more, loud male voices. As they got nearer, she could make out the words.

'You bastard Micksy,' someone shouted.

'Shut it, Keenan. What about your girlfriend, eh? Your older woman?'

'Leave it, you tosser.'

'That the best you can get, eh, Keenan? She must be at least fifty. And is she still a virgin?'

There was the sound of scuffling, more shouts, jeering laughter. Agnes backed against the wall by the window, then peered round a fraction. The courtyard was floodlit, and people walked across it towards the gate. The evening shift, Agnes supposed, giving way to the dawn shift. From the archway she could see another group of people arriving, and for a moment the two lines met, exchanged a few words, their long shadows mingling in the arcs of light. Agnes saw Billy Keenan by the gate, his laughing face caught in the glare, before he turned and sloped off home up the hill.

There was silence again. Agnes thought about Baines. Mad with grief, Evelyn had said. Madness, Agnes thought, is usually based on reason. Agnes put on her gloves and placed the chair under the chimney flue. She climbed up, then braced herself with her back against the brickwork. She wedged one foot on the bricks, then the other further up, and found she could climb far enough to hold on to a ridge inside the flue. Then she found a foothold, and was soon about a yard inside the chimney.

It was pitch dark. She'd left her torch on the desk. She gripped the ridge with one hand and with the other felt around the edge of the flue. Her hand touched something. She fingered it. A square edge. Paper. She pulled it out, and realised she was holding a bundle, tied with tape. She tucked it into her trousers, and climbed back down the chimney, dropping on to the hearth. She picked up her torch and shone it on to her find.

There was a label attached to the tape. 'A52N' it said.

Chapter Eighteen

Agnes picked up her phone, glanced at her clock, put the phone down again. It was 2:34 a.m. Nina wouldn't thank her for waking her now. Even though what she had to tell her was important. Very important.

Agnes looked at the curled old paper spread out before her, its pink tape hanging down. It was a Deed of Trust, made out in the name of Jeremiah Baines and dated 1869. She read through it again, the ornate Victorian language winding around her mind, trying to assure herself of the truth of what she'd read. That Jeremiah Baines, in honour of his own beloved and devoted wife Dorothea, who had suffered her own loss of sight with such faith and fortitude, does hereby declare that any of his employees, and any employee of Allbright's hereafter, who do lose their sight while in the service of the mill, shall be recipients of a sum of money, the amount to be decided hereafter . . . And such money shall be entrusted to their descendants insofar as children and grandchildren . . .

Agnes put the pages down again. David, Mark and Nina. All grandchildren of people who have lost their sight, employees of Allbright's. And Mark's eyes . . . and Nina's attack . . . and David's photograph . . .

Her clock flashed 2:40 a.m. Still too early to phone Nina and tell her – tell her what, exactly? That she was owed money? Perhaps she got the money, perhaps Louisa did, and the Snaiths, perhaps it was all paid direct, so straightforward that they'd neglected to mention it. Perhaps this document meant nothing at all.

But then why hide it up the chimney?

Agnes lifted the pages, flicking through to the end, looking for some sign that the trust was annulled. The parchment gave way to thick, inky paper, which gave way to typeface. She saw the signature 'William Baines', the date, 'September 1954'. She read the text above it, then read it again. It seemed to say that as at present there were no employees or descendants who met the criteria for receiving the trust moneys, and as the mill was short of funds, the money kept in trust was to be made available for the financing of redundancies. But in order not to break the terms of the trust as set down by his great-grandfather Jeremiah, any future employee who was found to comply with the terms would be granted one hundred shares in the company, as would their children and grandchildren as laid down by Jeremiah.

David, Mark and Nina were entitled to shares in Allbright's. David, Mark and Nina could stop Turnbull selling the company. Mark could have stopped Turnbull selling the mill. If . . .

Agnes felt very cold. She stood up and switched on her heater, and sat by it, pulling her cardigan around her. Perhaps she should phone the police. But what would she say? That Anthony Turnbull was so desperate to sell the mill that he'd followed Mark to the moors and –

And perhaps Anthony Turnbull didn't know about this document. Perhaps all he knew was that Baines had hidden something that was connected to the sale of the mill.

And Reg, she thought. Had one of Reg's relatives lost their sight?

It was 2:59 a.m.

She undressed and got into bed. She lay awake, staring at the ceiling, for a long time, before settling into an uneasy sleep.

Before dawn she tried David's mobile number but a recorded voice said it was switched off.

She phoned Nina, and a sleepy voice answered.

'I'm sorry, it's early –'

'Too right it is.' Nina sounded cross.

'It's important.'

'Did you put my files back last night?'

'Yes, but this is more important – can I come round?'

'Now?'

'Yes.'

'If you must. I'll get dressed.'

They sat with mugs of tea. Nina read and re-read the pages that Agnes spread before her.

'Did you know anything about this?'

216

'Nothing at all.' Nina turned another page. 'It's – it's unbelievable. It must have just been convenient to Baines to forget about it, as no one was around who knew.'

'I suppose with the mill needing the cash –'

'And there's my mum, you said –'

'And Ernest Coulter, who was David and Mark's grandfather . . .'

Nina raised her eyes from the parchment. 'But people still knew about the trust in his days, judging from this.'

'He'd have got the money, maybe. But then, after the war, there were so many other pension things . . .'

'Mmmm. Maybe. I can't take it in.'

'It means you're still in danger. And David.'

'But why?'

'Because you have a share in the mill.'

'If all this is true. It's a big if.'

'Baines hid it. Turnbull's looking for it. It must still be true.'

'Oh God. Shall we tell the police?'

'I suppose so. Although I'm not sure what we say.'

'That Turnbull's on the loose and he's a mad man.'

'It might not be –'

'I want him out of the way. He's been really odd recently.'

'Nina, they won't arrest him immediately, even if we tell them. There's no evidence –'

'Funny that. If it was Jay, he'd be banged up in police cells before you could say Racist Police State.'

'But it's not Jay.'

'No, and Turnbull's not black.'

Agnes began to roll the papers up. 'What shall we do, then?'

'Dunno. I can't think straight. I ought to get Rosie up and get ready for work.'

'You can't go back there now.'

'Why not? As far as Turnbull knows, nothing's changed. That file's still missing, if that's the one he's after.'

'So you're really determined to go into work?'

'What'll he think if I don't?'

'I'll drive you, then.'

In the courtyard, two figures were shouting at each other, one elegant in camel coat and court shoes, the other wrapped in a skimpy denim jacket and high heels. Agnes turned into the car park and stopped the car.

'Patricia,' Nina said.

'And Lianna.'

'Who's she?'

They got out of the car.

'She lives on the estate,' Agnes began.

'Don't you call me a slut,' Lianna was shouting, teetering across the courtyard towards Patricia. Faces appeared at windows behind them.

'Coming in here, accusing my husband –' Patricia's voice was shrill.

'Listen to you on your high horse. All I've come here for –'

'You've come to make trouble, and you can bloody well go away again. Things are bad enough for Anthony without you –'

'Oh, poor, poor Anthony. Well listen to me, lady, your bloody Anthony promised me –'

'I'm not interested,' Patricia shouted.

'I've only come to get what's mine, what he said he'd give me!'

'I'm sure he said nothing of the sort. The idea that Anthony would make promises to a cheap tart like –'

'Tart am I? And what does that make you, eh? Who buys your clothes? Who pays for your bleedin' five bedroom three bathroom Jacuzzi bloody three acre pad, eh? And you think you're better than me – what're you doing here?' Lianna turned in astonishment as Agnes took hold of her arm.

'Perhaps that's enough, Lianna, don't you think?'

'I only want what's mine,' Lianna said.

Nina had gone to Patricia, and now put her arm around her and ushered her inside.

'And what is yours? Someone else's husband?'

'Maybe.'

They sat on the car park wall.

'All I want,' Lianna said, 'is what he said he'd give me.'

'And what was that?'

'He came to see me, right, 'cos he knew me from the sports centre, when we were all doing that, right, well, not me, but I knew I knew Mark and that, and he asked me about Billy Keenan, and them papers –'

218

'What papers?'

'Billy and Mark had some of the accounts for the centre, and did I know where they were, as I know Billy, and I said I didn't know, 'cos I don't, right, and I don't have much to do with Billy, like lots of folk round here, and he were dead nice to me, Turnbull were, and he give me some money, and he said he'd look after me, and he were talking about this flat he knew about, over Ilkley way, dead posh, he said I could have it –'

'When was this?'

'Day before yesterday. And so I waited yesterday, and nothing happened, and then – and then someone I don't want to see is trying to get to me, and I thought, if I could get away, that'd be it, then, I'd be able to get on wi' me life, and now that old slag of a wife of his says he's gone off somewhere, and I've nowhere to go, and he said, he promised . . .' Lianna burst into tears.

Agnes waited until her sobbing had subsided. 'I'd better take you home,' she said.

Lianna stood up, swaying on her high heels. She sniffed. 'They're all bastards in the end, aren't they?'

'Lianna?' Agnes opened the passenger door for her, and Lianna got in. 'It wasn't Turnbull who—'

'Who beat me up?' Lianna laughed. 'No, it weren't. Why? D'you think he's the sort?'

'Right now, I don't know anything about that man at all.'

They drove to Lianna's house. As they approached, Lianna covered her face with her hands and burst into tears again.

'I can't . . .' she was saying.

'Who are you scared of?'

She shook her head.

'Lianna – if you tell me, I can help –'

'No one can help.' She took her hands from her face.

'Why was Turnbull promising you a flat?'

'He thinks I know more than I do. Billy's got something he wants. These papers. Turnbull's desperate for them. If I get Billy to hand them over, he'll help me.'

'Is it Billy you're frightened of?'

'No.'

'Who is it?'

'I'll tell you why I'm scared. 'Cos it's me, in the end. What I do to myself, with the smack an' that, in the end, it's me, in't it.' She opened the car door. 'Thanks for the lift.' She got out of the car and slammed the door.

On the drive back, Agnes found herself making plans for Lianna: she'd find her a convent house, she'd find her some kind of employment in the school, she'd get the convent to book her into a rehab unit, she'd ask Julius if he could find her something in London, away from all this, away from her dealer or pimp or whoever he was. In her mind she had rescued Lianna, had seen her start a new, clean life, before she realised that there was nothing she could do for Lianna. Nothing at all.

Patricia was sitting in Nina's office, dabbing at her face with a handkerchief. 'And I don't even know where he is now,' she was saying to Nina. She looked up as Agnes came into the room. 'Nina says you know that girl?'

'Yes. Lianna Vickers. She lives on the estate.'

'Do you think Anthony really made her those promises?'

'Do you?'

Patricia looked at Agnes, looked down at her hands which were screwing the handkerchief into a ball. 'I don't know. All I know is that I don't know my husband at all.'

'He's been gambling,' Nina said, bringing Agnes a mug of coffee.

'I wouldn't mind that so much,' Patricia said, tearful again, 'if it wasn't for – for . . . and to treat my father like that, to abuse his trust . . .' She started to cry again.

Agnes glanced at Nina. 'Anthony's borrowed heavily on the back of the mill,' Nina said.

'I opened a letter yesterday,' Patricia said, between sobs, 'because it said P Turnbull, but it was meant for him, they'd got the initial wrong. It was a final demand for tax on his other company. It's thousands. He hasn't got it. He's gambled it away. I went to his office then, he has a room in the house, and went through the desk. There's bills there, unopened, bank statements, VAT stuff – it's terrifying. I have nothing, it turns out. He's spent it all under me. It's like finding that I don't have a husband at all, why didn't he tell me, he could have confided in me, I'd have helped him . . .'

Nina went to her and put her arm round her. 'You have the mill.'

'For all I know he's sold it too.'

'He can't sell it without you, can he?'

'I've signed all sorts of documents recently, I keep thinking, what if there was some small print, something I overlooked . . . it's like having a stranger as a husband, he's so – he's so different, the Anthony I married was so generous and funny and full of life . . . and this one's just – he seems so detached now, so panicky, and I haven't seen him for two days now . . .'

'It'll be all right,' Nina said, gently.

'But Andrew said – Andrew McInnes, he's our solicitor. We went to sign a deed thing about Jo and Marcus, a few weeks ago, Daddy and me and Anthony. Oh, Daddy's such a fool. Such a stupid old man. Fancy trusting that pillock of a husband of mine . . . the only person who can run this place is Daddy, or family. True family. And he's signed Marcus out of it, and he tried to sign Jo out of it too. I'm such a stupid stupid bloody fool . . .' She started to cry again.

'He can't sell it,' Nina said, then glanced at Agnes.

'How can you be so sure?' Patricia said.

Nina took a deep breath. 'Because Agnes found an old document that your father had hidden up the chimney.'

'Found a what?'

'It may not mean anything,' Agnes said.

'That my father had – what is it?'

'It's about a trust –'

'It may be very dangerous,' Agnes interrupted Nina.

'But what? Why would he?'

'If you don't mind,' Agnes said, 'I think we should talk to your father about it, before we do anything else. I'll tell you more then.'

Patricia looked from one to the other with tearful, mascara-smeared eyes. She nodded. 'This evening, then? I'll phone him, I'll let him know we're coming.'

The school was on the edge of hysteria, with girls packing bags, endless streams of taxis and luggage and last-minute panics. Agnes found Charlotte in her room. On her bed was a large, expensive suitcase. It contained some neatly folded underwear and a couple of books. Charlotte was staring at it vaguely, and looked up when Agnes put her head round the door.

'Packing?'

'Sort of.'

'When are you going?'

'Tomorrow morning.'

'It'll be nice to see your parents.'

'Perhaps.' Charlotte folded a T-shirt and put it in the case.

'You can get some perspective on things.'

'But they don't know, do they? I've played it down to them, and now they'll be expecting to see me get on with my life like it was nothing at all, as if Mark meant nothing at all . . . at least here people know how much he meant to me, I can talk about it here . . .' She sat down on her bed.

Agnes put the suitcase on the floor and sat down next to her. 'You can always phone me here if you need to talk.'

'Will you be here?'

'Sure. I'm not going anywhere.'

Patricia pushed open the main gate, and was greeted by the dogs, who quietened instantly on seeing her and sniffed around Agnes instead. Agnes followed Patricia through the open back door, the darkened porch she'd last visited with Elias.

'Daddy?'

'Ah, there you are.' A light came on in the hall and William Baines was standing there. He was wearing a shabby jacket and crumpled trousers, and his hair was dishevelled.

'You remember Agnes, don't you?' Patricia began.

'You work with my other daughter, don't you?' Baines was staring at her.

'That's right. Before she left.'

Baines shook his head and with a shuffling gait led them into the drawing room.

'She left,' he echoed. He knelt in front of the gas fire and lit it, then switched on an ornate lamp that stood by the hearth, but the room still seemed dingy and chilled. He stood by the hearth, leaning against the heavy mahogany fireplace. 'She said she had to go. But it was my fault.'

'Daddy, perhaps Agnes would like—'

'Patricia knows, don't you? It was my fault she went. Everyone knows. Everyone can see that now. I can see that now. But I couldn't see it then.'

'Daddy—'

'I have been blind.'

'Please, Daddy . . .'

'I tried to make her –'

'Sherry?' Patricia said brightly, getting up. 'Or perhaps you'd prefer –'

'I tried to make her into something she couldn't be. She means so much to me, she was so precious to us, to Hannah . . .' Uttering his wife's name seemed to weary him, and he sat heavily into a chair.

'Shall I put the kettle on?' Patricia stood, helpless, her fixed smile fading as she looked at her father.

'I'll help you,' Agnes said, taking Patricia's arm and leading her from the room.

In the kitchen, Agnes said, 'Do you think we should tell him we found the document?'

'I don't know. He seems so – so fragile . . .' Patricia blinked back tears. 'Does he need to know?'

'I need to ask him if it's still valid.'

'Andrew can tell you that, our solicitor.'

'Perhaps that's best. I'm worried that if we tell your father now, he might think that you'll –'

'That I'll tell Anthony – that I'll betray him?'

'It sounds awful.'

Patricia shook her head. 'It's all such a mess, I just don't know what to do. The idea that Nina – and David – it's so hard to take it all in. And I suppose it's Anthony that he was hiding it from.'

'It must be.'

'Let's not say anything now, he seems so upset, and what with Mother's anniversary . . .'

Baines was sitting exactly as they'd left him. He was staring at the floor.

'We thought we'd have sherry instead,' Patricia trilled, pouring two very large glassfuls and handing one to Agnes. 'Do you want anything, Daddy?'

He looked up, and smiled at her. 'I have one daughter,' he said. He turned his head slowly to face Agnes. 'I still have one daughter.'

Chapter Nineteen

'The number you have called is not available. Please try again later.' Agnes switched off her phone, wondering how much longer David was going to stay out of reach. Not knowing where he was made her anxious. Perhaps I'll ask Janet Cole if she's heard from him, she thought, going into the shower, reaching for her Givenchy shower gel. Or maybe I'll get his address from Nina and go and call on him. Or maybe he's up in the hut on the moors, with Joanna, hiding.

Hiding from what?

The shower filled with steam, and in her mind she saw the moors shrouded with mist.

At breakfast she sat with Rachel Swann.

'It's your last chance to spy on me,' Rachel said, taking a small mouthful of dry cornflakes. 'I'm off home later today.'

'How does that feel?'

Rachel put down her spoon. 'Awful. Having to field endless questions about my progress, having my exam results relayed to all my aunts and uncles in enormous detail, being nagged about homework and practising . . . Can't I just stay here?'

'It's only a couple of weeks. Anyway, I warned them off.'

'You did what?'

'When I wrote to them. You can see the letter if you want. I told them that you were in a fragile state and must on no account be asked any questions about your schoolwork, your future or any related matter.'

'That's fantastic.'

'And that you, in turn, would try to eat.'

Rachel stared at her plate.

'It's fair, isn't it?'

'S'pose so.' Rachel picked up some cornflakes with her fingers.

'I wonder what we'll talk about instead.'

Agnes wandered to the staff-room and sat down with a cup of coffee. She flicked idly through a newspaper. The phone rang and she picked it up.

'Agnes, there's a call for you, hold on,' said Mary Watson.

'Agnes, thank God you're there!'

'Patricia?'

'I'm at my wits' end, Anthony's been arrested, I heard early this morning, he was held in police cells last night, oh God, I can't bear it –'

'Patricia – what for?'

'He was found drunk and disorderly in Bradford, in Manningham, I can't stand it, God knows what he's been doing . . . he'd been to a casino apparently, they picked him up in the small hours, they're holding him, he's lost the car somewhere, I've got to go and pick him up, will you come too . . .?'

'Yes, of course. Stay there, I'll come and get you. And pack some clean clothes for him while you're waiting.'

Anthony Turnbull shuffled out of his cell, staring at the ground. Without looking at Patricia he handed her a foul-smelling carrier bag.

'It was nice you brought him something else to wear,' the duty sergeant said. 'He weren't a pretty sight last night, were you, sir? Sign here, please.'

Turnbull's fingers shook on the pen.

'The press were on to us,' the sergeant said. 'Word had got out. We've tried to fend them off, but you might get some of 'em snooping around, just thought I'd warn you.'

'Thank you,' Patricia managed to say. She took Anthony's arm and followed Agnes to her car. As they passed a rubbish bin, she dropped the filthy carrier bag into it.

Anthony said nothing throughout the drive home. Patricia watched him get out of the car, saw him into the house, then insisted that Agnes drive her to the mill. She seemed sharpened, brought into focus by the events of the morning.

'Nina,' she smiled, walking into the office. 'I need that order for Pengelly on the ten by twelves today – and is the black acrylic in yet, it's getting late? And has Michael in sales heard anything back about the grey fleck worsted . . . I'll go and ask him.'

'What's got into her?' Nina asked, as Patricia swept down the stairs.

'Turnbull was found drunk and disorderly last night, after a two-day binge. We've picked him up from Bradford police station.'

'Wow. And what did her Dad say about the deed?'

Agnes flopped into a chair. 'We didn't tell him in the end. It's pitiful, Nina, a man like that, so frail now, so eaten up with guilt. We decided it was better if he continued to think the deed was hidden.'

'So we don't know –'

'Patricia's going to ask their lawyer about it.'

'Didn't Baines say anything?'

'Only that he blames himself about Jo running away. Only that he was blind and now he can see.'

Nina looked at Agnes, then frowned and went back to her typing.

Agnes wandered over to the filing cabinet and looked up the name Chadwick from the files she'd returned to Nina. Chadwick, Ray. She pulled it out. Date of birth, 13 October, 1921. Died 19 August, 1951, aged 29. Bald facts encompassing a lifetime of suffering. She turned to the medical history section, knowing already what she was going to find. There it was, the doctor's letter. 'Nervous exhaustion. Recommend a few weeks away.' The date was April 1947. Ray returned to the mill in October 1947.

All three. Reg, Ernest and Ray.

Nina's typing came to a halt. 'Haven't you got anything better to do than browse through confidential files, you nosy cow?'

Agnes put the file away. 'You're right. I have.' At the door, Agnes said, 'Remind Patricia to phone her solicitor.'

In the courtyard she listened to the rhythmic hum of the spinning sheds, and thought how odd it was that the work went on regardless, the inexorable process that turned the raw fleece into yarn, tonnes and tonnes of it per day, per hour, per minute, as if all the human drama of the mill played itself out to an unseeing, unfeeling, mechanised presence.

She drove to the police station and asked to see Janet Cole.

'You heard about Turnbull, then,' Janet said, showing her to a chair in the cramped office.

227

'Yes. Janet – has David Snaith been in touch with you?'

'No. Not for weeks. Not that I can think of. Mind you, I've been out on Morton's Crag a lot these last few days.'

'He was sent a photograph, didn't he show it to you?'

'No. What photograph?'

'Of the athletics team, it has Reg and Mark in it – and him. And someone had ringed him.'

'But – he should have—'

'And now I can't get hold of him, there's no answer . . .'

'We'll send someone to call on him. I'm glad you told me. I've been watching Mark's pair of peregrines. We thought we'd better go back to the beginning, watch for anybody behaving suspiciously around the nest.'

'And have you seen anyone?'

'No one. But the birds are grand, I could stay up there all day, you know.'

'Talking of Mark . . .' Agnes pulled Jeremiah Baines's Deed from her bag. 'There's something else I wanted to show you.'

On the way back to the school she drove past Florence Chadwick's house. She hesitated, then parked outside and tried the bell.

'Oh, it's you.' Florence peered at her, then stood back to let her in. 'I don't get many visitors. Our Danny says I shouldn't just open the door to anyone, but it makes you feel like a prisoner, don't it, all them bolts and chains and peep-holes. Have a cup of tea, love.'

'I wanted to ask you –' Agnes followed her into the kitchen. 'Something more –'

'About the mill? I doubt I'll be able to help, love, my memory's not what it was.'

'About Ray – and Ernest, and Reg – they seemed to get into some kind of trouble, just after the war.'

Florence carried the tea tray shakily into the front room. 'It's like I told you, love, they came back changed men. Always rowing, always quick to anger.'

'But I noticed from the mill records, they were all absent for a time.'

'Well, it were their health, my Ray, like I told you, his chest . . .' She lowered herself into a chair.

'But Reg too?'

Florence stirred sugar into her tea. 'I don't remember Reg being poorly. He weren't the type.'

'Can you remember why they might have all had a period of leave, in 1947 it was?'

Florence held her cup and saucer neatly on her lap. 'That were a bad time, those years after the war. A right bad time. Nightmares, my Ray used to have, on and off right up to his death, sobbing an' that, fast asleep, it right broke your heart to see it. Sometimes he'd call out, No, No. Wouldn't remember a thing the next day, I stopped asking him after a while, it only made him worse.'

'Did this happen as soon as he got back?'

'Not at once, no. To start with he seemed quite normal. Making an effort, I think he were. After a few months, then it started.'

'It must have been very difficult.'

'Aye, it weren't easy. Full of rage, he was, and hatred. Hated the Japs. And the Germans, after the war. Hated anything German, even anything that seemed German, like Jacob's Cream Crackers, I kept telling him, it's not even a German name, but it got to him for some reason. He weren't sane, you see. You hear more about it now, don't you, how people re-live terrible things they've suffered, and when I think about him and the others, just boys, out in that jungle, seeing God knows what – these days they'd claim for compensation, wouldn't they. We had nowt in those days, though, none of this counselling stuff you get these days. Funny how things change. You see, I can feel sorry for him now, but at the time, it were difficult, living it day by day.'

'And your neighbour, Millie –'

'She had it difficult too, worse than me.'

'And her grandson –'

'Mark, aye. Terrible business. Hit her very hard. She's got no one now, Daphne gone, and Robert and now Mark, tragic that is, only David, he's a good boy, keeps an eye on her, he were over there just yesterday evening, I popped round and saw him there.'

'David?'

'D'you know him?'

'A bit, yes.'

'Nice lad.'

'Was he – is he OK?'

'Seemed to be, love. They were playing Scrabble. Aye, seemed happy enough.'

* * *

Then why isn't he returning my calls, Agnes thought, driving back to the school. She'd missed lunch, again, and Rachel would be about to leave.

Rachel was standing by the steps with a huge suitcase.

'Hadn't you better wait inside, it's starting to rain?'

'The taxi said he'd be here any minute.'

They stood side by side, gazing along the driveway. The chestnut trees were flecked with green. A car appeared at the gates and slowly approached.

'There's your cab.'

'Yes.'

The car pulled up and the driver got out. 'Miss Swann?'

She nodded. He busied himself fitting the case into the boot, then opened the door for her. Her hair was misted with the rain. She turned to Agnes, gave her hug, then got into the car.

Perhaps his phone has run out of batteries, she thought, next morning, trying David yet again. Perhaps I should just walk up to the hut and wait for him. She put her phone in her raincoat pocket and went to get the car.

'Oh, hello love, you've just caught me.' Maureen stood aside to let her in.

'Is Billy around?'

'You've just missed him, he's over at Kitty's, she had a dripping tap, he often helps out with bits and pieces for them like that, her and her mum, and now her mum's gone, she seems to call on him more. Tell you what, we'll go down there, I'm due at the mill later, we can go from there. I'll just get my coat. To be honest,' she added, as she locked her door behind her, 'it's started up all sorts of rumours, him being friends with Kitty, just because he's a lad and she's a woman. I mean, I know they're close, and she does rely on him more now, but what I say is, it's none of anybody else's business, if two people try and find a bit of happiness together. If there's any truth in it, it might be the making of him.'

They passed the corner of the street, the red railings of the community centre straight ahead of them.

'Terrible shame that community centre,' Maureen said, 'nothing's come of that, you know. Like everything round here.

And it were so good for the kids, you know, like Billy, he turned a new leaf with all that.'

'Was he friends with Mark?'

'Well, that's what were so good, because like I said, there were no love lost between the Keenans and the Coulters, that were his mum, right, she were a Coulter.'

'What was the reason for that, then?'

'Oh, some feud. They say one of the Keenans stole a Coulter girl, years back, before the war, when they were all working in the other mill, across the valley there, Conningby's, closed down about twenty year ago now. The Coulters were chapel, you see, didn't take kindly to the Irish. These things stick, you see. So it were nice to see Mark and Billy getting on, water under the bridge, I don't hold with bearing grudges myself. Here we are.' Maureen pushed open the door. 'Kitty? It's me, love.'

'You after your Billy? He's still here.' Kitty came to the door. She looked at Agnes, and Agnes saw her face, her drawn, edgy features, the nervousness around her mouth.

'Hello, we met before, at Maureen's.'

Kitty tried to smile, and showed her into the living room.

'Sister Agnes wants a word with our Billy,' Maureen said.

'I'll call him, he's outside, something about the tap there.' Kitty went out into the kitchen.

The living room was cluttered, with the furniture squeezed together, and an oak cabinet in one corner which seemed to blot up all the light in the room. Maureen ran her fingers along the windowsill and looked at the dust on her fingertips.

'She's not looking after herself,' she murmured.

'Mother would have known,' they heard Kitty say from the kitchen. 'Something about a stop-cock, and where is it, and I know that Mother would have known, there's so much, you see, so much that's just gone with her . . .'

Billy appeared from the kitchen. 'Hiya, y'all right?'

Maureen stood up. 'I'll go and see to her, she's upset again.'

'Billy . . .' Agnes began, as he sat down opposite her. 'Those papers from the sports centre –'

'What about them?'

'You have them, don't you? You have the accounts, and Turnbull's nervous about them.'

'What if I do?'

'You can't keep them for ever, can you?'

'Right now, I'm keeping them.'

'What's in them?'

'Can't rightly say. Just boring old bits of paper, mostly.'

'So why do you need them?'

He grinned. 'Thing is, Sister, he owes me, does Turnbull.'

'So while he owes you, you're going to keep the papers?'

'Summat like that.'

'Something's going to go wrong, Billy. Turnbull's desperate, he might – he might –'

'Might what?'

'If you've got incriminating evidence, Billy –'

'Who says it's incriminating?'

'Shouldn't you go to the police?'

Billy laughed, showing two chipped front teeth.

'Billy – if you keep those papers, it's not just you who's in danger.'

He laughed again. 'Me, I'm used to trouble. Round here, you know, anything could just go up in flames.'

'But –'

'Nice of you to be concerned,' he said, standing up. 'I've got to go now, got to see a man about a tap washer.' He lumbered out of the door.

Agnes was left alone. She could hear Maureen and Kitty talking in low voices in the kitchen. She glanced around the room, at the collection of pottery milkmaids arranged on the mantelpiece, at a stack of audiobooks from the library; she could see several Barbara Cartlands among the titles. And another book. *Soaring Glory – The Peregrine Falcon.* Agnes picked it up, glanced through it. 'Chapter One, a Pedigree Ancestry; Chapter Two, Beloved of Kings; Chapter Three, Habitat and Breeding . . .' Agnes turned to the title page. From the library stamp, it appeared to have been borrowed about two months before.

Agnes quickly replaced it, then went into the kitchen to tell Maureen that Billy had gone.

She drove back to the school. A lone figure was sitting on the wall by the gates, a suitcase at her feet, her hair tied back at her neck. Agnes got out of her car.

Leonora was smiling at her. 'Don't say anything, this time I'm allowed to be here.'

'Are you going today?'

The girl nodded. 'My taxi will be here in a minute.'

'You'll miss the Maundy Thursday vigil tonight.'

'Mummy will probably drag me off to our local church – I'm sorry, Sister –' Leonora put her hand over her mouth, shocked at her own lapse of good manners. 'I mean, Mummy and I will attend our service at home . . .'

Agnes smiled. 'Will it be OK, going back, do you think?'

'I've no idea. It'll all be difficult, I suppose. Unless they pretend to be as they were. Come to think of it, they were pretending then anyway. Oh, I don't know, it's so confusing.' She swung her legs, staring at the ground. 'Just so long as they don't want me to be bridesmaid.'

They heard the hum of a motor engine, and a taxi appeared at the gates. Agnes helped Leonora down from the wall, and carried her suitcase to the waiting car.

'And will you still try to run away next term?'

Leonora laughed. 'Depends. I might run away altogether, not even come back next term.'

'What are the odds?'

Leonora frowned, considering. 'As things stand, about fifty-fifty.' She got into the car, her legs tucked neatly under her, then opened the window and smiled at Agnes.

'I won't put money on it, then,' Agnes laughed, waving her off as the car pulled out of the drive.

And what are the odds for me, she wondered, heading to her room. Fifty-fifty? Either I'll go, or I'll stay. Place your bets now.

Her footsteps echoed in the deserted corridors.

She sat at her desk and dialled James's number. It rang for a long time, then she heard him answer.

'James –'

'Agnes?'

'Are you all right?'

She heard the smile in his voice. 'Yes, of course I am. I was outside, and I heard the phone.'

'I just thought I'd see how you are.'

'Well, I'm just the same.'

'Good.'

'And you? How are you?'

233

'Oh, OK. It's Maundy Thursday.'

'Am I supposed to know what that means?'

'It's the commemoration of the Last Supper.'

'Ah. So it's Good Friday tomorrow?'

'That's right.'

'See, I'm learning.'

'James, I'm going to phone Julius now.'

'Right.'

'OK?'

'Sure.'

'I'll – I'll let you know what he says.'

'Sure. Whenever.'

'Bye.'

'Have a nice Maundy Thursday.'

She sat and stared at the phone, looked at her watch, stood up, put on the kettle, sat down again. She dialled Julius's number.

'I'm sorry –' she began, as he answered.

'Do all our conversations have to start that way these days?'

'But Julius, I know you're busy, I'm about to go to chapel myself, it's just –'

'Just what?'

'I need to – I need to decide.'

'Tonight?'

'Well, no, not quite tonight. But James hasn't got time on his side.'

Julius was quiet for a moment. 'He must understand he can't rush you.'

'He's trying not to.'

'If he really cares . . .'

'Julius, it's important that I see my mother.'

'Agnes, that's two weeks. They'd allow you that. It's just the world cruise bit that I can't quite see. Why give everything up just to feel sea-sick for weeks, just to eat far too much food and spend weeks cooped up with people you can't stand?'

'Julius –' In her mind Agnes saw Leonora sitting on the wall. 'If I don't go –'

'If you don't go, then that will be something to work with.'

'But the sense of loss . . .'

'Life is loss.'

234

'Even to live without joy?'

'Joy will come. Renunciation is essentially a joyful state.'

'I wish I was so sure.'

'So do I.'

Agnes smiled.

The chapel was stripped of all ornament, the altar was bare. There were fewer candles lit, and Elias moved in near darkness as he prepared the sacrament for the evening vigil. Agnes sat with the sisters, the resident members of staff and the few girls whose circumstances required them to stay at school for the holidays. She reflected on the passover, the message of redemption through sacrifice. She listened to the gospel reading, the Lord washing the feet of His disciples; the bread and the wine, the body and the blood; the sense of waiting, the inexorable playing out of the prophecy that would end in betrayal and death.

She glanced up at Elias. In the shadows he seemed restless, unshaven, dishevelled, and as his eyes met hers, she saw his despair. Through the murmured prayers she could hear other whispers, other voices, the call of birds of prey across the moors, Lianna's angry shouting, the guttural swagger of Billy Keenan, the touch of Baines's fingers upon his daughter's arm. And Patricia saying, It is the anniversary of Mother's death . . . And Evelyn saying, It is the anniversary of Hannah's death . . . Mad with grief, she'd said. I still have one daughter, Baines had said. William and Hannah, Joss had said.

Elias's voice rang out and banished the whispered confusion. '. . . Turn to me and take pity on me, for I am wretched and alone.'

Agnes, kneeling in the darkened chapel, felt suddenly afraid.

Chapter Twenty

'No, I'm not working today.' Nina's voice on the phone was indignant. 'It's Good Friday, *you* should know that.'

'I need to check something at the mill.'

'Agnes, what is it about those files? I've sat in the same room as them for months now and I still haven't acquired wisdom.'

'Nina, it's all about the mill and the family . . .'

'So you keep saying.'

'Could I borrow your key?'

'There's no need. Patricia said she'd be in today. Ever since Anthony fell apart she's become a new person, really taken charge.'

'How is Anthony?'

'She hasn't mentioned him. Not a word. She says "I" instead of "we" now.'

After chapel Agnes went to join Teresa in the staff room. The chill grey stone of the corridors seemed to echo with melancholy. They sat in silence, sipping their coffee, nodding in greeting as the occasional staff member joined them. Agnes heard a door slam, a man shouting, hurried footsteps, raised voices, and then the staff-room door flew open and Billy Keenan stood there, swearing, with Mary Watson at his side.

'I'm sorry, Sister, I tried to –'

'They wouldn't let me see you –'

'– tried to explain he needed an appointment –'

'Here. Have these.' Billy was holding a large cardboard box, and now he dropped it. It landed heavily on its side, spilling papers across the doorway.

'It's all right, Mary.' Agnes stood up. 'Thank you.' She knelt and gathered the papers back into the box.

Billy looked down at her, his face fixed in its habitual sneer.

'That bastard Turnbull. He owed me, he did, and now he's gone, and no one does that to me, right, no one scarpers off wi'out paying me what I'm owed. I warned him, I did.'

Agnes picked up the box and led Billy out into the corridor. They sat side by side on a couple of chairs.

'So he was defrauding the community centre?'

Billy nodded. 'Aye. It's all there. His signature, for stuff what he never bought. Building materials, that kind of thing. I should know. And Mark must have known too.'

'Why? Why did Turnbull want to defraud the centre? He really believed in it.'

Billy shrugged. 'Takes a lot to keep believing, up there. It gets to you after a while.'

'And I can have these?'

He met her eyes. 'In't no good to me, now. He in't going to pay me.'

'How do you know?'

'Saw him, didn't I? Over at Lianna's. He's there.'

'At Lianna's?'

'Aye. And drunk. I threatened him, I did, and he just laughed. He said it were all over for him. Nothing left, he said. Made me right angry. No one laughs at me. I could torch the fuckin' place and he'd still be laughing, I reckon.'

'And what good would that do?'

He looked at her. His eyes flashed steel. 'It would make me feel better. A whole lot better.' He smiled.

'Billy – why not take this stuff to the police?'

''Cos they wouldn't believe me.'

'And you want me to take it instead?'

'I don't give a toss what you do with it. It means nowt to me now. It only had a value s'long as Turnbull could pay up. It's just rubbish now.' He stood up, smoothing his trousers, then turned to her and offered his hand. 'Pleasure doin' business with you.'

'How are you getting back?'

'Dunno. Walking, I suppose.'

'Do you want a lift? I'm going to the mill.'

'Sure. Sound.'

She dropped him off at the edge of the estate.

'Billy . . .'

'What?'

'Don't do anything stupid.'

He opened the car door, then turned to her and smiled. 'What's the difference, eh?'

'But –'

'Depends how I feel, see.' He got out of the car. 'You see, Turnbull's made me angry. Very angry.'

'Can't you feel sorry for him?'

Billy looked at her, his eyes blank with disbelief. 'Him? Why should I?'

Agnes met his gaze. She couldn't think of anything to say.

'Thanks for the lift. See ya.' He shut the car door. As she pulled out towards the mill, she could see him in her mirror. He was still waving.

Hanson, Kitty. Hanson, Esther. Agnes pulled the files out and put them on Nina's desk, then sat down in Nina's chair.

Kitty Hanson. It was a very thin file. Date of Birth, 9 September, 1951. Joined the mill at the age of eighteen. Had taken time off recently to nurse her mother.

Esther Hanson. On the front the name Meyer was crossed out. Born July, 1926. Joined the mill at the age of fifteen. Married Frederick Hanson in 1948. One daughter, Kitty, born 1951. Her husband died in 1970. Esther retired in 1979 due to ill health. There were some pension details, ending with her death at the end of last year.

Agnes leafed through the sparse, yellowing pages. Work, marriage, motherhood, widowhood, death. An unremarkable life. The last page, tucked away behind the others, was a memo, dated September 1947, headed Re: Meyer, Esther:

'Regarding the incident which has been of some concern to this company, I have suggested to the unfortunate woman that she might now put this matter behind her. I have stressed that these are difficult times for us all, and the war has left many people in distressed circumstances, but that rather than looking back, we are all better served by looking forward to a new future. She has agreed that the matter might now be dropped.'

The memo was signed, Douglas Styring, Office Manager, and copied to Mr Baines.

Agnes closed the file. She stood up and went over to the window, blinking against the sunlight. After a few moments she returned to the file, re-read the last page, closed the file and returned it with Kitty's to its place. She checked to see if any other files had the name Meyer. Finding none, she left Nina's office and went to look for Patricia.

The door of the main spinning shed swung shut behind her. Agnes stood in the surge of noise. The uniform banks of machines stretched endlessly away from her. She could see Patricia, far off, a tiny figure in high heels. Around her people moved according to her gestures, checking bobbins, carrying boxes, as if subject to her choreography. Agnes began to walk towards her. In an altogether different place, Elias would be preparing the chapel for Good Friday. It seemed odd, Agnes thought, to recall the Passion of Our Lord amongst all this impervious metal. It had no place here, as if the raw rituals of blood and pain and sacrifice and death had to be left outside the door, or risk being crushed under the wheels of this clean, inexorable steel.

Patricia saw her, and began to walk towards her.

'The office was unlocked –' Agnes began.

'I wanted to see you anyway. I'm worried about Daddy.' Patricia's voice was shrill above the noise.

'What's happened?'

'His housekeeper, Isabel, she phoned me this morning. Let's go somewhere quieter.' Patricia led her out into the courtyard, which seemed empty of sound after the vibrations of the spinning sheds.

'Isabel said Anthony came to see Daddy last night, and they had some kind of argument, and Daddy was very upset afterwards. They were shouting about Jo, apparently, both very angry. And Anthony was drunk, surprise, surprise.' She stared at her feet.

'What were they saying about Jo?'

'I've no idea. I can't think what she'd have to do with anything. And then after Anthony had gone, Daddy went up into the attic, all by himself, and started carrying stuff around, and then he was hanging paintings on the wall downstairs, and poor Isabel tried to stop him, she was frightened for him, she said, she thought he'd injure himself, but he wouldn't listen, muttering things, she said.'

'What things?'

'He was saying, "It's what she'd have wanted." He kept saying it, apparently. I wish she'd called me at the time. And now he's vanished.'

'Since when?'

'She said his bed hadn't been slept in. And she hasn't seen him since last night. And the dogs have gone, apart from poor old Greer, of course. I could kill Anthony, it's all his fault, wading in and upsetting an old man. When it's me he should be angry with, I'm the one trying to override his claim to this place.'

'Does he know?'

'I haven't told him. I haven't seen him, you see.' She picked at a speck of fluff on her jacket. 'After the police fiasco – he went. Don't know where. Don't care actually, although I suspect that blonde piece. And now upsetting Father . . .' Her eyes filled with tears. 'Bloody liability, that man,' she muttered, fishing in her pocket for a handkerchief. 'Can't think what possessed me to . . .' She began to cry.

'I'm afraid –' Agnes said. 'I heard today that he'd been –'

'What?'

'He was defrauding the community centre. Billy Keenan gave me back all the papers that he'd stolen from Mark's place.'

'Well, that just proves it, doesn't it. And the awful thing is, I had no idea. You see, he never used to be . . . when I met him . . . he was lovely. Really lovely . . .' She sobbed into her handkerchief, and Agnes gently patted her shoulder.

'Is it possible for you to take back his share of the mill?'

'I'm trying to. It's difficult, he's named personally by Daddy. I've been on to Andrew about it, he's seeing what he can do. But now I don't know where Daddy's got to, I'm so worried about him, and I'm furious with Anthony, it's typical of that stupid bloody idiot that he should go upsetting Daddy at such an awful time . . .'

'I could call on your father, if you like.'

'Could you? That would be such a help. You could talk to Isabel, see if there's any news.'

'And you should phone the police and report your husband missing.'

241

Patricia looked up. 'I'm not sure I care enough about him to do that.'

'Patricia – if he's dangerous . . .?'

'Do you think he is?'

'I think he's unstable, yes.'

Patricia shrugged. 'All right, then. As long as they promise not to return him to me when they do find him.'

Agnes tentatively pushed open the gate, bracing herself to be greeted by the dogs. There was silence. She went up to the front door and rang the heavy bell. There was no answer.

Greer, she thought.

She went round to the side door, and pushed it open, then crept inside. Sunlight fell in dusty parallels across the parquet floor. She heard a low growling, and saw Greer lift his head in his basket. 'Greer . . .' she whispered, going to him. She saw him twitch his nose, still growling at her unfamiliar presence. Gently she placed her hand on his head. 'Greer . . .'

What could an old, blind dog tell her? Greer grew quiet and settled back to doze, as if to point out to her the futility of her quest. She stood up, and realised that something about the hallway had changed. The plain wood panelling was hung with paintings. Two paintings. The still lifes from the attic, hung one either side of the fireplace.

Agnes stared at the grapes and the lemons, so glowing with life that they seemed to light up their corner of the hall. Then she looked at the other painting, the rich velvet tablecloth, the clock, the book; the skull. There was something final about such a gesture; to hang these paintings in the hall, on the anniversary of his wife's death – and then to disappear.

Agnes hurried from the house, so gripped by anxiety that she ran down the drive, and almost gasped with shock when she saw someone standing at the gates, watching her, a tall figure with a long coat and tartan scarf. She hesitated, then turned towards him, but he fled. When she reached her car he was nowhere to be seen.

She drove fast to James's house. Finding no answer, she went straight to the Campbells.

Evelyn opened the door. 'Agnes – what a lovely – oh, dear, are you all right?'

'What is it?' Agnes heard James's voice. 'You're pale, what's happened?' She felt his arm around her, and turned towards him, feeling the rough wool of his sweater against her face.

'Yes, I'm all right, it's Baines, I'm very worried . . . Patricia said he'd vanished, Turnbull upset him last night, but he's hung these paintings, it seems so symbolic, somehow, I'm sorry, I'm not making sense . . . And then I saw this man and I've seen him before . . .'

'We were just having lunch,' Evelyn said. 'Come and sit down, I'll get you a drink.'

'So he's really vanished?' James said, laying a place for Agnes.

'After Turnbull visited him, it seems. And the dogs aren't there, apart from the old one.'

'You must excuse Joss's absence,' Evelyn said. 'We're out of logs for the fire, he said he'd go and bargain with the Bradshaws, they've got loads.'

'Poor William,' James said. 'He must feel everything's gone wrong. He had a wife, three children, a mill – and now he's lost it all.'

'It's a sign of the times, Jim.' Evelyn smiled. 'These huge family businesses only work when there's an empire to support them, plenty of money swishing around. When times are hard they take everyone down with them. I'm speaking from experience, my grandfather used to have a farm machinery empire, sold tractors and things right across the world. That was in the days when you could, no competition, you see. Then we lost the colonies, the company lost its customers, couldn't change its ways, couldn't compete . . . you should have seen the damage. Bankruptcies, marriages breaking up, inheritance squabbles . . . My father was the wise one, he got out before the real ruin set in. Coffee?' She smiled, and stood up.

'No, allow me, I insist. I know your kitchen as if it was my own.' James got up and left the room.

'It's funny –' Agnes started to say.

'What?' Evelyn sat down and emptied the last dribble from the wine bottle into her glass.

'How those of us without families – well, speaking personally – what I mean is . . .' Evelyn was looking at her kindly. 'You see, living in community is so terribly difficult. I find it so, anyway.

And sometimes I see people who live in families, and I think, it must be easier. Like my friend Nina, and Rosie, and Nina's mum, they seem to get along OK. It appears so straightforward, in a family, doesn't it, who belongs where, who owes what to whom . . .' The words seemed to tumble from her mouth. 'And then you encounter this, and you realise, it's not straightforward at all, it's just like any community. Or maybe it's worse.'

'Oh, much worse, I think.'

'Why is that?'

'I think it's because one's expectations are higher. Like you, I only look at it from the sidelines. Not having children . . .' She gathered crumbs together on the tablecloth. 'For a long time I idealised it, the family, the children gathered around. I used to envy people with children, made myself ill with it sometimes. And it wasn't because I particularly liked children, because I'm not sure I do, but when people have children they seem to acquire a kind of ready-made unquestioning purpose in life, a focus to the relationship. When I think of how hard we've worked at our marriage, Joss and me, because there's been only us. Only us . . .' She stopped, breathing hard. 'And it's worked. It's been tough at times, but – we've really made it work.' The eruption of feeling seemed momentarily to have overpowered her, and Agnes watched her struggle to regain her composure. The high colour in her cheeks faded back to gentle rose, her face settled once more into polite attention. She spoke again. 'Not that it's like your life. It must be much more difficult, your way.'

'I wouldn't say that. In the end, it's just life, isn't it.' Agnes smiled, and the two women sat in companionable silence, both vaguely wondering how James could be taking so long to make a simple pot of coffee.

'What made it more difficult,' Evelyn said suddenly, 'was that I've always known I was the one who couldn't. Have children, I mean. I went through a few desperate years, terrible painful years, and I went to my doctor, secretly, and he referred me. And to cut a long story short . . . Anyway . . .' She smiled, gazing down at the rug at her feet. 'It resolved things for me a bit, but then I had the dilemma of whether to tell Joss. On several occasions I nearly did.'

'What stopped you?'

'My own terrible, selfish impulses. I was frightened of losing him. I thought he might go off and find someone else to have children with.' Her voice shook slightly, and her cheeks coloured with the strength of her feeling. She smoothed her skirt, making small sweeping movements with her delicate fingers. 'It stayed on my conscience. In a way, it always has done. Although, he, in his turn . . .'

Agnes waited. Evelyn had raised her eyes and was now looking directly at her. Then she shook her head and smiled. 'The funny thing is, now I think Joss prefers it this way. He says he likes to have me to himself.'

James came into the room bearing a tray. 'I couldn't decide between Kenyan and Colombian,' he said. 'And now here's Joss, and I've only made enough for three.'

'Bradshaw's got enough bloody hazel to see us through the next ice age.' Joss came into the room, his face flushed, his hair flecked with bits of tree bark. 'I'd love a cup, thank you, James.' He took the largest mug. 'And the Radleighs have been spreading malicious gossip about poor old William, I've a good mind to take out an injunction against them, gone completely off his rocker, they're saying, one of their cronies was out walking her dogs at crack of bloody dawn this morning, ghastly beagle things, caught sight of him with his two dogs. Poor chap was only taking the air, but by the time the Radleighs had finished with the story, he was stark raving mad, shaking his stick at the sky, talking to himself . . . Didn't even recognise the old trout. Come to think of it, I'd act crazy if any of the Radleighs' set hove into view while I was up on the moors . . .' He drained his mug and refilled it from the coffee pot, then sat down, glowing with good humour.

'Joss . . .' Evelyn spoke quietly, and he turned to look at her. 'Joss – they might be right, for once. William's housekeeper says he's gone missing. And he was very upset last night, apparently.' Joss met her gaze, suddenly serious. 'And it is Good Friday,' she added.

'I know it is. Do you think I'd forget that?' He turned away from her, staring at the rug at his feet.

'I'll make some more coffee,' James said, standing up.

'Poor William,' Joss said, suddenly subdued.

'Joss.' James touched Joss's shoulder. 'I think after our coffee we should drive over that way and look for him.'

Joss glanced up at James and nodded.

'I'll wait here,' Evelyn said, and looked across to Agnes.

'I've got to be in chapel in an hour,' Agnes said. 'But James has got my phone number.'

The fading daylight drained the colour from the altar window, as if the light of the heavens was being gradually extinguished. Agnes heard Elias's voice ring out through the chapel.

'He is despised and rejected of men; a man of sorrows, and acquainted with grief . . . Surely He hath borne our griefs, and carried our sorrows . . .'

Agnes allowed the words of the Gospel readings to surround her, as the story unfolded of the darkest hour, the suffering to end all suffering. When she went forward to kiss the foot of the cross, her face was wet with tears.

After the service she went straight to her room and knelt in prayer. Outside it was dark, and the silhouetted trees shivered in the chill wind. When her phone rang, it made her jump.

'It's Evelyn. They've just come back, but they're going out again. They saw him.' Agnes heard her voice catch. 'He's in a very bad way. He didn't seem to see them, although they were right up close to him. Joss said he was calling his wife's name . . .' Again her voice faltered. 'The dogs won't leave his side, they were growling, even though they know us. Joss was very upset. They're getting warm clothes and stuff and going back. I've phoned Patricia too.'

'Thanks.' Agnes could barely speak.

'Joss said . . . to see him like that . . . such a man . . . it's pitiful . . . I'll phone you again.' The line went dead.

In her mind, Agnes heard a voice that seemed to be Elias's reciting the Twenty-Second Psalm. 'My God, I cry to You by day but You do not answer; and by night also, I take no rest . . .' The window rattled with a gust of wind, and she glanced up at it. Beyond the lights of the courtyard she could see the dark slopes and hollows of the moor, receding into the black sky. 'O go not from me, for trouble is hard at hand; and there is none to help . . .' She thought of William Baines, alone with his dogs, cast out on the moor.

The phone rang and she snatched it up.

'Agnes, it's David.'

'David – but – Thank God –'

'She's gone, I was only away a couple of hours, oh God . . .'

'What – who?'

'Jo . . . Oh my God, please help . . .'

'Where are you?'

'At the hut.'

'I'm on my way.'

Chapter Twenty-One

Agnes found she was hammering on Elias's door, thumping with both fists. He opened the door in astonishment.

'Agnes?'

'Listen, you must come, they're up on the moors, Baines and Jo and Turnbull. Oh God, David's just phoned me, please –' her breath could carry no more words.

'I'm sorry, I'm not quite with you.'

She noticed his eyes were red, as if he'd been crying. 'There's no time to explain, please, only you know where he'll go, please –'

'Baines?'

'He's mad, please, there's no time, and Turnbull's up there too –'

'Agnes . . .' His eyes looked huge against the pallor of his face. 'If I go back there . . .'

'We must go now.'

'I can't go back. Please don't ask me . . .'

She walked past him into his flat, picked up his coat from the hook by the door and handed it to him.

'You're asking more of me than you realise,' he said. He took the coat and put it on, all the time holding her gaze with his own. She handed him his gloves. His hands shook as he put them on.

He followed her to the car, and got in wordlessly. She accelerated hard out of the school on to the main road. As they turned off the road towards the moor, she heard him murmur, 'There is no past, there's only the present.'

She glanced at his hands, which were still shaking. 'Elias – I'm sorry – I had to – they need us –'

He murmured something. She thought he said, 'I shall go mad.' He clutched the thick wool of his coat to quieten his hands. She parked the car at the track and they walked fast up to the hut by the light of her torch and the clouded half moon.

The hut was in darkness and there was no smoke from the chimney. She knocked at the door. 'David?' she whispered. The door opened a crack.

'Thank God,' David breathed. He saw Elias, and blinked.

They sat by the light of David's torch, crouched by the chill stone of the grate. The sparse light intensified the angles of his face, hollowed with exhaustion and fear.

'I wanted to go after her, but then I found this.' He handed her a note and Agnes pointed her torch at it. It was scribbled in charcoal:

'Don't follow me. Please. You are in more danger than you know. Please stay away. Jo.'

David took the note back. 'I don't know what to do. I don't know where she's gone, or why. We've been here for days, and she's been really calm. That's why I didn't phone you, Agnes, it's been wonderful, it's been like a holiday. But yesterday she went back to her father's house, she had a meeting with Andrew and today she's been really agitated, going on about Turnbull and the mill, and then I thought maybe he'd come for her, but then, why the note?'

'Were there signs of a struggle?'

'No, none at all.'

'She's protecting you,' Agnes said.

'From Turnbull? But –'

'You see, you can stop him selling the mill. And he knows that. He's known it for some time.'

'*Me?*'

'There was a trust. Jeremiah Baines in the mid-nineteenth century married a woman called Dorothea Culverton. He adored her, they had loads of kids. But she became blind. And he was so touched by the fortitude with which she bore it, that it became his cause. To the extent that anyone working at the mill who lost their sight was paid an allowance from a trust he set up, and if they left the mill or died it was paid to any living children or grandchildren of that person.'

'But that's – why me? And no one else knows about this –'

'In the fifties it was transmuted into shares. And then quietly forgotten about. There was a good thirty years when no one claimed it, it didn't apply to anyone, and it was forgotten.'

'My grandfather –'

'Exactly.'

'So I own . . .'

'You have a small share of Allbright's. Enough, with you and your brother and Nina Warburton, who's the other living recipient of this trust – enough to prevent Turnbull selling the mill.'

David sat back on his heels. He stared at the empty hearth, at the grains of soot which fell from time to time from the chimney. 'So where has she gone?' he said at last.

'This meeting with Andrew,' Agnes said. 'What happened?'

'She said that Turnbull had betrayed her father. She was very angry with him.'

'Was her father there?'

'No, and she was very worried about that too. And Patricia's at her wits' end, apparently, her life has fallen apart.'

'Did she say anything about meeting Turnbull?'

'Meeting him?' David turned worried eyes to Agnes. 'But no one knows where he is.'

'Perhaps she does. Perhaps she's going to try and talk to him.'

'Oh God.'

Elias stirred. 'We must find William,' he said. 'She'll have gone after him.'

They both looked at him. 'Oh God, of course,' David said.

Elias stood up, and they followed him out of the hut. David lit the path before them, but Elias pushed the torch away. 'No,' he whispered, 'no light . . .' He was trembling. The moonlight touched the side of his face with silver. Agnes felt a sudden terrible fear, that she was indeed asking too much of him; that it would prove to be more than he could bear.

They walked, stumbling at times against the uneven ground. After a while Elias led them away from the path, climbing steadily, negotiating every rabbit hole, every muddy stream as if they were totally familiar to him. Agnes wasn't sure how long they'd walked, maybe a mile, maybe more, when the air was cut through with a terrible cry. A human cry, a primeval deep-voiced howl of grief. Agnes and David froze. But Elias began to shake, as if the cry had echoed in his deepest self, and then he answered the voice with a low sob of his own.

'Elias . . .' David took a step towards him, but Agnes put her hand out to stop him. She felt sick with fear; with guilt.

Again came the howl. Elias called out – 'William . . .' and then broke into a run, following the cry, stumbling over the rough ground, David and Agnes close behind. 'William,' he was shouting, and then, 'Kate, oh God, no, not Kate, no . . .' and he was sobbing and running, and the wind seemed to take up Baines's cry and sound it across the moor into the distant clouds.

They ran with their torches on, stumbling down a slope towards a hollow edged with spindly trees. Agnes was aware of a figure slumped on the grass, of Elias approaching, and as she and David reached the scene she saw in the beam of their torches Baines sitting on the ground. His clothes were torn, and his face was streaked with mud. His hair was matted, twisted with leaves. He was staring, unseeing at Elias; and in his arms he was cradling the blood-soaked form of Joanna.

Elias stood, frozen to the spot, staring at Joanna. His face wore an expression of bewilderment. David rushed to her, grabbed her wrist and shouted at Agnes, 'There's a pulse, for God's sake – there's a pulse!'

Agnes pulled out her phone and dialled 999. 'Is she breathing?' she called to David.

Baines stared down at his daughter in his arms and smiled, softly. 'No,' he whispered. 'No breath. No life.'

'Yes. Sort of . . .' David bent over her.

Agnes heard the operator ask where they were. 'Near Silsden – yes – hang on – Elias, tell me – where are we?'

Elias stirred and said, 'Laithe's Hollow. Near Holden Beck.'

She repeated his words into the phone. 'One injured, very seriously, head injuries, attempted murder . . . Yes, I'm sure. Right. Thanks.' She hung up.

'No,' Baines was murmuring again, 'no life . . .' he shook his head and cradled Joanna closer. At his side his dogs whimpered.

One of them went to Elias, and Elias put out his hand absently and touched the soft fur of the animal's head, and murmured, 'Greer.' Then he looked at the dog as if seeing it for the first time, and again Agnes saw a look of puzzlement.

'How's her pulse?' she asked David.

'Steady. Ish.' David sat by Joanna, holding her hand.

They waited. The wind had quietened, and the moon rose in the sky. Agnes sat on the ground. Elias stood, transfixed. In the silence, Baines began to sing a lullaby, gently rocking the still form of his daughter, his words rising in a cracked voice. 'Sleep, little darling, do not cry . . .' Then he stopped, and stroked her face, smiling down at her.

David began to talk to Joanna. 'Stay with us,' he murmured, 'stay with me, don't leave, please don't leave me, I love you, Jo, I always will, stay here for me . . .'

Baines raised his head and stared into the distance, lost in grief. Agnes took his hand. 'Mr Baines – she's alive,' she said, staring into his eyes, willing him to understand. But he gazed beyond her to some other grief, some other loss. He looked towards Elias, and Agnes saw their eyes meet in recognition.

The breeze whispered with David's murmuring. Agnes strained her ears to hear the helicopter, willing it to come. Then she was aware of another sound, of footsteps approaching. A tall figure was descending the slope towards them. Agnes could make out very little about him, but she saw Elias see him, saw Elias start with terror and cry out, his hands clutching at his coat. As the figure came into the circle of torch light, Elias leapt to his feet and fled towards the dark reaches of the moors as the whirring hum of the helicopter sounded in the distance.

The man approached. Agnes saw his face was cut and bruised. He was wearing a tartan scarf. 'You must be Agnes,' he said, gasping for breath. 'I'm Marcus.'

Chapter Twenty-Two

The dogs left Baines's side and ran to Marcus, licking his hands, bringing him towards their grieving master as if somehow he might help.

'Is she –' Marcus said, looking towards Joanna.

'She's alive,' Agnes said, raising her voice above the noise of the helicopter which circled above them. Then it was landing, the white searchlights searing the grassland, the blades spinning, flattening the ground beneath them. Men jumped to the ground with stretcher, blankets, oxygen. As they surrounded Joanna, her father stumbled to his feet and tried to fight them off. Through the noise of the engine Agnes could hear his roars of rage. David tried to restrain him and was flung backwards. The dogs left their master and circled Joanna, escorting her as she was lifted on to a stretcher and taken inside the helicopter, and David was talking to one of the men and then he too climbed into the helicopter which took off, its swirling blades slicing through the air above the head of Baines who stood shouting and boxing the air, calling out and sobbing into the night as his daughter was taken from him.

Marcus hesitated next to him. He took a step towards him, his hand stretched out. Baines turned and looked at him, then looked at Agnes. 'She's gone,' he said, to no one in particular. He took a few steps in the direction of the helicopter, then stopped and bent down. He touched the flattened grass where the helicopter had landed, an expression of wonder on his face. Agnes could hear the sirens of police cars as they reached the road, and a police helicopter approached and began to circle overhead.

Marcus watched Baines, and his eyes welled with tears. 'He doesn't know who I am,' he said.

Baines was kneeling on the ground, pulling up the grass in handfuls and arranging it in a neat pile like a miniature pyre. His

255

dogs lay one at each side of him. From time to time they glanced back to Marcus. Agnes approached him. 'Mr Baines,' she tried again, 'Jo is alive. They've taken her to hospital.'

He shook his head. 'She's gone. I sent her away. It's my fault . . .' His hands pulled at the grass.

'We must try to get him away from here,' Marcus said. 'The hut, maybe?'

'He doesn't know who we are, he'll refuse . . .'

'We can't leave him here.'

Agnes turned to see three police officers running down the slope of the hollow. She went towards them, but they had seen Baines, kneeling calmly on the ground, his coat soaked with his daughter's blood. They stood over him. Slowly he raised his eyes to them. The dogs snarled.

Clumsily, awkwardly, he got to his feet. He smiled. 'Gentlemen,' he said, and held out his hands to them.

'No –' Agnes intervened. 'Not him. He's very ill. He's confused, and in shock. He needs treatment.'

'It's Mr Baines, from Allbright's, isn't it?'

'He found his daughter, badly injured, he's very upset . . .'

'And you are?'

'Sister Agnes from St Catherine's School.'

'He was first at the scene, you say?'

'For God's sake.' It was Marcus. 'You need to find Anthony Turnbull. I saw him. I saw the fight. He was beating the hell out of my sister. He ran off towards Millhouse.'

The policeman let go of Baines. Baines turned to them, still smiling. 'I had a son once, gentlemen,' he said, his voice slow and soft. 'Once I had a son. And two daughters. And a wife . . .' His words were choked by a sob.

There was a burst of noise from the police radios. The police conferred, briefly, and then two ran back to the cars and drove off fast. The third stayed to take details from Agnes and Marcus, and then he too left.

Baines had sat down again on a rock, and was staring straight ahead. Marcus went to him and helped him to his feet. Baines looked at him. 'You seem – do I know you – perhaps, familiar . . .?'

'Come and get warm,' Marcus said, his eyes filling with tears.

The police helicopter still circled overhead. Baines allowed his son to lead him to the track that led down to the hut. Agnes followed, the dogs bobbing at her feet. The moon was sinking in the sky, and at the horizon's edge the sky was turning pale.

They reached the hut, and Agnes found matches and lit candles, and then placed paper and wood in the grate and lit the fire. Marcus pulled the mattress near to the hearth and helped his father on to it. Baines allowed Marcus to take off his damp coat, raising each arm limply in turn like a child. Marcus put his coat and boots to warm by the fire and covered his father with blankets. 'Sleep, now,' he whispered, and Baines obediently settled down and closed his eyes. The two dogs settled at his feet. From time to time they opened an eye to keep watch.

Agnes soaked a handkerchief with cold water and handed it to Marcus. 'You seem to have taken rather a bruising,' she said.

'Oh, yes, that.' He tried to smile, dabbing at the side of his face.

'Turnbull?'

Marcus nodded. 'He's off his rocker. Bloody hell, I thought he was going to kill her.'

'What happened?'

Marcus shook his head. 'Long story. I don't quite know where to start. Some time ago, Jo told me that Dad wanted to hand the mill over to her and Pat.'

'Weren't you consulted?'

'No. Didn't surprise me, though, and I was glad to be out of it. Like Jo, she did the right thing too, refusing it. I thought old Turnbull and Patricia were welcome to it. But then just the other week, Jo told me about Turnbull trying to sell it. I was very angry. And it seemed – I dunno – I was surprised that Anthony should do that, go against Dad's wishes like that. I thought he was a decent bloke. And then I heard how Dad was so upset, and I started keeping an eye on him – there was no point calling at the house, he'd only have kicked me out, but I hung about a bit, just checking . . . And I was there when Turnbull called the other night. And he – *bastard* – he threatened Dad. Said he was selling the mill regardless, he'd got the Deeds, apparently, all but one, and he was trying to get Dad to hand over some file, and Dad said it wasn't there, and he wouldn't tell him where it was, and this went on for some time, I was outside the window – crazy, isn't it – lurking around in the grounds of my own house like God knows what . . . And then Turnbull started going on about Jo, and

David, and I didn't catch it all – he seemed to be blaming them. And Dad – oh God, it was terrible then, Dad was crying, pleading with him to leave Jo alone, really frightened for her, I think – and Turnbull stormed out. And I was left, watching Dad, crying, and he was calling for my Mum . . .' Marcus suddenly buried his face in his hands. 'And –' his voice was choked with sobs – 'And I couldn't go to him. I knew that if I went in – he'd throw me out. And I couldn't bear it.' His words were lost in weeping.

Agnes took his hand. After a while he grew calmer, and raised his head. They both looked across to William, who lay sleeping, peacefully.

'And the fight?' Agnes asked.

'Oh, yes. The fight.' He smiled. 'I surprised even myself. Jo phoned me – it must have been yesterday – and I told her what I'd heard, the row between Dad and Anthony. She was furious, it's years since I've seen her so angry, she was in a terrible state. She said she was going to sort Anthony out. I said she was mad, it was too dangerous. But she wouldn't listen, and she said I wasn't to tell David, because he was in danger too. I don't know what she meant by that. I think she knew that Turnbull was looking for her on the moors, and she went to find him. God knows what she thought she could do, but they were – they had a kind of understanding – it goes back years . . . All I know is that when I got here I saw Pat's car parked on the track back there – Turnbull must have "borrowed" it. And I ran. I kind of knew where they'd gone – and I saw Turnbull, and followed him, and got there just as he was punching the lights out of Jo – Oh God! She was on the ground, screaming. It was awful, if he's not sent down for that there's no justice – and I launched into him, and she got up, and ran off after Dad, and I stayed with Anthony, I was trying to – God knows – I thought I could restrain him till the police got there, but he got away – and then I caught up with Jo and Dad – and you were there . . . And Elias . . .'

'Hang on – *Jo* ran?'

'Yes. Superhuman, I think. She was really injured . . .'

'And then collapsed with your father?'

'Suppose so.'

'But she seemed so badly hurt – and why should Turnbull fight her?'

'Because he's a bastard. And because something had driven

258

him mad. It had obviously all built up, Joanna not letting him take her name off the Deeds, and also – he was shouting at her about them being made for each other.'

Agnes hesitated, then said, 'This "understanding" they had . . .'

Marcus met her eyes. 'It was a long time ago.'

'An affair?'

'Sort of. Well, yes. She was pretty crazy in those days, and lonely.'

'Was he already married to Patricia?'

'Yes. And – you see, he was OK, in those days. We all liked him. And he and Jo had this kind of teasing, bantering relationship . . . looking back, it was obvious, there was this kind of electricity between them. I'm amazed we didn't see at the time, I don't think Patricia ever suspected. But then he and Pat got all kind of aspirational, and the business grew, and they bought that horrible bungalow . . . he could have been a great guy, you know. And now he's stark raving mad.'

'And he thinks she's made for him?'

'After she met David, things cooled between her and Anthony, and now she rather despises him. And he's realised that, I think. I think that added to his madness on the moor, he was just yelling at her, and punching her, God, it was awful, the man should be put away for years.'

Agnes got up and stoked the fire, then turned to Marcus. 'He's ruined, you know. Bankrupt.'

Marcus looked up in surprise.

'He's been borrowing from the business for years. Gambling debts, apparently. He thought the mill would save him.'

Marcus laughed, emptily. 'The mill? What century is he living in?'

'And when he found it wouldn't, he tried to sell it. And he managed to squeeze out you, and Pat, nearly – and he was trying to get round Jo. But he couldn't squeeze out David.'

'David?'

'And Nina. And David's brother Mark.'

'I don't get you.'

'That's the Deed he wanted from your father. There's an old Trust document, a legacy, and those three are, or were, entitled to shares in the mill. It's with the police now.'

Baines stirred in his sleep and turned over, and Marcus went over to him to cover him up again. There was a rustling noise outside. Marcus glanced at the door. The two dogs at Baines's feet opened their eyes and sat up, whining. The door began to open. Agnes saw the patchy grey fur, the sightless eyes of the old dog Greer, as he nudged the door open and stumbled through it, sniffing his way, limping slowly, painfully, across the floor, making little whining noises. He went straight to Baines, licked his face once, then lay down, his face next to his master's, and fell into exhausted sleep. The young dogs quietened and lay down again. Agnes heard Baines murmur the old dog's name.

Agnes looked at Marcus. His face was wet with tears. Outside the sky was pale with the dawn.

Chapter Twenty-Three

They sat like that for some time, listening to the settled breathing of the old man, the louder, laboured breath of his old dog. Agnes's phone rang, and the sound was so odd, so intrusive, that for a moment she wondered what on earth it could be. She fished out the phone from her pocket and answered it.

'Agnes, it's David.'

'David –'

'Good news. She's recovered consciousness. She seems OK. She smiled at me.' He was almost laughing.

'Thank God.'

'She's asking after her father.'

'He's here, with us, me and Marcus, we're in the hut, he's sleeping.'

'I'll tell her he's fine, shall I?'

Agnes hesitated. 'Sure. Tell her he's fine.' She rang off. 'That was David. She's OK.'

Marcus looked across to his father. 'When he wakes up, tell him she's alive.'

'It should be you.'

Marcus shook his head. 'Not yet. I must go, before he wakes.'

'But . . .'

'No, really, believe me. Not yet. I can't risk upsetting him again. If he sees me –'

'What is it then, that's driven you both so far apart?'

He sighed. 'It's another long story. I was a fool. When my mother was dying . . . I said things . . . things I shouldn't have said. She was wonderful, you see, we all spent time with her in that room, during her last weeks, and she was so serene, so kind of reconciled . . . and there was something she said, about a letter she'd written me, she'd entrusted Dad with it, and now I understand that she wanted him to wait until he'd gone too, but at the time I was so

261

desperate about losing her, I wanted her to stay . . . I demanded to see it, and it upset them both, and then I was angry with him and I blamed him for her getting ill, for neglecting her in favour of the mill . .. I was a fool. And he's never forgiven me. I just didn't want her to go . . .'

'No. I can imagine. I know someone . . .' Agnes broke off as her phone rang again.

'Where are you?' James's voice sounded strained.

'Here. I mean – oh God, I'm so glad to hear you.' Agnes felt like bursting into tears.

'Are you OK? We lost him, we've had an awful time, we called the police in the end . . .'

'I'm OK. I'm at a hut on the moors, I'll give you directions, have you got a pen, it's not far from you at all.' She gave instructions, then rang off.

Marcus stood up. 'Your friend can help get Dad back home, can't he?'

'Do you really have to go?'

'Yes.' He glanced nervously at his father, then said, as if it was an excuse, 'It's not fair on my wife, we've got a young baby.'

'But – I wanted to ask you – how did you know where to find your father last night? Why Laithe's Hollow?'

Marcus shifted on his feet.

'Elias knew too,' Agnes said.

'Yes.'

'This riding accident,' Agnes persisted. 'This person who was killed—'

'Kate. She was my girlfriend at the time. And Dad was at the scene too, it was his horse, it was him who destroyed her, one of his favourite mares, she was. Elias blamed himself, he took it really badly. He went kind of crazy, he disappeared, it turned out he was living at the stables, sleeping in the straw. Then he left the area. I hadn't seen him since. Until – until last night. When I saw him last night, I was so glad . . . I wish he'd stayed.' He reached down for his coat, and put it on.

'Do you have to go now?'

'Really. I must. If Dad sees me –'

'It's for you, isn't it. It's to protect you, not him. In case he recognises you . . .'

Marcus looked down at her. He nodded. 'If he sees me and –

and rejects me again – I couldn't bear it, Agnes. I'm sorry. I'm a coward . . .' His eyes filled with tears. He turned towards the door. 'Look after Greer for me.' He tied his scarf around his neck and stumbled out into the morning. Agnes heard the call of a bird high above the moor.

The candles of the night had burnt right down to their wicks. She went round the hut, blowing them out, then sat quietly, waiting. She listened to the breathing, and was suddenly aware that she could hear only one rhythm, one breath, in, out. She looked across at Baines, who was sleeping quietly. At Greer, who was still. Quite, quite still. She saw that the young dogs had moved and were now lying next to him.

She went to the dog, and buried her fingers in his fur, feeling his fading warmth, feeling her eyes well with tears. She stroked his nose, tears rolling down her face. And at Easter, too, she thought, wondering why that should occur to her now.

James found her there, crying silently. He took her in his arms, and she sobbed, 'He's dead,' and James said, 'No he isn't, he looks fine,' and Agnes cried out, 'Not the man, you fool, the dog,' and then she was laughing through her tears.

'We must get them both back home,' James said.

They sat by the makeshift bed. Baines stirred, opened his eyes, closed them again.

'We shouldn't wake him,' Agnes said. She went over to the kettle, and filled it with water, and stoked up the fire under it.

They waited. Agnes made tea for them both, and told James about the events of the night, about Joanna, the helicopter, the police searching for Turnbull. As she put down her empty mug, she said, 'Oh my God.'

'What?'

'The school. They'll wonder where on earth I am. I haven't given them a second thought . . .'

James looked across at her and their eyes met. 'You have a phone,' he said.

'The batteries are low,' she said.

Baines stirred. 'My poor, poor dog,' he said. 'My Greer.' He opened his eyes. 'My dog,' he said, addressing James and Agnes. 'Come all this way to die. Courageous to the end.' He raised himself up on one arm, and the young dogs sat up and wagged their tails.

263

'Mr Baines . . .' Agnes said.

'You look familiar,' he said to her, then suddenly went white and sat up. 'Jo!'

'She's OK. She's in hospital. She has head injuries, but she's conscious –'

'I must go to her—' He tried to stand, but his legs gave way and he sat down heavily again. 'And Marcus,' he mumbled, 'I thought I saw Marcus . . .'

'Mr Baines –' James stood over him, holding his coat and shoes. 'If you'll allow me . . .' James put the shoes on the old man's feet, helped him on with his coat, and then put one arm under him and raised him to stand upright. Agnes saw the exhaustion in James's face, the shadows around his eyes.

She covered the dying embers of the fire with ash, while James helped William outside to his car which was parked by the track, next to Agnes's. He came back in, picked up the still form of Greer, and carried him outside, followed by the two young dogs. Agnes locked the hut behind them.

They drove to Baines's house. The dogs jumped and circled with glee as William led them all round to the side door, which Isabel had locked. He bent and retrieved a key from under the mat, and let them in. Agnes went straight to the phone and called the school, fending off all enquiries from Mary Watson, and saying firmly she'd see them in the next couple of hours. Then she phoned the mill, and got Nina.

'What the hell's going on?' Nina sounded indignant. 'I was called in here at crack of dawn, I had to dump Rosie on Jay, Patricia's vanished, police swarming the place looking for Turnbull, and all sorts of rumours about Mr Baines running amok up on the moor . . .'

'I'll tell you as soon as I can. Nina – stay where you're safe, Turnbull's still out there and he's dangerous. Does anyone know where Patricia is?'

'No one.'

'If you see her, tell her her sister's at the General Infirmary, and her father's back home. They're both OK.'

She rang off.

Baines had poured three large whiskies. He handed one each to Agnes and James. They settled down in the old chairs, in the gloom of the lounge. Greer was lying in state on the velvet plush of the old sofa, the two dogs sitting at his side. Agnes got up and went over to the window, and pulled on the curtain cord. The curtains parted, heavily, reluctantly, raising a cloud of dust, and sunshine poured into the room.

'It's Easter Saturday,' she said, for no apparent reason.

Chapter Twenty-Four

Yawning, Agnes parked the car in the school grounds. She got out and went straight to Elias's flat and knocked at the door. There was no answer. It was after ten, and she'd missed morning chapel.

She walked slowly back across the drive to the school. Her shoes were soaked with dew, and the birds chirped noisily from the chestnut trees. She breathed in the freshness of the morning, clenched her fists at her sides and went straight to Sister Philomena's office.

'Thought you'd eloped,' Philomena said, looking up from her desk. 'You gone, Elias gone, the morning service a wash-out – jumped to conclusions, don't you know. I had to do the readings, made a pig's ear of the whole bally show.'

'No, not eloped,' Agnes felt suddenly very tired.

'And look at you. Half a tree in your hair. Off you go now, old chap, explanations later. I expect they'll be colourful, as usual.' Philomena opened a book on her desk and started making notes in the margin.

Agnes closed the door softly behind her.

She went to her room and lay on her bed. She wondered how William was now. She'd left him with James half an hour ago, both engaged in animated discussion about the breeding of gun dogs. Agnes and James had explained to him the events of the night, and he'd listened quietly, every so often looking across to Greer. When Agnes got up to leave, he stood up with her. Clumsily, he'd reached out and taken her hand in his. 'I – I had to –' he shifted on his feet. 'I thought I had to look for Hannah. I was a bit confused. She's dead, you see. I can see that now.' Agnes met his eyes. His expression was calm, almost serene. He nodded, and let go of her hand. 'Yes. I can see that now.' He went back to his place to refill the whisky glasses, and Agnes had slipped away.

Now, lying on her bed, she dozed for half an hour, then got up and showered and put on fresh clothes. She made some coffee and toast, and sat at her desk. She dialled Janet Cole.

'It's Agnes. Any news?'

'Turnbull, you mean? He's either being hidden by someone, or he's left the area.'

'Have you seen Joanna Baines?'

'Yes, we went to talk to her earlier. She's doing very well.'

'Is David with her?'

'Yes, he is.'

'He's still in danger, isn't he?'

'We're aware of that, yes.'

'Has anyone seen Billy Keenan?'

'Funny you should ask that. There were a couple of small fires on the estate last night. Just the odd car, you know. But we recognised the style – it's his way of communicating, by smoke signal. If you see him, can you let us know?'

Agnes finished her toast and went back to the car park. There was still no answer at Elias's flat. She got into the car and drove to the estate, to the Keenan home.

Maureen answered the door. 'No, I in't seen him, love,' she said, ushering Agnes inside.

'I didn't think so.'

'Couple of cars torched last night,' Maureen said, turning the sound down on the television.

Agnes sat down in an armchair. 'Yes, so I heard.'

'And the mill all upside down, coppers everywhere.'

'Turnbull's gone missing.'

'GBH on his sister-in-law, I heard.'

'Your grapevine's fast, isn't it?'

For the first time, Maureen smiled. 'Cup of tea, love.'

Agnes followed Maureen to the kitchen. 'I wanted to ask you – there was an incident at the mill last December, involving Billy and your friend Kitty – some kind of fight, I think—'

'A fight? With our Kitty?' Maureen shook her head. 'I can't imagine that – ooh, wait a minute, I know what you mean. Our Billy took the blame, again, and it weren't his fault neither.'

'What happened?'

'It were just after her mother died, and a couple of the lads up there, bored wi' baiting the Pakis, starting taunting our Kitty, saying things like, aye, well, that's one Kraut less in the world – you have to remember, Kitty don't go out of her way to make friends with folk, and her mother was even more withdrawn, not a popular woman at all. Poor Kitty, she were that upset, screeching at them, she were, throwing things, I've never seen her so angry – and then Billy waded in and told them to shut it, and it ended in a fight of some kind, couple of eyes blackened, and of course he got the blame. Always does, you see. But he likes Kitty, like I told you, he couldn't stand by and see her treated like that.'

'Why Kraut? I mean, why was that the taunt?'

'Oh, just one of those things. People always said her mother was German, she was called Meyer. No proof at all, spoke proper and all. But she was so quiet, she never bothered to account for herself, folk could think what they like as far as she was concerned. She were a difficult woman.'

Agnes left the estate and drove down the hill towards the town. She passed Florence Chadwick's street. She pulled in and sat in her car, thinking. She looked across to Number 54, the house on the corner where Millie Coulter lived. She got out of her car and rang on Millie's bell. There was no answer. She pulled a page out of her notebook, scribbled a note, then changed her mind and screwed it up in her pocket. She went back to her car and drove to James's.

'I bet you haven't slept.' James looked at her with concern.

'I dozed a bit this morning. How about you?'

'I had a couple of hours. Are you hungry? It seems to be lunchtime.'

'And how's William?' Agnes asked, as she helped James make some sandwiches.

'He seems much better. He talked to Jo on the phone, which cheered him up a lot. Evelyn went over to make him some lunch, and Isabel will be back on Monday. And Patricia arrived with a huge suitcase and seems to be moving back in. So the poor chap can't move for women wanting to look after him.'

'Does he regret the mill?'

James arranged the sandwiches on a plate. 'He said he'd been a stupid old fool.'

Agnes followed James into the dining room. 'But he'd lost Hannah, he couldn't think straight.'

'That's what I said. I wanted him to see that it wasn't his fault.

Also, that daughter of his, Patricia, she could run twenty mills by the looks of her. I'm sure it will work out OK in the end.'

Agnes poured two cups of coffee. She put the coffee jug down, frowning. 'It's not over yet.' She looked up at James. 'Is David still with Joanna?'

'I think so, yes.'

'Do you mind if I phone him?'

'Sure, go ahead.'

David's voice on the phone was cheerful. 'Agnes, hi, thanks for everything yesterday – she's so much better, it's wonderful . . .'

'And are you OK?'

'Me? Of course, why?'

'That photo you were sent—'

'Oh, that, it's OK—'

'I don't think it is. Can you make sure you stay with people, David? Don't go anywhere alone.'

'But they're after Turnbull, they'll get him soon, it'll be OK.'

'*Please.*'

'Yeah, well, I'm here for now. I've got a camp bed and everything.'

'Good.'

'And by the way, can you tell your art dealer friends to choose their moment with more care.'

'What do you mean?'

'They phoned me, your London friend, what's his name, first thing this morning. Demanding another meeting – apparently, they want to see more of my stuff. I had to tell him that a) it was a Saturday, and b) my partner is in hospital and needs me with her – but he was most insistent. Rude even. Strange, I thought.'

Agnes laughed. 'You've obviously got a fan. Athena said he was in love with the North. I'll have a word with her.'

'Thanks. Come and see us soon.'

'I will.'

Agnes rang off. James poured her some more coffee. 'They sound fine,' he said.

'They are. Now there's just Turnbull to worry about. And –'

'And what?'

Agnes sighed. 'Elias.'

'Yes.'

'And I still don't know . . .'

270

'What don't you know?'

'I keep thinking about peregrine falcons.'

'William told me about Elias. There was a riding tragedy, apparently.'

'Yes.'

'William had to destroy his horse, he said. He shot her himself.'

'Yes.'

'And he gave away all the other horses, he told me. His neighbour took them in, there's a stables just across the way from him.'

Agnes looked at James. 'What's the neighbour called?'

'I've no idea. It's a livery stable. Why, what now?'

Agnes passed her hand across her forehead. 'Nothing. I don't know. It's just – Elias – he's missing at the moment. It's just a crazy thought I had.' She yawned. 'I'd better get back to the school, I can't miss the evening office as well.'

At his door, they held each other. 'Come back soon,' James murmured.

The nuns shuffled into the chapel and sat down, awkward in the absence of Elias. There was a moment's hesitation, in which glances were exchanged, and then Sister Teresa stood up and went to the lectern. Agnes stared up at the white vaulted ceiling, at the statue of Our Lady.

'. . . Though I walk through the valley of the shadow of death, I will fear no evil: For You are with me; Your rod and Your staff comfort me . . .'

Agnes shifted in her place, unable to shake off the feeling that there was somewhere else she ought to be.

Afterwards she went straight to her room. She paced to and fro, her mind working to sort out a tangle of thoughts. She stopped still, then suddenly went out, through the quiet corridors to the office. She went to the shelves, picked out a copy of the Yellow Pages and looked up Stables, Livery. She copied a couple of addresses down on a scrap of paper.

She went back to her room, put on a warm jumper, grabbed her coat and a torch and went out, taking the car without a second thought, even though the light was still on in Philomena's office.

She drove out of the town, towards Baines's house. She passed the end of his drive and then slowed down and followed the road towards the moor, leaving the lights of the town behind her. A sign said Burghley Stables. Livery. She stopped.

She reversed the car into a muddy gap by a gate where it couldn't be seen, and got out. She began to walk up the track that led to the stables. A dog barked, some way off. She kept to the grass, so as not to crunch the gravel underfoot.

This is mad, she thought. I'm crazy. He won't be here.

A dog barked again, nearer now, and she tried to keep calm. She heard the whinny of a horse, answered by another, and she followed the sound, round the back of the house.

There was sudden growling, very near, and Agnes froze. She could see a dog, tethered, jumping at its leash. She walked on into the yard, between neat rows of stalls, watched by the gentle equine eyes of their occupants.

'Elias?' she whispered. I'm crazy, she thought. What the hell am I going to say when the owner comes to set the dogs on me?

She heard a whinny. A cough. A human cough.

'Elias?'

Again the cough. She went towards it. A tall bay with a white stripe nodded at her.

'Elias? Is that you?' She stroked the nose of the horse, and peered over the door into the darkness beyond. Two eyes met her own. Murmuring softly to the horse, Agnes opened the stall and went in. Elias was crouched in the hay, shivering. He stared away from her. She sat down next to him and took his hands. He didn't look up.

'Do they let you stay here?' She didn't know what else to say.

'The groom knows me.' He coughed again. 'Harry. He was Baines's man, Jack took him on when he took the horses.'

'But –'

'He understands, Harry does. This is Adelaide. I rode her when she was a three-year-old. She's an old lady now.' The mare nodded in response to her name, and Elias reached out and touched her leg.

'Elias – we must get you out of here.' She hadn't meant to be so abrupt, and he let go of her hands.

'No.'

'You can't stay here.'

'I have nowhere else to go.'

'Elias –'

272

'No. You made me go back, you made me – I can't, I told you I can't, you didn't listen . . .'

'Elias, please . . .'

'If I leave here I shall die.'

She placed her hand carefully on his arm and looked into his eyes. 'Elias. You won't die. There is no going back. What happened has happened. It's the past.'

His gaze was hollow and distant. He had retreated so far away, she wondered how she'd be able to bring him back. And it's my fault, she thought.

'Are you hungry?' she tried.

He shrugged. 'Perhaps. I can't tell.'

'Elias – please come with me.'

He shook his head.

'In Laithe's Hollow . . .' she began, unsure how to go on. She looked at him. He had wrapped his arms around himself and was shivering, rocking to and fro with cold or fear or both.

'Did you love her very much?' Agnes heard herself say.

Elias stopped still. He stared at her. Then he nodded.

'And you couldn't tell Marcus?'

Elias didn't move. After a while she heard him say, 'I watched her die.'

Agnes's voice was a whisper. 'Show me. Please.'

After a moment, Elias stood up. He patted the horse, whispered into her neck, stroked her, then silently unlocked the stall, whispering goodbyes to his mare as he locked it behind them. Agnes followed him across the yard to the wooden fence. Elias climbed over it and set off across the field, Agnes hurrying to keep up. It was a damp, cloudy night, and her face was wet with the mist, but Elias seemed to know the way.

After a while Agnes recognised the path that led to the hut, but they carried on, climbing upwards, following the way they'd taken the night before. Then they were descending towards the Hollow. Elias stopped suddenly. He was staring into the distance. He raised his arm and pointed.

'There,' he whispered.

Agnes strained her eyes in the darkness.

'That's where we were.' He shivered. He seemed so thin and cold that Agnes feared for him, but she took his hand.

'Come on,' she said.

They made their way in the direction he'd pointed, skirting the edge of the Hollow until they reached a dry stone wall. Elias suddenly dropped to the ground, his hands over his face, a sobbing noise coming from his throat. 'I killed her,' Agnes heard him say.

'No –' Agnes said, but he was shaking his head, saying, 'It was my fault.'

'Tell me,' Agnes said, her hand on his shoulder.

'We were riding, here, the four of us, me, Kate, Jo and Marcus. She was Marcus's girlfriend, he adored her.' He took his hands from his face. 'She was a better rider than him, and we used to show off, her and me. And I loved her. And – and she loved me. We'd become – we'd become lovers. I think Jo knew, even then. And that day – this wall – you see up there, where it's raised, it's quite high, I said, let's jump it, and Jo called out not to, there was a ditch the other side, it had been flooded. And the worst thing was, I knew, I knew it was dangerous, but I wanted the others to see us doing something together, something crazy, something that excluded Marcus. I wanted Kate to tell Marcus it was over, I knew we should be together, and I wanted him to see . . . So – so we went over it.' He put his hands to his face again. 'I'll regret it as long as I live,' he said.

'Go on,' Agnes said.

'My horse cleared the ditch, I don't know how, and landed well, even though it was very wet. Kate came after me, and landed very badly, right into the ditch. Her horse slipped, then bolted, terrified, badly lame – shot right past me, I could see something was very wrong, and then down in the Hollow – the horse fell, with Kate under her.' Elias was shaking, and Agnes took off her coat and wrapped it around him.

'I got there first,' Elias went on. 'The others came round by the gate. By the time they arrived . . .' His eyes filled with tears. 'I knew I was watching her die. And it wasn't just . . . it wasn't only . . .' He was weeping openly now, unable to speak, and Agnes held him. She knew what he was going to say.

'It was your baby,' she murmured.

He nodded. 'She'd only told me a day or two before. Marcus didn't know. She was a few weeks pregnant. She knew it was mine. That's why she was going to tell Marcus it was over, she was going to be with me . . . Jo went for help and Marcus took her in his arms, and held her and all the time I wanted to fight him out

274

of the way, I wanted to be the one holding her, holding them both, I knew, I alone knew . . . I hated him for being there, for being in my place . . . Once she opened her eyes and she looked straight at me, and her eyes had this kind of pleading look – I nearly went for him then, so that I could be there, be with her, but I was a coward. I had to stand and watch her die, knowing it was two deaths. And there was no one else I could tell.' Agnes felt his body wracked with sobs. After a while he said, 'I've never loved anyone else. She was my life.'

They sat for some time, sheltered from the wind by the wall behind them. Elias grew calmer. He sat up, gathering Agnes's coat around him. 'And William had to come and shoot his horse,' he said suddenly. 'That's why I thought he might come back here.'

'Let's go and get warm,' Agnes said.

She led them to the hut, fishing in her pocket for the key, and once again she lit the fire and the candles, once again she made tea over Joanna's grate. They drew near to the flames, and Agnes saw their glow reflected in Elias's face as the colour returned to his cheeks and his shivering ceased.

'I couldn't face Marcus afterwards,' he said. 'I couldn't begin to tell him. He still doesn't know. He wanted to be friends, he couldn't understand . . .'

'But now – it's different now. He's got a new life, hasn't he? A wife, a baby . . .'

Elias nodded. 'We were young. Him and Kate, it wasn't serious.' He stared into his mug of tea. 'But it was for me. For us. My life ended with hers. That's why I ended up at the school. Before I met Kate I was considering the priesthood. She put a stop to all that, but then – without her . . . so that's what I became. Of course, I'm no good at it, I can't be. They don't trust me with a parish . . .' He tried to smile.

'You are good at it,' Agnes said, quietly. 'You were wonderful with Charlotte.'

He shook his head. 'How can I be good at it? My life ended then. You can't be open to God's love if you're just marking time.'

'You can't be open to God's love if you haven't suffered.'

He looked up at her, and his eyes reflected back to her the flickering of the flames. After a while he said, 'You'd better have your coat back.'

'No, I insist. Not until you pay for the dry cleaning.'
He smiled.

They left the hut and set off back across the moor. The sky was beginning to turn pale, and the ground underfoot was fresh and green in the light of the new day.

'Were you really going to stay at the stables?'

Elias shrugged. 'I don't know. I wasn't thinking straight. I just knew I couldn't go back to the school. Couldn't go anywhere.'

'And now?'

He shook his head. They walked in silence for a while, their footsteps marking a quiet rhythm. He stopped suddenly and turned to her, and she saw he was laughing.

'It's Easter Sunday,' he said.

'What's so funny?'

'Do you think Philomena can manage without me?'

Agnes smiled. She looked at the view beneath them, at Baines's house just visible beyond the fields, at the estate beyond. There was an odd glow in the sky.

'Oh God,' she said. 'The estate's burning.'

Chapter Twenty-Five

She found she was running through the streets towards the smoke which seemed to billow from behind the houses. She could hear sirens.

'Where are we going?' Elias called, breathlessly, behind her.

'It's Billy Keenan,' Agnes said, between puffs of breath. 'And Turnbull's in there, I'm sure.' Then there were police cars, and someone said, 'I'm afraid you can't go in there, Madam.'

There was a cordon of police tape. Beyond it Agnes could see columns of smoke, could hear the crackling of timber, the shouting of voices. She looked around for Janet Cole.

'I need to see someone, I know someone's in there –'

'It's all under control, Madam. No one's been hurt. Now it's best if you go home.'

'But –'

'Really, Madam, I can't allow you past.'

'Come on.' Elias took hold of her arm.

'But you don't understand, Turnbull's hiding there, and there was Reg, you see, and Nina, and Billy knows – and there was the book, about the falcons . . .'

Elias was leading her away. 'You can't go in there, Agnes.'

'But –'

'I haven't eaten for about three days, and we're expected at chapel in an hour.'

Agnes fidgeted in her place, trying to concentrate on the Easter readings. She watched Elias placing the wafers and the chalice ready on the altar, and tried to settle her mind, to become receptive to the redemptive presence of the Lord.

'Thus says the Lord,' she heard Elias read from Isaiah. She tried to block out the images of burning timber, of Billy and

Turnbull at the heart of the flames like demons, of birds of prey hovering above.

'I will make a way even through the wilderness,' she heard Elias say. 'I will provide water in the wilderness, and rivers in the barren desert . . .'

Sunlight poured through the East window, drenching the altar with colour. 'With joy you will draw water from the wells of salvation. And you will say in that day, Give thanks to the Lord, call upon His name . . .'

Agnes looked up, and met Elias's gaze. The light from the window behind him streaked his hair with gold. He smiled at her, and she smiled back, until Teresa threw her an odd look and she bowed her head in prayer instead.

Later, she lay on her bed, fighting sleep. She'd tried to talk to Janet Cole, who was out of the office, and no one else felt able to tell her what was happening on the estate. She'd phoned Baines, to talk to Patricia, but there was no answer there. She thought of going back to Billy Keenan's house, but there was no point bothering Maureen just because her son was an arsonist. And then there was Kitty Hanson. And her mother. And Billy springing to her defence last December, when she was newly bereaved.

The phone rang.

'Sweetie, I'm missing you.'

'Athena –'

'You sound tired.'

'I haven't slept for days.'

'No, neither have I.' She giggled. 'We've been in Paris, me and Nic, and Simon came too in the end, we went on the train, only just got back. Sweetie, it's fantastic, the train, you should try it, door to door in three hours, incredible, chugs along all the way to the South Coast, but once you're in France, amazing . . . we only had three days there but it felt like ages . . .'

'How nice.'

'You do sound tired. Shall I phone another time?'

'Things are rather complicated here.'

'Have you decided about your lovely man?'

'No.'

'Sweetie, if I were you –'

'Yes. I know. If you were me.'

'I'll phone tomorrow. Love and kisses.'

Agnes hung up. Something was not quite right. Something about going to Paris on the train.

Agnes snatched up her phone and dialled Athena.

'It's me. Listen – you were away on Saturday?'

'Yes, I said.'

'Simon too?'

'Yes. He and Nic get on so well. It's really annoying.'

'So Simon didn't phone David?'

'David?'

'David Snaith, the artist?'

'No, of course not, he's been away from the office. Why? Agnes? Agnes, are you there?'

Agnes stood, holding the phone. She thought of the library books in Kitty's front room.

'Athena – I'll talk to you late. 'Bye.'

She dialled David's number. It was switched off. She phoned the hospital and eventually spoke to Jo, who said he'd gone home to get clean clothes and things. 'Shall I say you called?' Jo asked.

'Yes, can you say –' Agnes hesitated, reluctant to worry her. 'Can you ask him to phone me as soon as he can. And – if anyone asks to see him about his art – can you make sure he speaks to me first? Thanks.'

She hung up, and paced her room. Then she picked up her coat and went out.

She parked her car at the edge of the estate, and got out. An acrid smell hung in the air, and she could see a couple of police cars on the street corner. She set off up the main street. The community centre was a burnt-out shell, with large beams of charred timber hanging between twisted metal. As she passed it a group of children ran giggling from behind it, a dog at their heels. She turned off past Reg's old house, to Lianna's.

She hammered on the door. Eventually there was the sound of bolts being drawn, and a voice said, 'Who is it?'

'It's Sister Agnes.'

'Oh. You.'

'Can I come in?'

The door opened a crack. 'S'pose so.'

Agnes went into the front room. The curtains were slightly drawn, and the place seemed cleaner and tidier. 'I expect the police have been bothering you, looking for Turnbull.'

'They're always bothering me, makes no difference who they're bleedin' lookin' for.'

'Silly, isn't it. Even if you were hiding him –'

'Which I'm not.'

'No, of course not. But even if you were – they'd only have to search the rooms to find him.'

'They did. Didn't find no one.'

'But he's wanted for terrible things, Lianna.'

'Don't make no difference to me.'

'Two murders and two attempted murders. Reg, Mark, Nina and Jo. Even though I know as well as you do that he didn't kill anyone.'

Lianna flopped into a chair and lit a cigarette. The ashtray at her elbow was spotless. 'He did over his sister-in-law.'

'Yes.'

'He's in a terrible state about it. Cryin' and that. Says he loves her.' She drew hard on the cigarette. 'Do you think he does? Love her?'

'Perhaps he does.'

'Is she pretty?'

'I don't know. I suppose so, yes.'

'Does she love him?'

'Anthony? No, she has someone else. She's devoted to him.' Agnes heard a slight noise in the kitchen.

'Is she serious about this bloke?'

'Yes. He's at her bedside all the time.' Agnes raised her voice slightly. 'He's saved her life. She loves him very much.'

Lianna's features softened, and her face lightened with her childlike smile. 'Will they get married?'

'Oh, I think so, yes.' Agnes saw the doorhandle move a fraction.

'That's not what he says, Anthony. He says they're made for each other. He sits where you are and goes on about her, it in't right, is it?'

'I think perhaps Anthony's life has gone rather awry.'

'I don't know why I put up wi' it. Maybe because he's got no one else.'

'He can't stay here for ever.'

'That's what I keep telling him. But he goes on about this Jo, as if she's going to make everything all right for him. Do you think she will?'

'No,' Agnes said, as loudly as she could without sounding unnatural. 'I think Jo is perfectly happy without him.' As she spoke the kitchen door flew open and Anthony stood there. He seemed thinner. His suit was filthy, and buttoned unevenly. His eyes burned out from the pallor of his face.

'What the hell do you know about it?'

Lianna flinched, and swung round to face him. 'I didn't tell her, honest!'

'How dare you come in here and tell me what Joanna thinks?' He didn't take his eyes from Agnes, and she saw how he smouldered with hatred and rage.

'You attacked her—' Agnes tried.

'I was – it was all so— I was trying to protect her . . .' He ran his hand across his face, and for a moment the rage left him. 'She needs me,' he said.

'She needs David,' Agnes said, as calmly as she could.

He shook his head. The gesture was exaggerated. 'You know nothing about it,' he said.

'Do you remember when we had lunch?' Agnes tried again. He frowned and shook his head, and she realised he wasn't pretending. 'You took me to a lovely restaurant.' She saw the bewilderment in his eyes. He sat down heavily on a chair. 'We talked about forgiveness,' she went on. A flicker of recognition passed across his face. 'Then you got a phone call, and you became distressed. And that night, Nina Warburton was attacked, in an incompetent and cowardly manner. Surely you remember that bit?'

'If you've come here to accuse me, you can leave now.' She saw the anger returning, saw him hang on to it, clinging to it as the only reality he knew.

'It was desperate, wasn't it, Anthony – that just because Mark had been killed, you thought you'd follow suit. And Billy Keenan's friends were willing—'

'I didn't mean—' she heard him murmur. 'When I talked to those lads, I didn't mean that they should . . .' He rubbed his forehead, blinking.

'And David – were you going to do the same to him?'

'I – I don't know . . . I wasn't thinking straight. I spoke to that lad, we talked about money, I remember that, I just thought, if only they were all out of the way, these obstacles, if only the mill just wasn't there any more. I wanted it to be over, you see, I just wanted it all to end . . .'

'And so you asked that lad to attack Nina?'

Anthony stared at her, then nodded. 'Yes. I must have done.' He bit his lip. 'That rope, the knots, he showed me. I must have asked him to . . . and then I came to the mill and saw her there, in the night, so frightened . . . terrible. But it was William, you see, it's his fault, I went to see him, I tried to explain, it was the missing document, you know, I knew he'd got it, I searched high and low for it, and when I challenged him he said everything rested with Jo. He said he was counting on her. So I had to get it from her. I found her on the moors, I tried to explain, that night, on the moor, that it was her future, my future . . .'

'He didn't mean that Jo had the document. He meant – he was speaking about his own state of mind . . .' Agnes saw the anguish behind Turnbull's eyes, and imagined him confronting William, both men half-crazed, despairing, one lost in grief, the other facing bankruptcy; neither able to understand the other. 'Anthony,' she tried, gently, 'if you turn yourself in, you'll only be charged with assault—'

'No, GBH, at least,' Lianna piped up, helpfully. 'And conspiracy to murder, even if old Doddsy did bottle out at the last moment, he could still give evidence against you.'

Agnes sighed. Turnbull was slumped in his chair. He looked confused. 'You see,' Agnes said, 'as things stand they're likely to charge you with two other murders, Mark's and Reg's.'

'But I didn't –' he sat up, agitated. 'I didn't mean any harm. The truth is, Agnes . . .' his hands were working in his lap. 'The truth is, I can't quite see where I am in all this. Somewhere it all went wrong.' He sighed, and smiled, an uneven, distant smile. 'I remember now, that lunch. Forgiveness.' He nodded. 'Forgiveness, I remember. But things had gone wrong for me. The mill, you see, was the answer to it all, I thought. But the sums didn't add up. And I was borrowing more and more, and the mill . . . I used to have these dreams, about drowning, a dead weight around my neck, used to wake up shouting . . .' he laughed, an odd, dry laugh. 'Millstone, they say, don't they? Millstone round your neck . . .' He raised his eyes to meet hers, but he seemed to be looking beyond her. 'And then I planned to sell it, it seemed the only way, and I realised the old trust would prevent me, and then Mark was found dead. And – and then it began to make sense. It was as if it was all falling into place, somehow, and I felt that if I just took things a bit further myself . . .' His voice tailed off, and he stared into the distance.

'And Jo?'

'I knew she'd understand.'

'Does she know any of this?'

'I tried to tell her on the moor that night, I knew she'd gone after her father, I caught up with her. We were lovers, you know.'

'Once. A long time ago.'

'But it lived on.'

'For you, perhaps.'

He looked at her then, and his eyes flashed with anger. 'For her too. On the moor, I knew she'd listen then, I told her we should be together, I told her I'd sell the mill, the site could be worth millions, we could go away, leave it all behind, I told her all this, I knew she'd understand once I explained, she knows we have to be together . . .'

'And what did she say?'

Turnbull pulled at the buttons on his jacket. He glanced at Lianna, and then stared at the floor. 'She didn't give me time to explain.'

'Anthony, I know what she said. She said she doesn't want you to sell the mill.'

'She's all I had left. I tried to tell her . . .'

'And that's why you went for her?'

'I can't – she didn't —'

'And she said she didn't love you.'

'No—'

'Didn't she?'

Turnbull met her eyes with a gaze that was now clear and focused. 'I don't think you know what you're talking about,' he said. His voice was level.

Agnes felt Lianna shrink away from him. She took a deep breath and said again, 'Anthony, she doesn't love you. You have no future with her.'

Turnbull stood up, his eyes still fixed on her.

'She doesn't love you. She loves David.' Agnes wondered whether he was armed. Turnbull took a step towards her. Agnes saw Lianna flash a nervous glance at her.

'No,' Anthony said, his voice like steel.

Agnes took a deep breath and said, 'Joanna loves David,' and at the same moment she flung herself sideways as Turnbull's fist crashed into the back of the chair where she'd been sitting. Agnes sprang to her feet, aware of Lianna shouting, of a strange roaring noise which she saw came from Anthony who was pummelling the back of the chair, crying, 'No, no . . .'

Lianna went up to him and calmly slapped his face. He stopped, straightened up, his hand to his cheek, his eyes staring in astonishment. Suddenly he began to cry, and Lianna wrapped her arms around him, and he laid his head on her shoulder.

'There, there,' she murmured, at the same time nudging her mobile phone towards Agnes with her foot. Agnes slipped out into the hall and called the police.

'It'll be all right,' Lianna was saying, when Agnes reappeared. 'You need time to think, Anthony. And when you come back, I'll be here.'

Lights flashed blue outside the window, and Agnes ran to open the door for the police, glad to see that Janet Cole was amongst them. Turnbull stood up and allowed himself to be handcuffed and led away to the waiting car.

'Treat him gently,' Agnes said to Janet.

Turnbull turned to her. 'My wife, you see . . .' his eyes welled with tears. 'My wife . . . I've rather let her down . . . Tell her I'm sorry.'

Agnes stood with Lianna in the doorway and watched him being driven away. Beyond the car, Agnes could see the burnt-out shell of a row of houses, a sign saying 'Dangerous Structure, Do Not Enter'. A thin column of smoke still rose in the distance.

'I'll miss him,' Lianna said. 'Bit of a nutcase, but at least he was company.'

Agnes turned to her. 'What will you do?'

Lianna shrugged. 'Just carry on, I suppose.'

'Isn't there somewhere you could go?'

'Where? Where am I going to go? I could run away from here, wherever I end up would be just the same. Or worse.' She tossed her blonde hair and Agnes was reminded of Leonora.

'Don't you have family?'

'Me?' Lianna snorted. 'Maybe once. Not now.'

'A mother?'

Lianna shook her head. 'If I ran to her, she'd kick me out soon as look at me.'

Agnes looked at the street which stretched away into the distance. She imagined Lianna walking along it, suitcase in hand, nowhere to go.

Lianna squeezed her arm and smiled. 'I'll be all right.'

Agnes walked slowly back to her car. In the car she phoned Jo again.

'Oh, Agnes, didn't David phone you? I gave him your message, he said he would. He's at his granny's.'

'His granny's?'

'She wanted to see him.'

'Millie?'

'That's right, he's there.'

Agnes drove fast to Myddleton Terrace and parked on the corner. She knocked at Millie's door. David opened the door and let her in.

Chapter Twenty-Six

It was dark by the time she reached James's house that evening.

'Happy Easter,' he said. 'You look terrible.' He ushered her into the house. 'You look as if you haven't slept for days.'

'I was out on the moor again last night,' she said, allowing him to take her coat. 'And then Billy Keenan torched the estate, and then Turnbull came out of hiding and gave himself up.' James was looking at her with an expression of concern. 'And I had to talk to an old lady about her memories. I've just come from there.'

'Surely this old lady's memories aren't that urgent?'

'I'm afraid they're very important indeed.'

'You ought to go home and rest.'

'And I wanted to see Evelyn.'

'Evelyn?'

Agnes nodded.

'She's here. We're discussing possible tenants for this house.' He looked suddenly weary.

She touched his arm. 'I'm nearly ready to decide,' she said. He turned and she followed him into the lounge.

Later, when Evelyn went to wash up, Agnes joined her.

'It's a sad business, James packing up his house,' Evelyn said. 'I just hope he has time to enjoy his travelling.'

Agnes took a tea-towel and began to dry the dishes. 'So do I,' she said, but her voice came out as a whisper, and Evelyn glanced at her. From the next room came the sound of Joss's booming laughter, and they both smiled at each other. 'I wanted to ask you –' Agnes said after a moment.

'What?'

'I don't know how to say this. Marcus – Baines's son – we talked all night, up on the moor.' Evelyn put a glass down on the draining board and fiddled with it. 'He said there was a letter,' Agnes went on. 'From his mother – to him, his father wouldn't let him see it, that's why they fell out, when Hannah died . . .' Evelyn was now looking at her directly, her gaze level. 'And I had to know – I realised – there was something about Joss, the way you are together, it just struck me –' Agnes saw Evelyn working to control her feelings, and she stopped. 'I'm sorry, this is impertinent, I shouldn't have raised the subject.'

'No, go on,' Evelyn said, her voice calm.

'I thought you might know what was in the letter.'

Evelyn turned to the sink. She carefully washed another glass and placed it on the draining rack. 'The letter,' she said, softly, 'is what you think it is.'

On the morning of Easter Monday, Agnes sat in chapel, wondering at the change in Elias. He read the service with a clear voice that resounded through the chapel, and, rather than hide behind his chair, he stood upright, surveying the small congregation with visible good humour. Afterwards he caught up with her as she left the chapel.

'You look tired,' he said.

'I can't do, I slept for about ten hours last night.'

'I thought I'd visit Jo in hospital this afternoon, do you want to come too?'

'I've got to be somewhere quite important this evening.'

'We'll be back in time for chapel.'

'OK.'

'You can give me a lift.'

'There's always an ulterior motive with you.'

'I was quite growing to like you, don't spoil it now,' Elias said, laughing.

In the car he turned to her. 'I hope you're going to stay at the school next year,' he said, suddenly.

'That's up to the order,' Agnes said.

'I'm not sure it is,' he said. 'I thought, perhaps, you were considering leaving.'

'How do you know?'

'Something Philomena said.'

'So now everyone knows that I'm feckless and disobedient?'

'It was nicer than that. She's quite concerned about you.'

'The thing is, Elias, God has seen fit to present me with a choice. I can either stay put. Or I can join an old friend of mine, who I've known since I was child, and help him to live out his last months in happiness, at the same time tying up some loose ends about my own life that badly need tying up. And having some fun in the process.'

'What are you going to do?'

'I wish I knew.' She turned on to the ring road towards Bradford.

'It's a lot to throw away, to give up this life,' Elias said.

'I know.'

'Just for a short-term decision.'

'But what is life for? What if I say no, and then regret it, and stay here and fester away in the order?'

'Maybe it's not festering; maybe it's learning to live free of the demands of the self. You see, if you learn to relinquish the self, you allow yourself to develop as God wants.'

'And is holing myself up here against my will really relinquishing the self?'

'All I mean is, life becomes clearer if we live with a sense that it could be taken from us tomorrow.'

'But then that's all the more reason to live. Why die in advance of death? Why not live first, as God has granted you life? It's like those paintings, Elias, the Still Lifes. They're the celebration of the material world, of God's creation.'

'But that's why there's the skull, the clock, to remind you that it's illusory, that it will pass.'

'Of course it will pass; but the objects in the paintings are here and now, aren't they? They're saying WE ARE. I AM. While we're on this earth, we should be joyful to be here. If I turn away from James, then I'm denying life.'

'If you accept this trip, you're denying faith.'

Agnes frowned as she thought about this. 'But if that's the case, then my faith becomes something empty, doesn't it? No longer a dialogue with a living God, just a set of rules.'

'I'm not sure I have a dialogue with God.'

'I'm not surprised.' They turned into the hospital driveway, and she smiled at him. 'It must be very difficult to communicate with the space between atoms.'

They passed along white corridors, following a series of signs, and at last came to Joanna's ward. She was sitting up in bed, her head bandaged, her eyes still swollen and bruised, but her expression when she saw them was cheerful.

'How nice of you to come,' she said, as they pulled up a chair each. 'You're looking very well, Elias.'

'It must be Easter,' he said. 'The renewal of the spirit. There's no need to look quite so sceptical,' he added, as Joanna smiled.

'And I gather my awful brother-in-law gave himself up.' She turned to Agnes.

'Yes.'

Jo shuddered. 'Even if he didn't kill the others, I'm going to make sure he serves time for nearly killing me.'

'You'll have to be a witness. You'll have to re-live it.'

'I re-live it all the time. Flashbacks. They tell me they go after a while. When I go to sleep it's worst.' She sipped at her glass of water. 'It's Patricia I feel sorry for. She was here earlier. All her hopes and dreams, just shattered.'

'How is she?'

'She's thrown herself into looking after Daddy and salvaging the mill from Turnbull's mess. She wants to talk to Marcus –' she stopped and glanced at Elias.

'I thought –' Agnes began, 'I thought he was disinherited.'

'Daddy might change his mind, she thinks.'

Elias cleared his throat. 'How is Marcus?'

'He's fine. He came to see me yesterday, with Rachel and the baby. Imogen. She's lovely, very sweet.' She looked across to Elias and briefly touched his arm.

'And where's David?'

'Oh, around. He's got some meeting this evening, about his work. Seems rather preoccupied. God knows where it is. He said something about going to see an art dealer in some old mill the other side of town.'

'I'm sure we'll find it.'

Joanna looked at Agnes in surprise. 'Are you going too?'

'Um, yes, I am.'

'Good. Look after him, it all sounds rather dodgy to me.'

Agnes drove Elias back to the school in time for the evening office, and then sat in the canteen with Sister Teresa over a plate of macaroni cheese.

'Are you all right?' Teresa asked her. 'You keep looking at your watch.'

290

'Oh – yes, fine, thanks. Got to be somewhere quite soon.'

'And you've left half your supper.'

'I'm not hungry at the moment.'

'It's like flu, it really is.'

'What is?'

'Anorexia.'

Agnes laughed. 'I've been neurotic for many years and I've never lost my appetite over it. I don't intend to start now.'

At seven o'clock Agnes parked the convent car outside Millie Coulter's house. She knocked on the door and Millie let her in.

'David's on his way,' Millie said, 'he just phoned.' She had the same angular face as David, the same bright eyes. She was wearing a smart red suit, which looked odd in the everyday comfort of her home. She showed Agnes into the front room. It was similar to Florence's, except it had a beige-tiled gas fireplace instead of a Victorian one. The two women stood in the room, both too nervous to sit down. There was a knock at the door, and then David came in. He looked pale. He smiled briefly at Agnes, and then said, 'Let's go, shall we?'

'Are you sure about this?' Agnes asked him.

He nodded.

'We should call the police first,' she said.

He shook his head. 'I want to know. I want to hear what happened. I must know.'

Millie looked at Agnes. 'It's up to him, isn't it? Let's go.'

They left the estate, and drove out of the town along the valley. They could see the chimney of Allbright's Mill receding in the distance, the lights of the town blinking beneath it. They reached the river, drove a little way along a private road, then parked. They were at a mill. Above them towered a huge old chimney, and beyond that they could see the ragged spokes of the old water wheel, still hanging on to the side of the building above the river.

There was no lighting. The mill seemed derelict, its vast emptiness and broken windows telling a familiar story of decline and bankruptcy.

'Are you sure it was here?' Millie whispered.

David nodded. He went up to a door, a huge chunk of oak in the side of the building, and pushed at it. It opened.

They were in pitch darkness. The windows were dark grey squares, receding away from them into the blackness. Agnes realised they were in the main weaving shed. They stood, straining their eyes to see. Agnes put her hand on the phone in her pocket. In the silence she could hear the sound of water dripping.

David moved forward, and his footstep echoed in the cavernous space. Nothing happened. They waited.

'What now?' Millie whispered.

Agnes felt her skin tighten at the thought that they'd walked straight into a trap. She wished she'd argued David out of doing it this way.

'I don't know,' she whispered back.

Then there was a sound. A creak of a door, at the far end of the mill floor. A strip of light appeared, so tiny it seemed to be miles away, then vanished again. Someone must have come through the other door.

'So you're here, then, David Snaith.' It was a woman's voice, faint, but resonating in the emptiness.

David took a few steps towards the voice. 'I'm here,' he said.

'And what's it like, not to be able to see?' The voice seemed nearer. 'Because that's what it was like for Mark, before he died. And for Reg. And that's how it will be for you.'

David stopped, and Agnes was aware of his tension. 'So it was you,' he said at last.

'It was me,' the voice said.

'You killed my brother,' David said, his voice betraying a tidal wave of pain and anger. Agnes touched his sleeve, fearful that he might try to attack, but he stayed where he was, his fists clenched at his side. Millie had stepped back into the shadows.

'Why?' David called. 'Why did you kill Mark? What had he ever done to you? Who are you?'

'It's what Mother wanted,' she said.

'Who the hell was Mother?'

'You know the photo. I gave it to you.'

'The – the athletics team?'

'You were the last. I knew what she meant, she didn't have to tell me.'

'But – Mark –'

'You were the only ones left, you boys and Reg. Ernest had gone, Ray had gone. No children, you see.' The voice wavered

292

slightly. 'Only you. You boys. The line, it had to be ended.'

'Because – because of my grandfather? But –'

'I promised her. After she died . . . I promised.'

Agnes was aware of movement, a hint of cold air, as someone moved through the mill from behind them.

'Her life was ruined,' the voice was saying, 'Father could never forgive her, even though she was innocent, even though it was all the fault of those bastard so-called –'

'Heroes?' Millie's voice rang through the mill, and suddenly all the lights came on. Millie was standing by the door, her hand on the mains switch. David was standing some feet in front. Beyond him, a long way away at the other end of the mill, stood the diminutive figure of Kitty Hanson. Agnes turned to see Billy Keenan, who'd appeared next to David, and who now looked from Agnes to Millie, trying to hide his surprise behind a look of cool amusement. He had one hand in his pocket, and Agnes realised he must be armed.

'Is that what you were going to say?' Millie walked towards Kitty. 'That my old man was a hero, along with Reg and Ray? A war hero, returning to the mill in glory, full of tales of bravery?'

Kitty stared at Millie open-mouthed.

'Or,' Millie went on, 'or were you going to say that my husband raped your mother? Just because she had what folk said was a German name? So he raped her, with his two best mates, in the jungle-crazed twilight world that they shared. Is that what you were going to say? Go on, then, say it. Tell us all about it. God knows I know enough of that man's brutality to last the rest of my life. But go on, we're here to listen.'

Kitty was standing quite still, looking from Millie to David to Agnes, blinking.

'Because if you're not going to, I will.' Millie took a few more steps towards Kitty. Billy hovered behind her, uncertain, his hand still in his pocket. 'I'll tell you,' Millie went on, 'what it was like living with a war hero, because I lived it, day after day after day. Those lads went off to war, three cheerful boys, and came back as three battle-scarred, half-insane, brutalised men.'

Kitty was breathing hard. She spoke with difficulty. 'Afterwards, Mother had to see them every day, she had to work next to them, after the – after it happened. At first they were off work for months, and she could forget, for a while. But then they were allowed back, no blame, no fingers pointed at them, to say what they'd done, what terrible terrible thing they'd done. The fingers pointed at Mother instead, because she was the woman, and the eyes, staring, everywhere she went, the eyes looking at her, saying, she's the one, she's the one they . . .' Kitty stopped, gulping air. 'All the rest of the time in the mill, she had to see those men, watching her, looking at her, knowing what they knew of her. It destroyed her, those eyes on her. It destroyed us all.'

'But why make Mark pay?' David said. 'Why make us pay?'

'Because I paid. I paid a hundred times over. And my mother, God rest her soul, paid a thousand times over, ten thousand times over, re-living what your grandfather and Reg and Ray did to her, having to see them in the mill, day in, day out. There was no justice, not in them days. No tribunals, nothing. She spent the rest of her life, knowing what they knew, watching them watching her. Sordid, shabby, dirty, bastards.' She paused for breath. Her face was pinched, expressionless. 'After her death, I didn't know what to do. And I was going through her things, and I found that photo. With those marks. And then I knew what I must do, I knew what Mother was trying to tell me I must do. Reg, I wanted him to be first, but then I heard about Mark and those birds, up at Morton's Crag and I realised it would be easy, up there. And I read about it, and pretended to be from that society, the bird one, and phoned him up, and warned him that his birds were in danger. And then I waited up on the moors. And then Billy here gave him a lift. It was easy. Reg was easy too, because he knew me. You were more of a problem, particularly once the police started their hullabaloo about it all. And then you were never alone. I got Billy to phone you about your paintings.'

Billy shifted uneasily on his feet.

'How did you do it?' David's voice was clear. 'And why – and how – his eyes –'

Kitty smiled. 'I was alone. Billy was nowt to do with it, were you, love? He was just the driver, he didn't know what I was going to do. He just dropped him off. Then I came up behind him, I knew where he'd be, there's a place that's just right for looking at the birds, and I knew he'd go there, and once he was there, kind of wedged against the rock, I came up behind him with my rope, and a knife . . . took him by surprise, you see.' Her fingers made little jabbing movements in the palm of her hand. 'And all the time I was thinking of Ernest, and Ray, and Reg, and what they did to Mother, they shut her in a storeroom one day, it had been building up for months, the taunts, the jeers, and she ignored it, and they got worse and worse, that's what she told me, and then one day they shut her in, and they took turns, she told me all about it when she was dying, she hadn't told a soul, she'd lived with the whispers all her life. Dad didn't want to know, she had to tell someone, didn't she?' Two spots of colour had appeared on Kitty's cheeks. 'It ruined her life,' she said.

Millie broke the silence. 'It makes it better, doesn't it, love?' She was now quite near to Kitty, with Billy close behind. 'It makes it better, if you've suffered, to pass it on. Look at David here, without his brother, living with a grief that'll never go away. And look at you, living all your life with a mother who'd suffered as Esther did, look at how that's written on your face. And your mother, barely out of her teens, a virgin, learning that everything that should be about love was about hate instead, and living out her marriage unable to forget. And look at my Ernest, at what he did, at how that's brought us all here, just because he, too, thought that if you can pass your suffering on, it goes away. So he passed it on to Esther. And to me.' She stopped, and Agnes saw her eyes filled with tears. 'My Ernest saw things in the war, things he could hardly bring himself to tell me, the worst that men can be. He saw bloodied bits of body, they looked like meat, he said, until you recognised a bit of face and realised you were looking at one of your mates. He learned what it was like to feel a knife slip into live flesh, to see someone gasping their last at his feet – and now you know that too, Kitty. That's what he passed on to you. And to me, he passed on all his fear and pain and anger, and he made sure I should feel it too.' She was breathing with difficulty. 'But you see,' she went on, 'he was wrong. If you pass suffering on, it doesn't go away. And in the darkest nights, when he was still asleep but living out his terrors, he'd toss and turn, and cry out, like a child, like a young boy crying for his mother, and as the nightmare subsided, he'd be weeping, real tears, and I'd take him in my arms and rock him, and soothe him, and he'd hold me, and gradually he'd grow calm, and settle back to sleep. And I'd take his arms away from me, and lie down next to him, and know that next day he'd have shut it all away again, and he'd be back to being the monster that I had to call my husband. But I know that in those nights, those nights when he'd call out like a child, all I felt for him was pity.' She stopped, her cheeks wet with tears.

Kitty's eyes were strangely bright. 'And do you expect me to pity him too?' she said.

Millie looked at her calmly. 'He ruined your life,' she said. 'It's not for me to tell you.'

Kitty looked from one to the other. She seemed diminished, a tiny, stooping figure in the empty mill. She began to shiver, and hugged her arms around herself. She looked to Agnes, who stood, her hand on her phone; to David, who'd moved to stand next to his grandmother; to Millie, who leaned against her grandson, exhausted; to Billy, who took from his pocket a large, sharpened kitchen knife, held it out for all to see, then dropped it on the floor and put his foot down firmly on it, as the noise of police sirens broke the silence, and flashing blue lights cut through the night outside.

Billy shrugged. 'I warned t'coppers. Told them this is where we'd be.' He looked at his watch. 'Bang on time.'

Kitty was strangely calm. The broken windows of the mill glinted with the headlight beams as she was helped into the waiting car. Agnes joined Billy in the next car, and Millie and David in a third, and they processed out of the millyard, leaving the mill in darkness once more.

'Why did you turn her in?' Agnes asked Billy.

'Don't rightly know. Seemed for the best. I've grown very fond of our Kitty. Known her all my life, she's been good to me. Since her mum died, we've got closer, my mates rib me about it, older woman and that, in't none of their business if you ask me. And then, t'other night, she told me, all about it. About Mark. Felt pretty bad about it then, as it were me who'd brought him there, not knowing what were goin' on. I think she thought it made me part of it, you know, like she wanted me to tell her she was right. She hadn't really taken in what she'd done. And Reg, she told me all about him, too. And I didn't know what to do. In't in my nature to turn someone over to t'coppers, but this were out of my league. And when she told me about her plans for David, I thought, better go along wi' it, let t'coppers in on it too. She needs help, don't she, I thought it the best way. Though, knowing this lot, they'll try to pin it on me.'

'I'll vouch for you,' Agnes said, seeing the two police officers exchange glances. 'But they can still get you for arson.'

'Oh, that.'

'Yes. That.'

Billy grinned. 'Sometimes I just feel like watching a nice fire.'

Once they'd been released from the police station, Agnes and David took Millie home. It was after midnight. They sat in front of her gas fire with mugs of tea. David looked up, as if he was about to speak, sighed, fell silent again. Eventually Millie said, 'It's funny how you can know something and not know it at the same time. If you'd asked me about poor Esther – if you'd asked me about that, all those years Ernest was alive, I'd have sworn blind I knew nothing about it. But then you came to me, and told me about Kitty. And when I put them lights on, and saw her, standing there in that mill tonight – I realised then that I knew it all the time. I knew what he'd done, him and the others. He never told me. I just knew it.'

David nodded.

Agnes sipped her tea. 'Do you think Florence knows?'

Millie frowned. 'I doubt it. But then again, perhaps, like me, she'll find out she knew all along.'

'And if she'd had children,' David said, 'or grandchildren – Kitty would have tried to kill them too.' He shook his head. 'I still can't believe it. Mark – that she did that . . .' he sighed, and Agnes saw that his hands were shaking.

'We should get you back to Joanna,' she said to him.

Chapter Twenty-Seven

'Sweetie, you're not listening to a word I've been saying.' Athena's fork was poised at her lips and she stared accusingly at Agnes.

Agnes blinked. 'I'm sorry.'

'I mean, just because you had to track down some batty old thing in a deserted coal mine –'

'– woollen mill.'

'Whatever. Anyway, that was two days ago, and she's all locked up now, and your artist friend is safe, and happily reunited with his girlfriend, and there I was telling you something really interesting, and you weren't even listening.'

'I was. You went backstage at some pop concert –'

'Not backstage, sweetie, I went to the party afterwards, try and pay attention, Nic's son is working for this lighting company, and he got me a pass, I've forgotten the name of the band, but do you know, I'm sure I saw George Harrison standing by the bar, I was wearing my cream suit, you know the one, with the black velvet collar – you're still not listening, are you? And you haven't touched your lasagne.'

'No, I'm not very good company at the moment.'

'Poor sweetie. You still haven't decided, have you?'

'I'm seeing James this evening.'

'And what will you tell him?'

'Probably, nothing. Again.'

She parked the car outside James's cottage. There was the scent of spring in the freshness of the April evening. She looked at his house, and imagined it empty. The thought was unbearable.

James opened the door. 'I heard your car.'

She smiled as he took her coat. 'Athena says I must give you an answer.'

'I like your friend Athena. And I've never even met her.'

They sat down to chicken casserole and salad. He poured her a glass of red wine. 'I don't quite know how to say this,' he said suddenly, getting up again, 'but I thought this might make it easier.' He handed her what looked like a slip of paper, and then sat down again opposite her, watching her.

Agnes took the paper and realised as she looked at it that it was an airline ticket, destination Nice. She looked at the date. 'But that's only a week away,' she said.

'I just wanted you to have it. That way we don't have to talk about it any more, you can just join me here in time to catch the plane – or even meet me at the airport, if you like, it's Manchester . . . I didn't want to make you miserable, putting pressure on you. I've paid for the ticket anyway, so it's no problem . . . what I mean is, oh God, this is more difficult, and I was trying to make it easier . . .'

Agnes got up and went over to him, and rested her hands on his shoulders. 'You're probably the most discreet and tactful person I know. James – I understand. I'll let you know in good time, you won't have to hang around at the airport waiting for me, I promise.' She put the ticket in her pocket and sat down in her place.

He sipped his wine, and then put down his glass. 'It's a shame the Campbells aren't here, they're very fond of you.'

'I like them too.'

'And so close, aren't they? Do you know what Joss said, the other day? He said that Evelyn had taught him what love really means. He said that once he thought he knew all above love, but it was only through her that he truly understood.' James glanced up at Agnes and smiled. 'Though he can't expect us to know what he means, two steadfastly unmarried people like us, can he?'

Agnes met his eyes, which were bright with amusement. 'But we do know what he means. It's not just in marriage that you learn about faith, is it? Evelyn loves Joss unconditionally, even knowing what he is, what he's done, and forgiving him, and loving him regardless – and from that he's learnt too, that she's the person he must be with.'

James was regarding her with a questioning look. 'Perhaps you know my friends better than I do,' he said.

Agnes hesitated. 'Some things become clear, that's all.'

★ ★ ★

It was late when she returned to her room, but she picked up her phone and dialled Julius's number.

His voice was sleepy. 'Only you would ring me at home at this time of night.'

'I have to talk to you.'

'Talk away.'

'James has given me a plane ticket for a week's time.'

'Lucky you.'

'Julius, please be helpful.'

'I am being helpful. First you phone me yesterday with tales of murderous women trapped in deserted mills, then you phone me to say you've accepted this plane ticket. There's nothing much I can say. If you've taken his ticket, then that's all decided, isn't it?'

'Don't be cross –'

'I'm not cross.'

'Just because I've got a ticket doesn't mean I'm going to go.'

'Ah, so I'm not sacked yet.'

'What on earth do you mean?'

'As your conscience. I'm still in a job, then.'

'You know I value your opinion.'

'You know what I think.'

'Yes.'

'Do you want this whole performance again? You phone me up to ask me what to do, because you want me to tell you not to go. So I tell you not to go. And a few days later we have to do it all again.'

Agnes went silent.

'Agnes?'

She sighed. 'The thing is – I can't imagine not going. What if he dies while he's away, without me? I'll always regret it.'

'This is between you and your God, Agnes.'

'And what's He going to say?'

'You'll have to ask Him. You see, it seems to me that all this is about faith. Deciding to stay may well make you miserable. But it's in the decision itself, the act of commitment, that it will become the right thing to have done.'

'It's a big gamble.'

'Yes, but look at the stakes.'

'If you met James you'd understand.'

'It's just as well I haven't, then. There'd be no one left to be your conscience.'

Agnes laughed. 'Poor Julius. It's a thankless task. Athena thinks I should go.'

'She always gets the fun bit.'

Agnes heard him yawn. 'Go back to bed,' she said.

When she walked into Nina's office next morning, Nina got up and gave her a hug.

'I wondered how you were,' she said. 'Coffee?'

Agnes surveyed the office. 'It looks different in here.'

'Yes, I made a few changes.' Nina found mugs and a jar of instant coffee. 'As someone who's on the board of the mill, I decided to arrange my office accordingly. No more personnel files, for example.'

'You're right, it's much clearer.'

'And I'm choosing some nicer furniture. Patricia's going to have the office next door, we're going to coordinate our colours.'

'And the others?'

Nina handed her a mug of coffee. 'What others?'

'David? Jo? Marcus – aren't they on the board too?'

'Jo's sticking with her decision not to take her share. David's not interested, we've got to find a way to buy him out. Marcus – we don't know. There's a party at Baines's on Saturday, you're invited, we're going to talk to him then.'

'But – you mean, Marcus is going to visit his father?'

'Yes.' Nina frowned. 'Any reason why not?'

'Well – yes – I mean, no. I don't suppose so.'

Nina stirred some sugar into her coffee. 'I have to say, I was very glad when Jo and David bowed out gracefully. Too many artists around. We'd have the whole mill turned over to modern sculpture and Hockney, like everyone else around here. Terrible nuisance when you've got a business to run. I've got my eye on uniforms,' Nina added.

'Uniforms?'

'Polyester suiting. Corporate identity, you see. All these banks, building societies, all those poor girls have to wear the same stuff. And it changes every year. It's a huge market. All we have to do is the maroon with grey fleck this year, the grey with blue fleck next year – and all my sales team has to do is sell the stuff. And armies.'

'Armies?'

'Middle East, that's the hottest area these days.'

'Nina, you're joking.'

'Joking? No I'm not.'

'But – armies?'

'Chill out, Agnes, I'm only dressing them. I've never yet heard of anyone winning a war just because their army got the nattiest rig.'

'Yes, but –'

'It's trade, Agnes. Look at this area. Look at how it's going down the tubes. What good is my conscience if it means my own next-door neighbour starves?'

Agnes stared at her.

'I'm right, aren't I?'

'Well, um – yes. S'pose you are.'

'Nina, how about those lovely maroon chairs—' Patricia came into the office clutching a catalogue, then stopped. 'Agnes – how lovely to see you.' She kissed her lightly on both cheeks. 'I've been trying to get hold of you, but your school doesn't seem to know where you are most of the time.'

'No, I'm playing truant these days. But the girls are back next week, then I'll have to show up.'

'I wanted to invite you to Daddy's on Saturday, about four, for tea, we don't want Jo to get tired, just a nice restful do, maybe use the garden if this lovely weather lasts. Even Marcus is invited, although Jo saw him yesterday, and he was a bit upset.'

'What about?' Agnes looked up, her cup halfway to her lips.

'Oh, something about an old letter that Daddy had given him, something from our mother. Anyway, can you bring Elias? I'd love to see him again.'

'I'll try. And, I wonder if I might suggest someone else you should invite?'

On Saturday afternoon, Agnes knocked at the door of Elias's flat. He opened the door to her. He was wearing a white shirt that looked expensive, and a dark green silk tie.

'Why are you laughing?' he asked, going to get his coat.

'I wasn't laughing.'

'You look just as silly.'

'I don't.' Agnes glanced at her black jacket and trousers and cream silk shirt. 'I look just right.'

'These are my best clothes.'

'I'm just not used to it, that's all.'

They went to the car. Agnes started the engine and pulled out on to the road. 'Patricia will be glad about the weather,' Agnes said. They drove away from the town, across the moors which were shot through with vivid green and gold in the afternoon sun.

The living room was transformed. Half the furniture had gone, and the floor was newly polished, the curtains drawn back. There were french windows open on to the garden. The dogs ran back and forth effusively, and when they saw Elias they jumped up at him in delight.

'Elias . . .' Patricia came over and kissed him.

'You haven't changed a bit,' he said.

'I thought priests were supposed to tell the truth,' Patricia laughed. 'Joanna, Elias is here.'

Joanna was lying on a couch by the window. She was wearing a velvet turban and a deep blue dress. David was sitting by her. He stood up and came over to Elias and Agnes, and hugged them both.

'Where's your father?' Agnes said to Joanna.

'He's out in the garden, under the apple tree. Some people arrived, I don't know who they are.'

Agnes glanced towards the window. 'They're early,' she said, walking past Joanna's couch and out into the garden.

William Baines was staring at the ground, scuffing the sparse blades of grass with his foot. Next to him stood Joss, who had his arms clasped awkwardly behind his back.

'. . . I gave him the letter,' Agnes heard William say.

'He – he knows?'

William nodded, and looked at Joss. 'I respect . . . You could have told him. You could have sought him out. You didn't. I respect that.'

'It was how she wanted it.'

Agnes stayed in the shade of the house, wondering where Evelyn was, and James.

'If you want me to go . . .' Joss said, but William shook his head.

'No, he'll be here soon. With his wife. They have a baby now.'

Joss stepped backwards, as if to catch his balance. 'William, I insist, I shouldn't be here, it's not for me to intrude . . .'

'She loved you.' William nudged his toe against the roots of the tree. 'She'd have wanted this.'

'But you – it's too much to ask of you –'

William looked up at him. 'Some days ago – a lifetime ago – I held my daughter in my arms. I believed – I believed that she was dead. But she lived.' He glanced back to the house, to where Joanna was laughing with Nina and Rosie, then looked at Joss. 'I've learned that nothing is too much.'

Joss extended his hand towards Baines, then let it fall at his side again. 'William – she loved you. In the end, she chose you.'

William looked at Joss for a long moment. Slowly he nodded. 'Perhaps.'

Evelyn appeared from the rose garden, arm in arm with James. James saw Agnes and smiled at her. 'Tell you what,' he said, loudly, 'I see that champagne is being served indoors.' William stared at him unseeing, then blinked, smiled, turned back to Joss, and led the way back into the house. Joss went to Evelyn and took her hand.

The words on her plane ticket seemed to sparkle in the light of the Anglepoise lamp. Destination, Nice. Agnes stared at it for a while. Then she pulled her dressing gown around her and knelt in prayer. She found her mind was buzzing with images from the afternoon, a series of tiny dramas unfolding before her: Marcus arriving at his family home, his car drawing up outside, the car door slowly opening as he got out. Elias standing there, waiting on the drive; the two men walking towards each other, then stumbling into each other's arms, laughing, patting each other on the back in a vague and awkward way.

She saw Marcus's wife Rachel, elegant in a long linen dress, carrying baby Imogen, being greeted by William, shaking hands with Joss and Evelyn. She saw Rosie, delighted at being allowed to carry Imogen around, proudly showing her to Nina like a new doll. She recalled Joss and Marcus catching sight of each other as Marcus came into the room, the dogs at his feet capering with glee, and how Joss and Marcus had stopped still, and even the dogs had paused a moment in their frantic delight, and had looked from one man to the other, sharing in their moment of recognition.

Perhaps they'd found time alone together, Joss and Marcus,

Agnes thought, trying to gather together some words of prayer. She smiled, remembering Rosie's tantrum when they'd caught her attempting to give Imogen a ride on one of the dogs. 'But she likes it,' Rosie had wailed, 'Baby wants to go on the doggie . . .'

Agnes concentrated on her breathing and quietened her mind. She remembered what Julius had said about bringing her dilemma to God. She summoned up an image of her future life, of years spent in the service of the order. She thought about James, at the ending of his life, needing her to be there for him. The ending of his life, she thought. It seemed so final.

An image flashed across her mind, the most enduring image of the afternoon; of the french windows, the velvet curtains dappled with the last of the sunlight; of Evelyn, standing by the window, holding Imogen in her arms and gazing at her in wonderment.

'What do you mean, riding?' Agnes stood in her dressing gown, yawning. 'You woke me to suggest that I go riding? When?'

'Today. Now.' Elias was smiling at her, leaning on the door frame of her room.

'What are we riding?'

'Horses.'

'Very funny. Whose?'

'A friend of Marcus's.'

'Marcus? We're riding with him?'

'Any objection?'

'I haven't been anywhere near a horse for several months. I'm bound to fall off.'

'No you won't. A gentle canter across the moor, it'll be fun.'

'I've had no breakfast.'

'I'll make you some toast.'

'It's raining.'

'You like the rain.'

'I've got nothing to wear.'

'Here you are.' Elias thrust a large plastic carrier bag into her hands. 'It's Jo's stuff, jodhpurs and boots.'

'They won't fit. And my shoe size is a seven.'

'So is hers. Try them on.'

'Absolutely not.'

Agnes pushed her horse on, racing ahead of the others. The misty rain against her face made her want to laugh with joy. She slowed her pace, settling into a steady trot to allow the others to catch up with her.

'And this was the woman who claimed she'd fall off.' Elias laughed.

'You ride well,' Marcus said.

'Thank you. I'm not as good as I was.'

The grassland sloped down steeply towards a small wood, and their horses slowed to a walk to negotiate it.

'I can't take it all in,' Marcus said, as if continuing a conversation with Elias. 'Last night, all I could think was that Imogen has got three grandfathers. And what's so weird, is that if all this hadn't happened with Jo, and Turnbull – if Dad hadn't handed over the mill – none of it would have come out, not for years.' A low branch brushed against Marcus's face, scattering raindrops.

'I was thinking,' Elias said. 'About Joanna.'

'She was theirs,' Marcus said. 'She was their reunion. I always felt she was most loved of us all, when I was little. I always felt I didn't belong.'

'So did I –' Agnes began.

'And me,' Elias said, and they all laughed, as their horses emerged from the wood on to a flat plain.

'Did your mother's letter explain why she fell in love with Joss?' Agnes asked.

'No. She said she wouldn't try and justify herself. She asked me not to judge anyone harshly.'

'I suppose if your father forgave her,' Elias said, 'it's not for anyone else to judge her.'

They gathered speed into a fast canter across a field, and Agnes realised they had come out by the drystone wall before Laithe's Hollow. Elias had come to a halt, staring into the distance.

'We can take the upper path here,' Marcus said, 'and go back the way we came.'

Elias shook his head. 'Let's go across the Hollow.'

'If you're sure.' Marcus flashed him a look.

They walked round by the gate, and skirted the Hollow. A damp mist clung in the air, although the rain had eased. A bird's cry sounded through the soft silence, and looking up, Agnes saw two peregrine falcons, circling above the horses as they crossed the long grass. Then they'd left the Hollow behind them, returning to the flatter reaches of the moor. Beneath them the town was a misty blur, etched in peaks of purple and grey.

'Some stories don't start where you think they should,' Marcus said, suddenly. 'They always go back further than you realise. Like Joss being my father.'

'Or like Kate,' Elias said, quietly.

Marcus glanced at him.

'And –' Elias went on, 'it's never just one story. I mean, it always turns out there's several stories, all intertwined.' He raised his eyes to meet Marcus's gaze.

Marcus smiled. 'That's life, isn't it.'

The sun broke through the clouds, and Elias squinted up at it. He turned his horse and broke into a fast canter, jumping the fence ahead, racing away across the field beyond. Marcus turned to Agnes, laughing. 'We're not letting him get away with that.'

Agnes leaned over her horse's neck as they sailed over the fence. She felt lighter than air.

Chapter Twenty-Eight

'All I seem to have done today,' Teresa said, sitting down in the staff room with a cup of coffee, 'is wipe people's tears. All these goodbyes, all these endless boxes of tissues . . .'

'They're bound to be a bit bereft at the start of term,' Colin Furse said. 'They're only little.'

'No, I meant the parents. Poor things, sobbing their hearts out. The girls don't seem to mind at all.'

'Is Charlotte back yet?' Agnes took a Bourbon biscuit from the packet on the table.

'Yes, about half an hour ago.'

'And Rachel Swann?'

'Yes, she came with the first train load.'

'How is she?'

'Who can tell? She smiled at me, at least.'

'And Leonora?'

Teresa checked her clipboard. 'No, not yet.' She looked up at Agnes. 'Shall we panic now or later?'

Agnes smiled. 'I've got a meeting with Sister Philomena this morning. I'll panic after that.'

At lunchtime Agnes avoided the canteen and went to her room, negotiating the corridors which were full of boxes and trunks and suitcases. She took down the photo of herself, with her hair tied back at the neck, the air of sullenness accentuated by the shades of black and white. She sat by the window, staring at her image. There was a knock at the door. Reluctantly she stood up and opened it. Elias was there, holding something large and rectangular wrapped in brown paper.

'I've brought you a present,' he said, coming into her room, then glanced at her. 'You've been crying.'

She shook her head.

'You saw Philomena,' he said.

Agnes nodded.

'Decision time?'

She nodded again.

'This had better be a going-away present,' he said. She was about to interrupt to explain, but he added, 'Or a staying-put present. Whichever is most appropriate. Here.'

She got up and went over to it, where he'd leaned it against her desk. She unwrapped the paper.

'It's one of Joanna's,' Elias said. 'A new one. Still roses, of course, some things don't change. And candles. But no skulls.'

Agnes saw a blaze of glowing colour, of crimson flowers, of oranges in a bowl, a candle at their side, its melted wax falling in white curves against the terracotta candlestick.

'No clock either,' she said.

'No.'

'Is it really for me?'

'I thought it was the best way of saying goodbye.'

'If only the answer was in this painting.'

'Perhaps it is.' Elias hugged her, and then was gone.

Nina was standing in her office, smart in high heels, flicking through a computer print-out. She looked up. 'Agnes, how nice – are you all right?'

'Yes, I'm fine.'

Nina was looking at her hard. 'Are you sure?'

'Yes, I'm sure.' Agnes sat down in a new maroon chair and swivelled to and fro.

'Coffee?'

'Yes please.'

There was a loud swishing noise, and Agnes looked up, startled.

'My new machine,' Nina said. 'Real ground coffee. I'm thinking of getting that bit you can add on that does frothy milk, what do you think?'

'I think that would be lovely. Listen, I just came to – to say goodbye.'

'Where are you going?'

'Away.'

'For how long?'

'I'm – I'm not sure.'

'Agnes – is something wrong?'

'No, no, it's fine. It's – um – it's fine.'

'Good.' Nina placed a cup of fragrant fresh coffee in front of her. 'As long as you're sure.'

'Yes, I'm sure. Nina – would it be all right if I phoned a taxi?'

'Of course. Where's the car?'

'I've – I've left it at the school. It's not mine to use any more.'

When the cab arrived, Agnes got up to leave, and Nina hugged her. 'Don't forget to write.'

'I'll send you postcards, to the Managing Director, Warburton Mills Inc.'

'Sounds about right,' Nina laughed.

She got out of the car at James's cottage. As the taxi drove away, she was aware of a silence, an emptiness about the house. She rang the bell, but no one came to the door. She walked round the house, to the back door, and tried it. It opened.

'James?' she called. The house seemed to echo, as if it had already become a blank space ready for the next occupants.

She wondered whether to check the date on her ticket, wondered whether perhaps he'd gone without her. She walked into the lounge, thinking of going straight to the airport, but then realised he was there, asleep in an armchair.

'James!' she said, overwhelmed with relief. She reached out and touched his hand. Slowly she took her hand away. She took a step backwards to a chair and sat down, still gazing at him. His posture was peaceful, his head leaning against the back of the chair, his eyes closed. In front of him stood the clock that he'd been so determined she return to her mother. Next to it was a mug of coffee, half drunk, and a plate with an apple on it, untouched. A bone-handled knife lay across the plate. The clock had stopped.

Still life, Agnes thought. *Nature Morte.*

Eventually there had been the flurry of activity to deal with, the fluttering hordes of officialdom that always surround a corpse. First she'd called the Campbells, who'd called Isabel, who'd called James's GP, who'd called the coroner, who'd sent the police.

'When did you find the body?' someone asked Agnes.

'Some time this afternoon. About one o'clock, I think.'

'But it's nearly five now.'

'I know.'

'What happened in between?'

Agnes tried to speak, fell silent. It was impossible to describe the eternity of the afternoon, the peace of the hours she had spent with James, just sitting, listening to the stillness in the room, sensing his departing presence, his farewell. 'I had to say goodbye,' she said.

Now she walked towards the gates of the school. The last of the sun dusted the chestnut trees with pink against the blue of the sky. She could see a figure sitting on the high wall by the gates. As she got nearer, she could see the hair tied back at the neck, the huge suitcase at her feet. 'You came back, then,' Agnes said.

Leonora nodded. 'You too?'

'Me too.'

Leonora jumped down. She looked at the tears that welled in Agnes's eyes, but said nothing. She picked up her suitcase in one hand, took Agnes's arm in the other, and they began to walk up the drive.

'Too late in the day, you see,' Leonora said.

'For what?'

'For running away.'

Agnes nodded. The birds in the trees called to each other in the gathering dusk.

'Elias will laugh,' Agnes said.

'Makes a change.'

They strolled towards the school. Leonora stopped to rest her bag. She looked up at the sky. 'Tomorrow, maybe,' she said. 'It'll be a fine day tomorrow. We won't take much, just what we need.'

'Just a small suitcase each.'

They reached the steps. Leonora tightened her grip on Agnes's arm as the front door slowly closed behind them.